DOODLES FROM THE BOOGIE DOWN

STEPHANIE RODRIGUEZ

COLOR BY ANDREA BELL

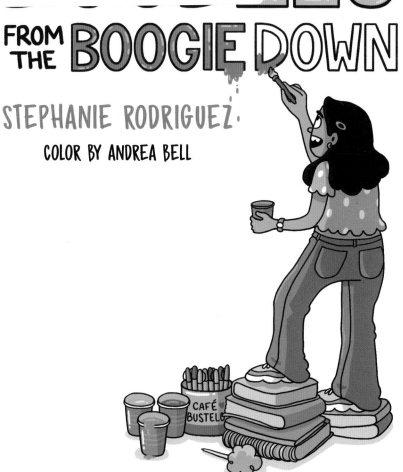

Kokila

KOKILA

An imprint of Penguin Random House LLC, New York

First published in the United States of America by Kokila,
an imprint of Penguin Random House LLC, 2023

Copyright © 2023 by Stephanie Rodriguez

Kokila & colophon are registered trademarks of Penguin Random House LLC.
Penguin Books & colophon are registered trademarks of Penguin Books Limited.

Visit us online at penguinrandomhouse.com.
Library of Congress Cataloging-in-Publication Data is available.

Manufactured in China

ISBN 9780451480668 (PBK)   10 9 8 7 6 5 4 3 2 1
ISBN 9780451480651 (HC)   10 9 8 7 6 5 4 3 2 1
TOPL

This book was edited by Joanna Cárdenas and designed by Jasmin Rubero.
The production was supervised by Tabitha Dulla, Nicole Kiser, Ariela Rudy Zaltzman, and Cherisse Landau.
Text set in Bupkis.

The artwork for this book was created digitally using Adobe Photoshop and Wacom Intuos
and with the support of assistant colorist Andrea Bell.

To all creative kids with big dreams, in NYC and beyond.

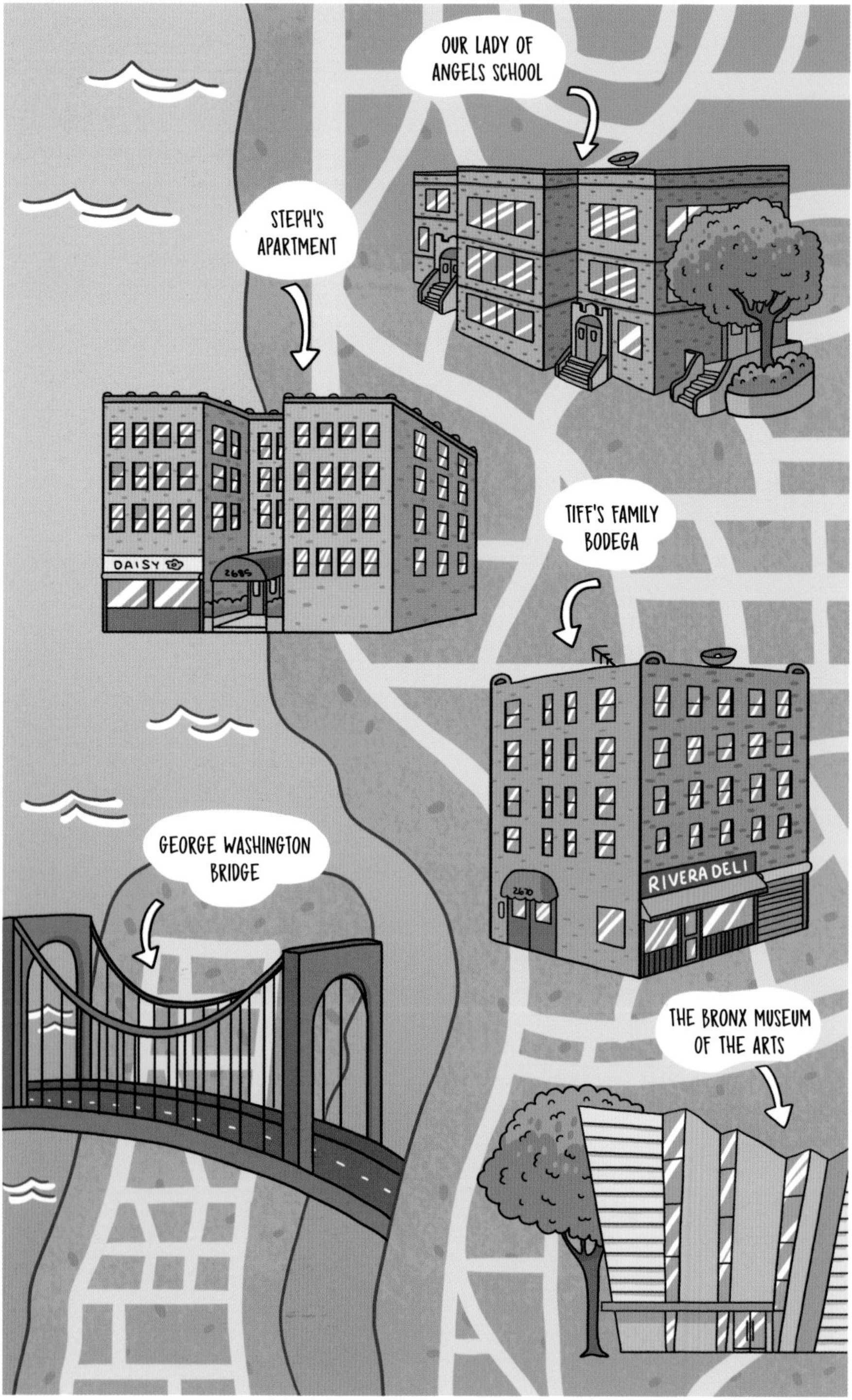
OUR LADY OF ANGELS SCHOOL
STEPH'S APARTMENT
DAISY
2685
TIFF'S FAMILY BODEGA
RIVERA DELI
2670
GEORGE WASHINGTON BRIDGE
THE BRONX MUSEUM OF THE ARTS

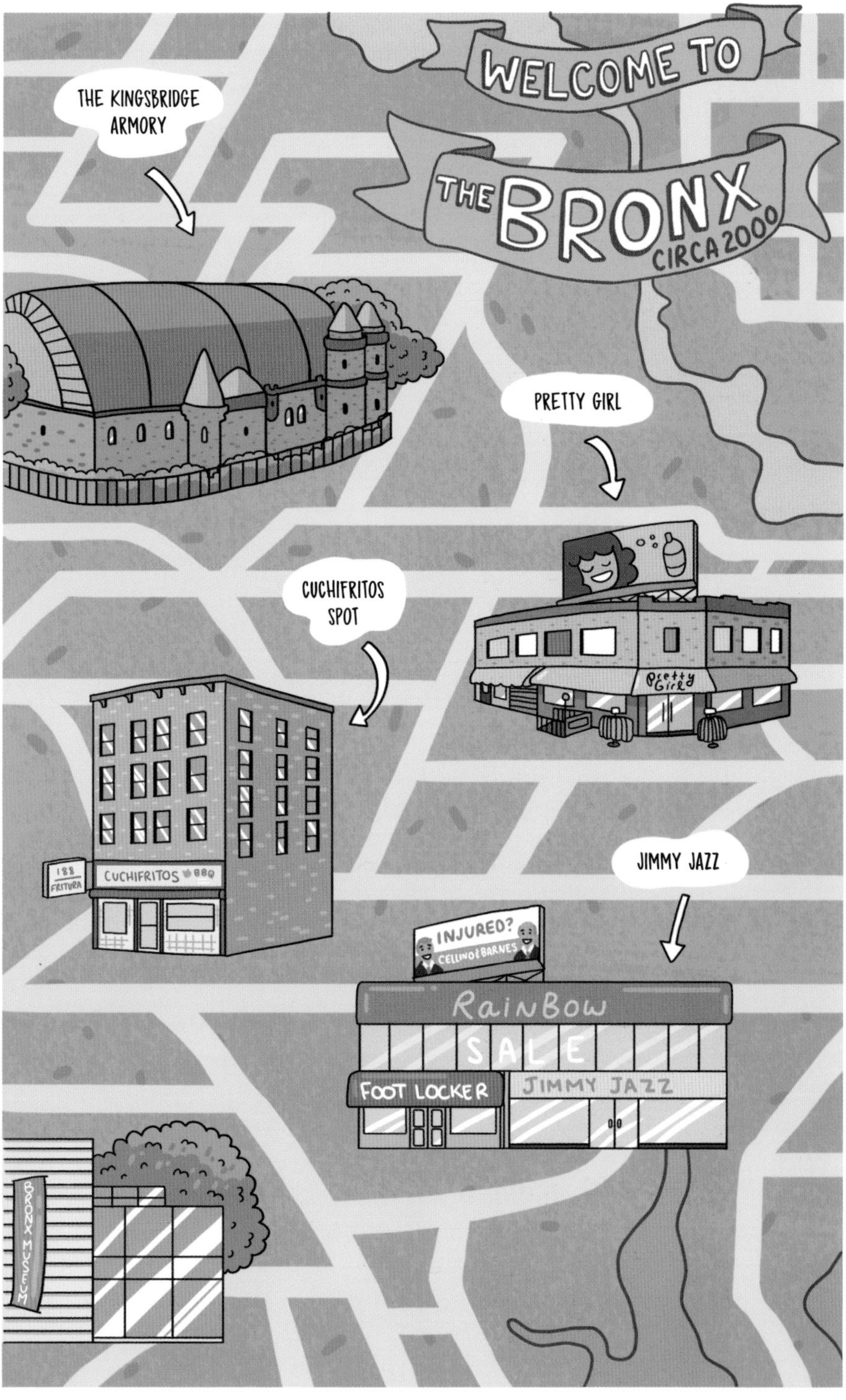
WELCOME TO
THE BRONX
CIRCA 2000
THE KINGSBRIDGE ARMORY
PRETTY GIRL
Pretty Girl
CUCHIFRITOS SPOT
188 FRITURA
CUCHIFRITOS BBQ
JIMMY JAZZ
INJURED?
CELLINO & BARNES
RainBow
SALE
FOOT LOCKER
JIMMY JAZZ
BRONX MUSEUM

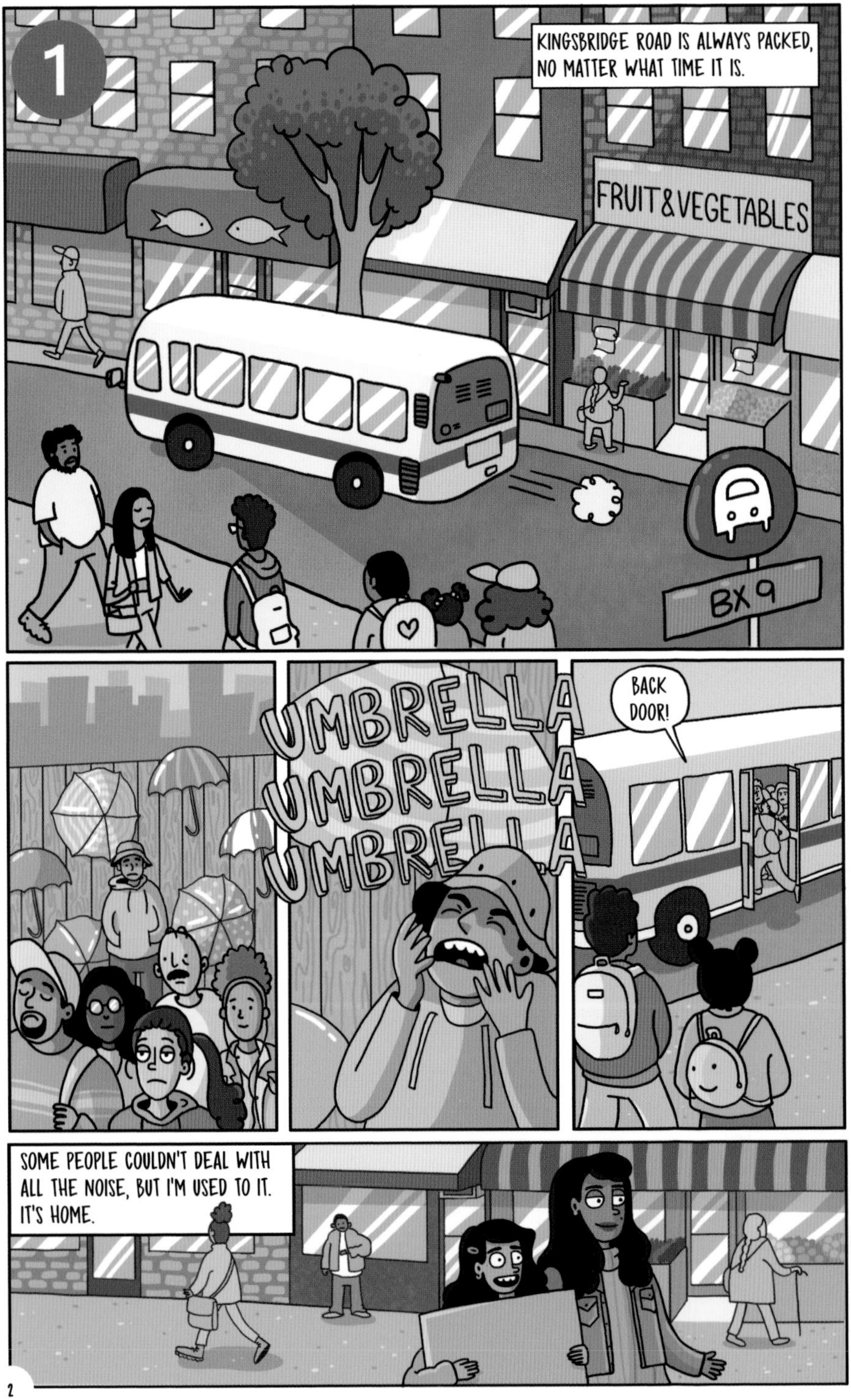
1
KINGSBRIDGE ROAD IS ALWAYS PACKED, NO MATTER WHAT TIME IT IS.
FRUIT&VEGETABLES
BX 9
UMBRELLA
UMBRELLA
UMBRELLA
BACK DOOR!
SOME PEOPLE COULDN'T DEAL WITH ALL THE NOISE, BUT I'M USED TO IT. IT'S HOME.

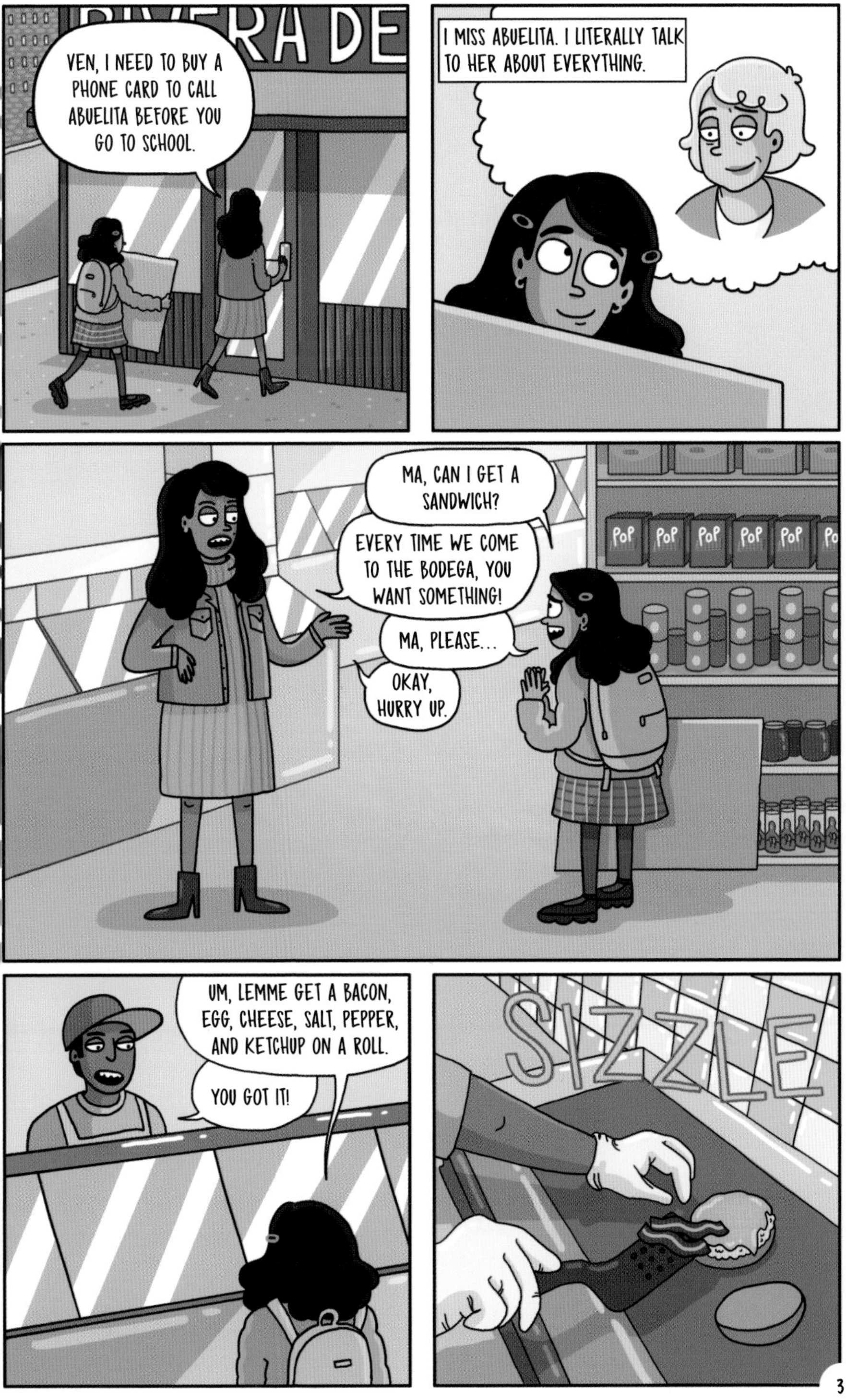

VEN, I NEED TO BUY A PHONE CARD TO CALL ABUELITA BEFORE YOU GO TO SCHOOL.
I MISS ABUELITA. I LITERALLY TALK TO HER ABOUT EVERYTHING.
MA, CAN I GET A SANDWICH?
EVERY TIME WE COME TO THE BODEGA, YOU WANT SOMETHING!
MA, PLEASE...
OKAY, HURRY UP.
UM, LEMME GET A BACON, EGG, CHEESE, SALT, PEPPER, AND KETCHUP ON A ROLL.
YOU GOT IT!
SIZZLE

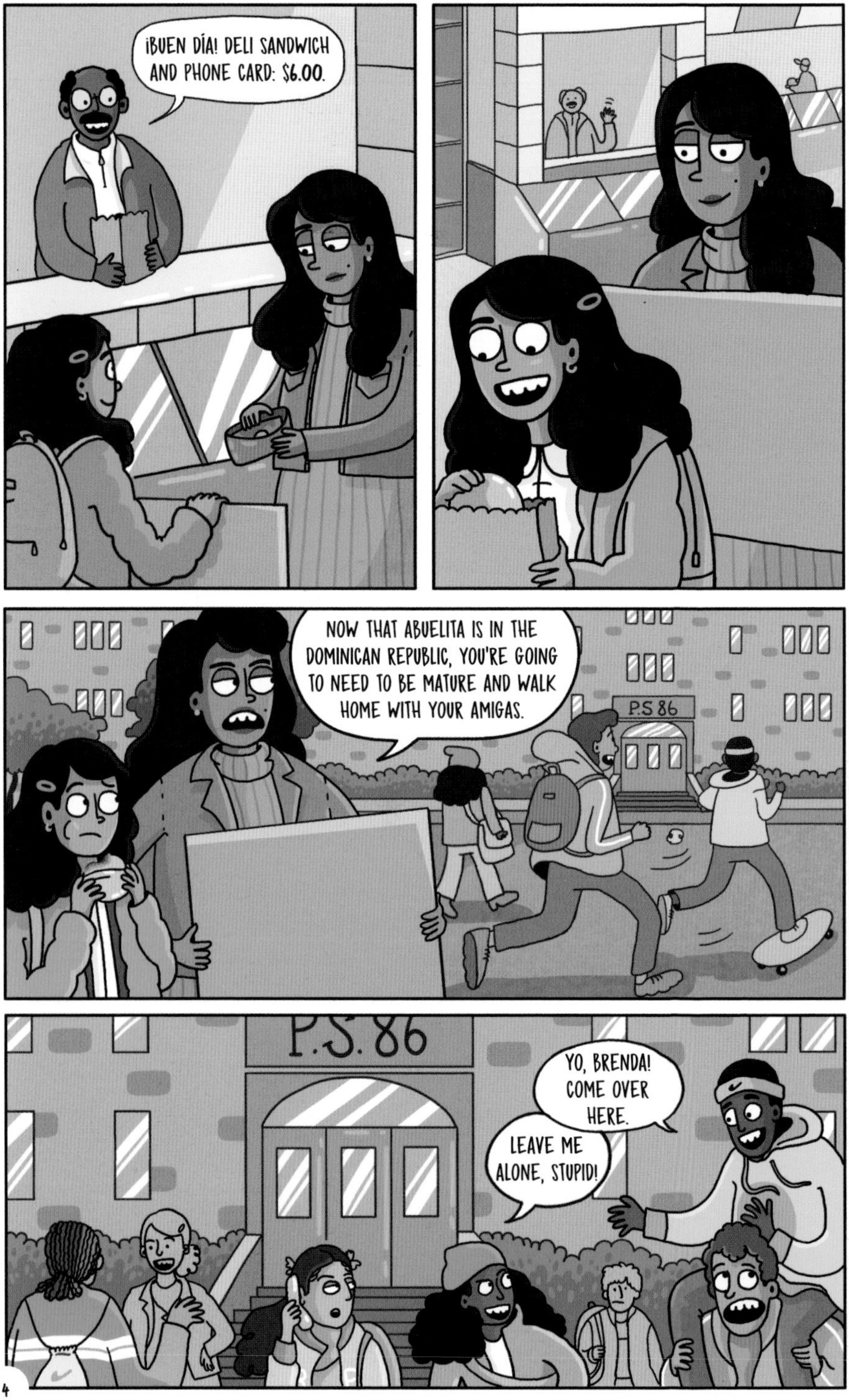
¡BUEN DÍA! DELI SANDWICH AND PHONE CARD: $6.00.
NOW THAT ABUELITA IS IN THE DOMINICAN REPUBLIC, YOU'RE GOING TO NEED TO BE MATURE AND WALK HOME WITH YOUR AMIGAS.
P.S 86
P.S. 86
YO, BRENDA! COME OVER HERE.
LEAVE ME ALONE, STUPID!

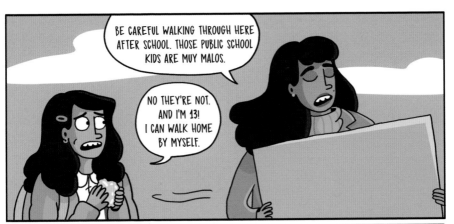

BE CAREFUL WALKING THROUGH HERE AFTER SCHOOL. THOSE PUBLIC SCHOOL KIDS ARE MUY MALOS.

NO THEY'RE NOT. AND I'M 13! I CAN WALK HOME BY MYSELF.

AT LEAST I CAN DROP YOU OFF.

¿QUÉ? YOU DON'T WANT ANYONE TO SEE YOU WITH YOUR MAMI?

UM... I DON'T KNOW...

I'LL STAND RIGHT HERE TO MAKE SURE YOU GET IN SAFE.

BUT, MOM...

5

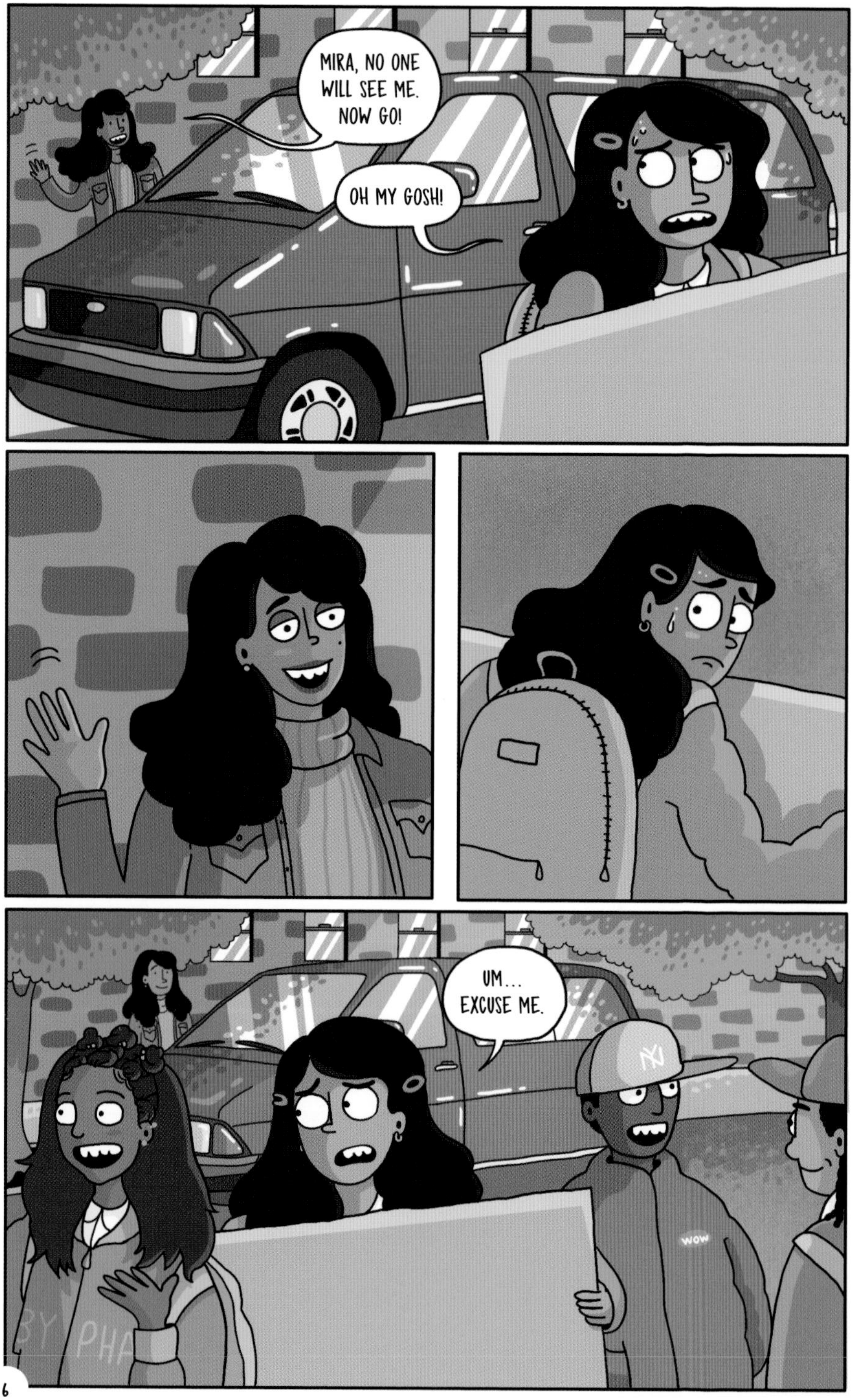
MIRA, NO ONE WILL SEE ME. NOW GO!
OH MY GOSH!
UM... EXCUSE ME.
WOW

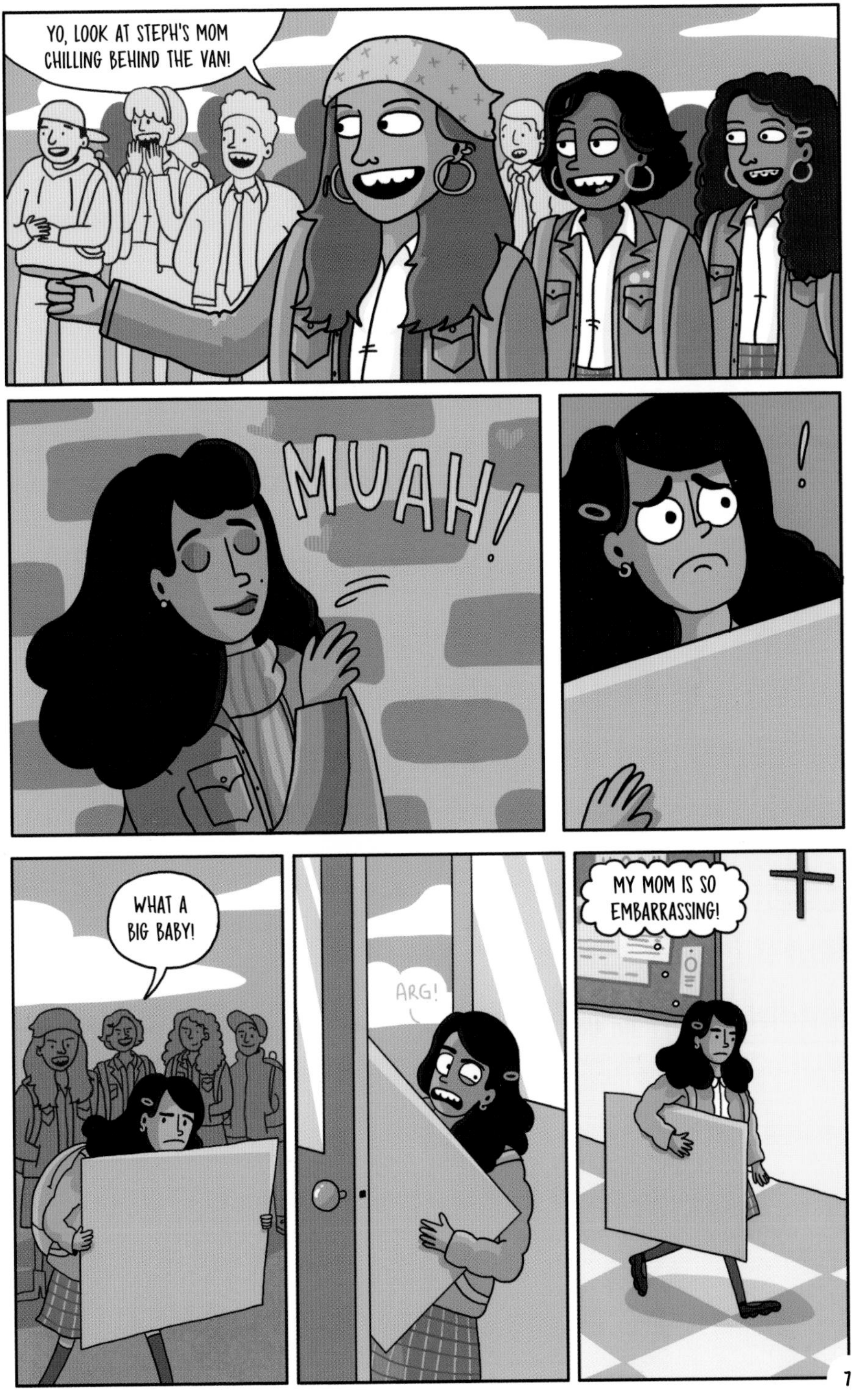
YO, LOOK AT STEPH'S MOM CHILLING BEHIND THE VAN!
MUAH!
!
WHAT A BIG BABY!
ARG!
MY MOM IS SO EMBARRASSING!

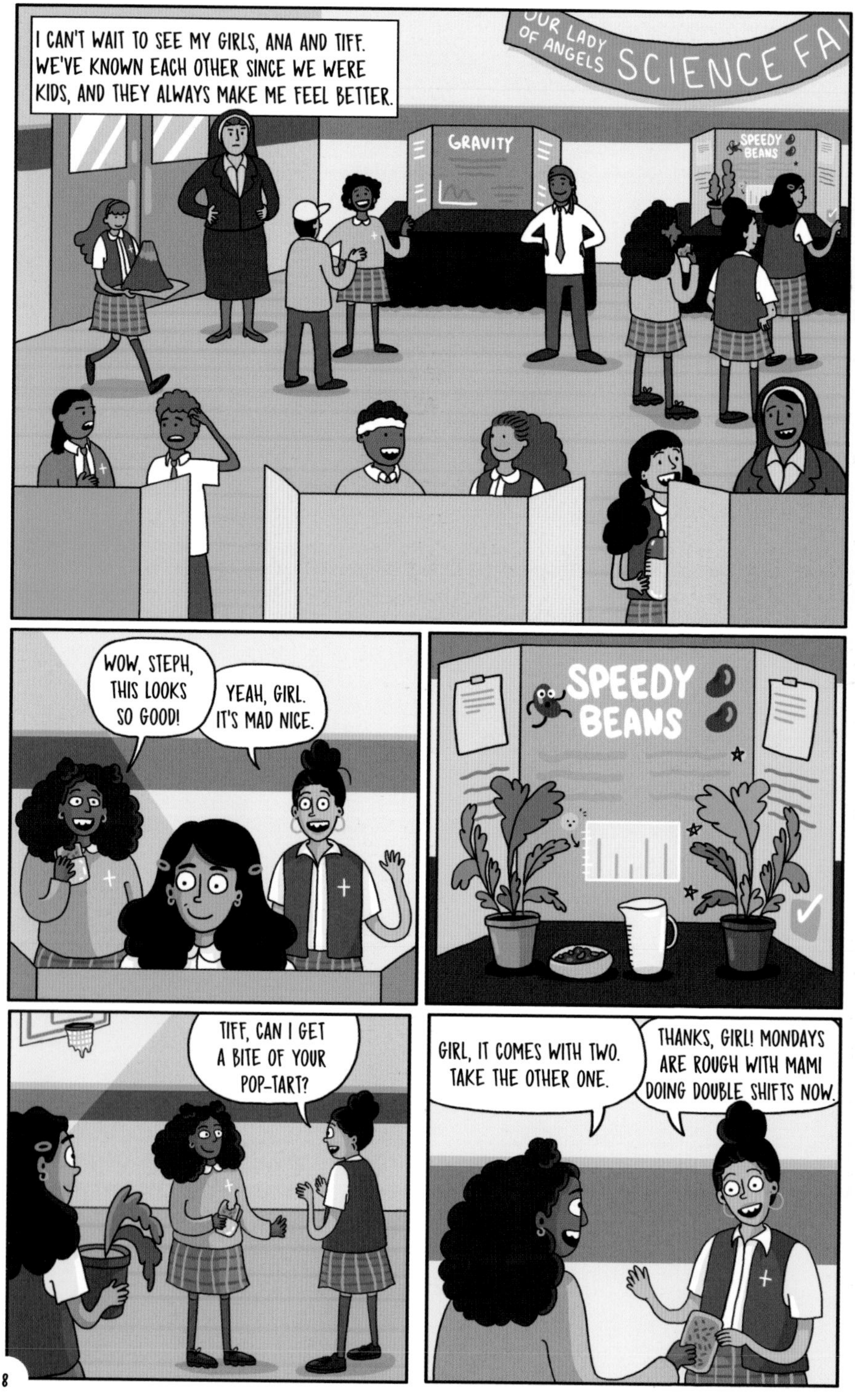
I CAN'T WAIT TO SEE MY GIRLS, ANA AND TIFF. WE'VE KNOWN EACH OTHER SINCE WE WERE KIDS, AND THEY ALWAYS MAKE ME FEEL BETTER.
OF ANGELS SCIENCE
GRAVITY
SPEEDY BEANS
WOW, STEPH, THIS LOOKS SO GOOD!
YEAH, GIRL. IT'S MAD NICE.
SPEEDY BEANS
TIFF, CAN I GET A BITE OF YOUR POP-TART?
GIRL, IT COMES WITH TWO. TAKE THE OTHER ONE.
THANKS, GIRL! MONDAYS ARE ROUGH WITH MAMI DOING DOUBLE SHIFTS NOW.

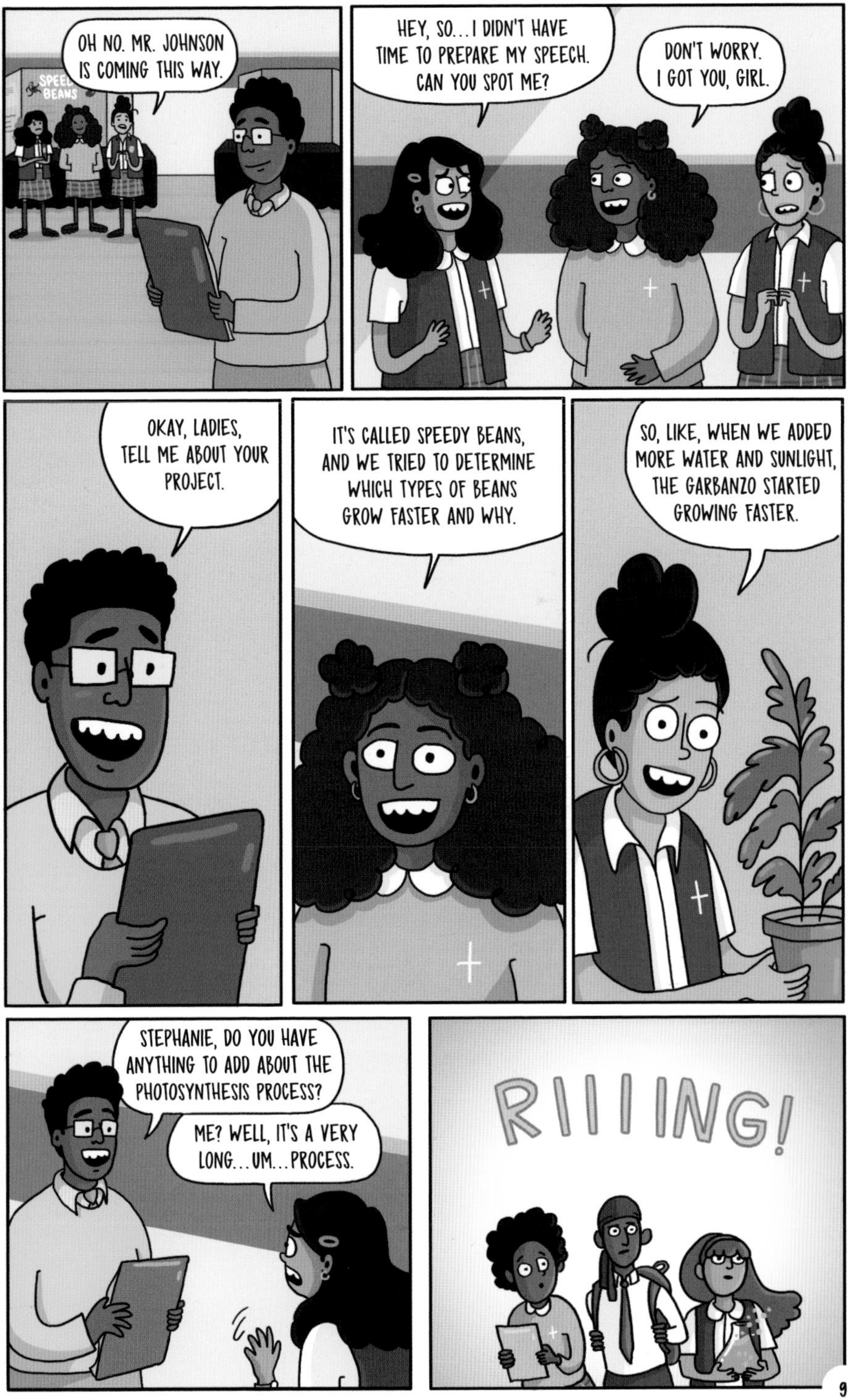
OH NO. MR. JOHNSON IS COMING THIS WAY.
SPEEDY BEANS
HEY, SO...I DIDN'T HAVE TIME TO PREPARE MY SPEECH. CAN YOU SPOT ME?
DON'T WORRY. I GOT YOU, GIRL.
OKAY, LADIES, TELL ME ABOUT YOUR PROJECT.
IT'S CALLED SPEEDY BEANS, AND WE TRIED TO DETERMINE WHICH TYPES OF BEANS GROW FASTER AND WHY.
SO, LIKE, WHEN WE ADDED MORE WATER AND SUNLIGHT, THE GARBANZO STARTED GROWING FASTER.
STEPHANIE, DO YOU HAVE ANYTHING TO ADD ABOUT THE PHOTOSYNTHESIS PROCESS?
ME? WELL, IT'S A VERY LONG...UM...PROCESS.
RIIING!

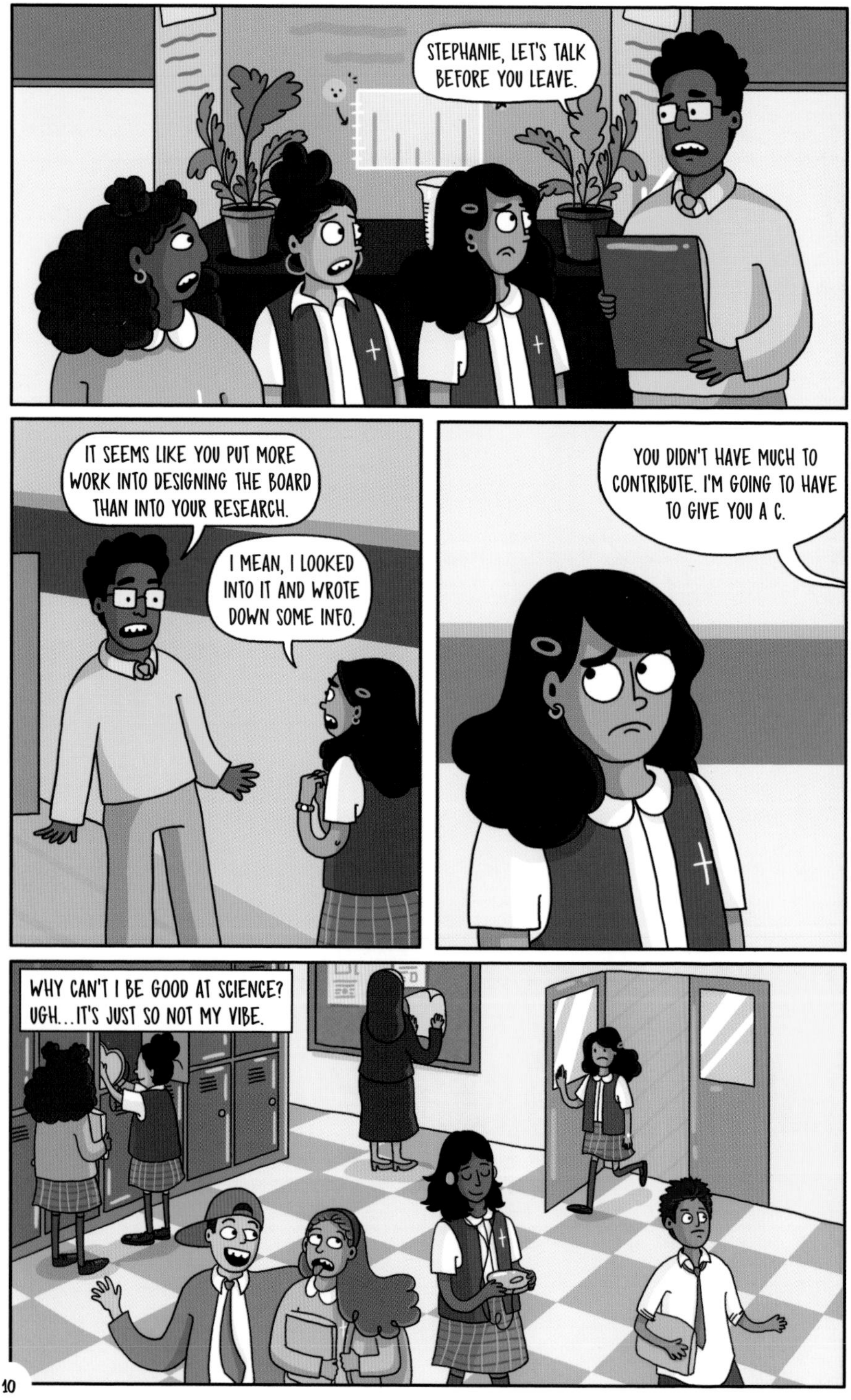
STEPHANIE, LET'S TALK BEFORE YOU LEAVE.
IT SEEMS LIKE YOU PUT MORE WORK INTO DESIGNING THE BOARD THAN INTO YOUR RESEARCH.
I MEAN, I LOOKED INTO IT AND WROTE DOWN SOME INFO.
YOU DIDN'T HAVE MUCH TO CONTRIBUTE. I'M GOING TO HAVE TO GIVE YOU A C.
WHY CAN'T I BE GOOD AT SCIENCE? UGH...IT'S JUST SO NOT MY VIBE.

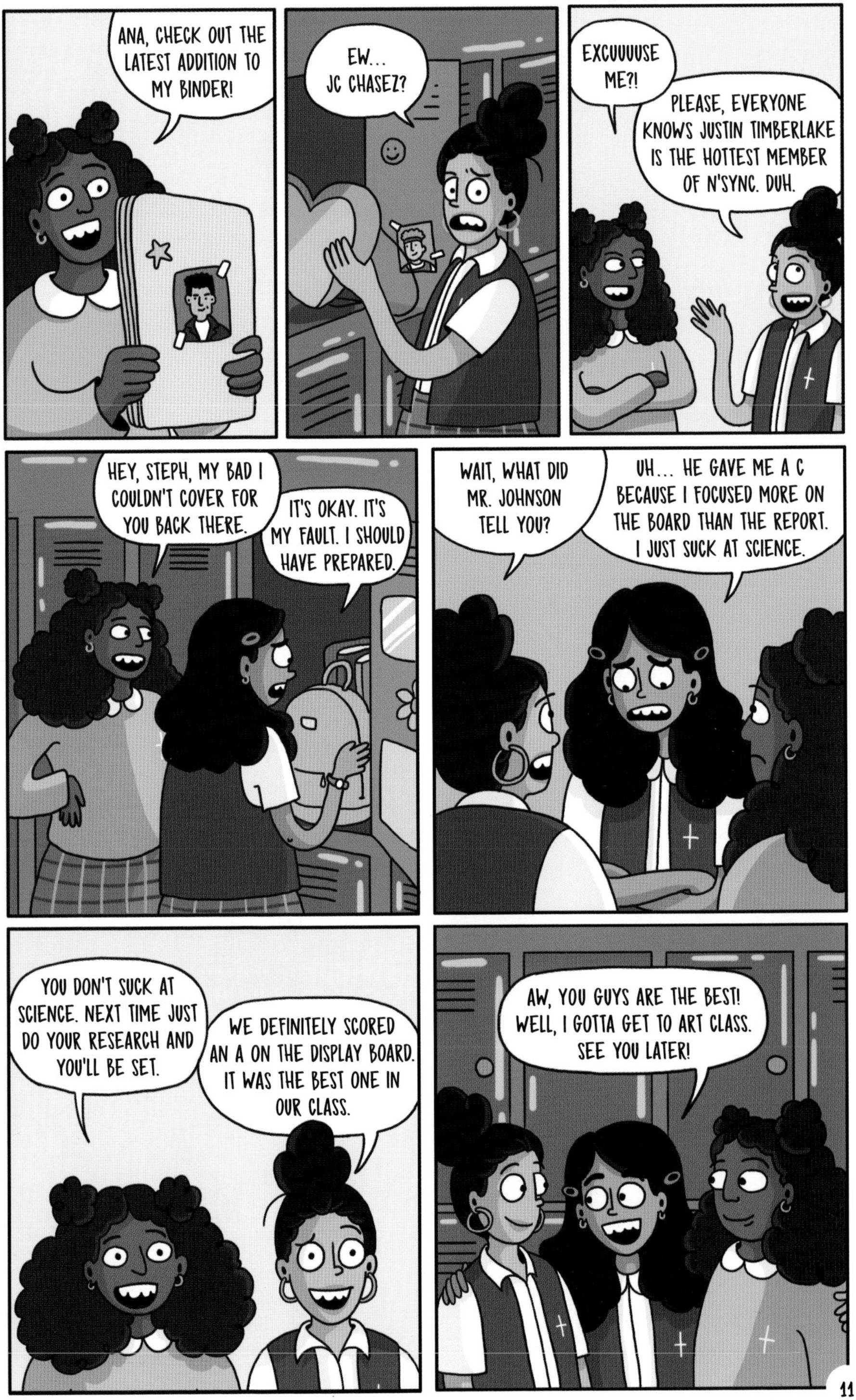
ANA, CHECK OUT THE LATEST ADDITION TO MY BINDER!
EW... JC CHASEZ?
EXCUUUUSE ME?!
PLEASE, EVERYONE KNOWS JUSTIN TIMBERLAKE IS THE HOTTEST MEMBER OF N'SYNC. DUH.
HEY, STEPH, MY BAD I COULDN'T COVER FOR YOU BACK THERE.
IT'S OKAY. IT'S MY FAULT. I SHOULD HAVE PREPARED.
WAIT, WHAT DID MR. JOHNSON TELL YOU?
UH... HE GAVE ME A C BECAUSE I FOCUSED MORE ON THE BOARD THAN THE REPORT. I JUST SUCK AT SCIENCE.
YOU DON'T SUCK AT SCIENCE. NEXT TIME JUST DO YOUR RESEARCH AND YOU'LL BE SET.
WE DEFINITELY SCORED AN A ON THE DISPLAY BOARD. IT WAS THE BEST ONE IN OUR CLASS.
AW, YOU GUYS ARE THE BEST! WELL, I GOTTA GET TO ART CLASS. SEE YOU LATER!

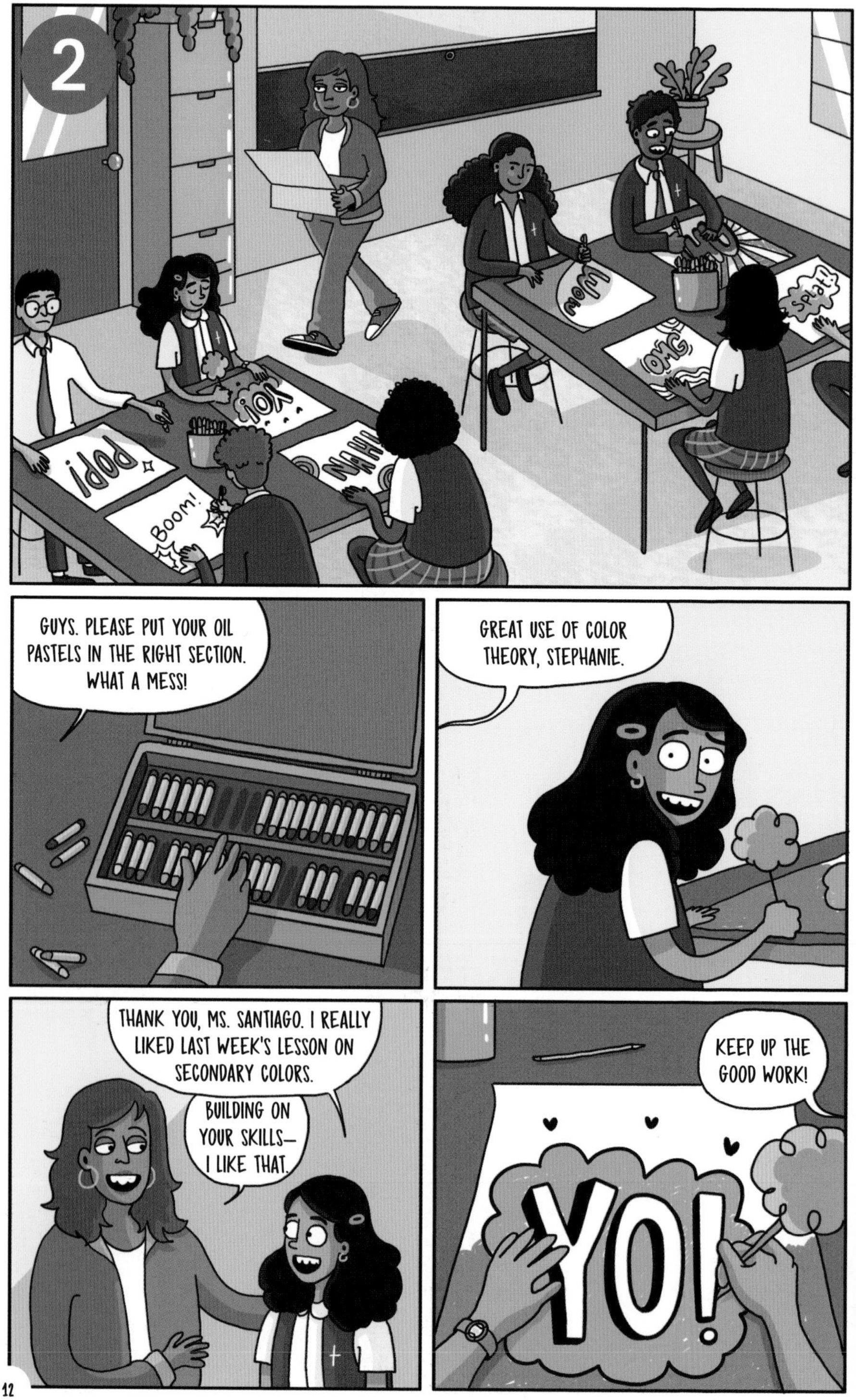
2
POP!
Boom!
YO!
WOW
OMG
Splat!
GUYS. PLEASE PUT YOUR OIL PASTELS IN THE RIGHT SECTION. WHAT A MESS!
GREAT USE OF COLOR THEORY, STEPHANIE.
THANK YOU, MS. SANTIAGO. I REALLY LIKED LAST WEEK'S LESSON ON SECONDARY COLORS.
BUILDING ON YOUR SKILLS— I LIKE THAT.
KEEP UP THE GOOD WORK!
YO!

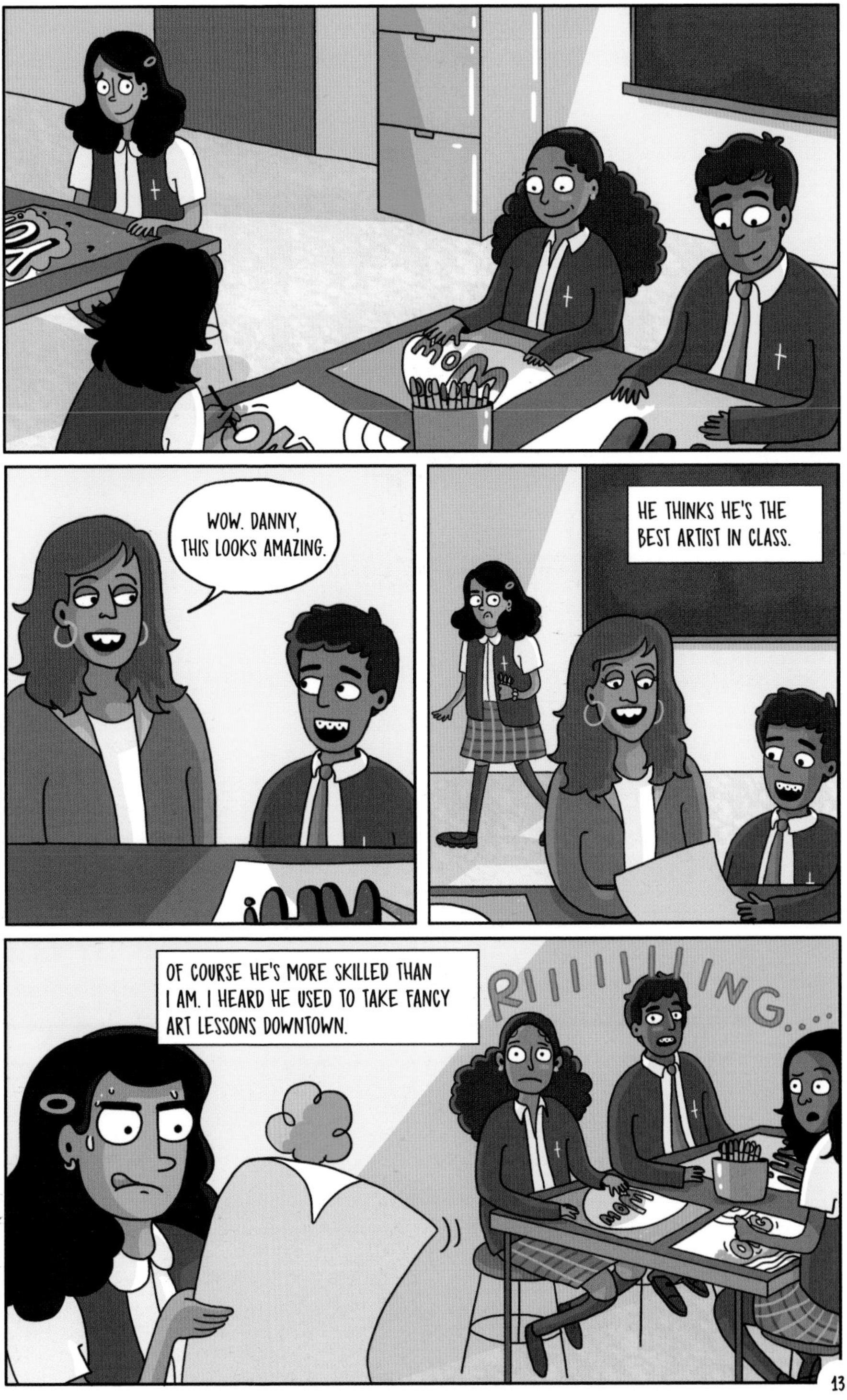
WOW. DANNY, THIS LOOKS AMAZING.
HE THINKS HE'S THE BEST ARTIST IN CLASS.
OF COURSE HE'S MORE SKILLED THAN I AM. I HEARD HE USED TO TAKE FANCY ART LESSONS DOWNTOWN.
RIIIIIIING...

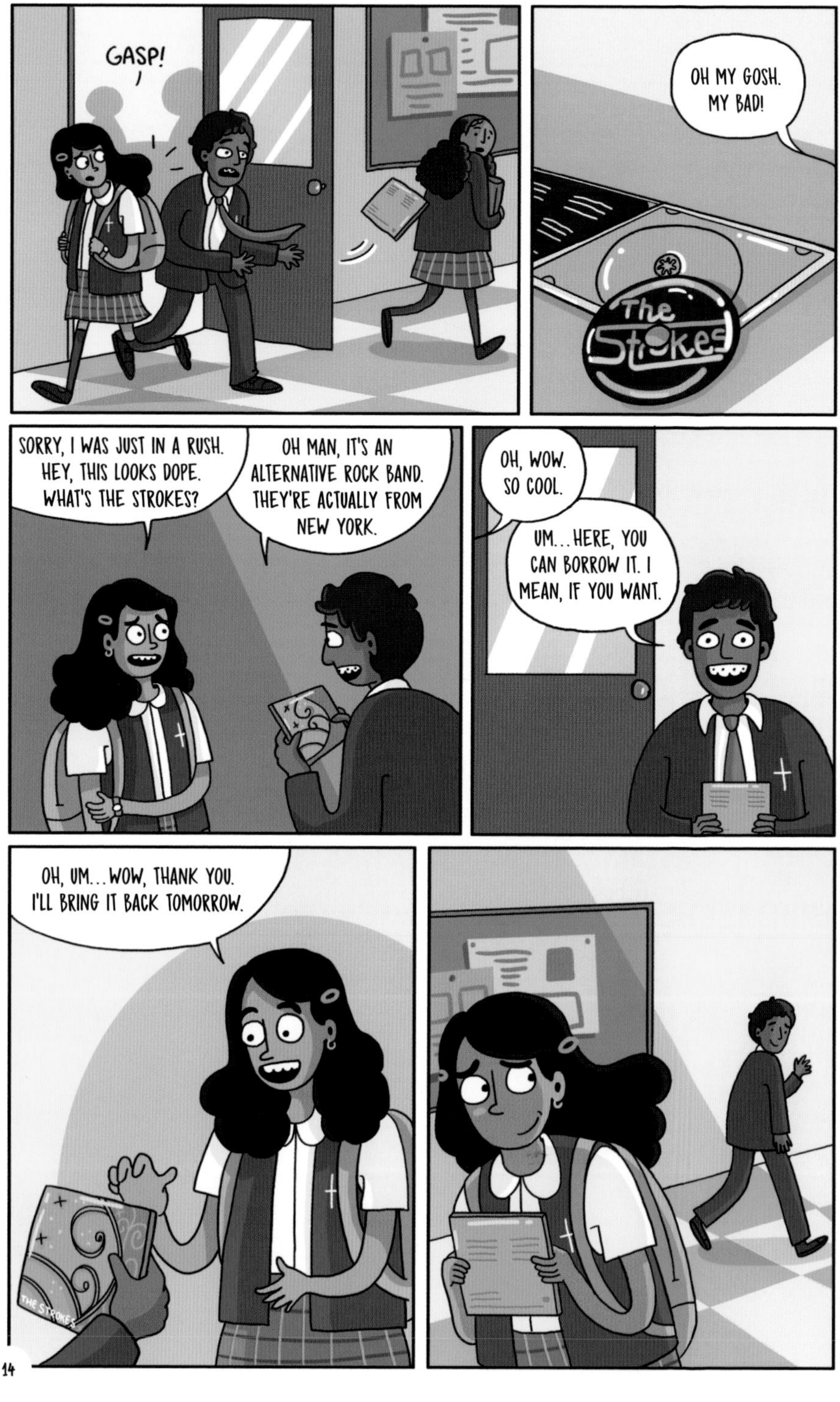
GASP!
OH MY GOSH. MY BAD!
The Strokes
SORRY, I WAS JUST IN A RUSH. HEY, THIS LOOKS DOPE. WHAT'S THE STROKES?
OH MAN, IT'S AN ALTERNATIVE ROCK BAND. THEY'RE ACTUALLY FROM NEW YORK.
OH, WOW. SO COOL.
UM...HERE, YOU CAN BORROW IT. I MEAN, IF YOU WANT.
OH, UM...WOW, THANK YOU. I'LL BRING IT BACK TOMORROW.
THE STROKES

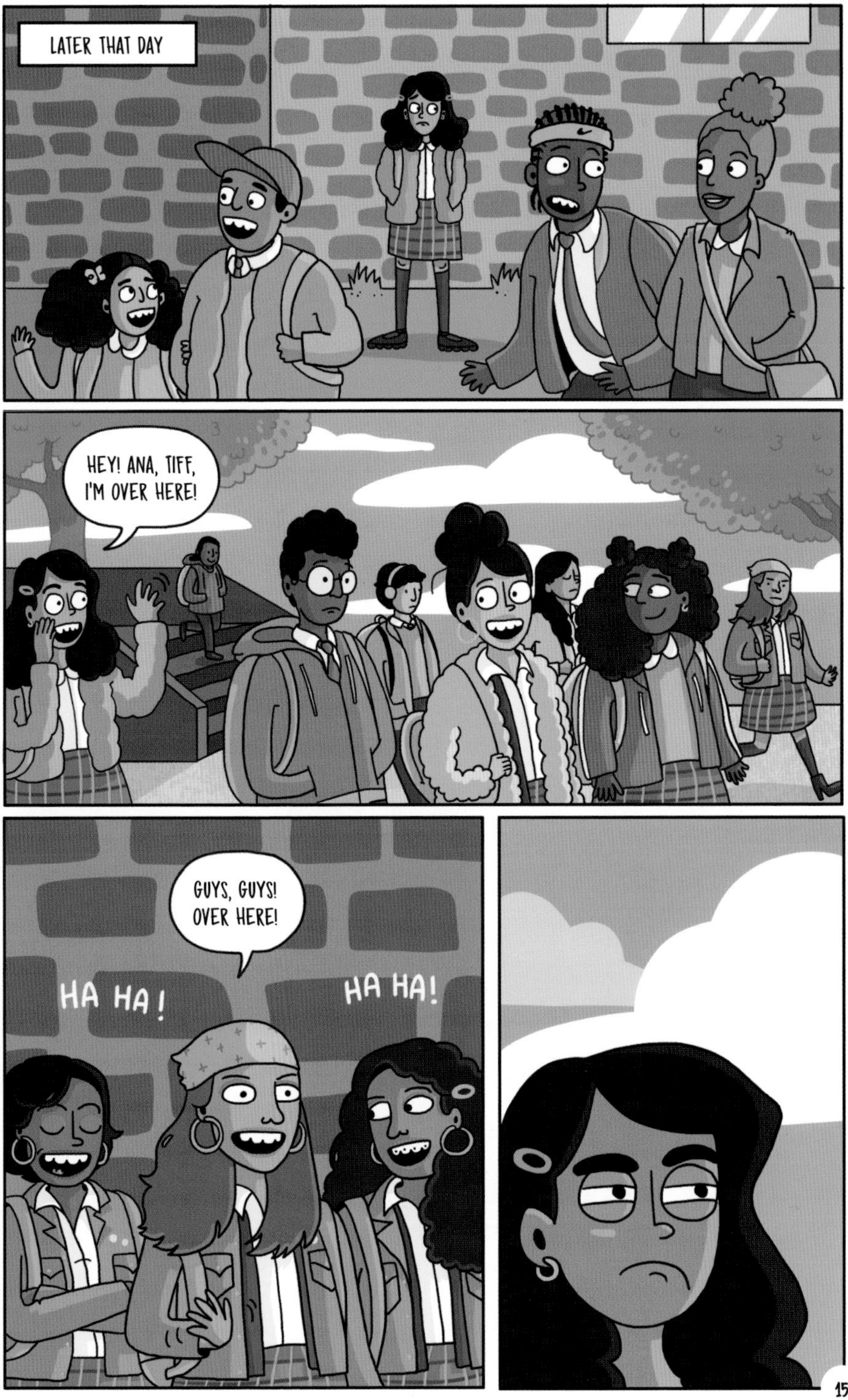
LATER THAT DAY
HEY! ANA, TIFF, I'M OVER HERE!
GUYS, GUYS! OVER HERE!
HA HA!
HA HA!

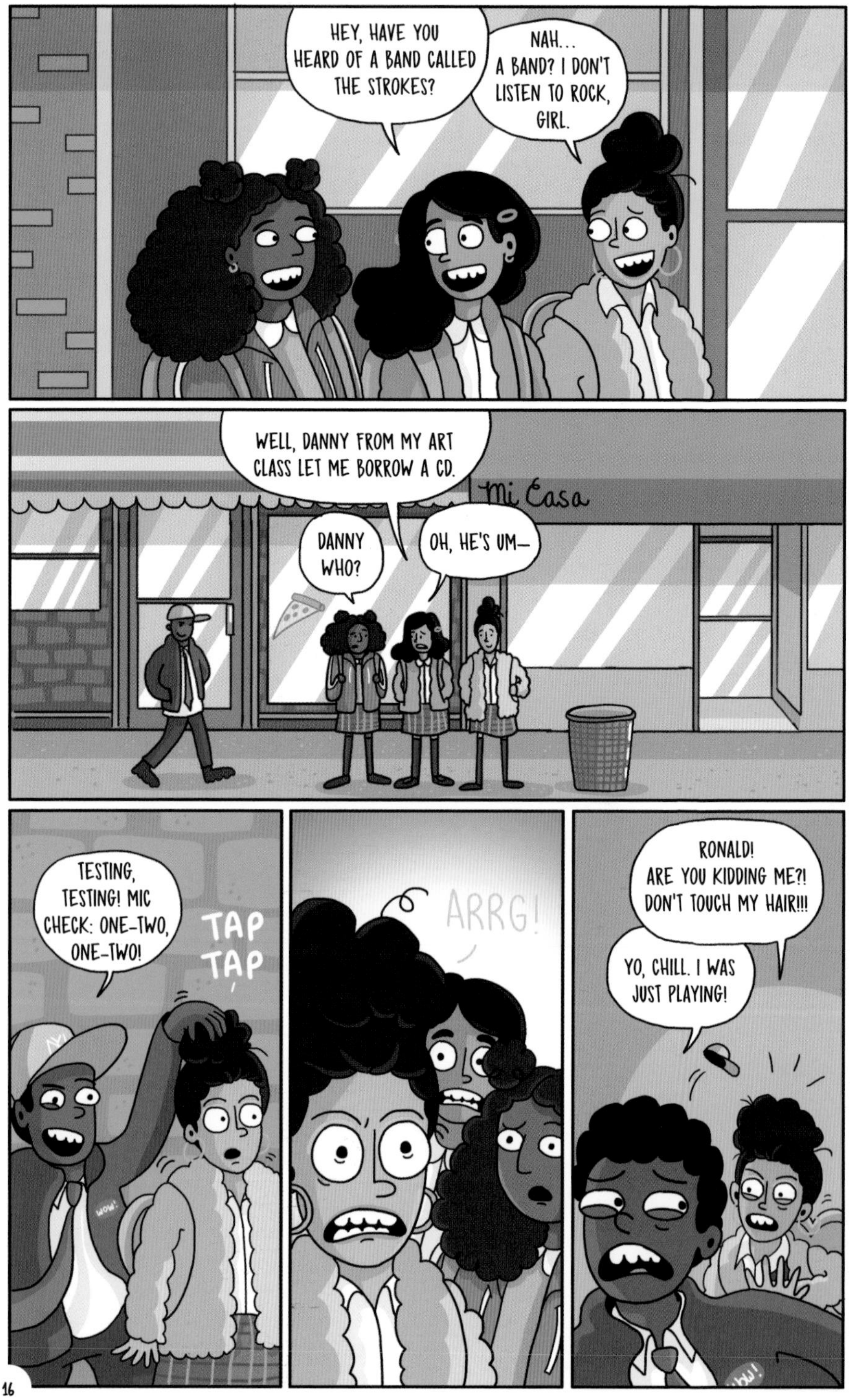
HEY, HAVE YOU HEARD OF A BAND CALLED THE STROKES?
NAH... A BAND? I DON'T LISTEN TO ROCK, GIRL.
WELL, DANNY FROM MY ART CLASS LET ME BORROW A CD.
Mi Casa
DANNY WHO?
OH, HE'S UM—
TESTING, TESTING! MIC CHECK: ONE-TWO, ONE-TWO!
TAP TAP
ARRG!
RONALD! ARE YOU KIDDING ME?! DON'T TOUCH MY HAIR!!!
YO, CHILL. I WAS JUST PLAYING!

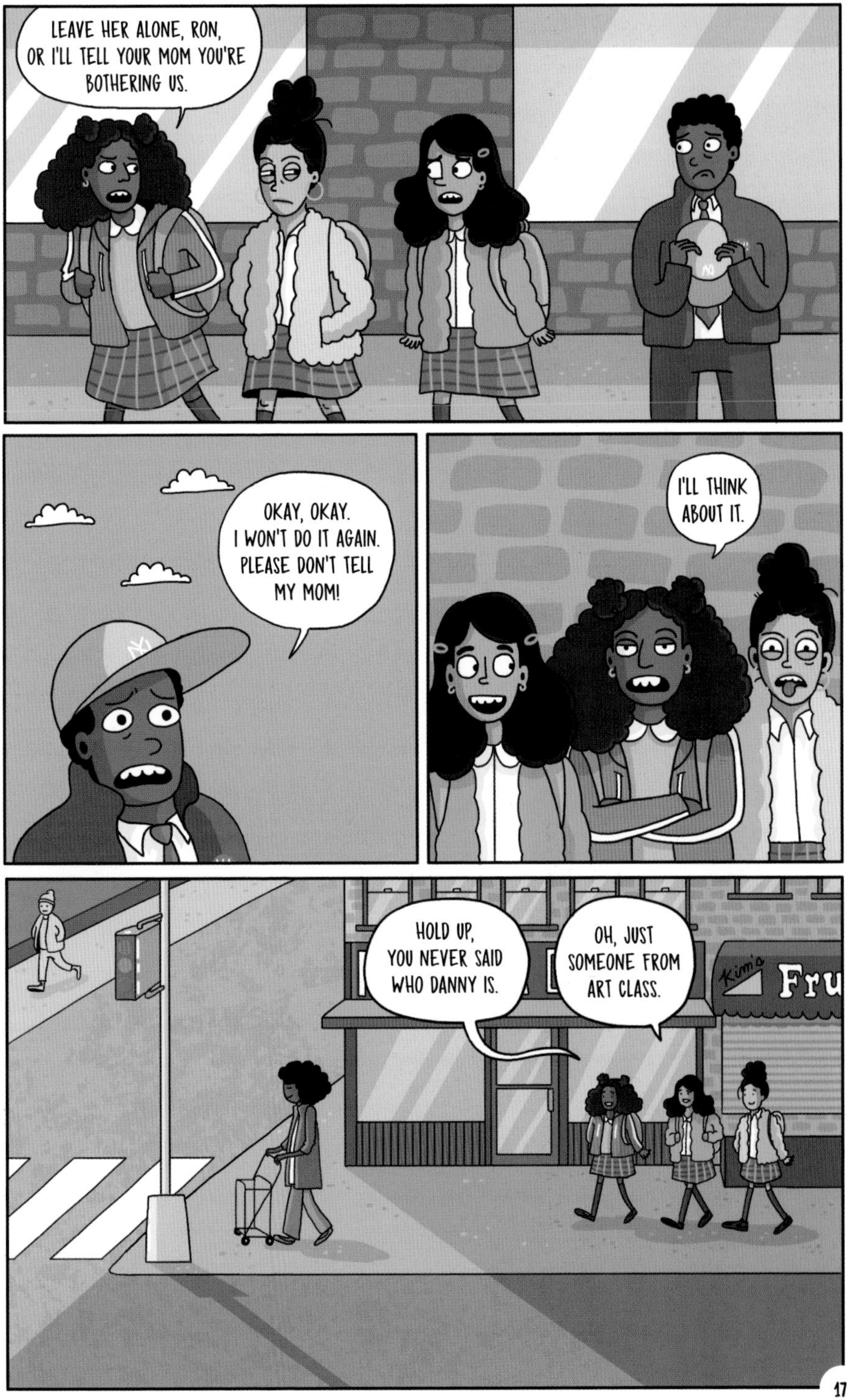
LEAVE HER ALONE, RON, OR I'LL TELL YOUR MOM YOU'RE BOTHERING US.
OKAY, OKAY. I WON'T DO IT AGAIN. PLEASE DON'T TELL MY MOM!
I'LL THINK ABOUT IT.
HOLD UP, YOU NEVER SAID WHO DANNY IS.
OH, JUST SOMEONE FROM ART CLASS.
Kim's
Fru

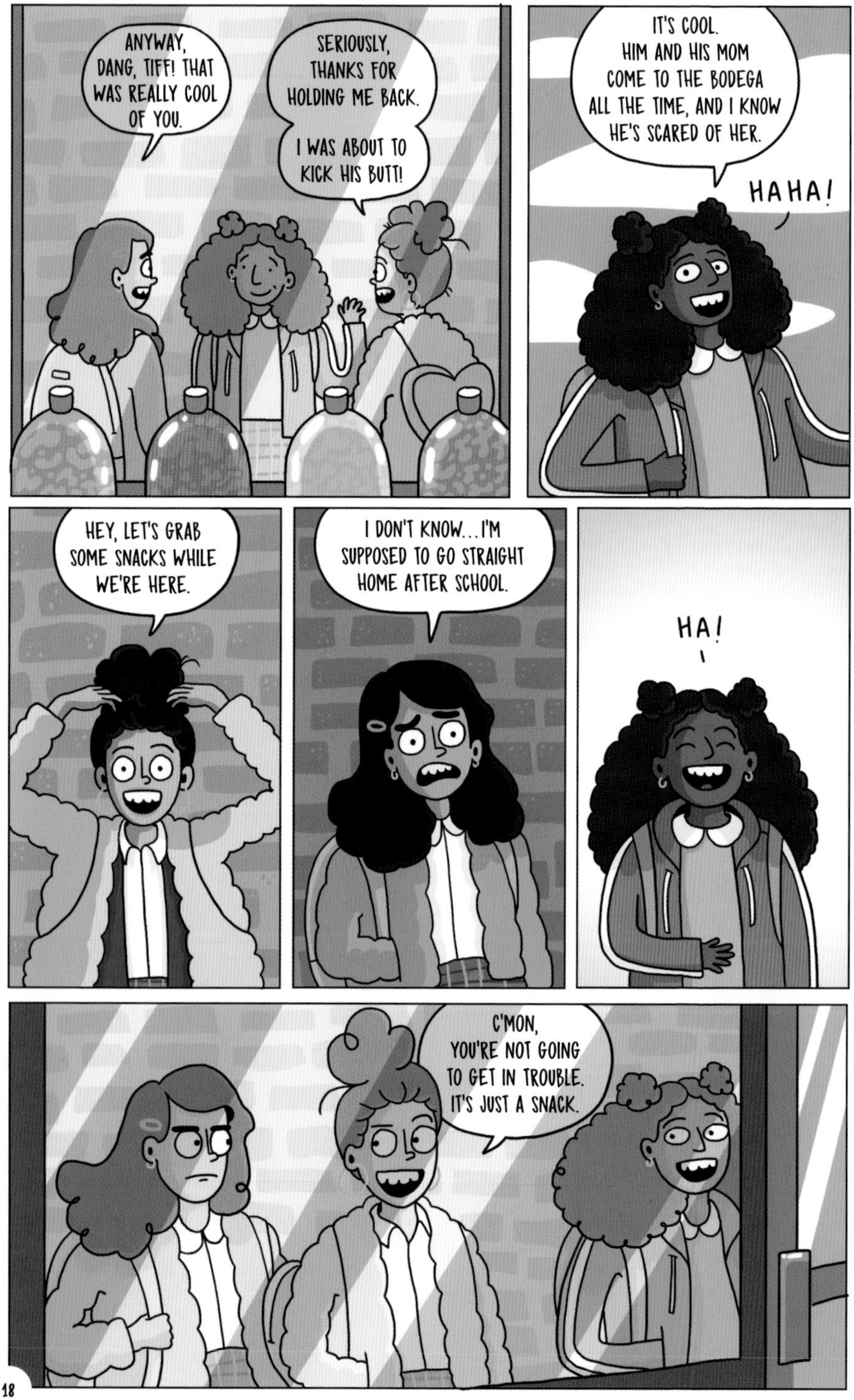
ANYWAY, DANG, TIFF! THAT WAS REALLY COOL OF YOU.
SERIOUSLY, THANKS FOR HOLDING ME BACK.
I WAS ABOUT TO KICK HIS BUTT!
IT'S COOL. HIM AND HIS MOM COME TO THE BODEGA ALL THE TIME, AND I KNOW HE'S SCARED OF HER.
HAHA!
HEY, LET'S GRAB SOME SNACKS WHILE WE'RE HERE.
I DON'T KNOW...I'M SUPPOSED TO GO STRAIGHT HOME AFTER SCHOOL.
HA!
C'MON, YOU'RE NOT GOING TO GET IN TROUBLE. IT'S JUST A SNACK.

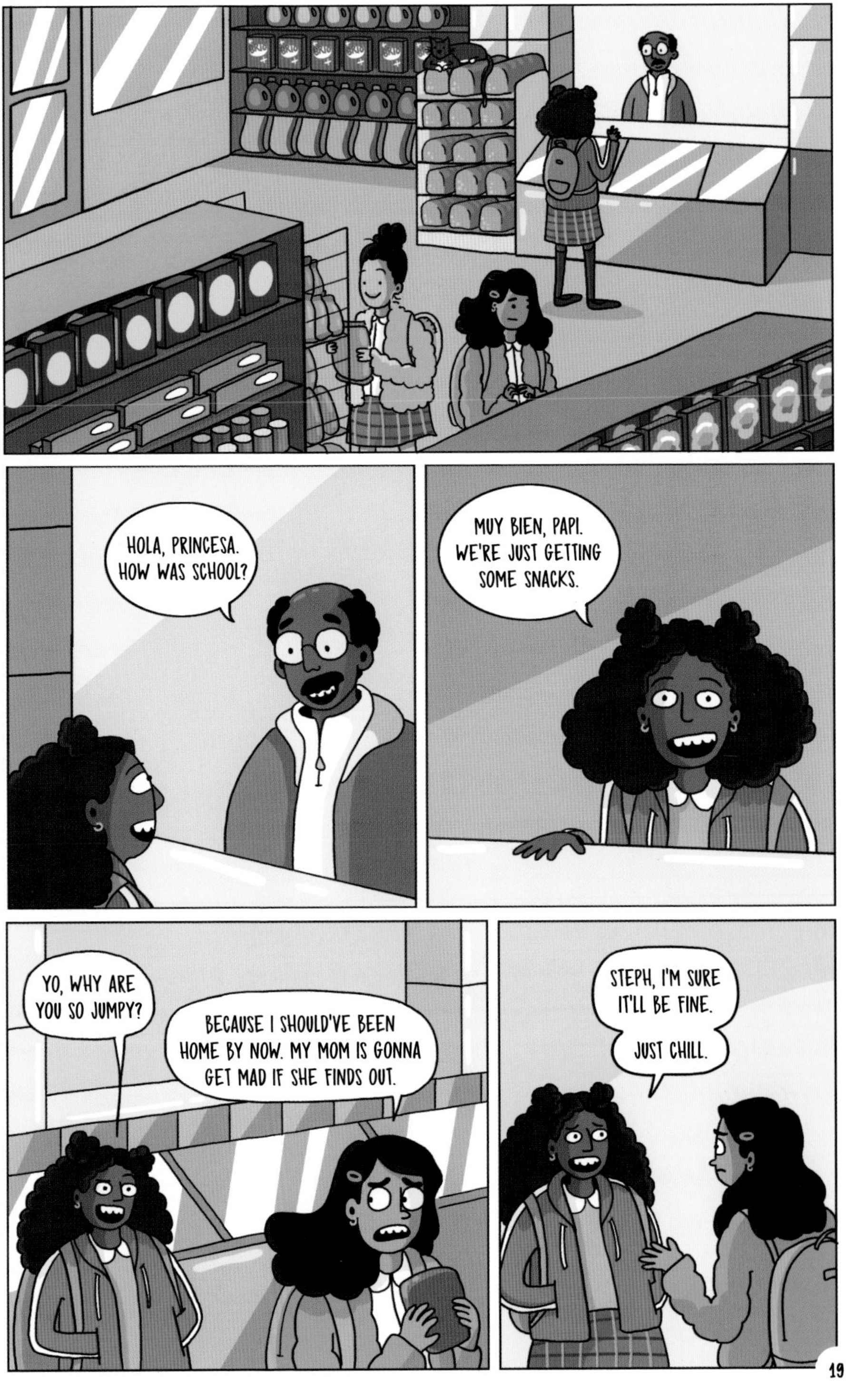
HOLA, PRINCESA. HOW WAS SCHOOL?
MUY BIEN, PAPI. WE'RE JUST GETTING SOME SNACKS.
YO, WHY ARE YOU SO JUMPY?
BECAUSE I SHOULD'VE BEEN HOME BY NOW. MY MOM IS GONNA GET MAD IF SHE FINDS OUT.
STEPH, I'M SURE IT'LL BE FINE.
JUST CHILL.

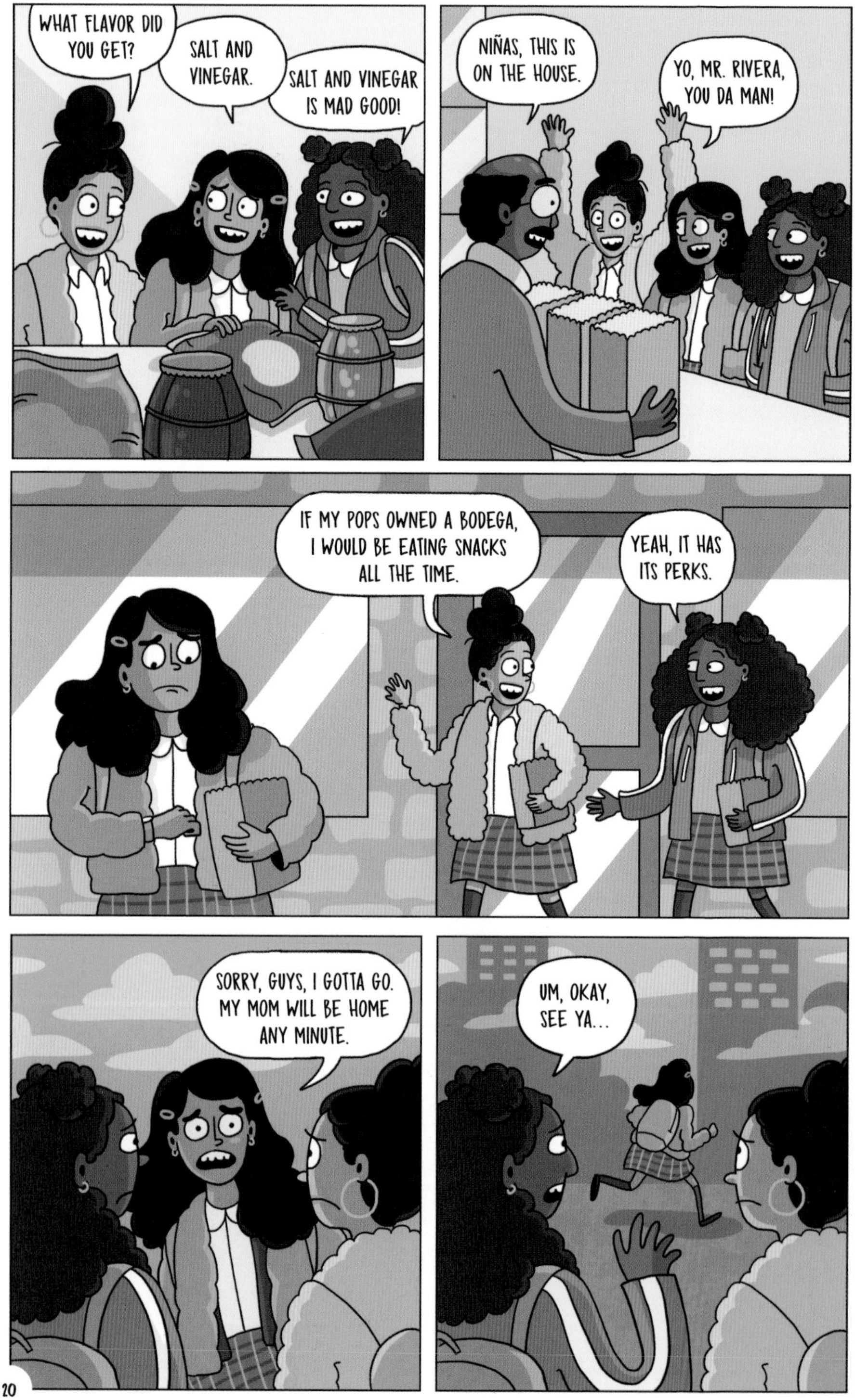
WHAT FLAVOR DID YOU GET?
SALT AND VINEGAR.
SALT AND VINEGAR IS MAD GOOD!
NIÑAS, THIS IS ON THE HOUSE.
YO, MR. RIVERA, YOU DA MAN!
IF MY POPS OWNED A BODEGA, I WOULD BE EATING SNACKS ALL THE TIME.
YEAH, IT HAS ITS PERKS.
SORRY, GUYS, I GOTTA GO. MY MOM WILL BE HOME ANY MINUTE.
UM, OKAY, SEE YA...

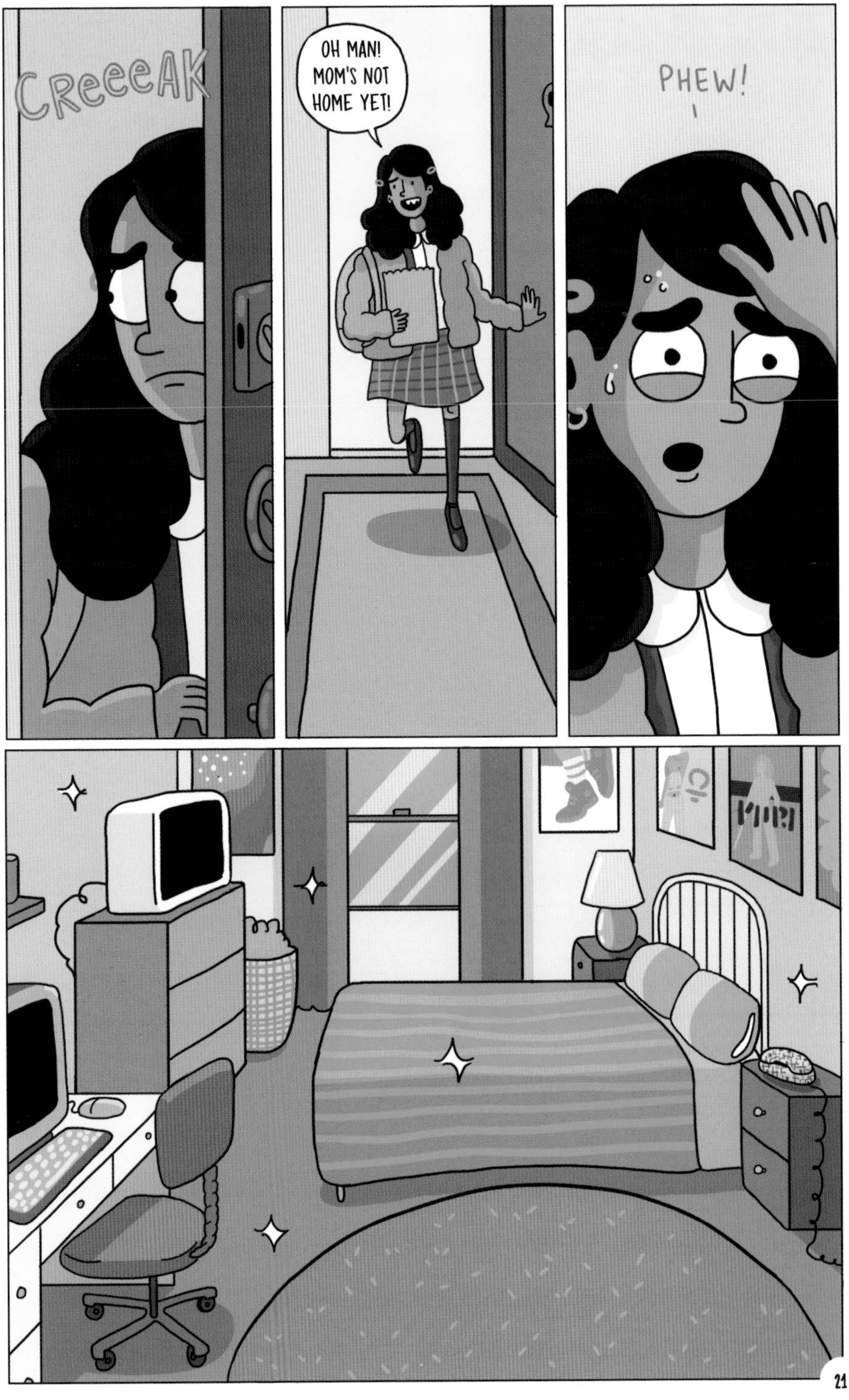
CReeeAK
OH MAN! MOM'S NOT HOME YET!
PHEW!

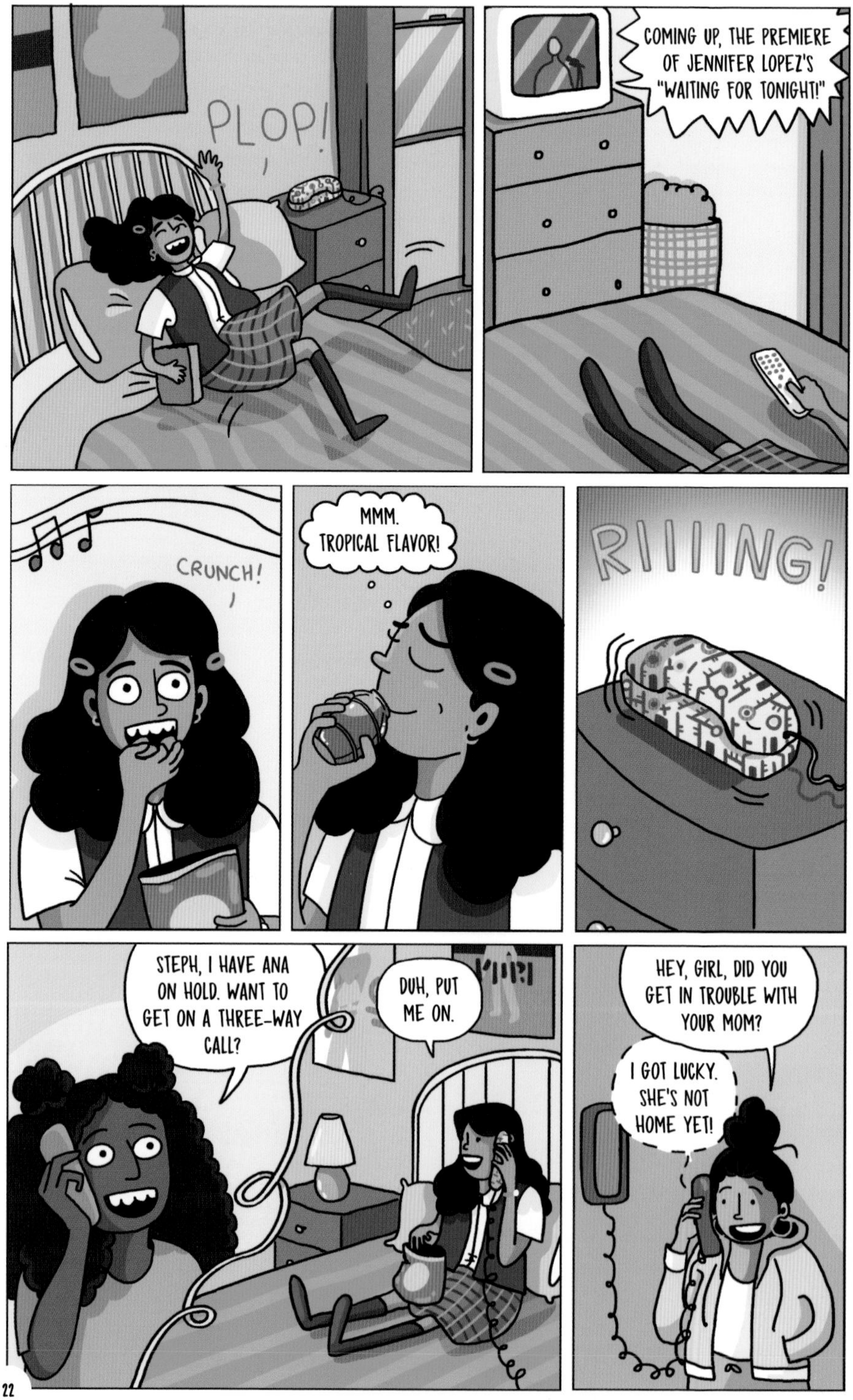
PLOP!
COMING UP, THE PREMIERE OF JENNIFER LOPEZ'S "WAITING FOR TONIGHT!"
CRUNCH!
MMM. TROPICAL FLAVOR!
RIIIING!
STEPH, I HAVE ANA ON HOLD. WANT TO GET ON A THREE-WAY CALL?
DUH, PUT ME ON.
HEY, GIRL, DID YOU GET IN TROUBLE WITH YOUR MOM?
I GOT LUCKY. SHE'S NOT HOME YET!

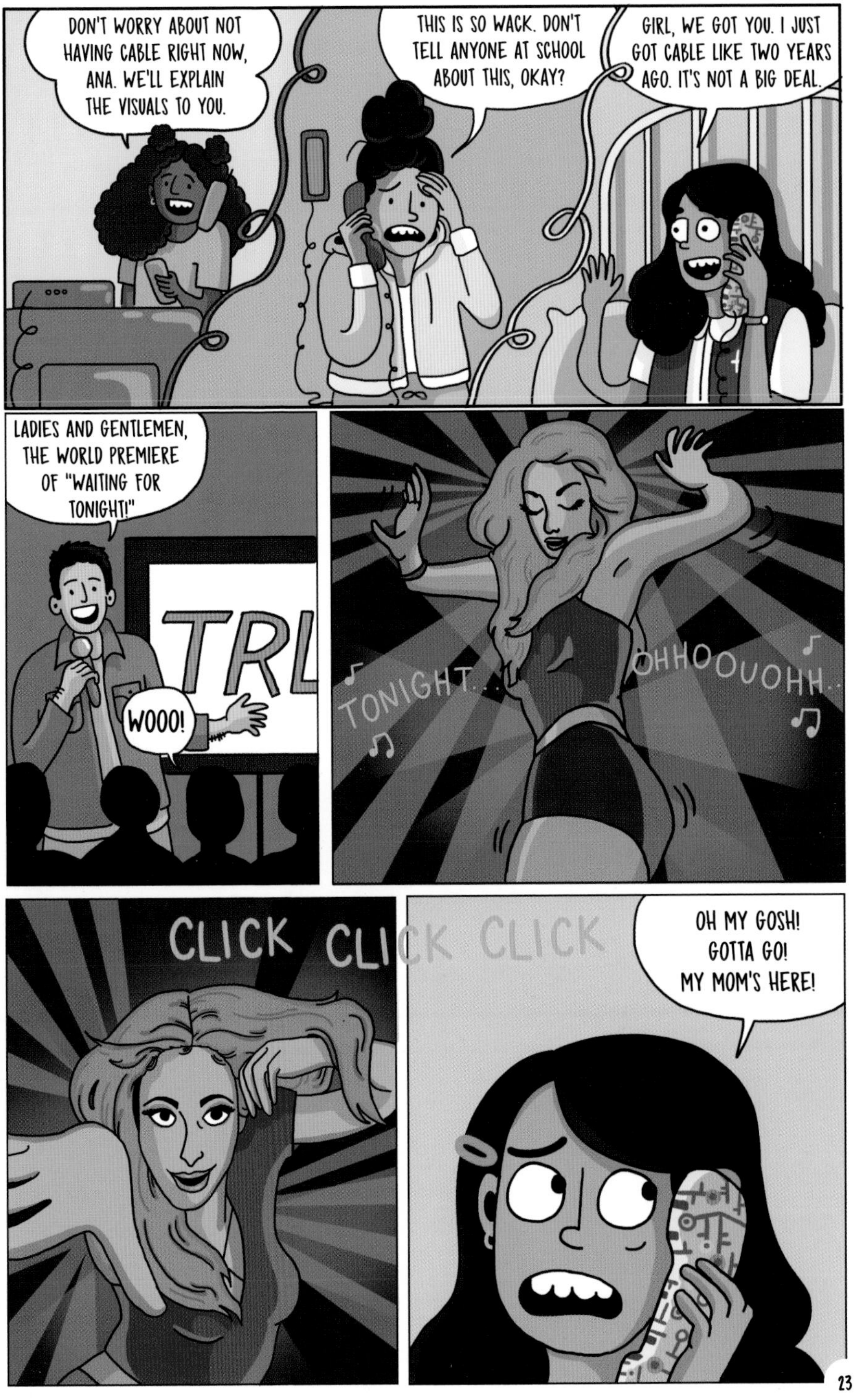
DON'T WORRY ABOUT NOT HAVING CABLE RIGHT NOW, ANA. WE'LL EXPLAIN THE VISUALS TO YOU.
THIS IS SO WACK. DON'T TELL ANYONE AT SCHOOL ABOUT THIS, OKAY?
GIRL, WE GOT YOU. I JUST GOT CABLE LIKE TWO YEARS AGO. IT'S NOT A BIG DEAL.
LADIES AND GENTLEMEN, THE WORLD PREMIERE OF "WAITING FOR TONIGHT!"
TRL
WOOO!
TONIGHT...
OHHOOUOHH...
CLICK CLICK CLICK
OH MY GOSH! GOTTA GO! MY MOM'S HERE!

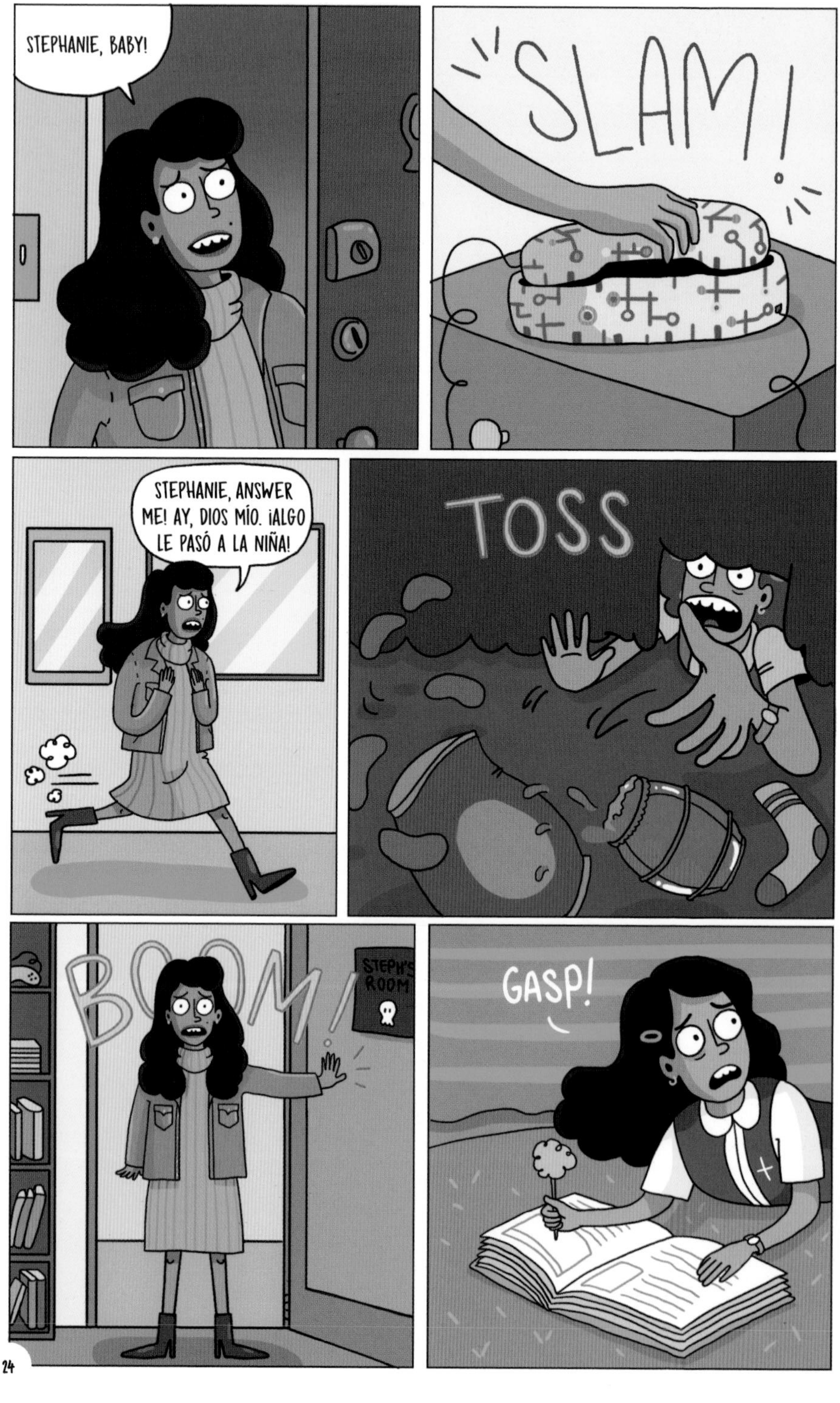
STEPHANIE, BABY!
SLAM!
STEPHANIE, ANSWER ME! AY, DIOS MÍO. ¡ALGO LE PASÓ A LA NIÑA!
TOSS
BOOM!
STEPH'S ROOM
GASP!

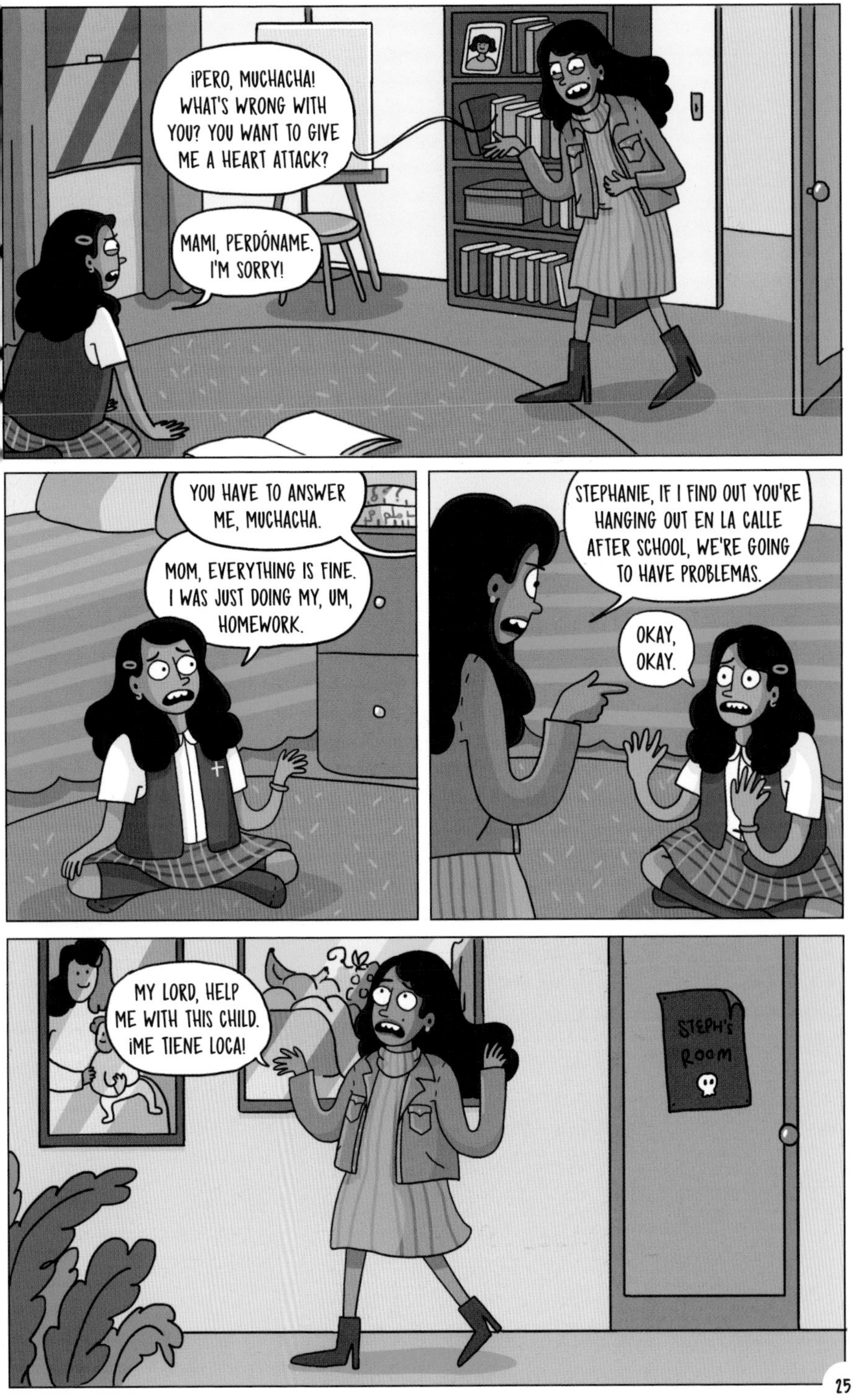

¡PERO, MUCHACHA! WHAT'S WRONG WITH YOU? YOU WANT TO GIVE ME A HEART ATTACK?
MAMI, PERDÓNAME. I'M SORRY!
YOU HAVE TO ANSWER ME, MUCHACHA.
MOM, EVERYTHING IS FINE. I WAS JUST DOING MY, UM, HOMEWORK.
STEPHANIE, IF I FIND OUT YOU'RE HANGING OUT EN LA CALLE AFTER SCHOOL, WE'RE GOING TO HAVE PROBLEMAS.
OKAY, OKAY.
MY LORD, HELP ME WITH THIS CHILD. ¡ME TIENE LOCA!
STEPH'S ROOM

LATER THAT NIGHT

Leo! Big changes are coming your way! Pero be aware of hurting loved ones!

DID YOU HEAR THAT? HE NEVER LIES.

LOOK HOW FEAS MIS HANDS ARE AFTER CUTTING HAIR ALL DAY.

RUB RUB

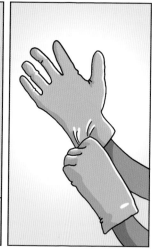

MA, YOU LOOK LIKE MICHAEL JACKSON WITH THOSE GLOVES ON.

HAHA!

MIRA, MUCHACHA. ¡RESPÉTAME! AND DON'T SIT SO CLOSE TO THE TV OR YOU'LL GO BLIND.

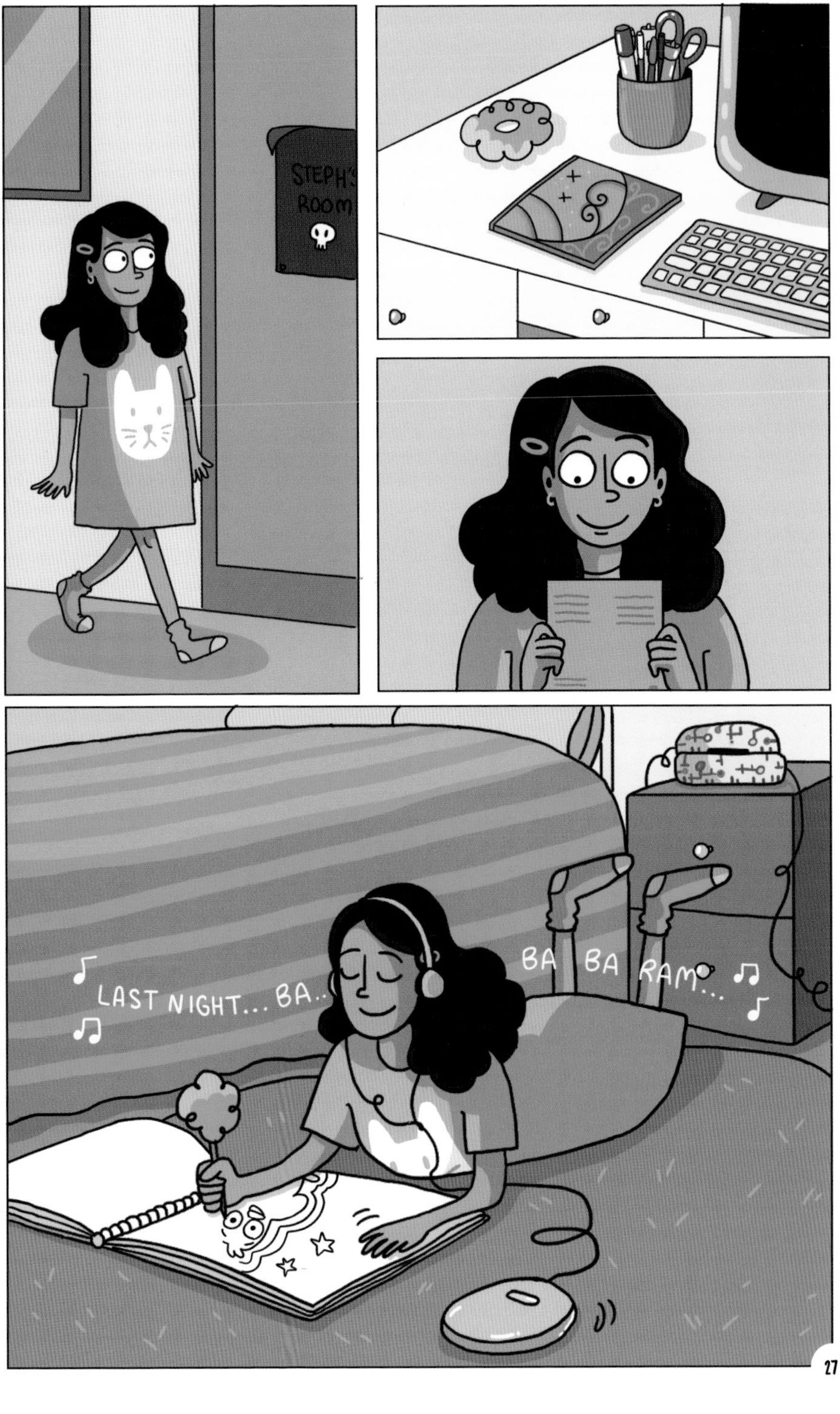
STEPH'S ROOM
LAST NIGHT... BA...
BA BA RAM...

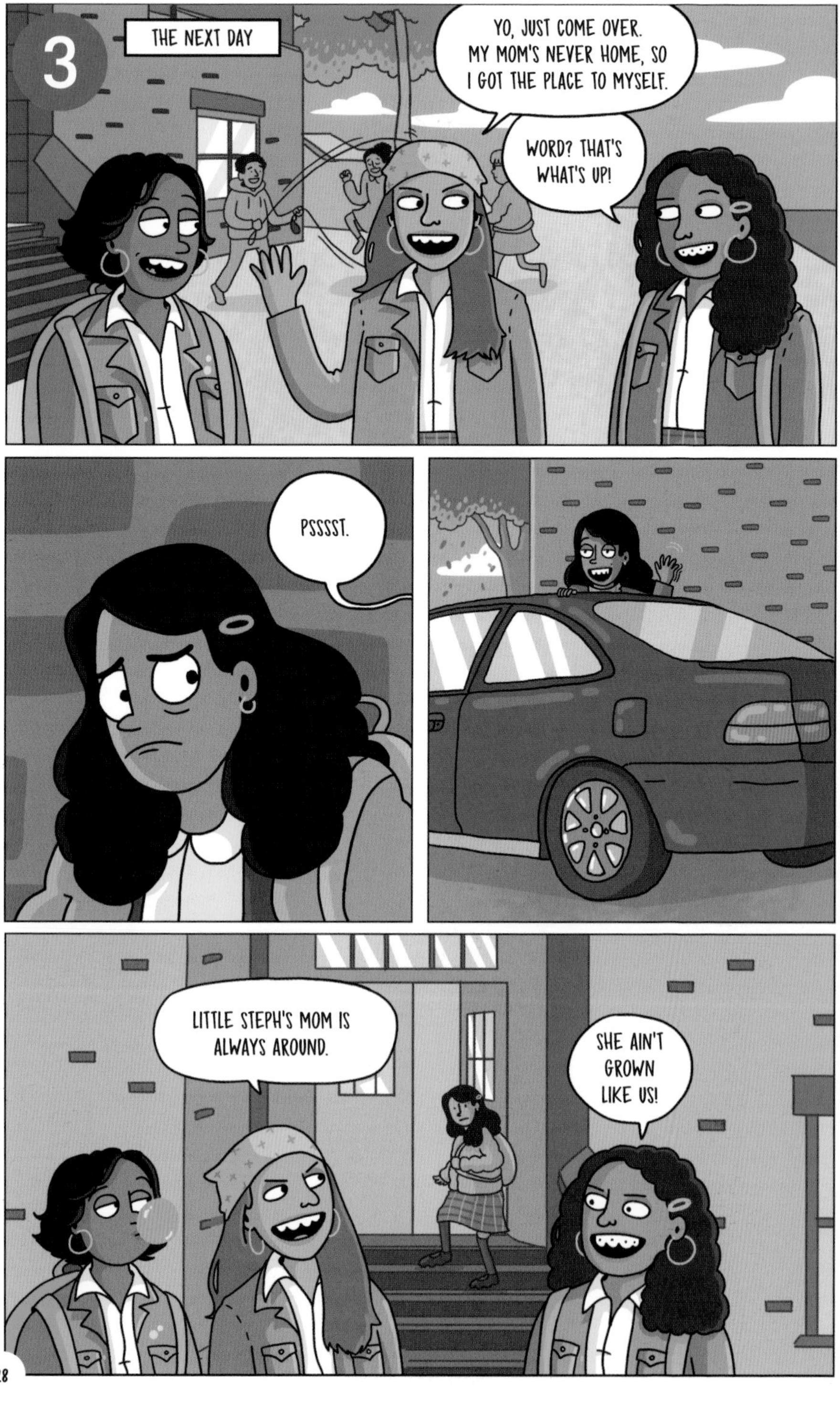
3
THE NEXT DAY
YO, JUST COME OVER. MY MOM'S NEVER HOME, SO I GOT THE PLACE TO MYSELF.
WORD? THAT'S WHAT'S UP!
PSSSST.
LITTLE STEPH'S MOM IS ALWAYS AROUND.
SHE AIN'T GROWN LIKE US!

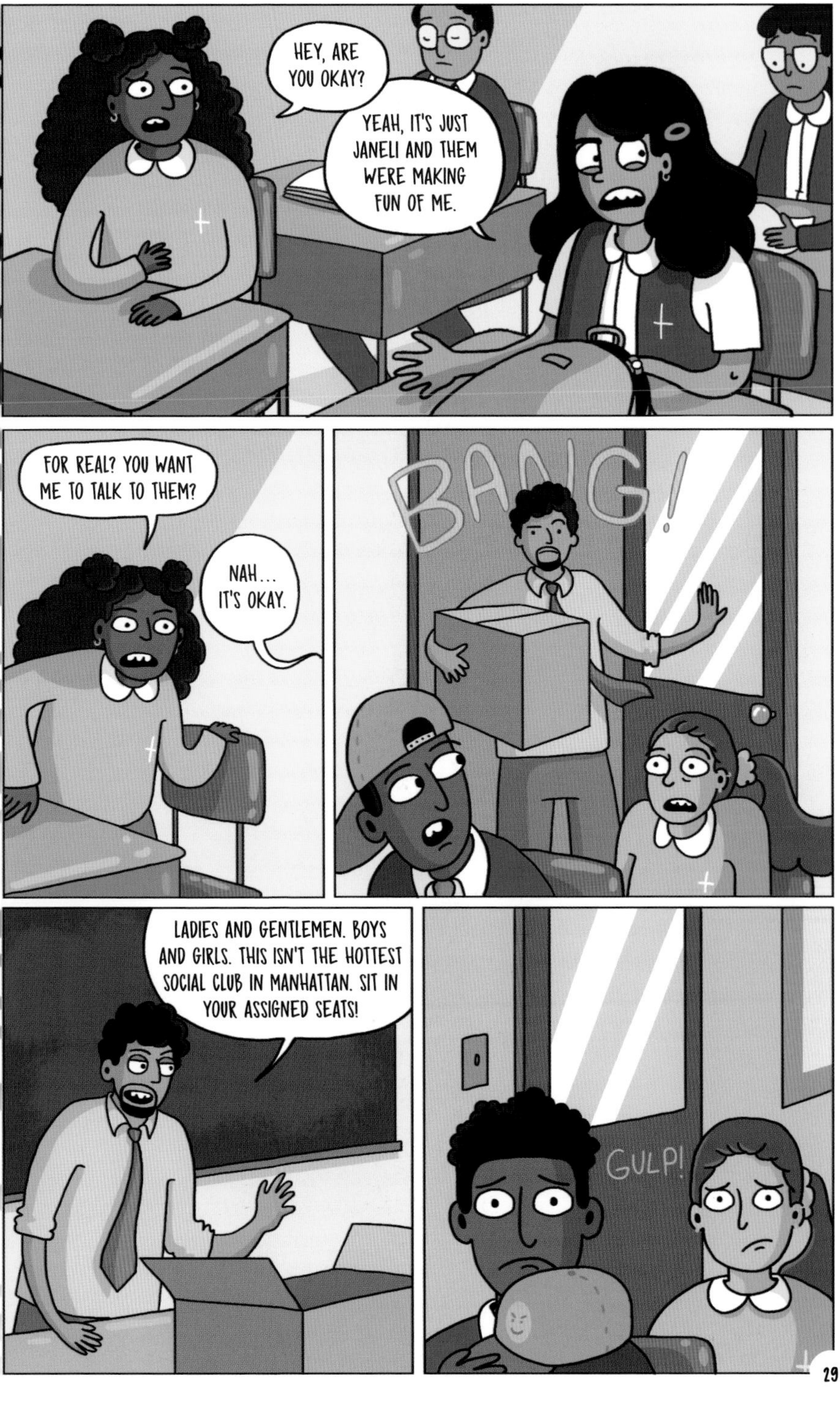
HEY, ARE YOU OKAY?
YEAH, IT'S JUST JANELI AND THEM WERE MAKING FUN OF ME.
FOR REAL? YOU WANT ME TO TALK TO THEM?
NAH... IT'S OKAY.
BANG!
LADIES AND GENTLEMEN. BOYS AND GIRLS. THIS ISN'T THE HOTTEST SOCIAL CLUB IN MANHATTAN. SIT IN YOUR ASSIGNED SEATS!
GULP!

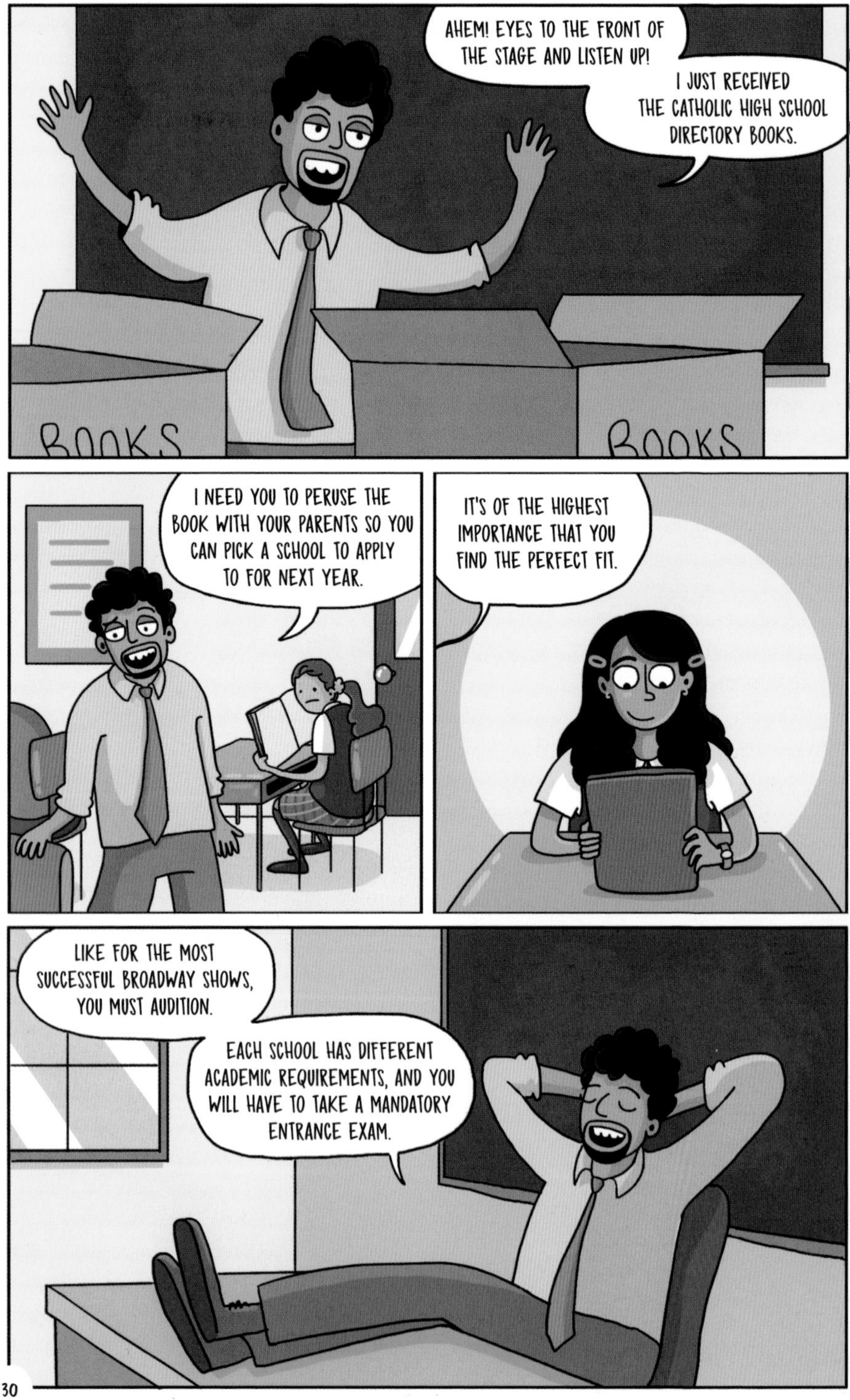
AHEM! EYES TO THE FRONT OF THE STAGE AND LISTEN UP!
I JUST RECEIVED THE CATHOLIC HIGH SCHOOL DIRECTORY BOOKS.
BOOKS
BOOKS
I NEED YOU TO PERUSE THE BOOK WITH YOUR PARENTS SO YOU CAN PICK A SCHOOL TO APPLY TO FOR NEXT YEAR.
IT'S OF THE HIGHEST IMPORTANCE THAT YOU FIND THE PERFECT FIT.
LIKE FOR THE MOST SUCCESSFUL BROADWAY SHOWS, YOU MUST AUDITION.
EACH SCHOOL HAS DIFFERENT ACADEMIC REQUIREMENTS, AND YOU WILL HAVE TO TAKE A MANDATORY ENTRANCE EXAM.

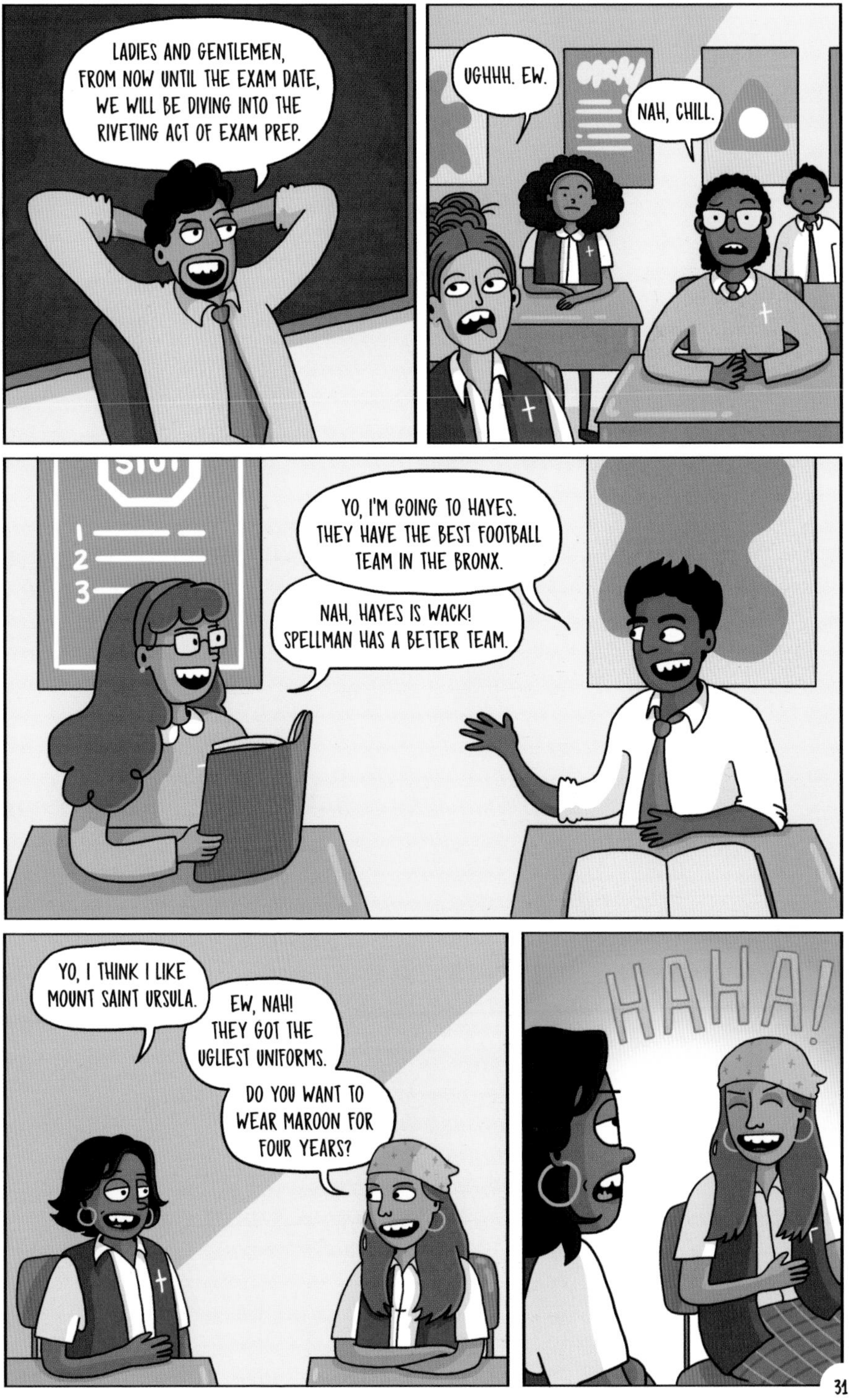
LADIES AND GENTLEMEN, FROM NOW UNTIL THE EXAM DATE, WE WILL BE DIVING INTO THE RIVETING ACT OF EXAM PREP.
UGHHH. EW.
NAH, CHILL.
YO, I'M GOING TO HAYES. THEY HAVE THE BEST FOOTBALL TEAM IN THE BRONX.
NAH, HAYES IS WACK! SPELLMAN HAS A BETTER TEAM.
YO, I THINK I LIKE MOUNT SAINT URSULA.
EW, NAH! THEY GOT THE UGLIEST UNIFORMS.
DO YOU WANT TO WEAR MAROON FOR FOUR YEARS?
HAHA!

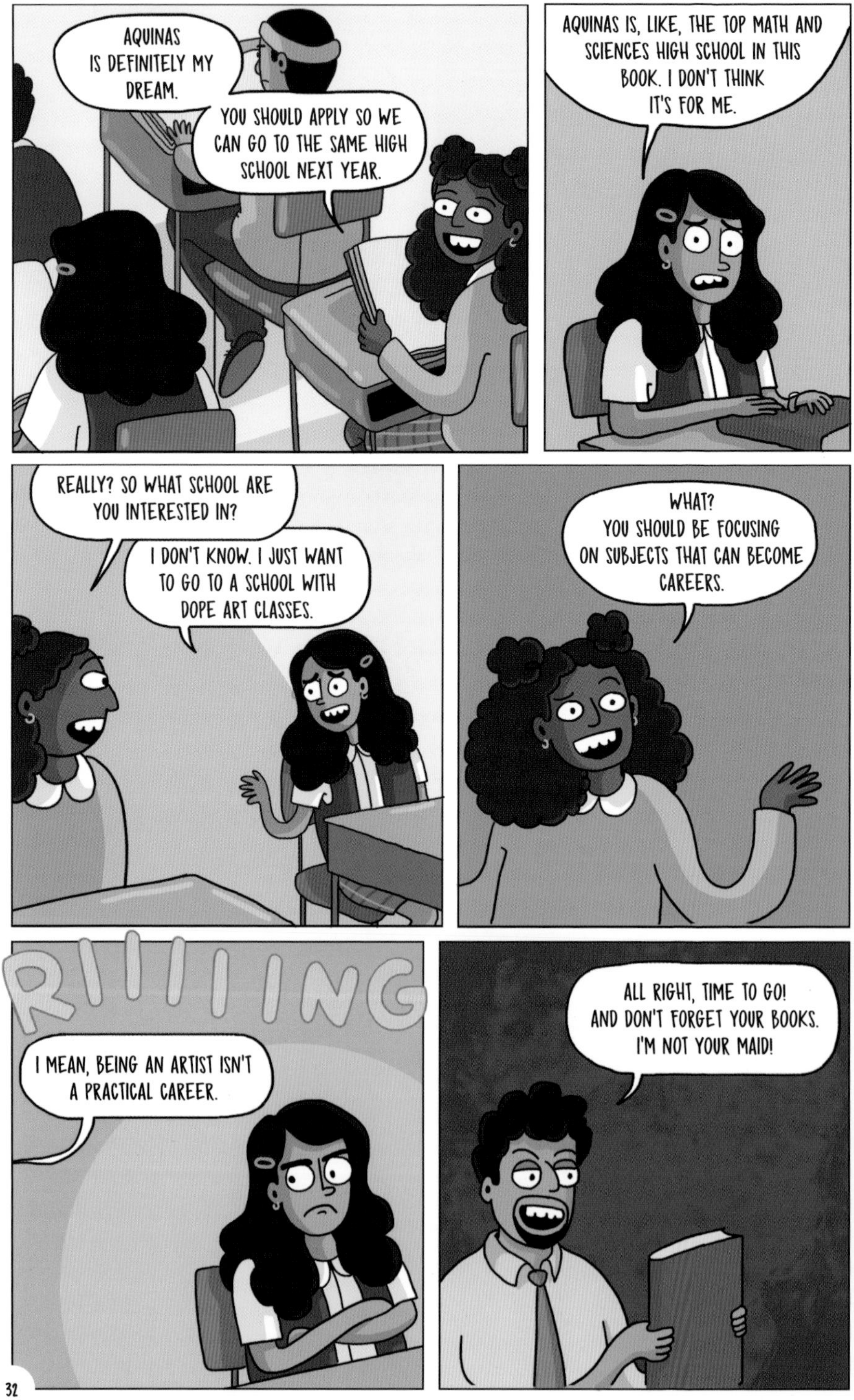
AQUINAS IS DEFINITELY MY DREAM.
YOU SHOULD APPLY SO WE CAN GO TO THE SAME HIGH SCHOOL NEXT YEAR.
AQUINAS IS, LIKE, THE TOP MATH AND SCIENCES HIGH SCHOOL IN THIS BOOK. I DON'T THINK IT'S FOR ME.
REALLY? SO WHAT SCHOOL ARE YOU INTERESTED IN?
I DON'T KNOW. I JUST WANT TO GO TO A SCHOOL WITH DOPE ART CLASSES.
WHAT? YOU SHOULD BE FOCUSING ON SUBJECTS THAT CAN BECOME CAREERS.
RIIIING
I MEAN, BEING AN ARTIST ISN'T A PRACTICAL CAREER.
ALL RIGHT, TIME TO GO! AND DON'T FORGET YOUR BOOKS. I'M NOT YOUR MAID!

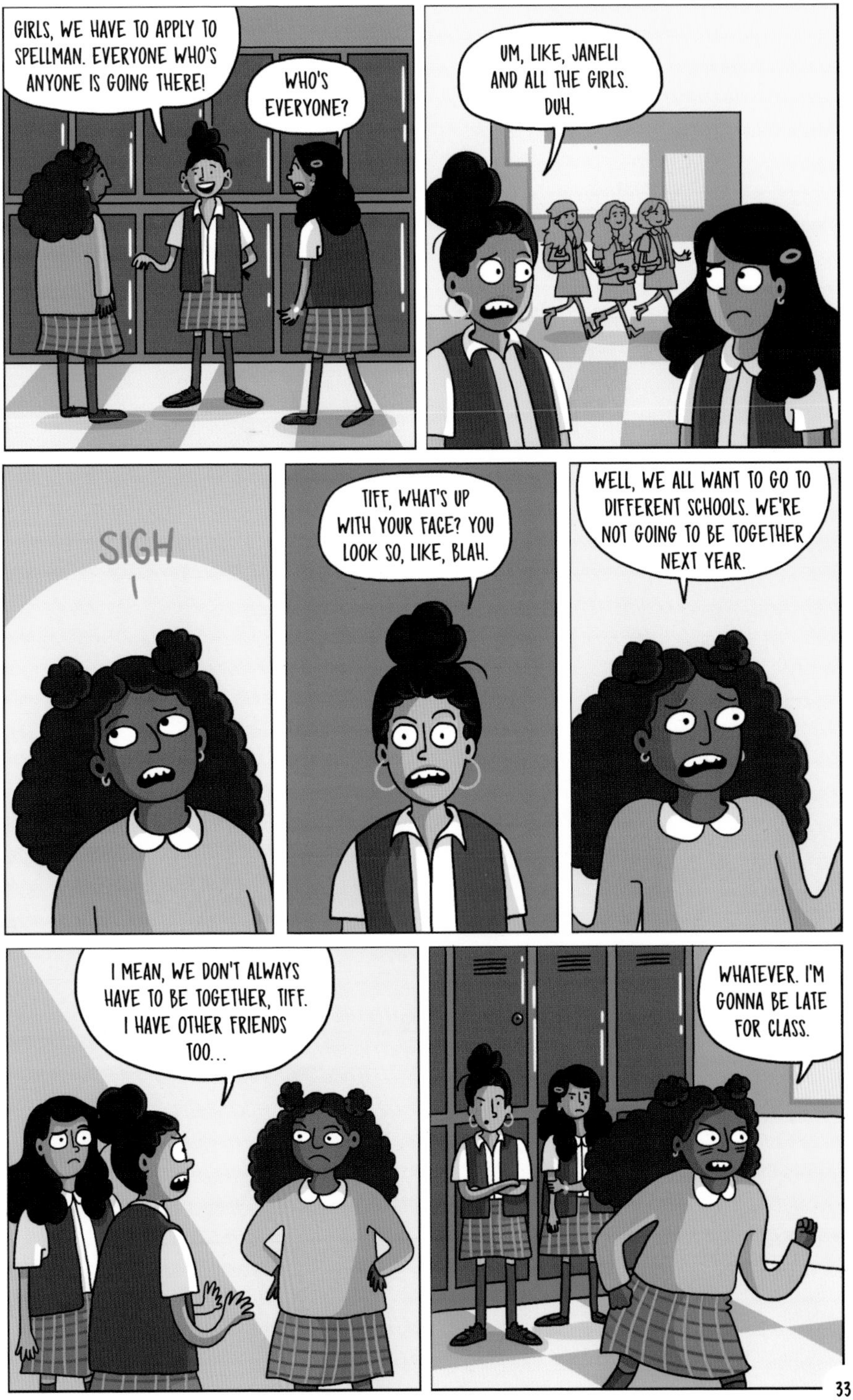
GIRLS, WE HAVE TO APPLY TO SPELLMAN. EVERYONE WHO'S ANYONE IS GOING THERE!
WHO'S EVERYONE?
UM, LIKE, JANELI AND ALL THE GIRLS. DUH.
SIGH
TIFF, WHAT'S UP WITH YOUR FACE? YOU LOOK SO, LIKE, BLAH.
WELL, WE ALL WANT TO GO TO DIFFERENT SCHOOLS. WE'RE NOT GOING TO BE TOGETHER NEXT YEAR.
I MEAN, WE DON'T ALWAYS HAVE TO BE TOGETHER, TIFF. I HAVE OTHER FRIENDS TOO...
WHATEVER. I'M GONNA BE LATE FOR CLASS.

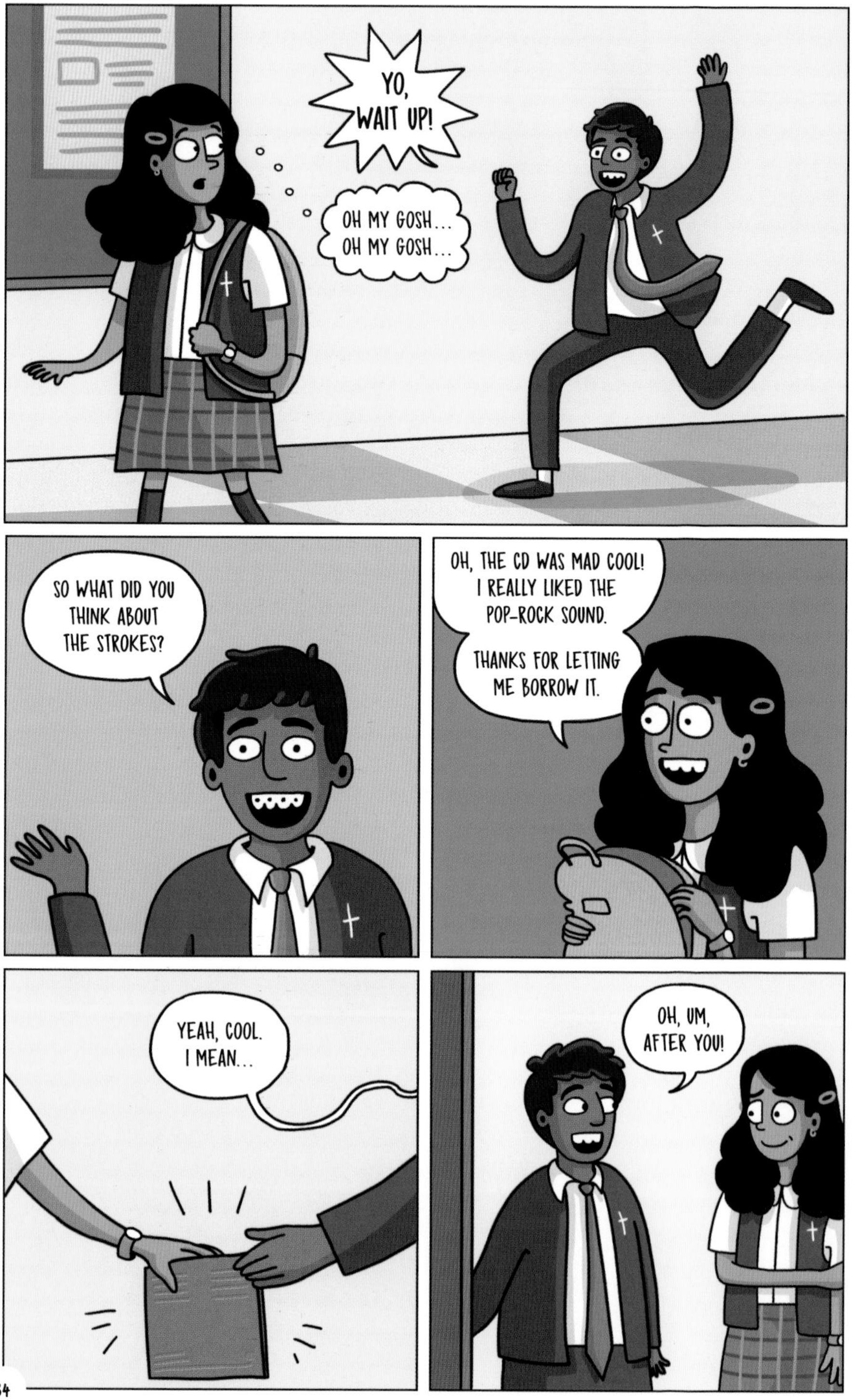
YO, WAIT UP!
OH MY GOSH... OH MY GOSH...
SO WHAT DID YOU THINK ABOUT THE STROKES?
OH, THE CD WAS MAD COOL! I REALLY LIKED THE POP-ROCK SOUND.
THANKS FOR LETTING ME BORROW IT.
YEAH, COOL. I MEAN...
OH, UM, AFTER YOU!

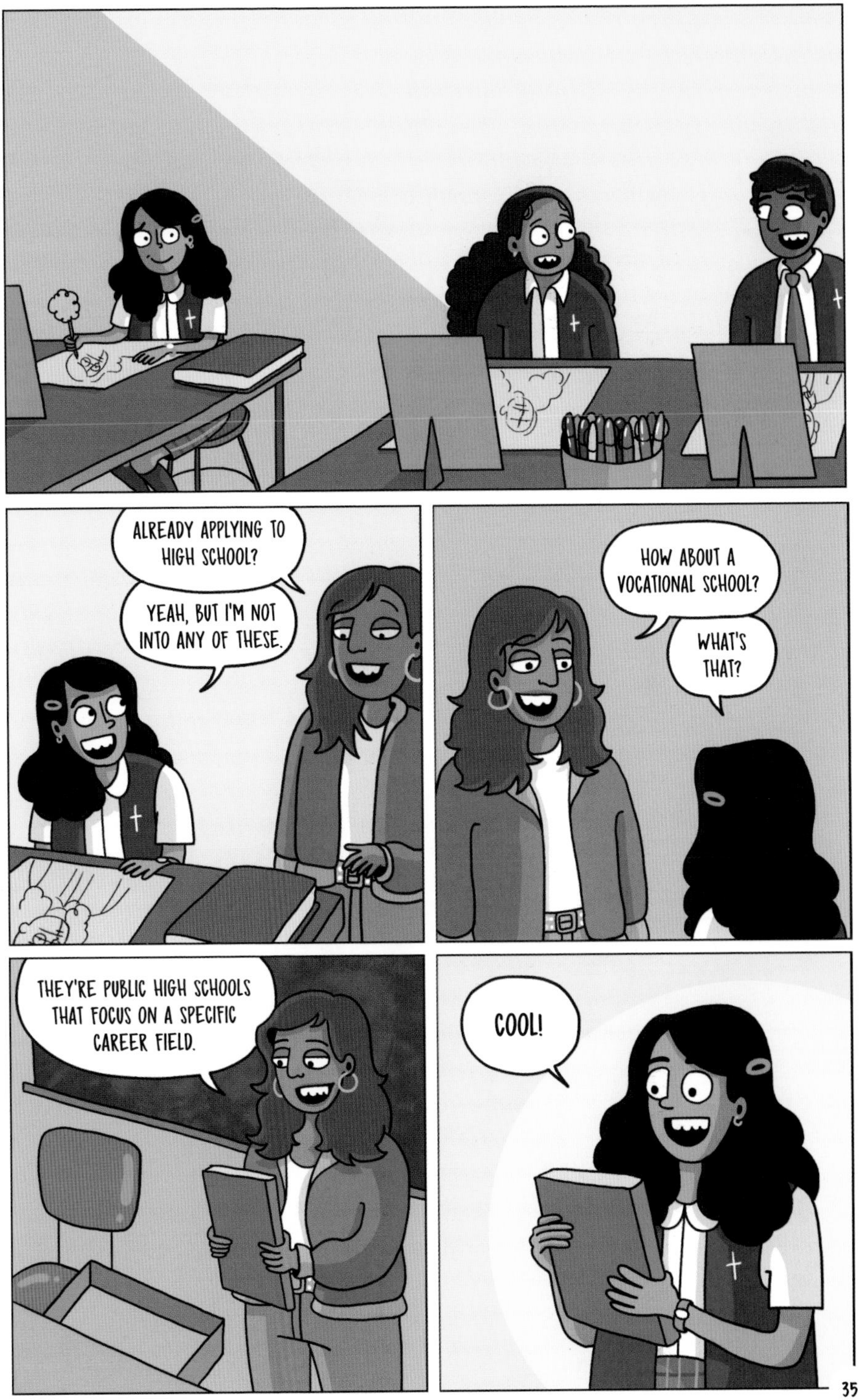
ALREADY APPLYING TO HIGH SCHOOL?
YEAH, BUT I'M NOT INTO ANY OF THESE.
HOW ABOUT A VOCATIONAL SCHOOL?
WHAT'S THAT?
THEY'RE PUBLIC HIGH SCHOOLS THAT FOCUS ON A SPECIFIC CAREER FIELD.
COOL!

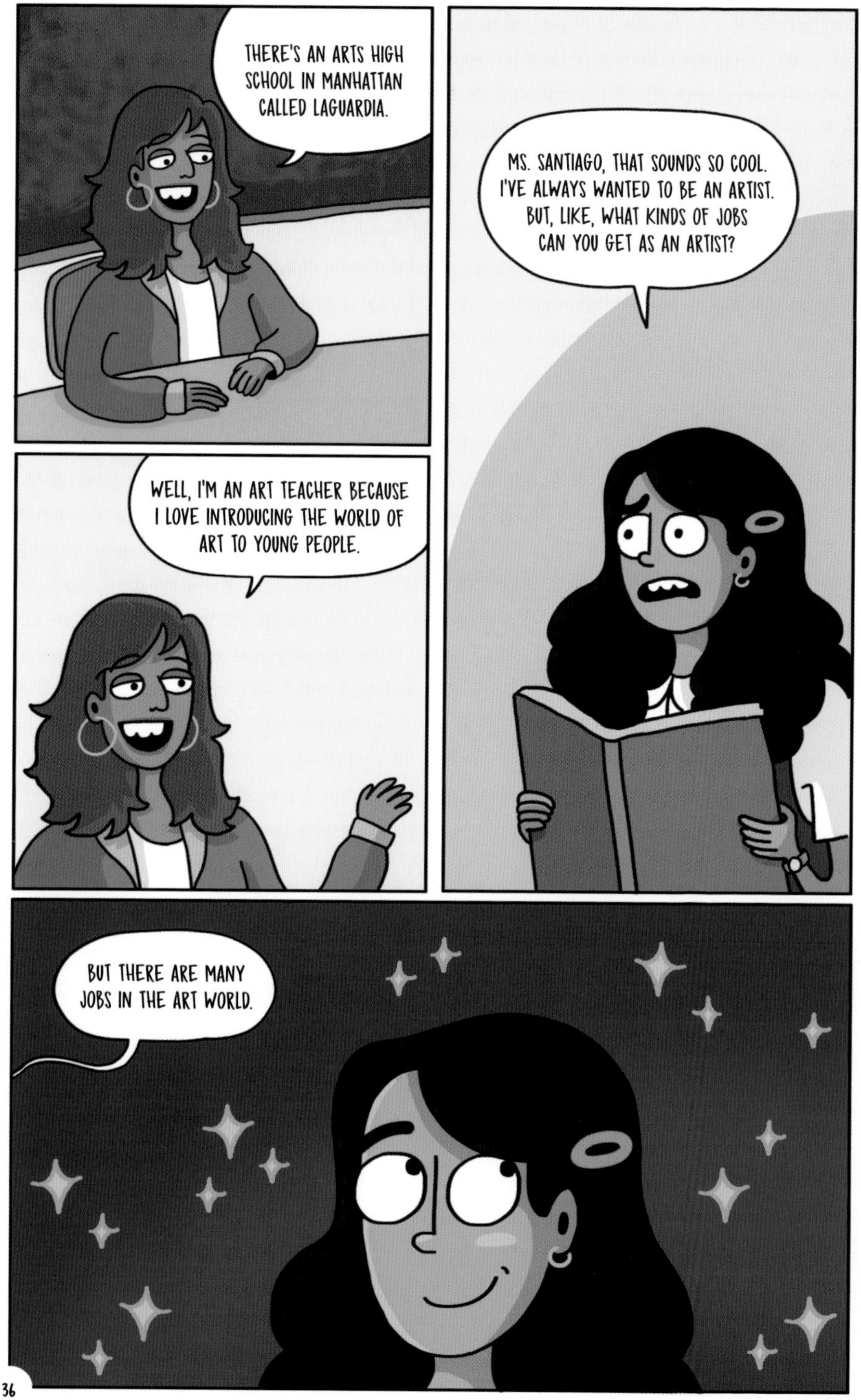
THERE'S AN ARTS HIGH SCHOOL IN MANHATTAN CALLED LAGUARDIA.
MS. SANTIAGO, THAT SOUNDS SO COOL. I'VE ALWAYS WANTED TO BE AN ARTIST. BUT, LIKE, WHAT KINDS OF JOBS CAN YOU GET AS AN ARTIST?
WELL, I'M AN ART TEACHER BECAUSE I LOVE INTRODUCING THE WORLD OF ART TO YOUNG PEOPLE.
BUT THERE ARE MANY JOBS IN THE ART WORLD.

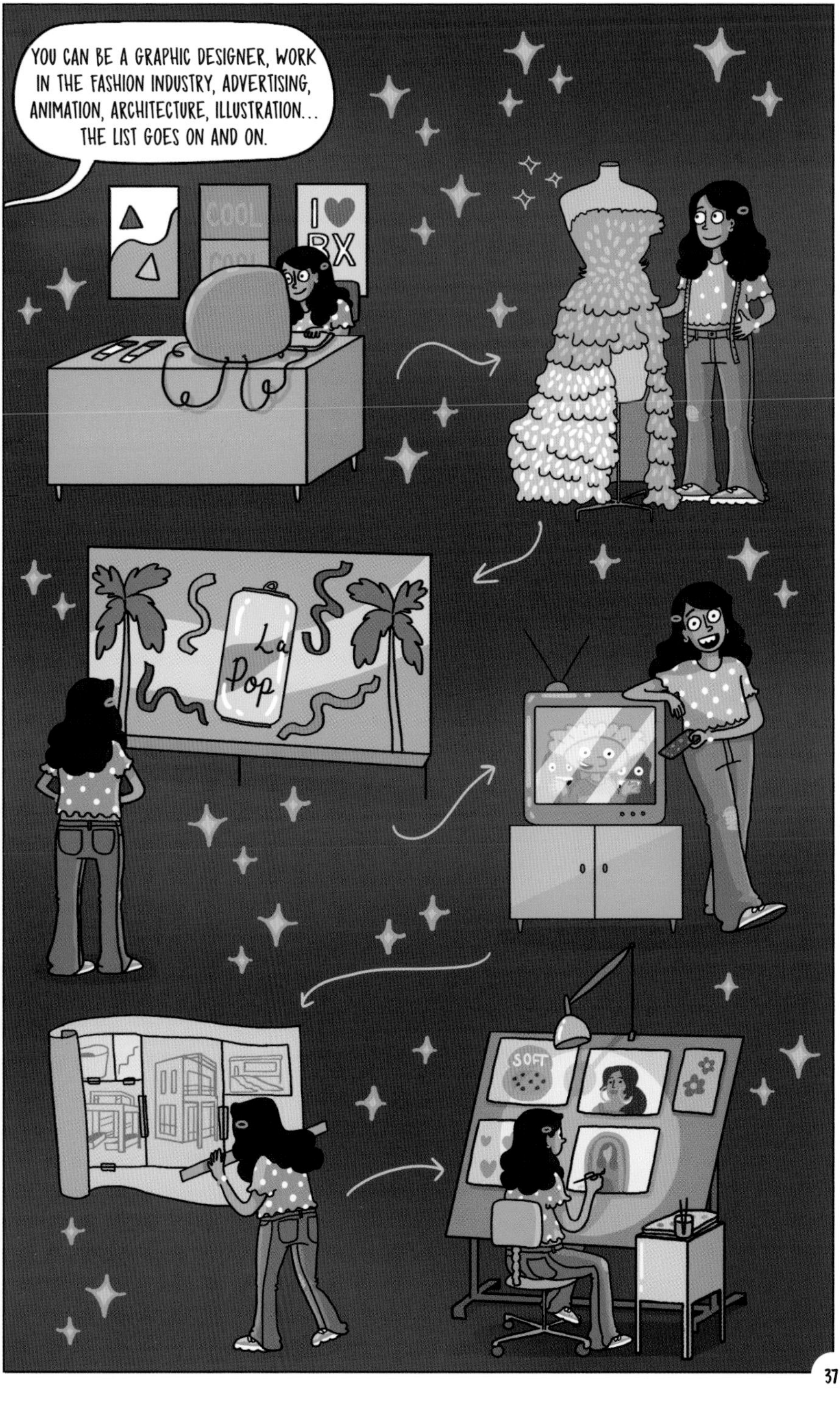
YOU CAN BE A GRAPHIC DESIGNER, WORK IN THE FASHION INDUSTRY, ADVERTISING, ANIMATION, ARCHITECTURE, ILLUSTRATION... THE LIST GOES ON AND ON.
COOL
COOL
I ♥ BX
La Pop
SOFT

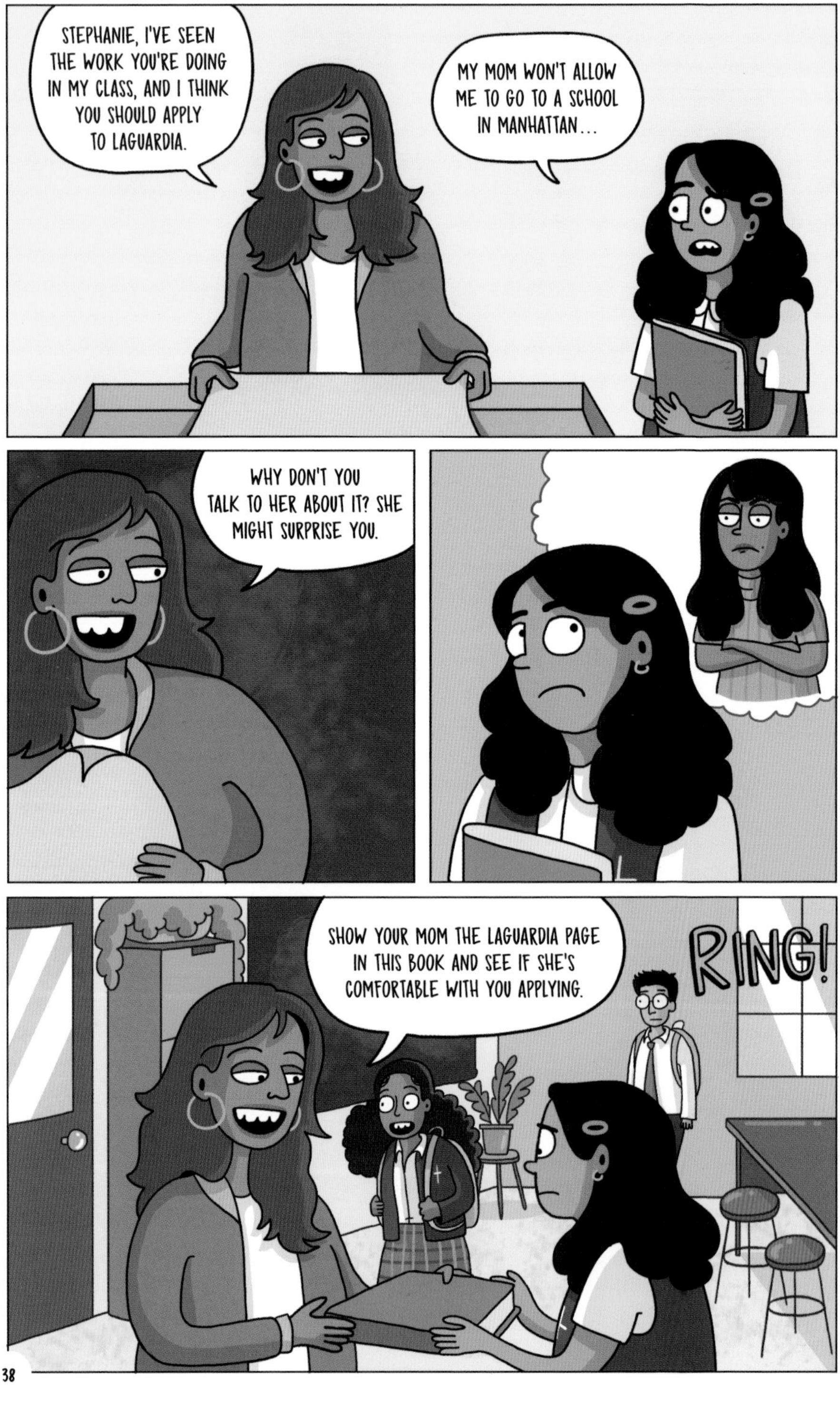
STEPHANIE, I'VE SEEN THE WORK YOU'RE DOING IN MY CLASS, AND I THINK YOU SHOULD APPLY TO LAGUARDIA.
MY MOM WON'T ALLOW ME TO GO TO A SCHOOL IN MANHATTAN...
WHY DON'T YOU TALK TO HER ABOUT IT? SHE MIGHT SURPRISE YOU.
SHOW YOUR MOM THE LAGUARDIA PAGE IN THIS BOOK AND SEE IF SHE'S COMFORTABLE WITH YOU APPLYING.
RING!

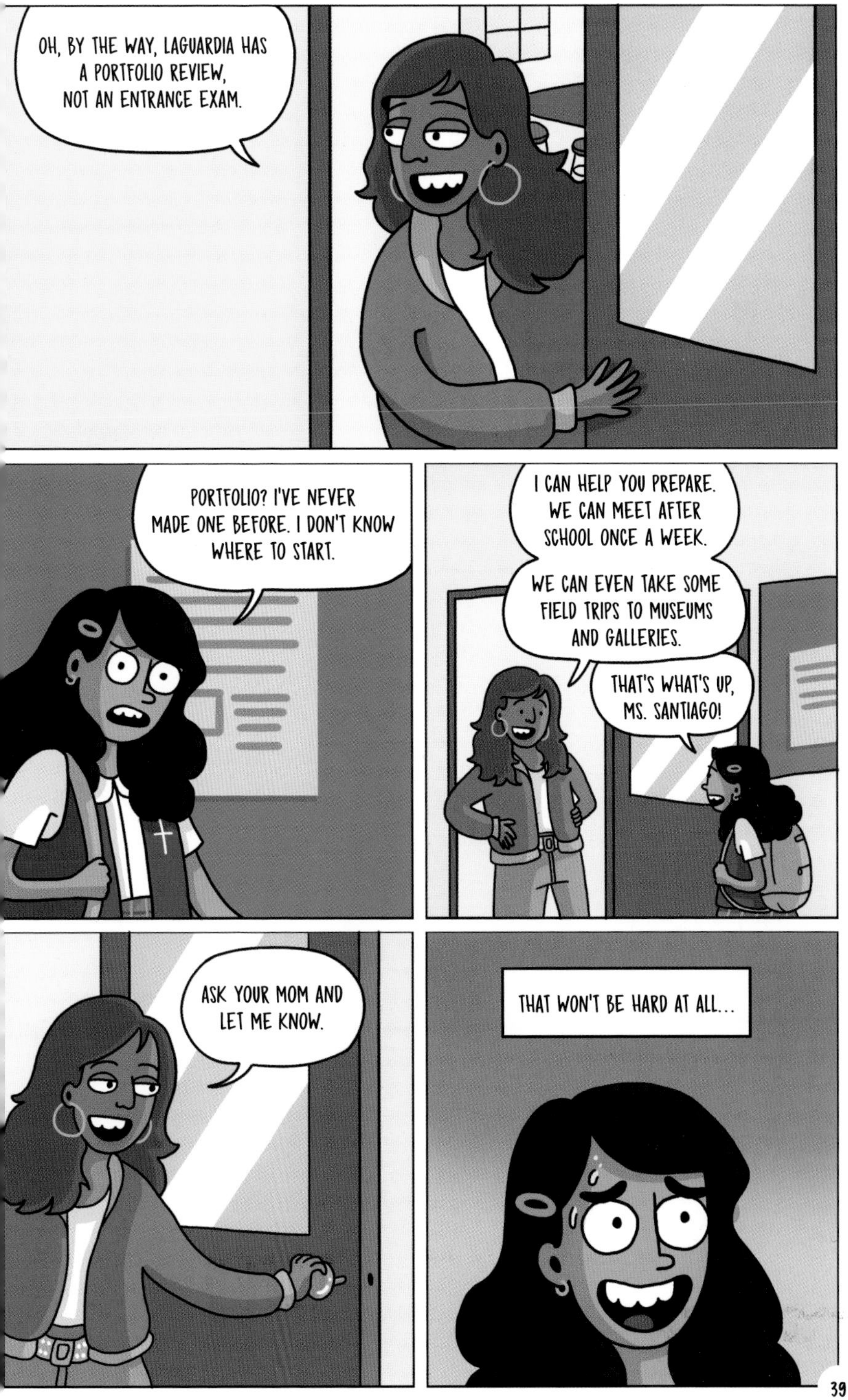
OH, BY THE WAY, LAGUARDIA HAS A PORTFOLIO REVIEW, NOT AN ENTRANCE EXAM.
PORTFOLIO? I'VE NEVER MADE ONE BEFORE. I DON'T KNOW WHERE TO START.
I CAN HELP YOU PREPARE. WE CAN MEET AFTER SCHOOL ONCE A WEEK.
WE CAN EVEN TAKE SOME FIELD TRIPS TO MUSEUMS AND GALLERIES.
THAT'S WHAT'S UP, MS. SANTIAGO!
ASK YOUR MOM AND LET ME KNOW.
THAT WON'T BE HARD AT ALL...

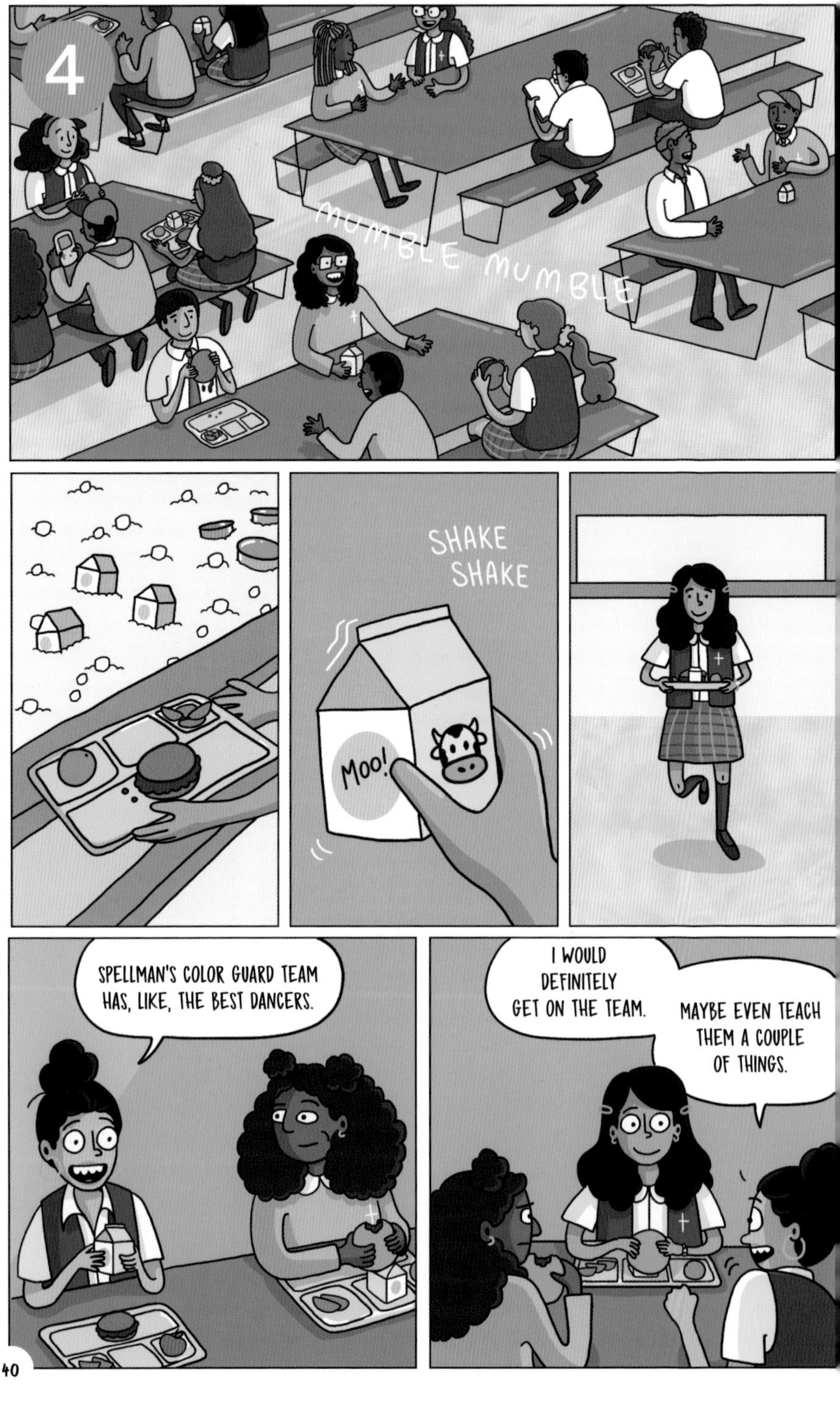
4
MUMBLE MUMBLE
SHAKE
SHAKE
MOO!
SPELLMAN'S COLOR GUARD TEAM HAS, LIKE, THE BEST DANCERS.
I WOULD DEFINITELY GET ON THE TEAM.
MAYBE EVEN TEACH THEM A COUPLE OF THINGS.

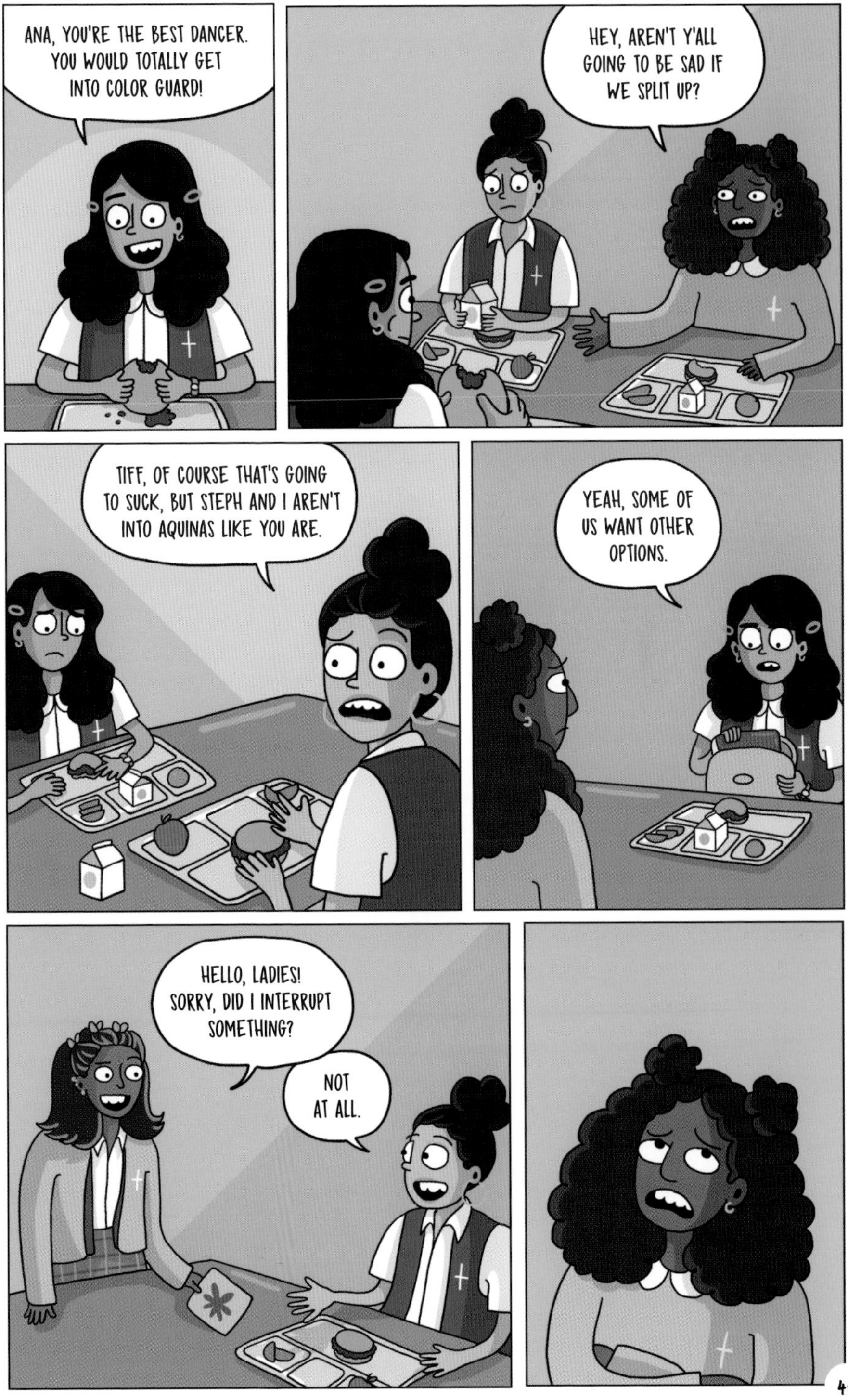
ANA, YOU'RE THE BEST DANCER. YOU WOULD TOTALLY GET INTO COLOR GUARD!
HEY, AREN'T Y'ALL GOING TO BE SAD IF WE SPLIT UP?
TIFF, OF COURSE THAT'S GOING TO SUCK, BUT STEPH AND I AREN'T INTO AQUINAS LIKE YOU ARE.
YEAH, SOME OF US WANT OTHER OPTIONS.
HELLO, LADIES! SORRY, DID I INTERRUPT SOMETHING?
NOT AT ALL.

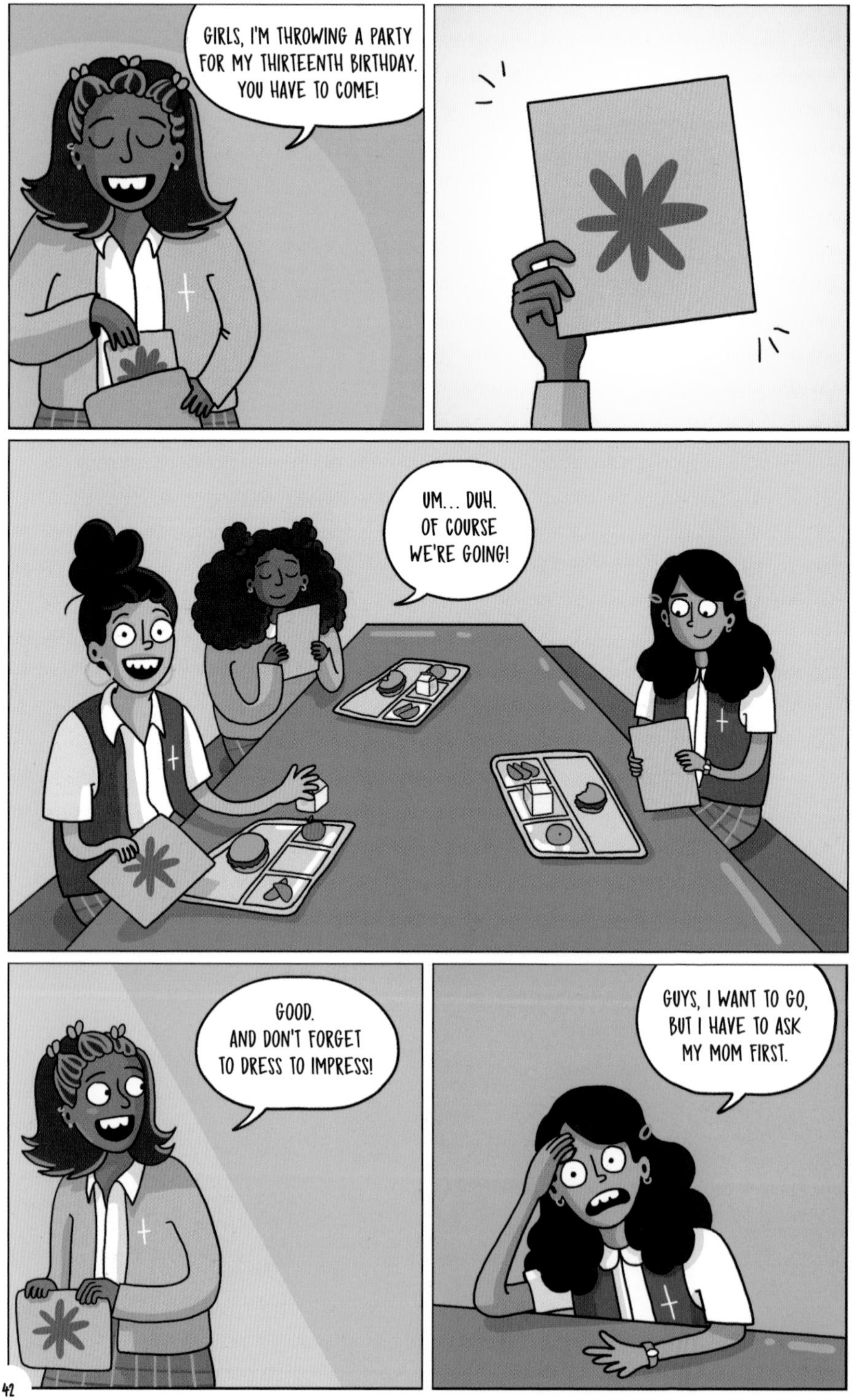
GIRLS, I'M THROWING A PARTY FOR MY THIRTEENTH BIRTHDAY. YOU HAVE TO COME!
UM... DUH. OF COURSE WE'RE GOING!
GOOD. AND DON'T FORGET TO DRESS TO IMPRESS!
GUYS, I WANT TO GO, BUT I HAVE TO ASK MY MOM FIRST.

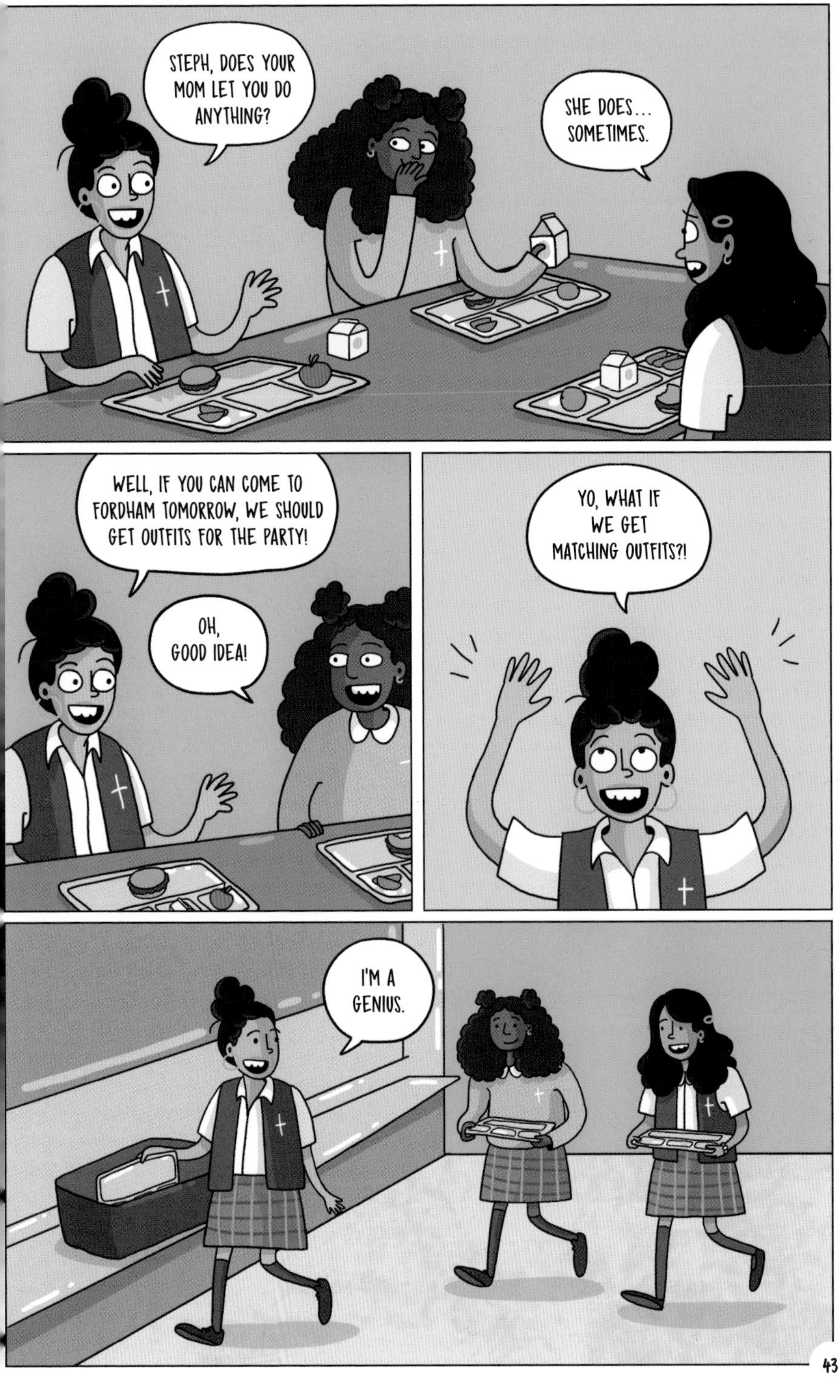
STEPH, DOES YOUR MOM LET YOU DO ANYTHING?
SHE DOES... SOMETIMES.
WELL, IF YOU CAN COME TO FORDHAM TOMORROW, WE SHOULD GET OUTFITS FOR THE PARTY!
OH, GOOD IDEA!
YO, WHAT IF WE GET MATCHING OUTFITS?!
I'M A GENIUS.

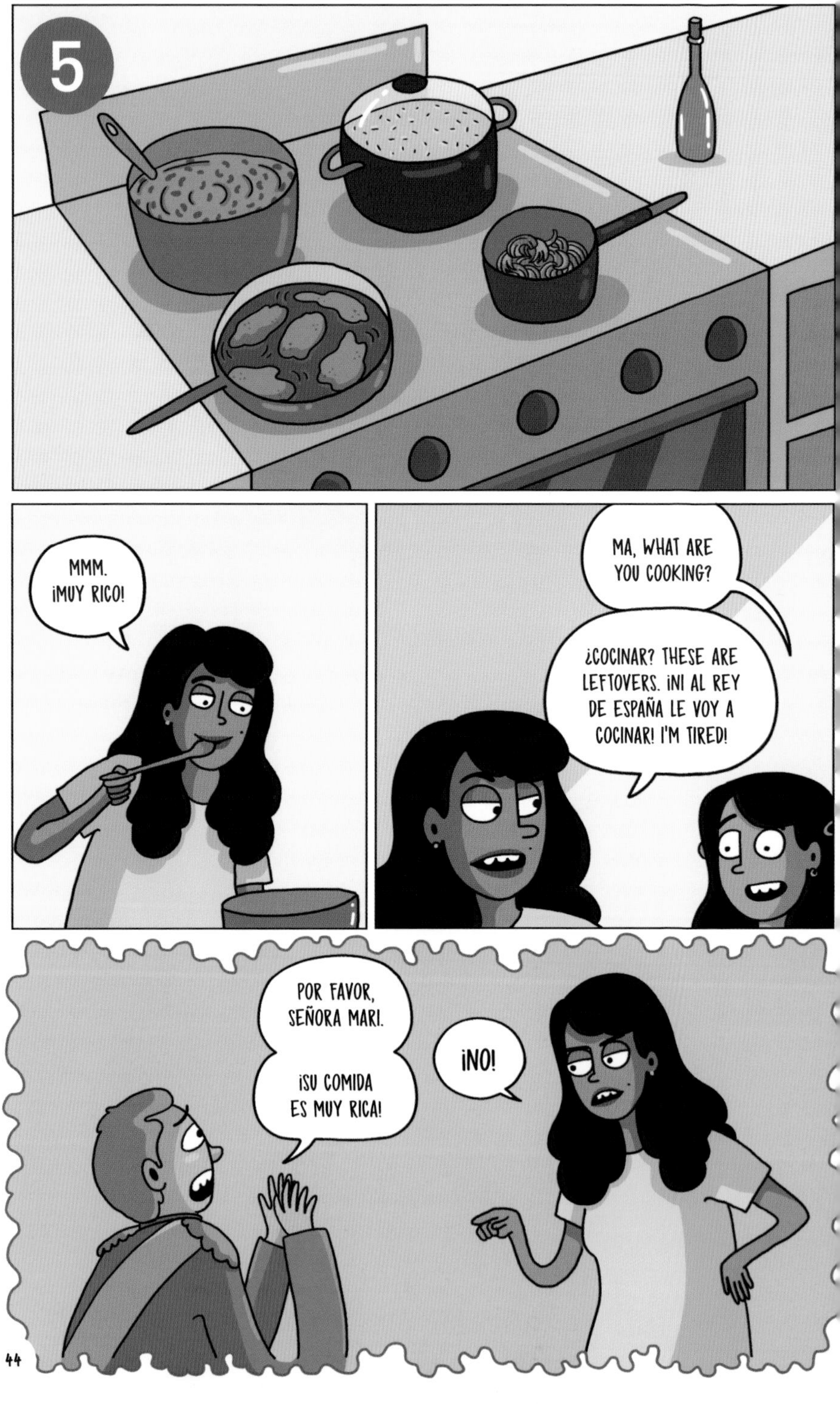
5
MMM. ¡MUY RICO!
MA, WHAT ARE YOU COOKING?
¿COCINAR? THESE ARE LEFTOVERS. ¡NI AL REY DE ESPAÑA LE VOY A COCINAR! I'M TIRED!
POR FAVOR, SEÑORA MARI.
¡SU COMIDA ES MUY RICA!
¡NO!

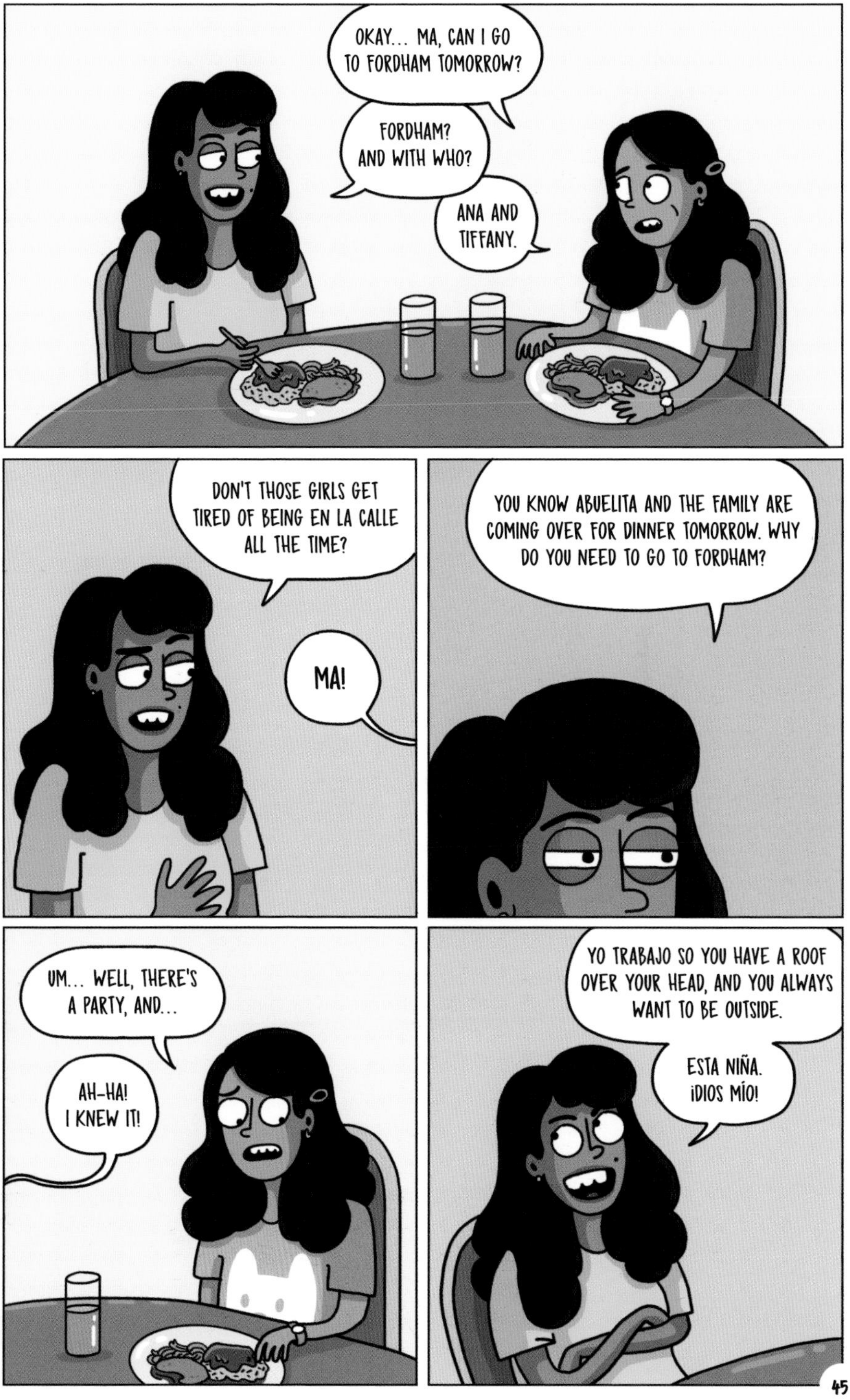
OKAY... MA, CAN I GO TO FORDHAM TOMORROW?
FORDHAM? AND WITH WHO?
ANA AND TIFFANY.
DON'T THOSE GIRLS GET TIRED OF BEING EN LA CALLE ALL THE TIME?
MA!
YOU KNOW ABUELITA AND THE FAMILY ARE COMING OVER FOR DINNER TOMORROW. WHY DO YOU NEED TO GO TO FORDHAM?
UM... WELL, THERE'S A PARTY, AND...
AH-HA! I KNEW IT!
YO TRABAJO SO YOU HAVE A ROOF OVER YOUR HEAD, AND YOU ALWAYS WANT TO BE OUTSIDE.
ESTA NIÑA. ¡DIOS MÍO!

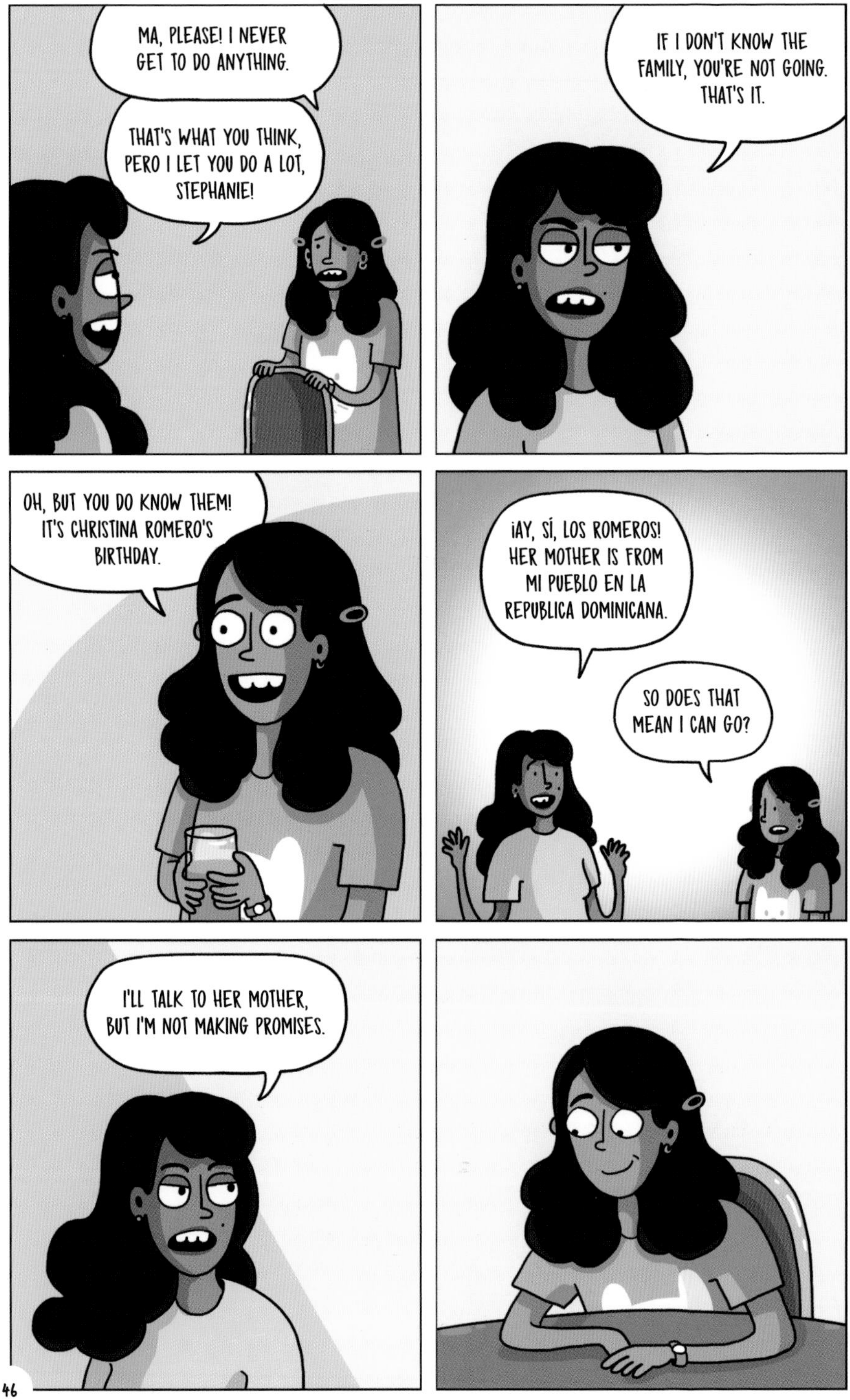
MA, PLEASE! I NEVER GET TO DO ANYTHING.
THAT'S WHAT YOU THINK, PERO I LET YOU DO A LOT, STEPHANIE!
IF I DON'T KNOW THE FAMILY, YOU'RE NOT GOING. THAT'S IT.
OH, BUT YOU DO KNOW THEM! IT'S CHRISTINA ROMERO'S BIRTHDAY.
¡AY, SÍ, LOS ROMEROS! HER MOTHER IS FROM MI PUEBLO EN LA REPUBLICA DOMINICANA.
SO DOES THAT MEAN I CAN GO?
I'LL TALK TO HER MOTHER, BUT I'M NOT MAKING PROMISES.

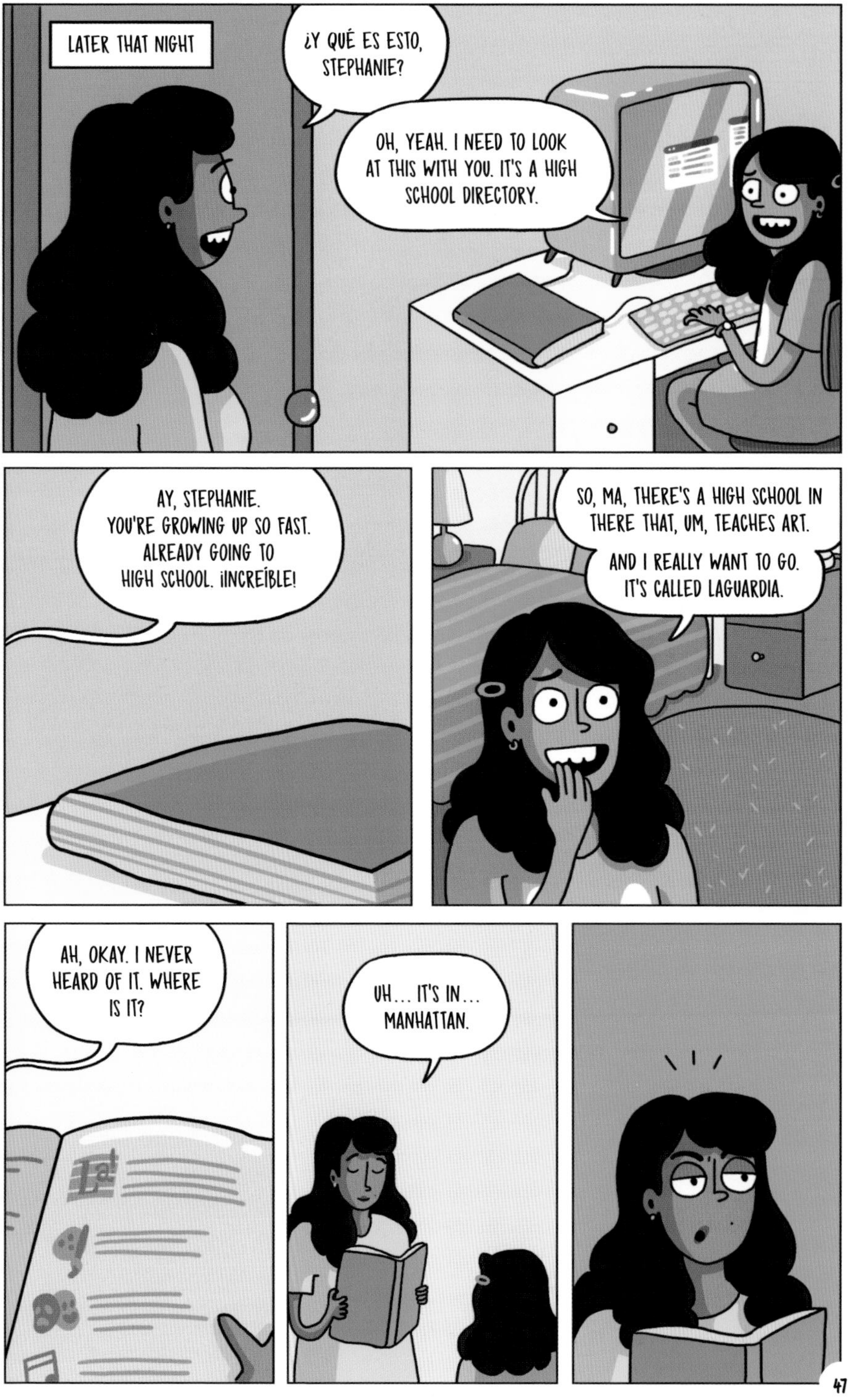
LATER THAT NIGHT
¿Y QUÉ ES ESTO, STEPHANIE?
OH, YEAH. I NEED TO LOOK AT THIS WITH YOU. IT'S A HIGH SCHOOL DIRECTORY.
AY, STEPHANIE. YOU'RE GROWING UP SO FAST. ALREADY GOING TO HIGH SCHOOL. ¡INCREÍBLE!
SO, MA, THERE'S A HIGH SCHOOL IN THERE THAT, UM, TEACHES ART.
AND I REALLY WANT TO GO. IT'S CALLED LAGUARDIA.
AH, OKAY. I NEVER HEARD OF IT. WHERE IS IT?
UH... IT'S IN... MANHATTAN.

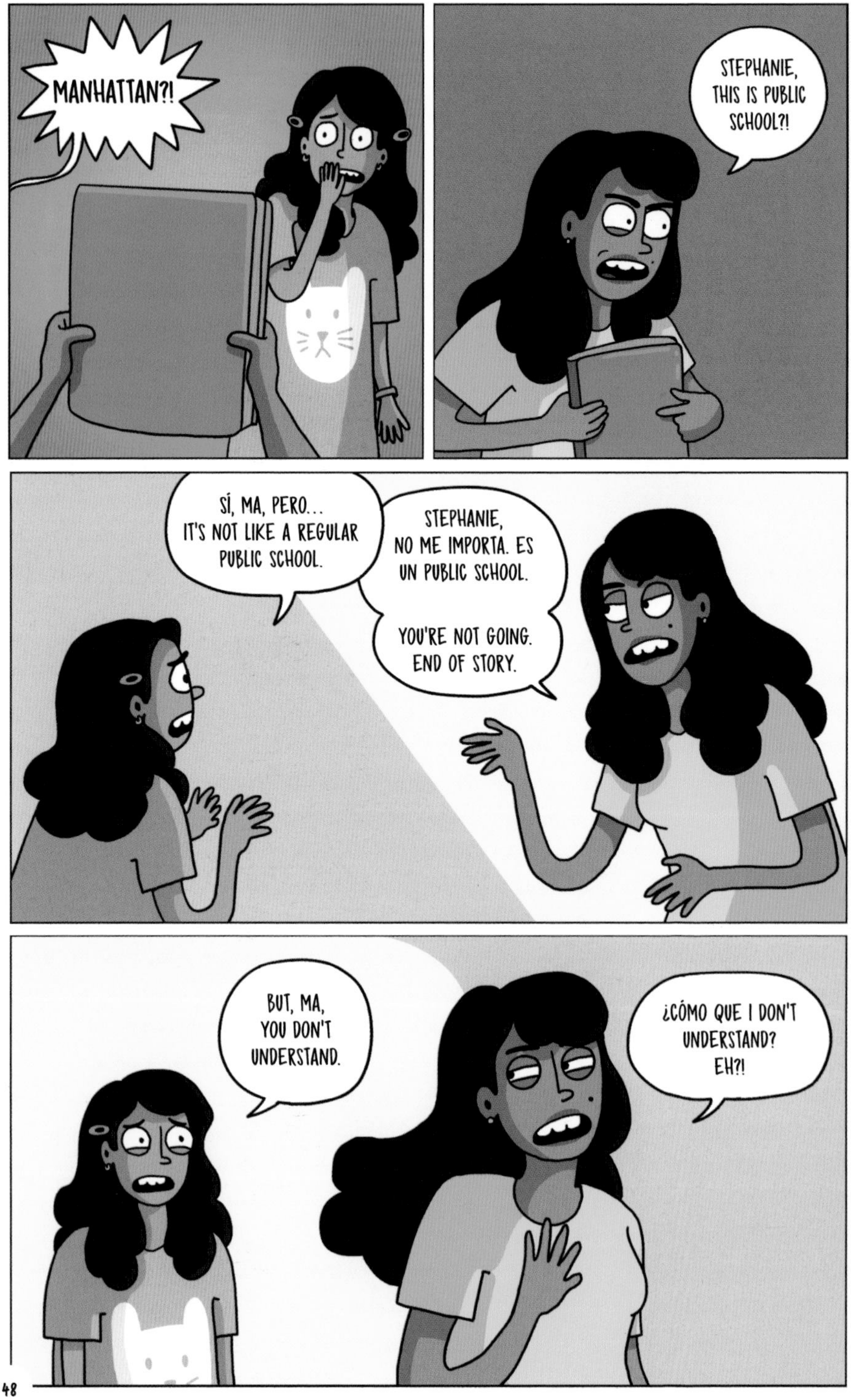
MANHATTAN?!
STEPHANIE, THIS IS PUBLIC SCHOOL?!
SÍ, MA, PERO... IT'S NOT LIKE A REGULAR PUBLIC SCHOOL.
STEPHANIE, NO ME IMPORTA. ES UN PUBLIC SCHOOL.
YOU'RE NOT GOING. END OF STORY.
BUT, MA, YOU DON'T UNDERSTAND.
¿CÓMO QUE I DON'T UNDERSTAND? EH?!

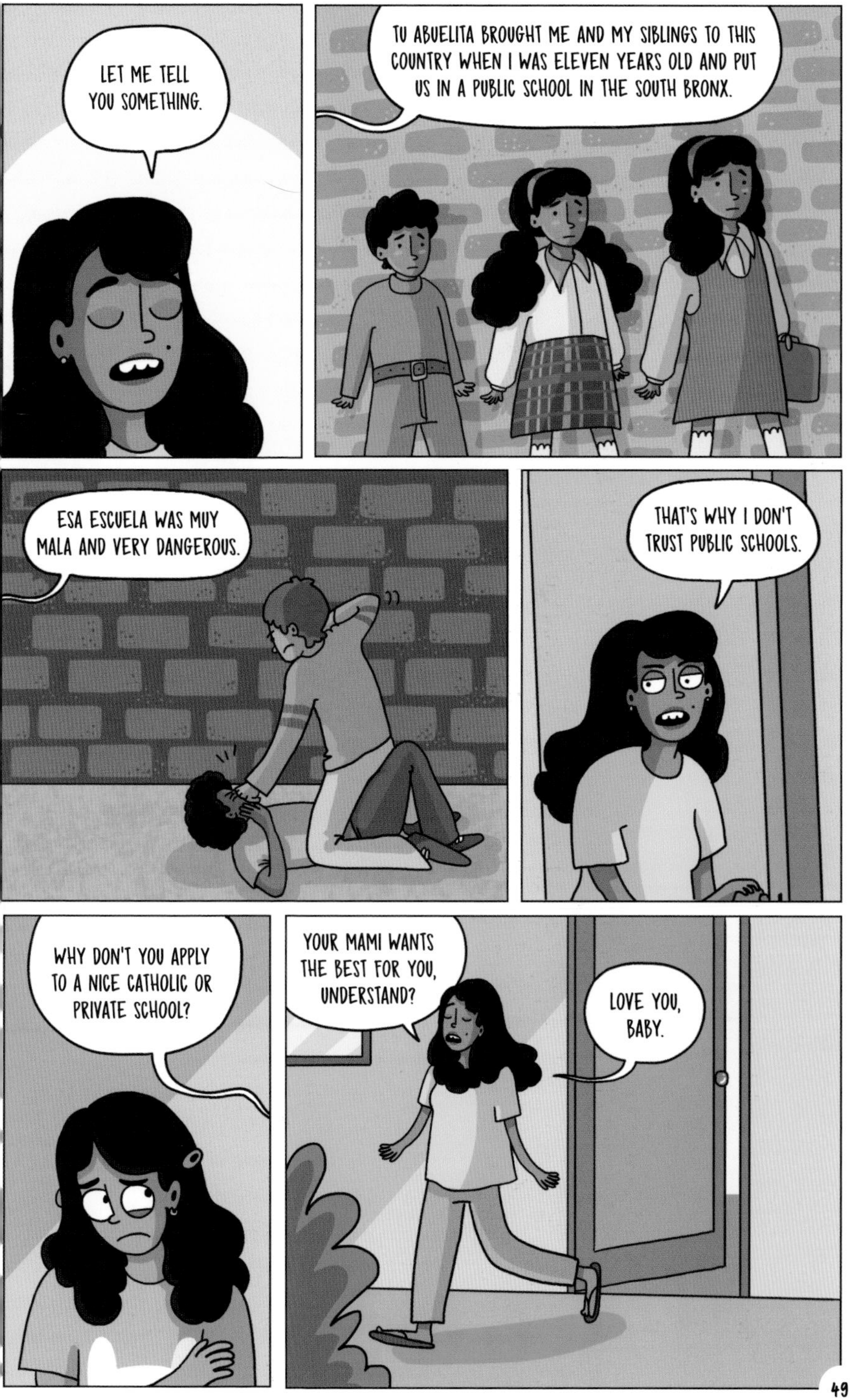
LET ME TELL YOU SOMETHING.
TU ABUELITA BROUGHT ME AND MY SIBLINGS TO THIS COUNTRY WHEN I WAS ELEVEN YEARS OLD AND PUT US IN A PUBLIC SCHOOL IN THE SOUTH BRONX.
ESA ESCUELA WAS MUY MALA AND VERY DANGEROUS.
THAT'S WHY I DON'T TRUST PUBLIC SCHOOLS.
WHY DON'T YOU APPLY TO A NICE CATHOLIC OR PRIVATE SCHOOL?
YOUR MAMI WANTS THE BEST FOR YOU, UNDERSTAND?
LOVE YOU, BABY.

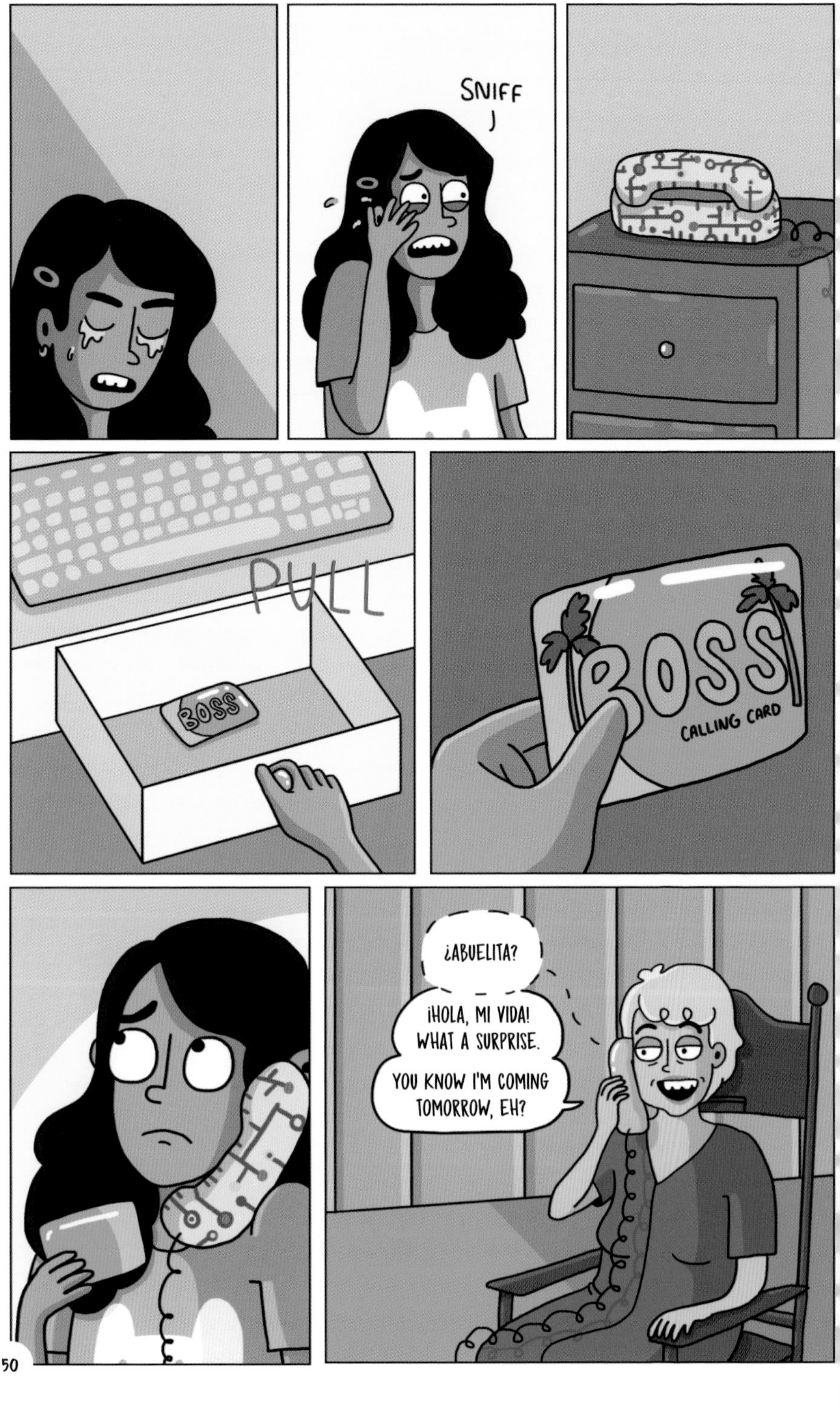
SNIFF
PULL
BOSS
BOSS
CALLING CARD
¿ABUELITA?
¡HOLA, MI VIDA! WHAT A SURPRISE.
YOU KNOW I'M COMING TOMORROW, EH?

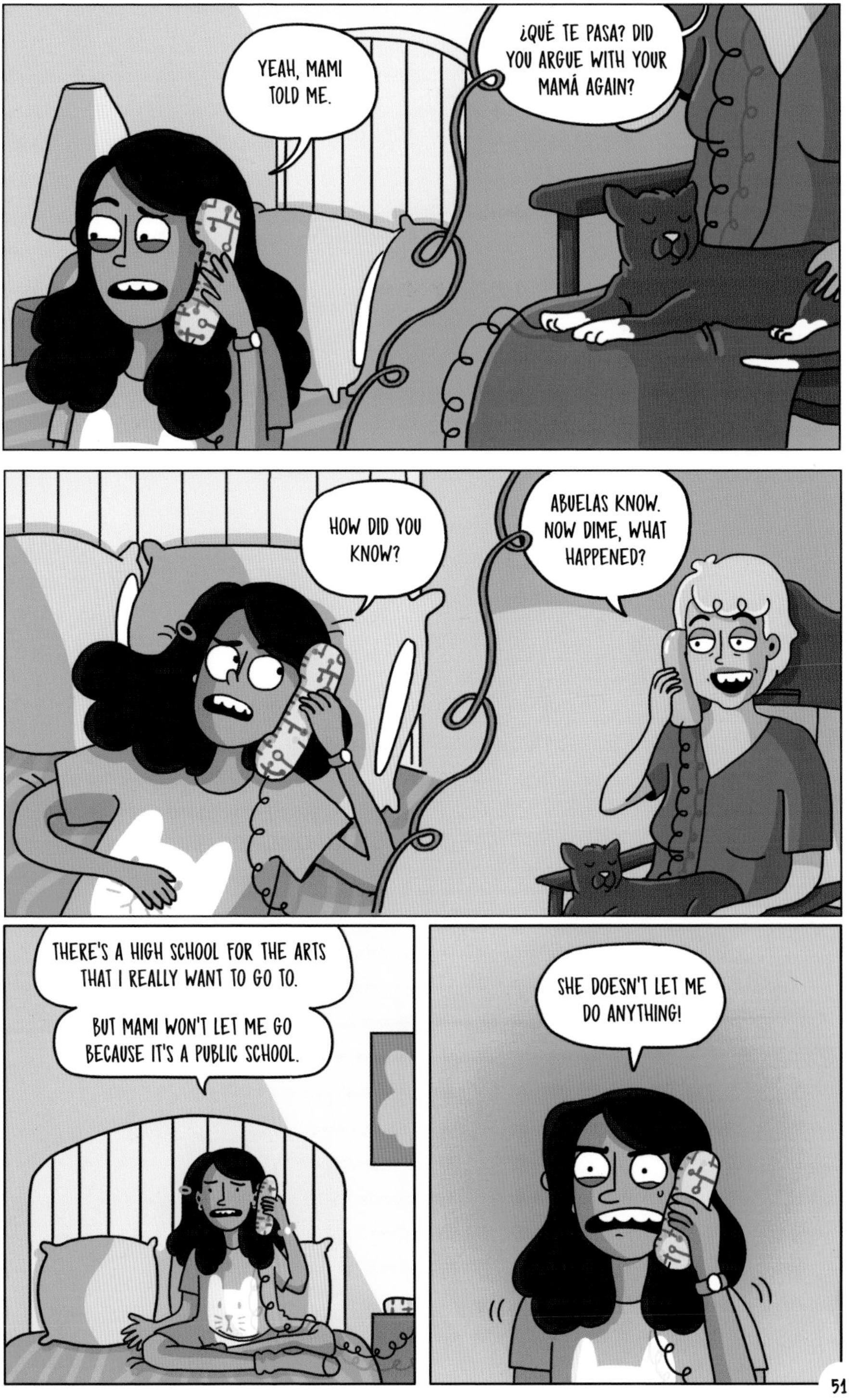
YEAH, MAMI TOLD ME.
¿QUÉ TE PASA? DID YOU ARGUE WITH YOUR MAMÁ AGAIN?
HOW DID YOU KNOW?
ABUELAS KNOW. NOW DIME, WHAT HAPPENED?
THERE'S A HIGH SCHOOL FOR THE ARTS THAT I REALLY WANT TO GO TO.
BUT MAMI WON'T LET ME GO BECAUSE IT'S A PUBLIC SCHOOL.
SHE DOESN'T LET ME DO ANYTHING!

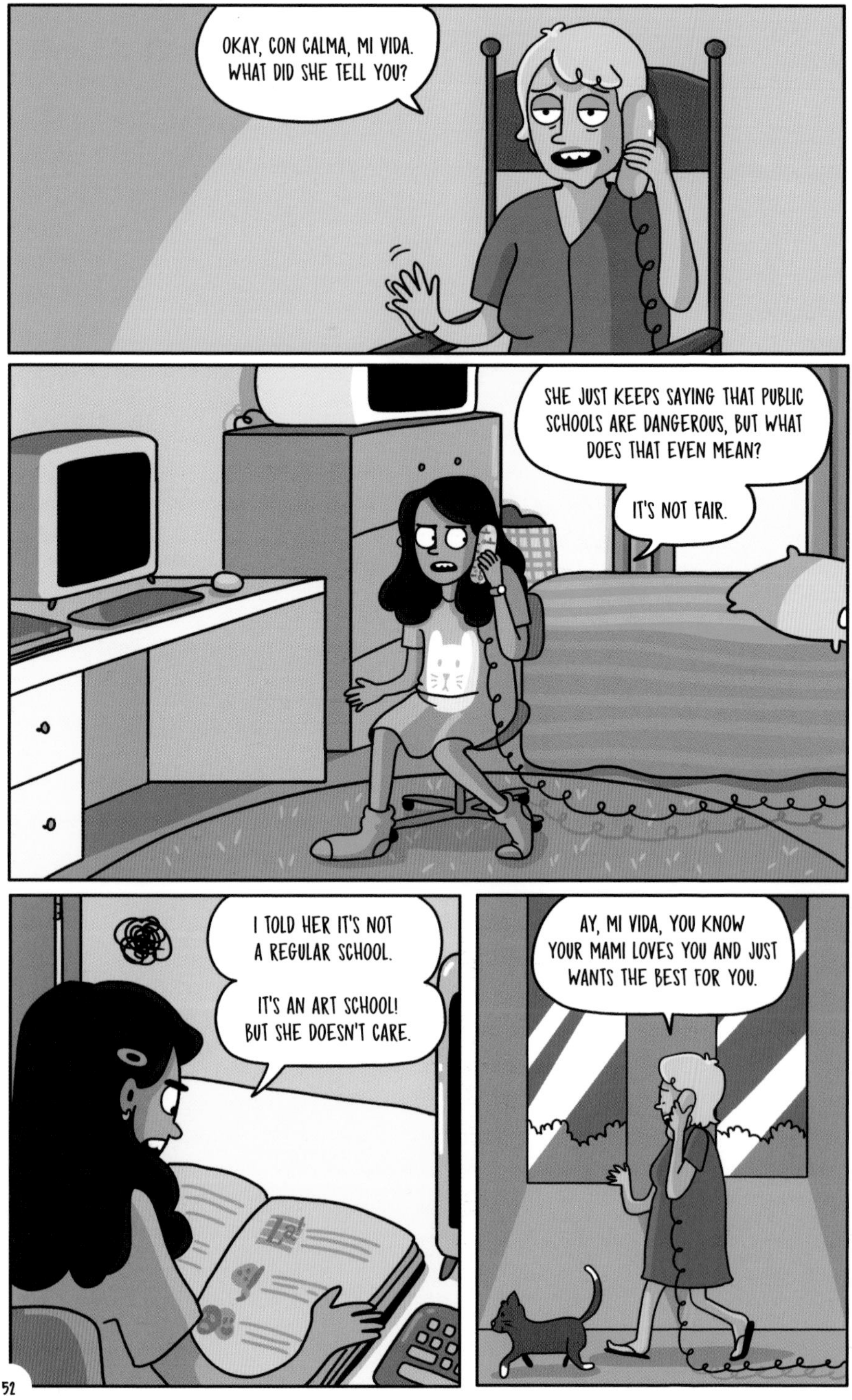
OKAY, CON CALMA, MI VIDA. WHAT DID SHE TELL YOU?
SHE JUST KEEPS SAYING THAT PUBLIC SCHOOLS ARE DANGEROUS, BUT WHAT DOES THAT EVEN MEAN?
IT'S NOT FAIR.
I TOLD HER IT'S NOT A REGULAR SCHOOL.
IT'S AN ART SCHOOL! BUT SHE DOESN'T CARE.
AY, MI VIDA, YOU KNOW YOUR MAMI LOVES YOU AND JUST WANTS THE BEST FOR YOU.

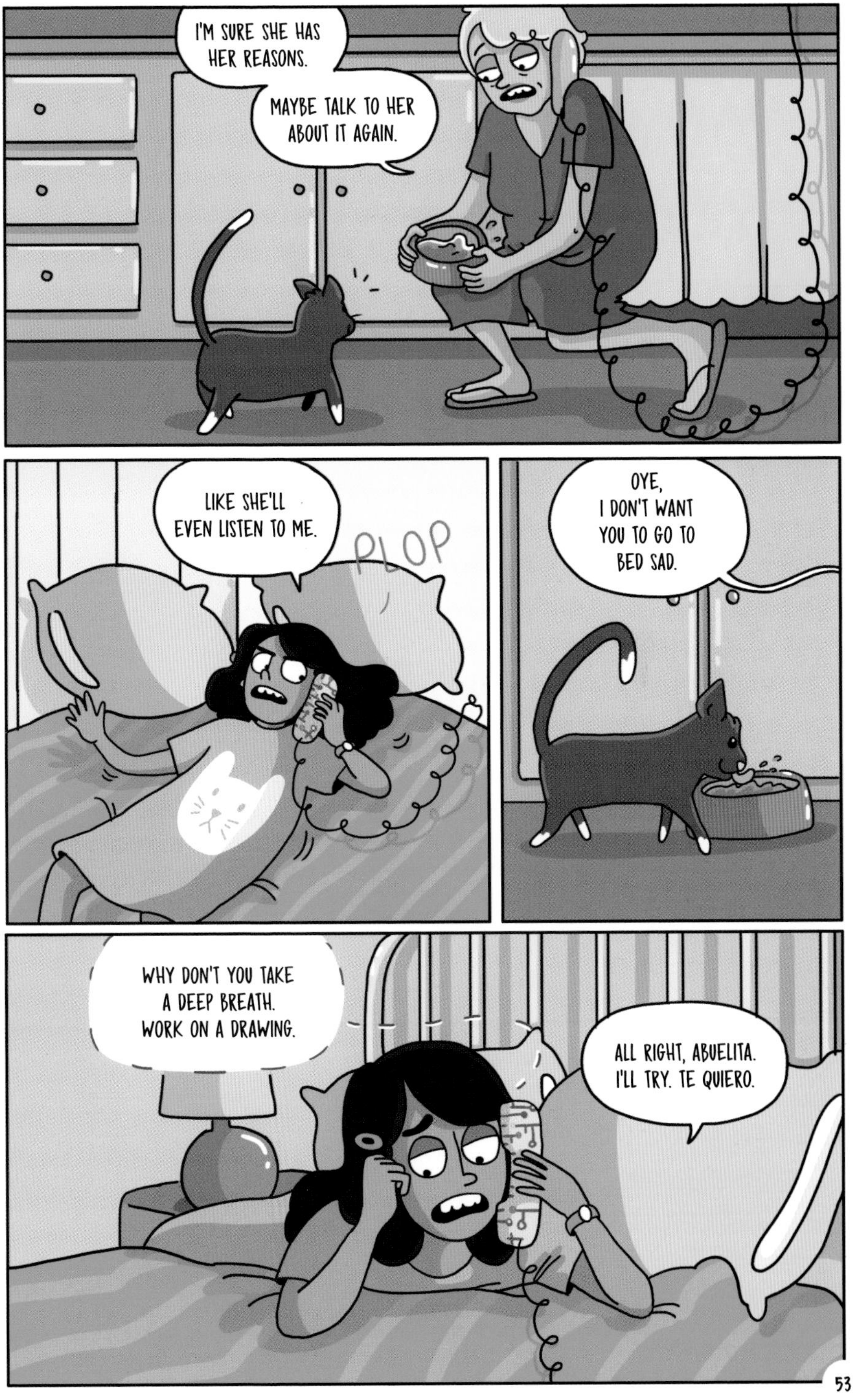
I'M SURE SHE HAS HER REASONS.
MAYBE TALK TO HER ABOUT IT AGAIN.
LIKE SHE'LL EVEN LISTEN TO ME.
PLOP
OYE, I DON'T WANT YOU TO GO TO BED SAD.
WHY DON'T YOU TAKE A DEEP BREATH. WORK ON A DRAWING.
ALL RIGHT, ABUELITA. I'LL TRY. TE QUIERO.

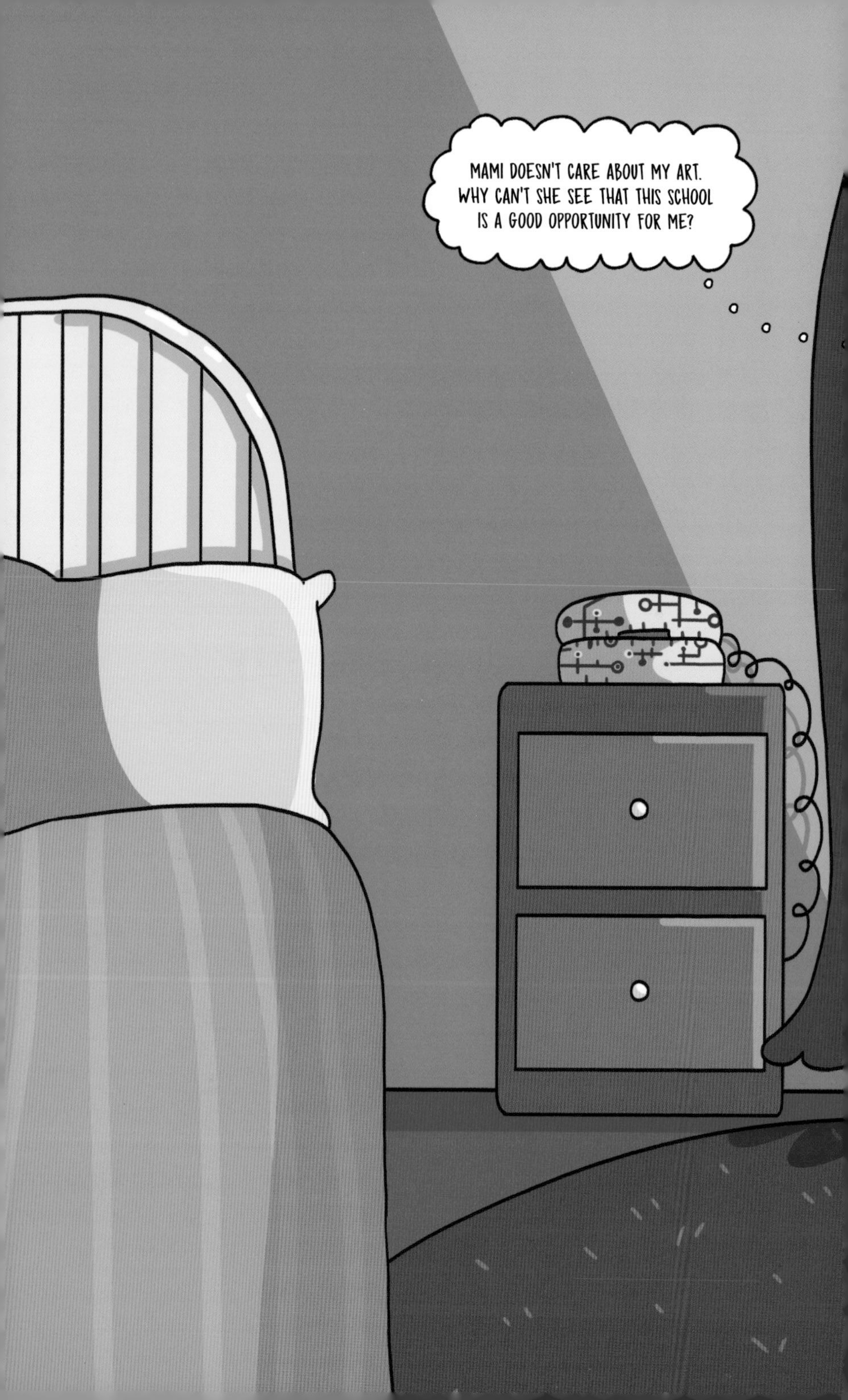
MAMI DOESN'T CARE ABOUT MY ART. WHY CAN'T SHE SEE THAT THIS SCHOOL IS A GOOD OPPORTUNITY FOR ME?

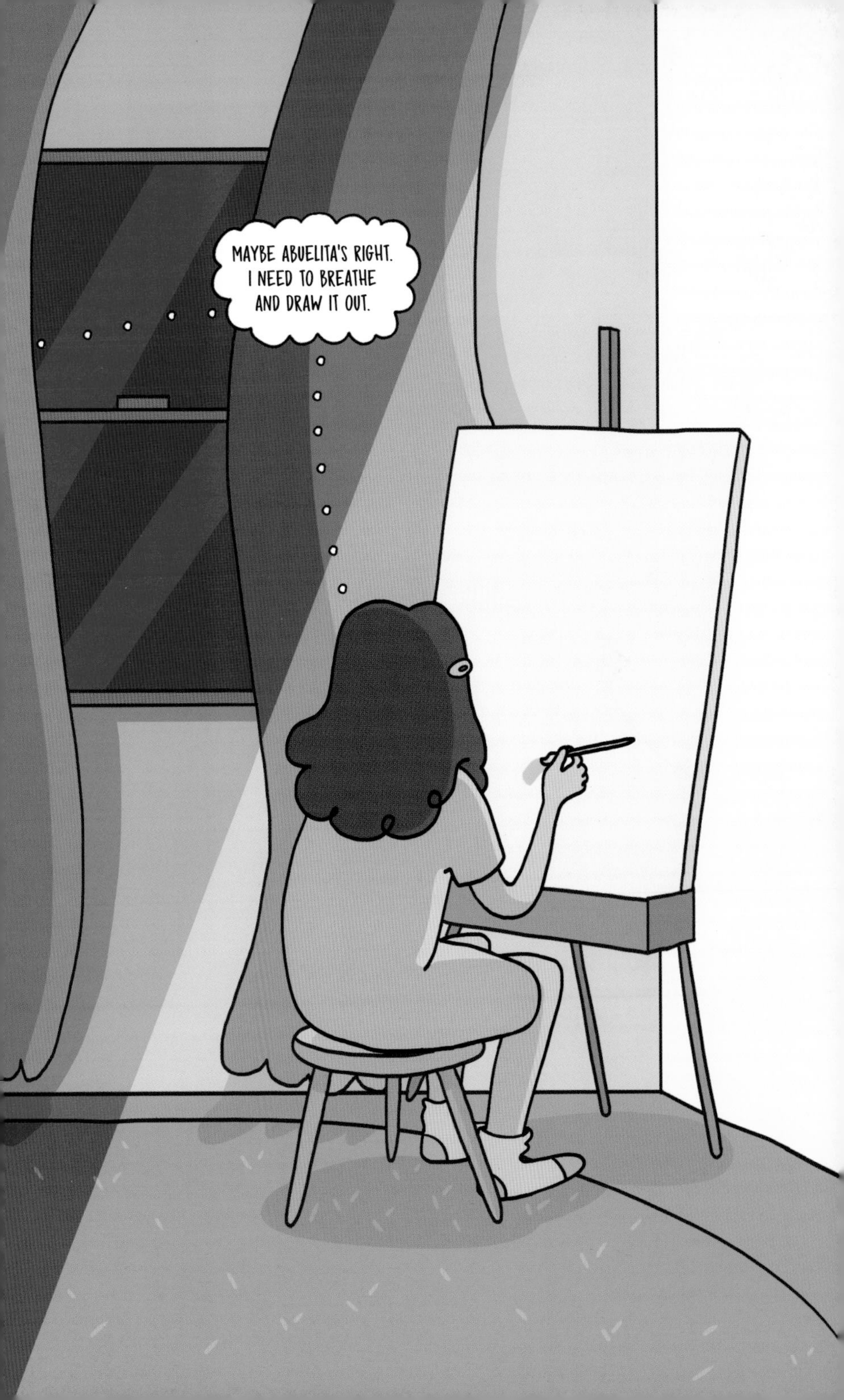
MAYBE ABUELITA'S RIGHT. I NEED TO BREATHE AND DRAW IT OUT.

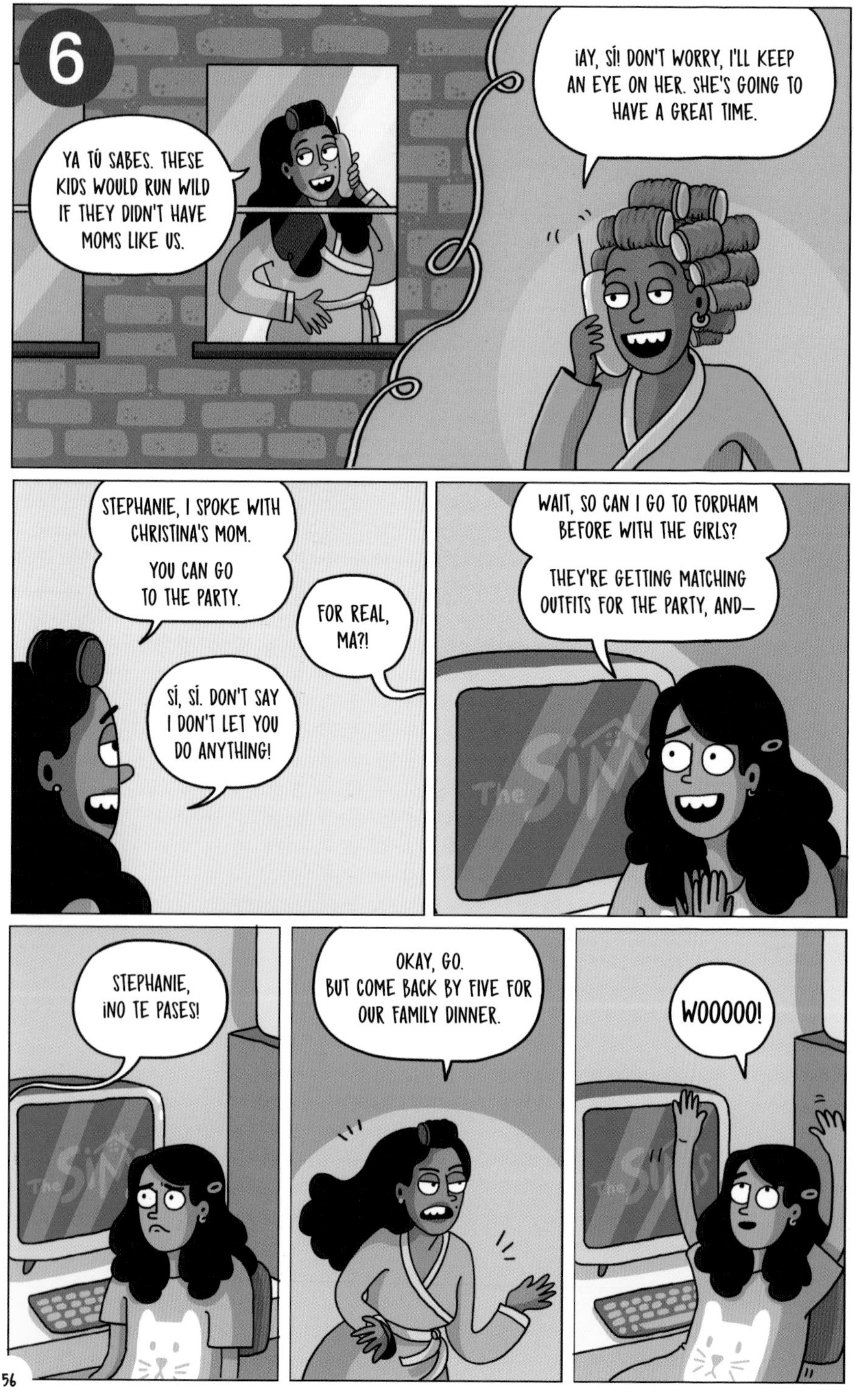
6
YA TÚ SABES. THESE KIDS WOULD RUN WILD IF THEY DIDN'T HAVE MOMS LIKE US.
¡AY, SÍ! DON'T WORRY, I'LL KEEP AN EYE ON HER. SHE'S GOING TO HAVE A GREAT TIME.
STEPHANIE, I SPOKE WITH CHRISTINA'S MOM.
YOU CAN GO TO THE PARTY.
FOR REAL, MA?!
SÍ, SÍ. DON'T SAY I DON'T LET YOU DO ANYTHING!
WAIT, SO CAN I GO TO FORDHAM BEFORE WITH THE GIRLS?
THEY'RE GETTING MATCHING OUTFITS FOR THE PARTY, AND—
STEPHANIE, ¡NO TE PASES!
OKAY, GO. BUT COME BACK BY FIVE FOR OUR FAMILY DINNER.
WOOOOO!

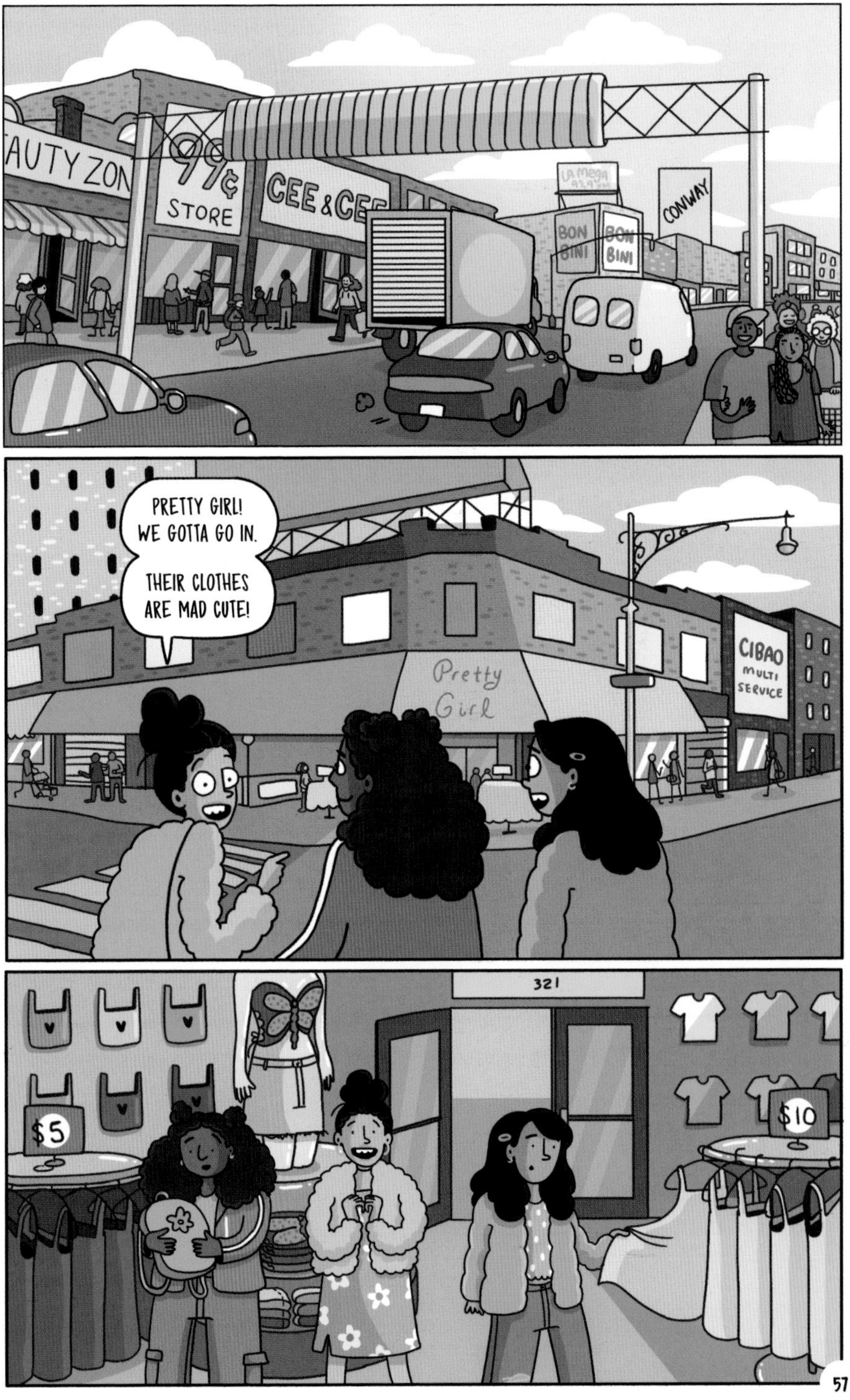
AUTY ZON
99¢ STORE
CEE&CE
BON BINI
BON BINI
CONWAY
PRETTY GIRL! WE GOTTA GO IN.
THEIR CLOTHES ARE MAD CUTE!
Pretty Girl
CIBAO MULTI SERVICE
321
$5
$10

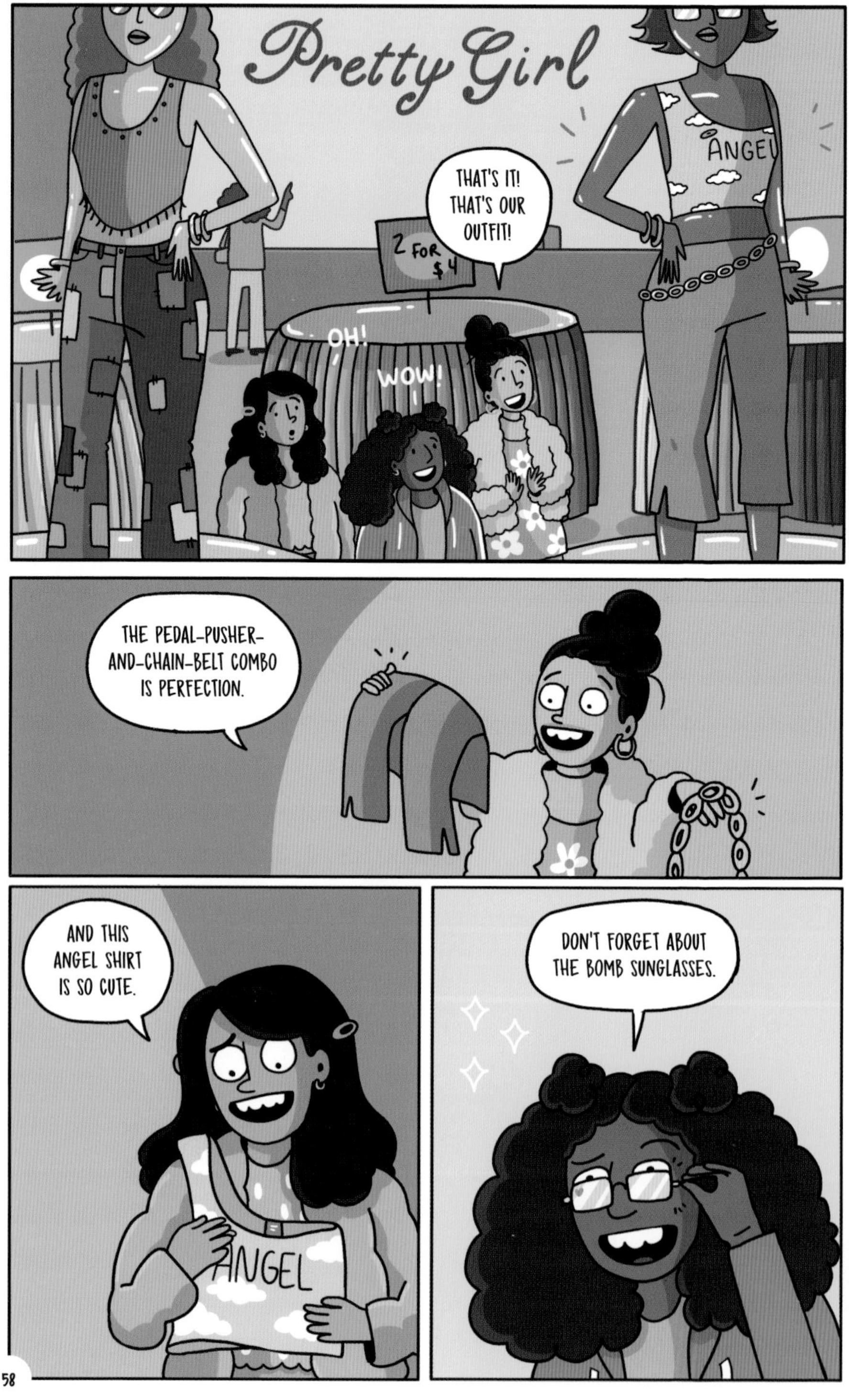
Pretty Girl
ANGEL
2 FOR $4
THAT'S IT! THAT'S OUR OUTFIT!
OH!
WOW!
THE PEDAL-PUSHER-AND-CHAIN-BELT COMBO IS PERFECTION.
AND THIS ANGEL SHIRT IS SO CUTE.
ANGEL
DON'T FORGET ABOUT THE BOMB SUNGLASSES.

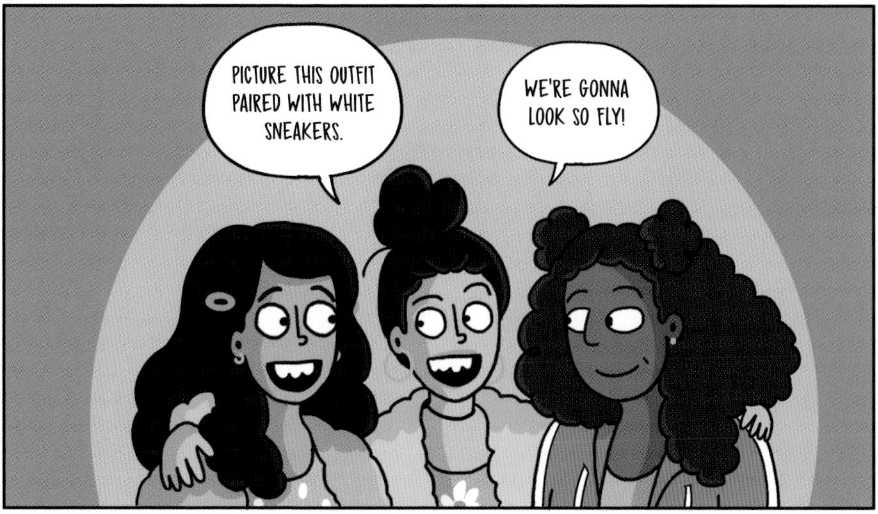
PICTURE THIS OUTFIT PAIRED WITH WHITE SNEAKERS.
WE'RE GONNA LOOK SO FLY!

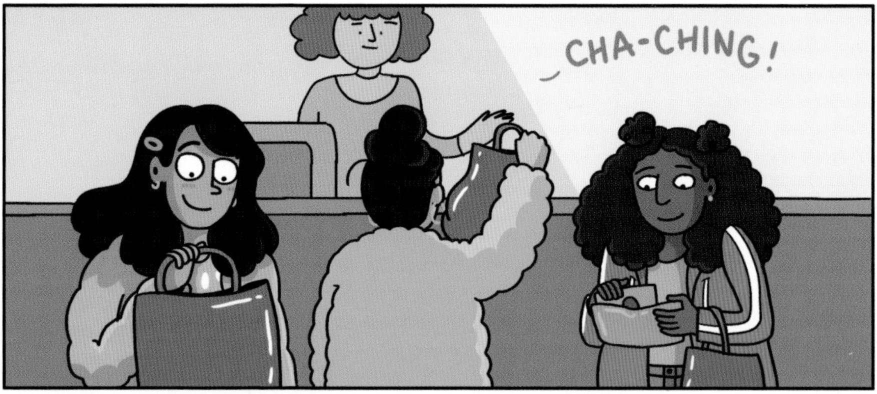
CHA-CHING!

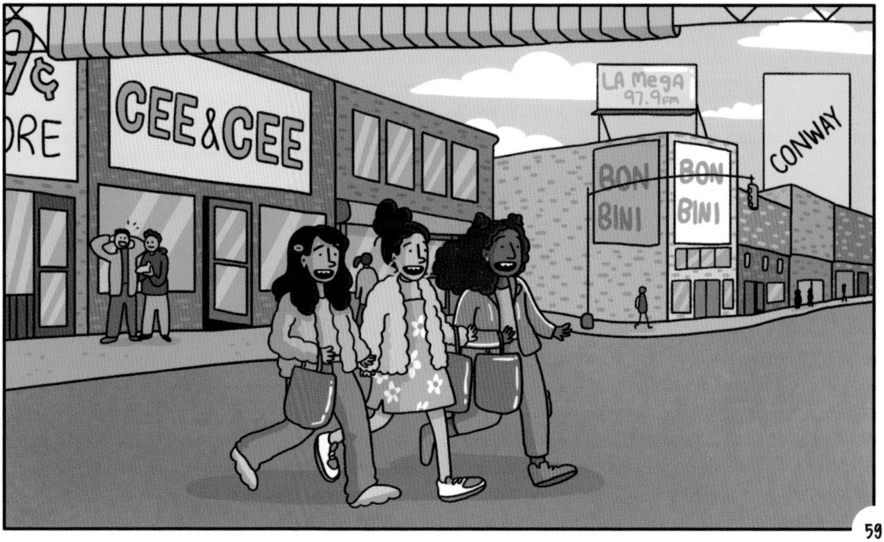
CEE&CEE
LA Mega 97.9FM
BON BINI
BON BINI
CONWAY

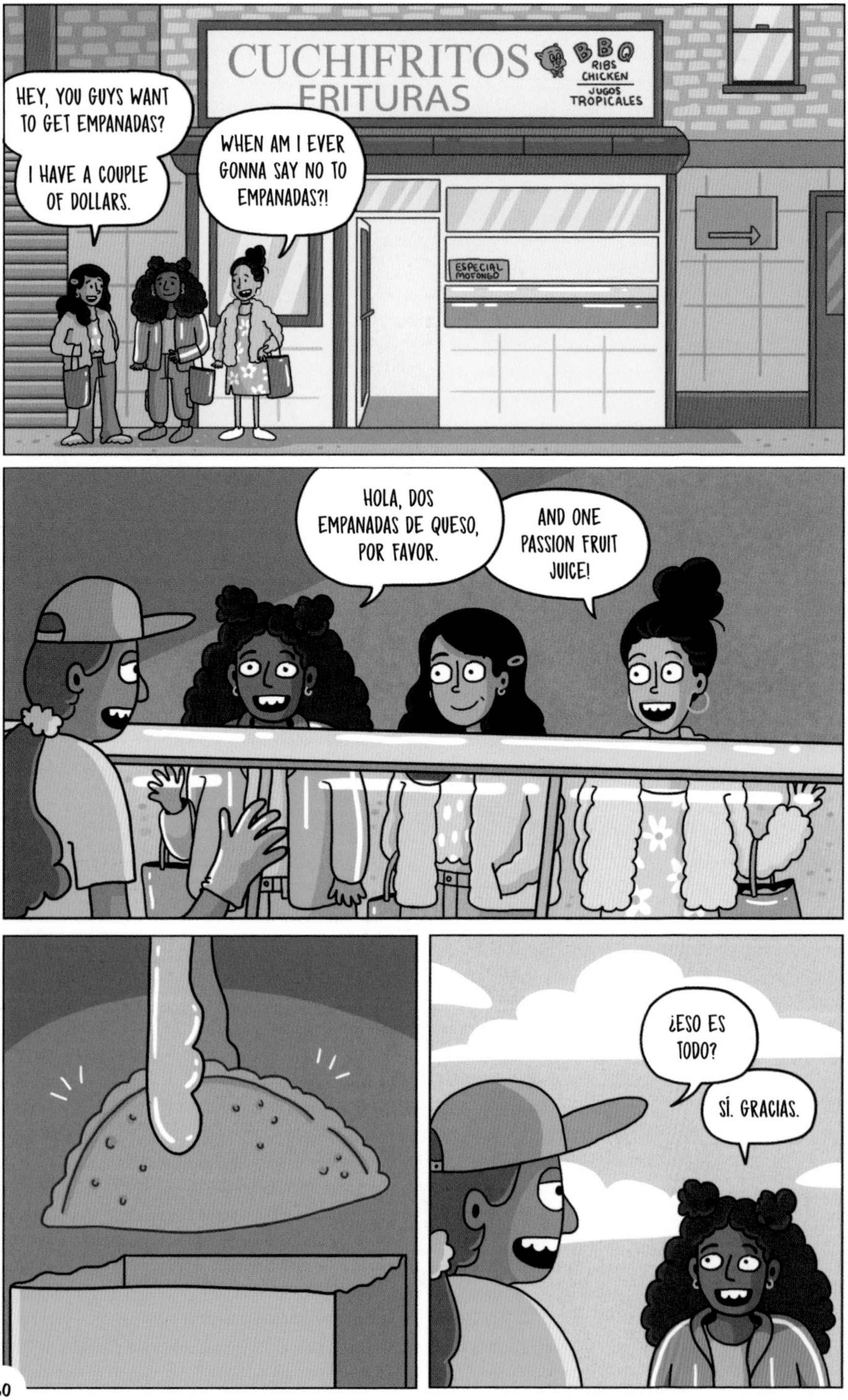
CUCHIFRITOS
FRITURAS
BBQ
RIBS
CHICKEN
JUGOS
TROPICALES
HEY, YOU GUYS WANT TO GET EMPANADAS?
I HAVE A COUPLE OF DOLLARS.
WHEN AM I EVER GONNA SAY NO TO EMPANADAS?!
ESPECIAL MOFONGO
HOLA, DOS EMPANADAS DE QUESO, POR FAVOR.
AND ONE PASSION FRUIT JUICE!
¿ESO ES TODO?
SÍ. GRACIAS.

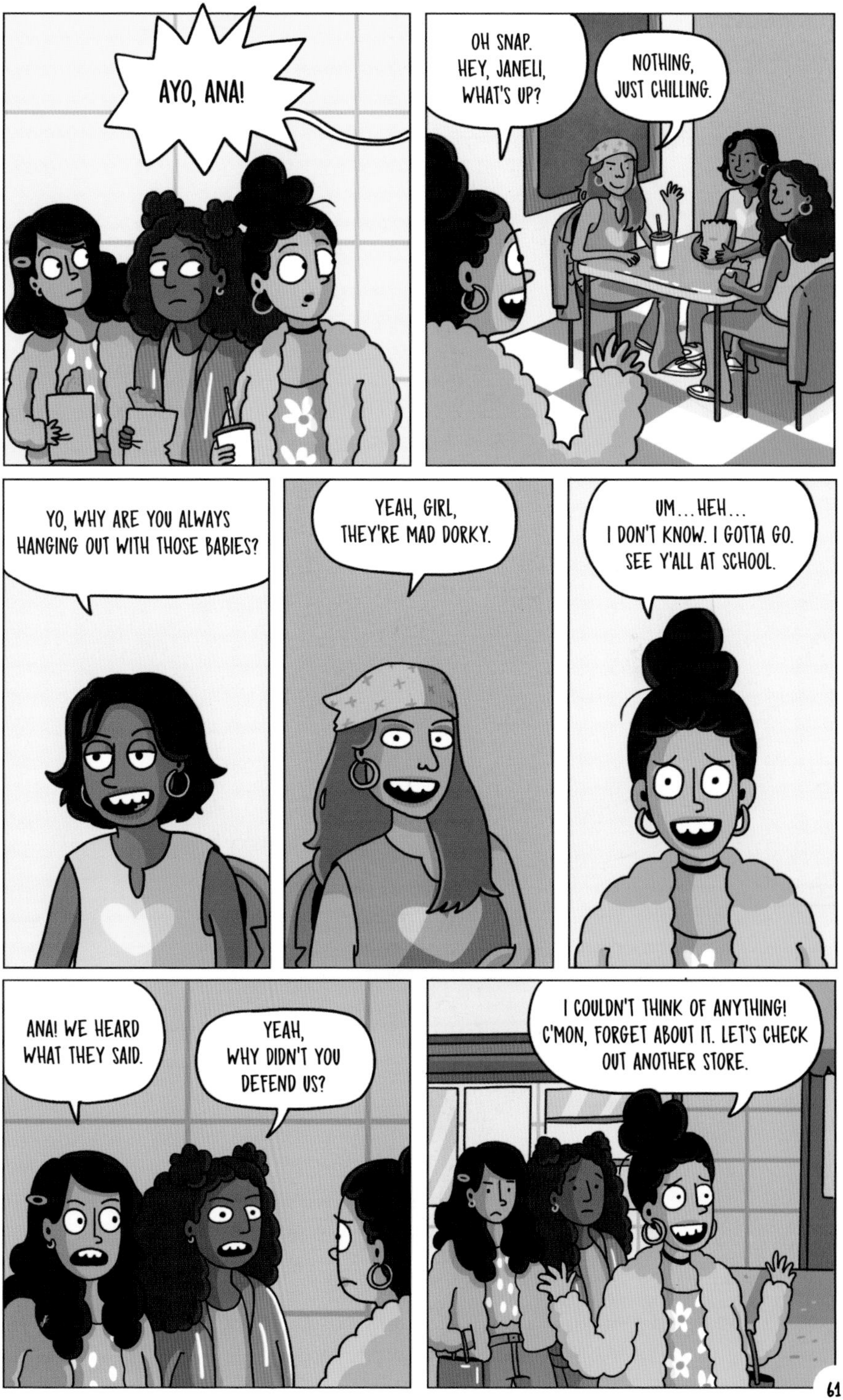
AYO, ANA!
OH SNAP. HEY, JANELI, WHAT'S UP?
NOTHING, JUST CHILLING.
YO, WHY ARE YOU ALWAYS HANGING OUT WITH THOSE BABIES?
YEAH, GIRL, THEY'RE MAD DORKY.
UM... HEH... I DON'T KNOW. I GOTTA GO. SEE Y'ALL AT SCHOOL.
ANA! WE HEARD WHAT THEY SAID.
YEAH, WHY DIDN'T YOU DEFEND US?
I COULDN'T THINK OF ANYTHING! C'MON, FORGET ABOUT IT. LET'S CHECK OUT ANOTHER STORE.

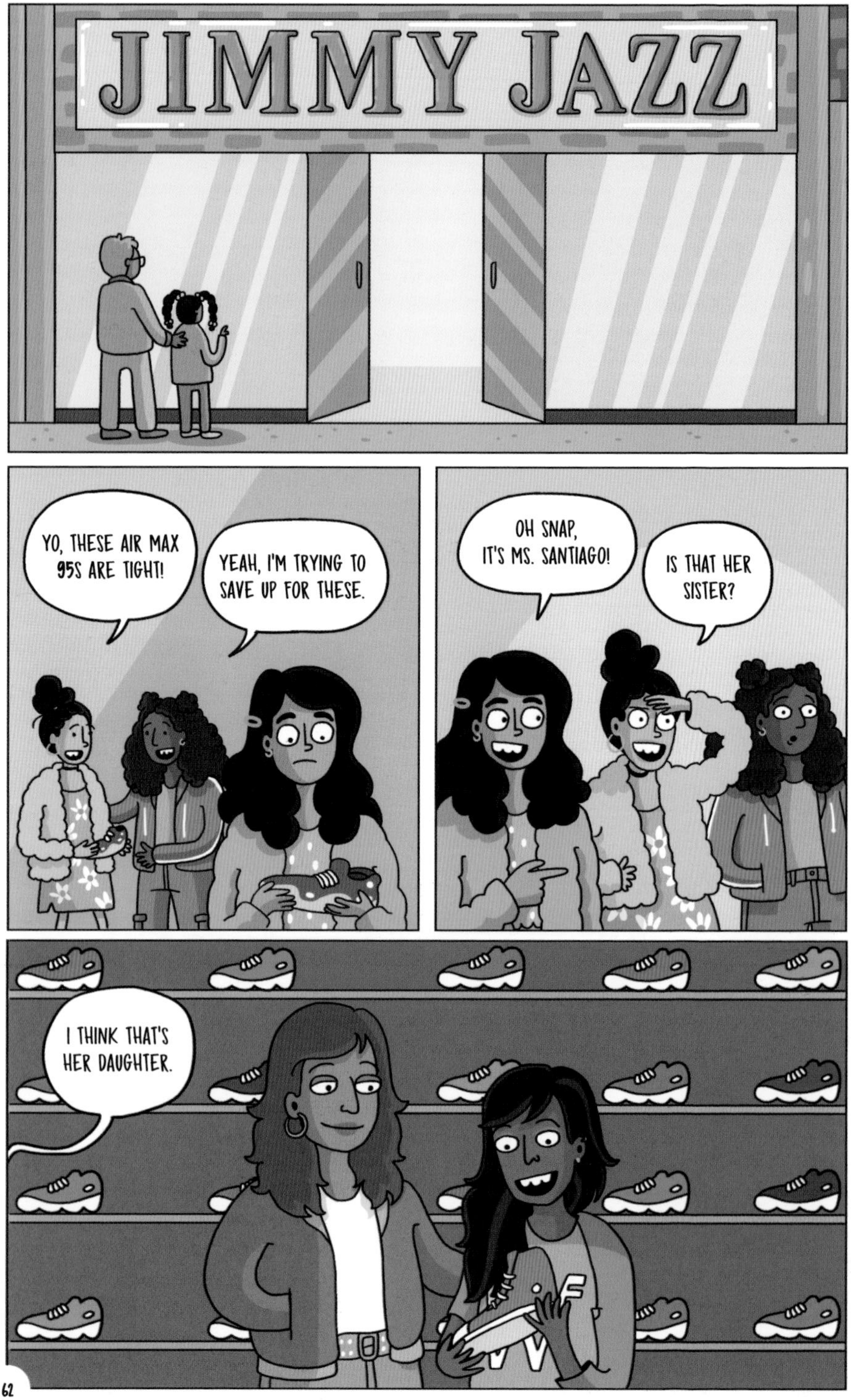
JIMMY JAZZ
YO, THESE AIR MAX 95S ARE TIGHT!
YEAH, I'M TRYING TO SAVE UP FOR THESE.
OH SNAP, IT'S MS. SANTIAGO!
IS THAT HER SISTER?
I THINK THAT'S HER DAUGHTER.

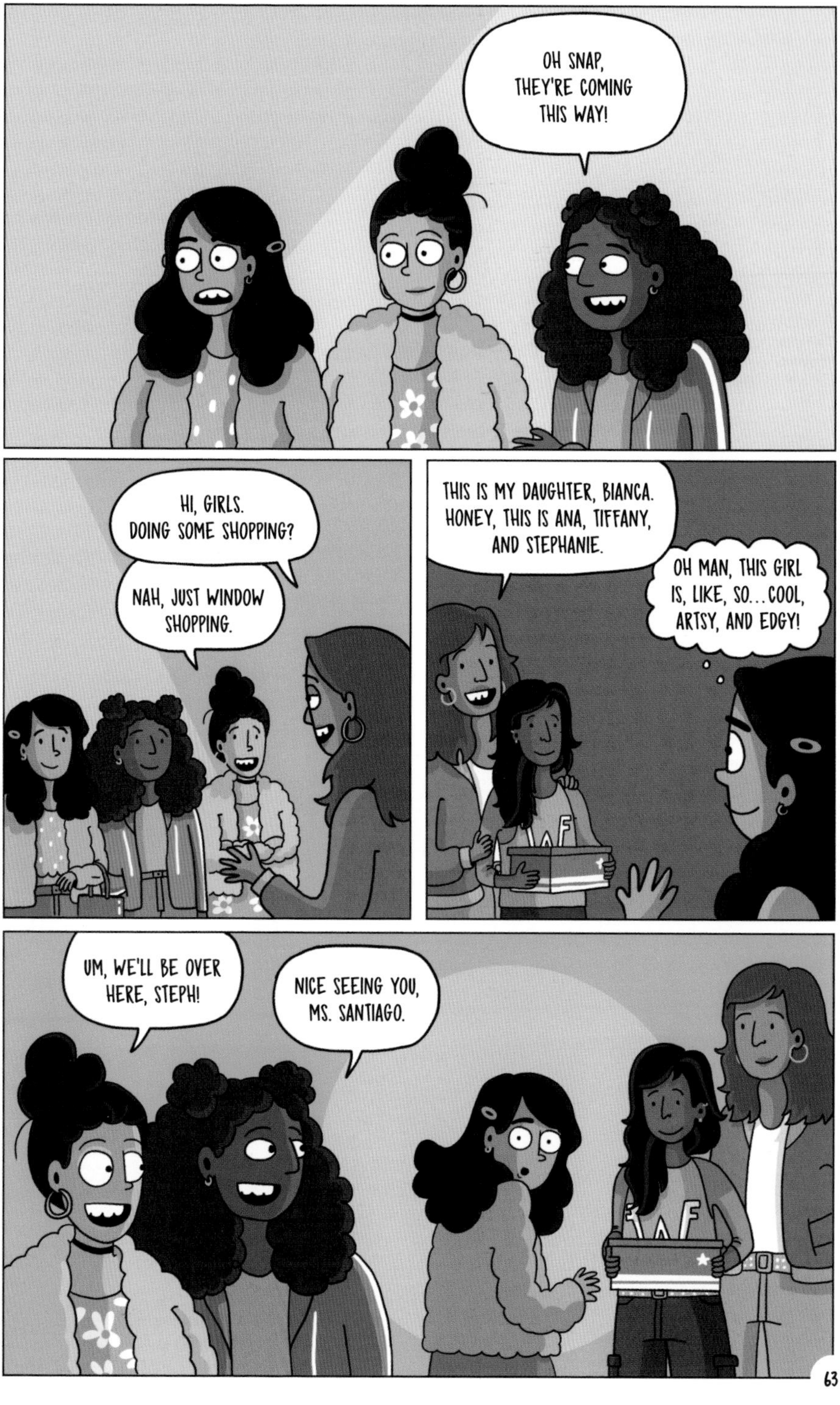
OH SNAP, THEY'RE COMING THIS WAY!
HI, GIRLS. DOING SOME SHOPPING?
NAH, JUST WINDOW SHOPPING.
THIS IS MY DAUGHTER, BIANCA. HONEY, THIS IS ANA, TIFFANY, AND STEPHANIE.
OH MAN, THIS GIRL IS, LIKE, SO...COOL, ARTSY, AND EDGY!
UM, WE'LL BE OVER HERE, STEPH!
NICE SEEING YOU, MS. SANTIAGO.

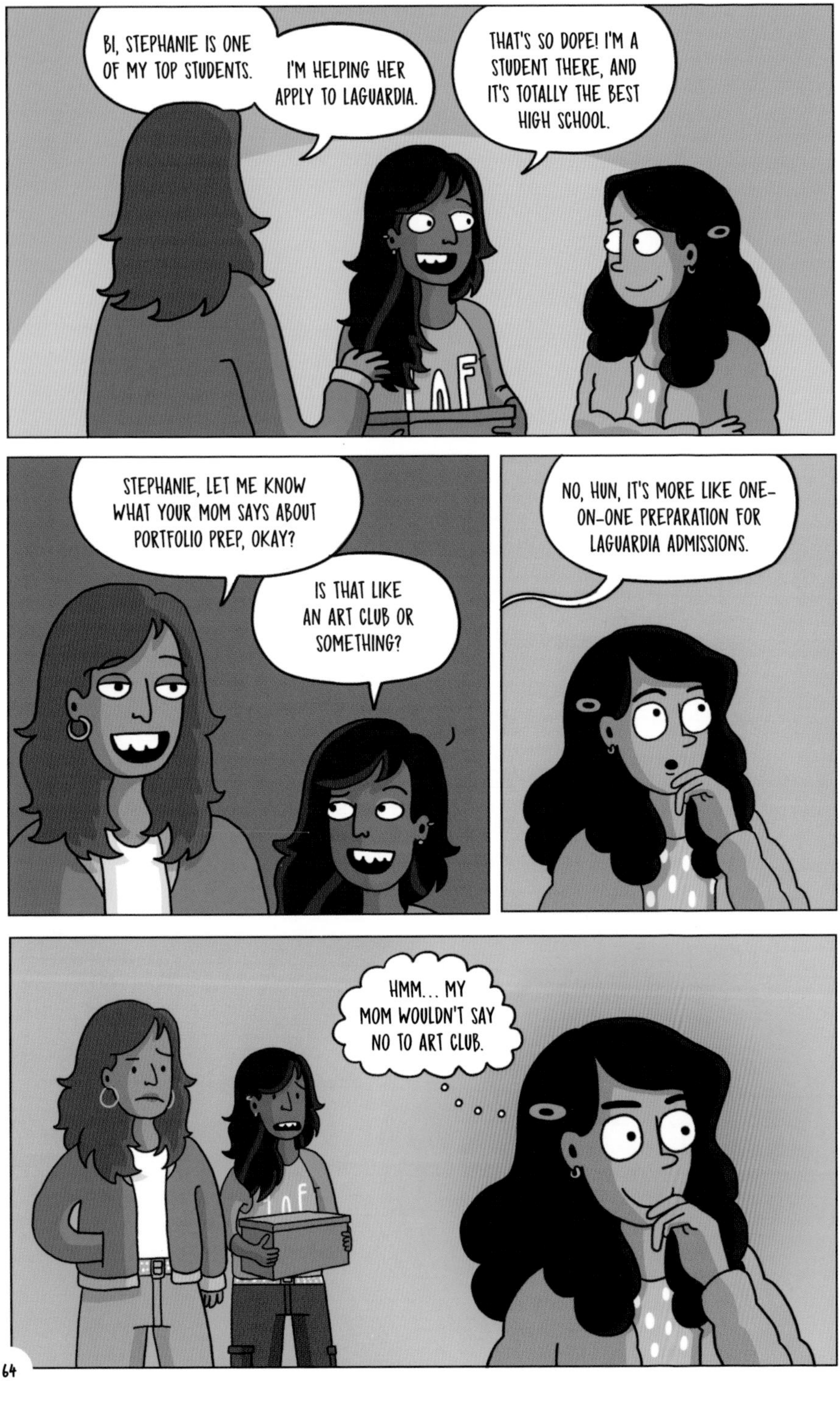
BI, STEPHANIE IS ONE OF MY TOP STUDENTS.
I'M HELPING HER APPLY TO LAGUARDIA.
THAT'S SO DOPE! I'M A STUDENT THERE, AND IT'S TOTALLY THE BEST HIGH SCHOOL.
STEPHANIE, LET ME KNOW WHAT YOUR MOM SAYS ABOUT PORTFOLIO PREP, OKAY?
IS THAT LIKE AN ART CLUB OR SOMETHING?
NO, HUN, IT'S MORE LIKE ONE-ON-ONE PREPARATION FOR LAGUARDIA ADMISSIONS.
HMM... MY MOM WOULDN'T SAY NO TO ART CLUB.

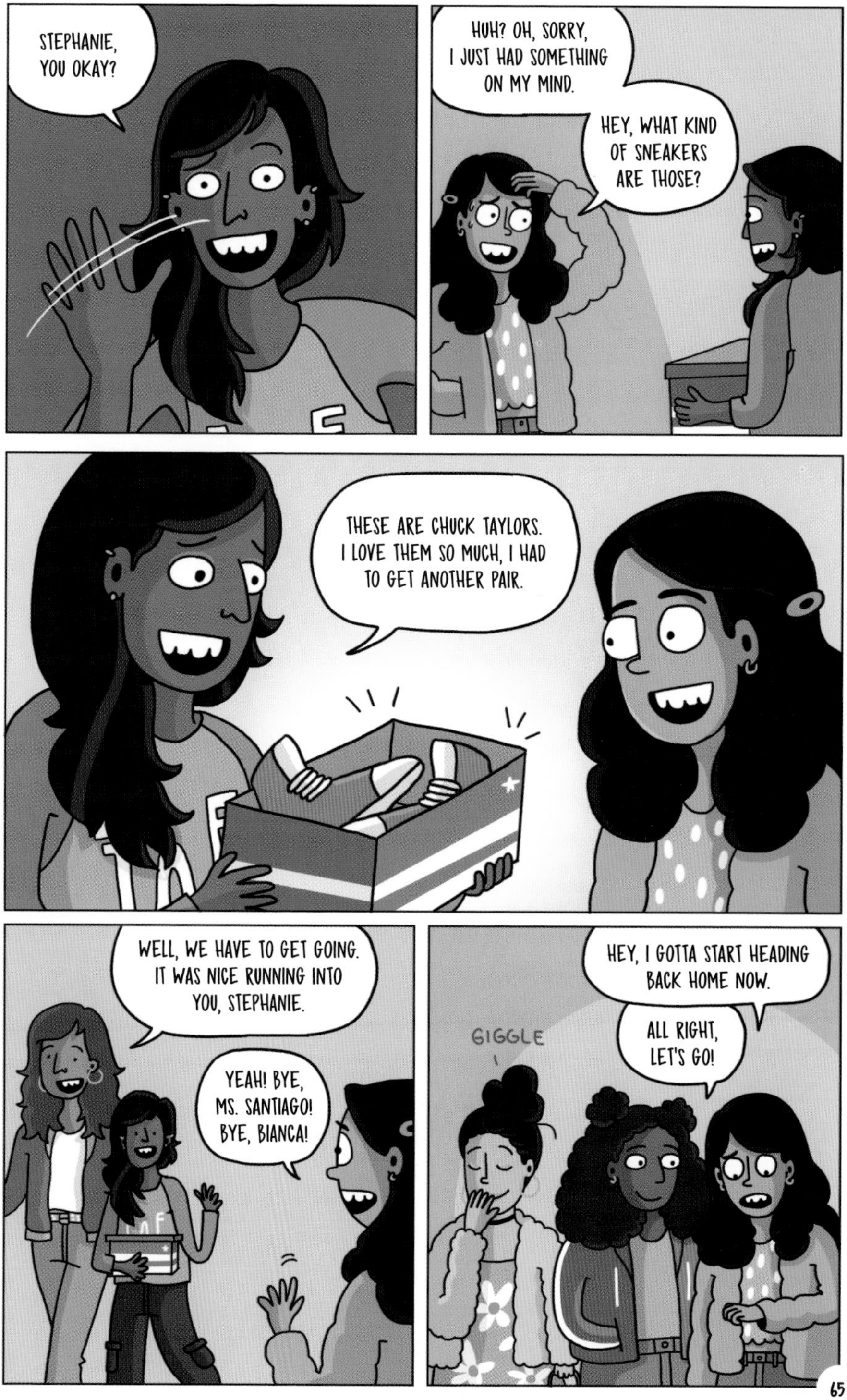
STEPHANIE, YOU OKAY?
HUH? OH, SORRY, I JUST HAD SOMETHING ON MY MIND.
HEY, WHAT KIND OF SNEAKERS ARE THOSE?
THESE ARE CHUCK TAYLORS. I LOVE THEM SO MUCH, I HAD TO GET ANOTHER PAIR.
WELL, WE HAVE TO GET GOING. IT WAS NICE RUNNING INTO YOU, STEPHANIE.
YEAH! BYE, MS. SANTIAGO! BYE, BIANCA!
HEY, I GOTTA START HEADING BACK HOME NOW.
GIGGLE
ALL RIGHT, LET'S GO!

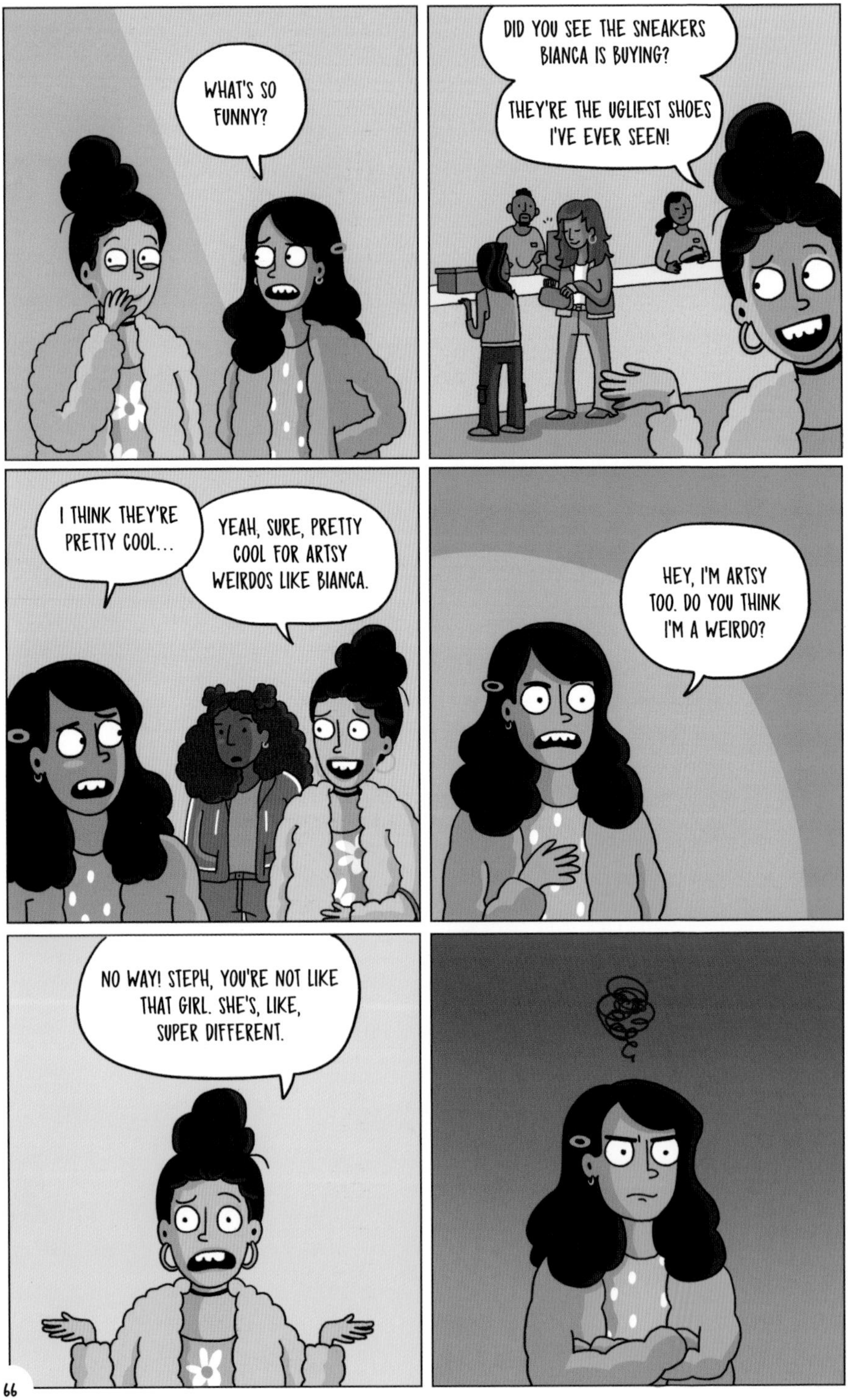
WHAT'S SO FUNNY?
DID YOU SEE THE SNEAKERS BIANCA IS BUYING?
THEY'RE THE UGLIEST SHOES I'VE EVER SEEN!
I THINK THEY'RE PRETTY COOL...
YEAH, SURE, PRETTY COOL FOR ARTSY WEIRDOS LIKE BIANCA.
HEY, I'M ARTSY TOO. DO YOU THINK I'M A WEIRDO?
NO WAY! STEPH, YOU'RE NOT LIKE THAT GIRL. SHE'S, LIKE, SUPER DIFFERENT.

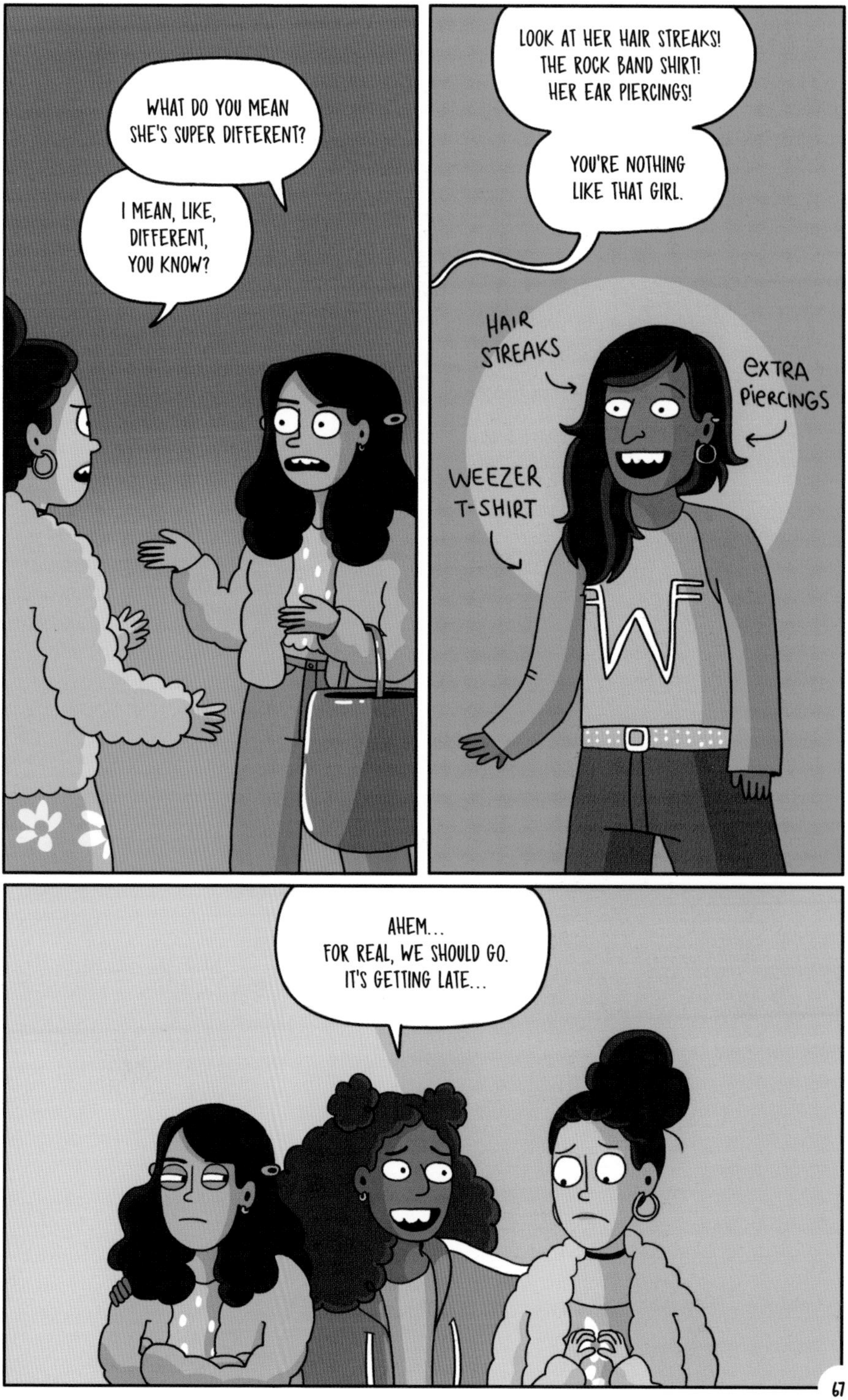
WHAT DO YOU MEAN
SHE'S SUPER DIFFERENT?
I MEAN, LIKE, DIFFERENT, YOU KNOW?
LOOK AT HER HAIR STREAKS! THE ROCK BAND SHIRT! HER EAR PIERCINGS!
YOU'RE NOTHING LIKE THAT GIRL.
HAIR STREAKS
EXTRA PIERCINGS
WEEZER T-SHIRT
AHEM... FOR REAL, WE SHOULD GO. IT'S GETTING LATE...

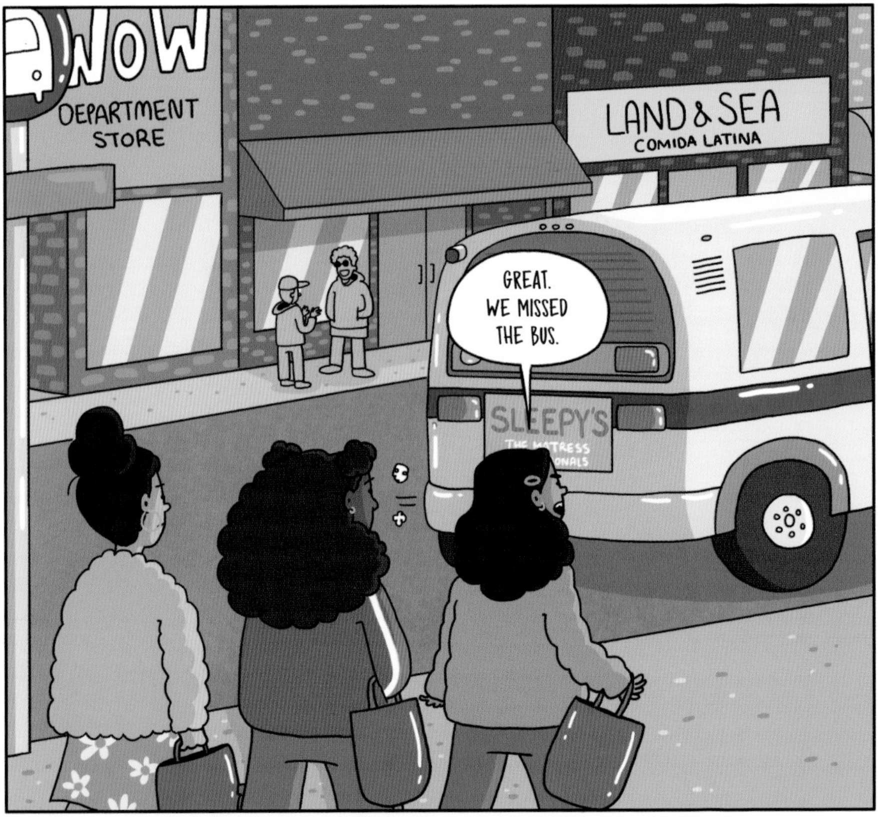
NOW
DEPARTMENT STORE
LAND & SEA
COMIDA LATINA
SLEEPY'S
GREAT. WE MISSED THE BUS.

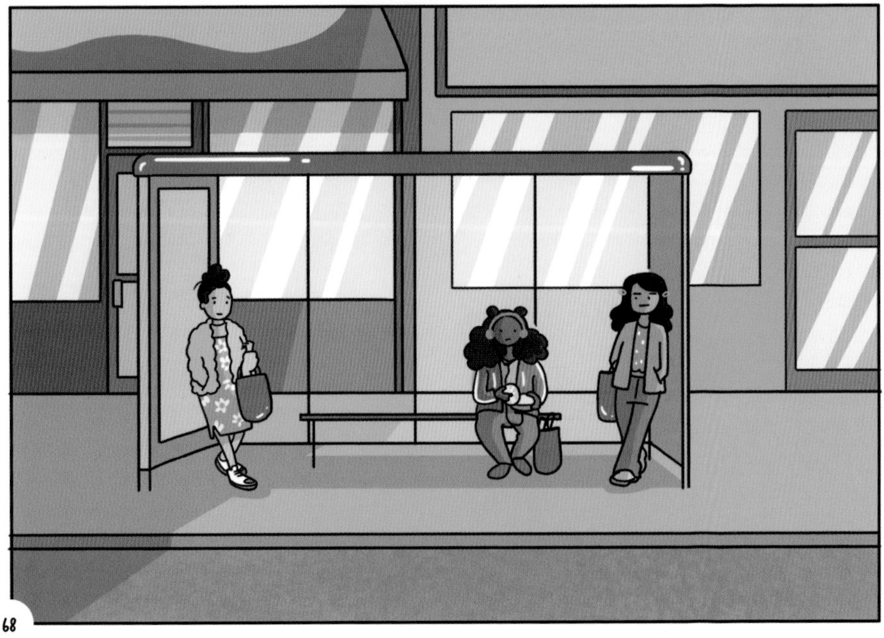

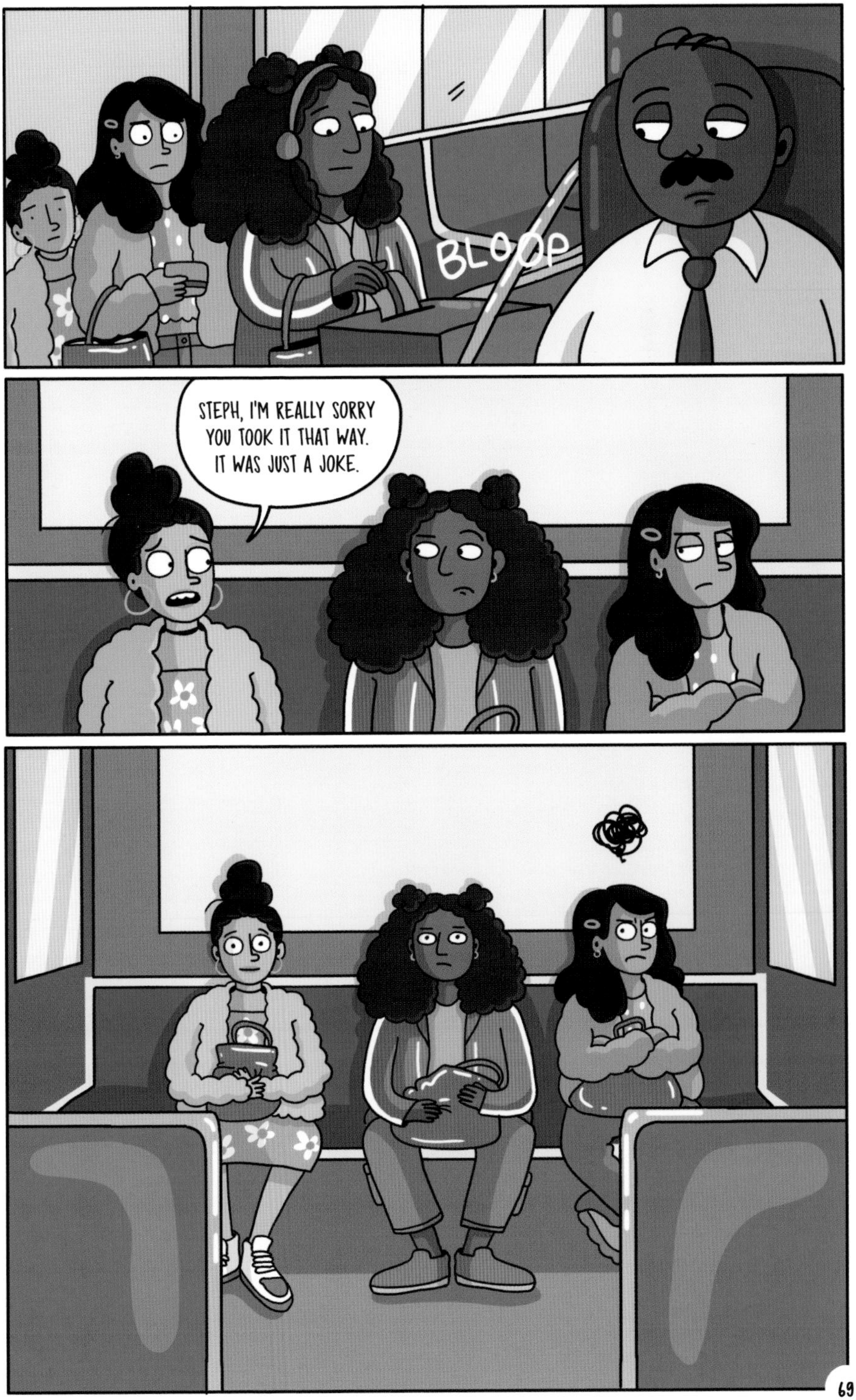
BLOOP
STEPH, I'M REALLY SORRY YOU TOOK IT THAT WAY. IT WAS JUST A JOKE.

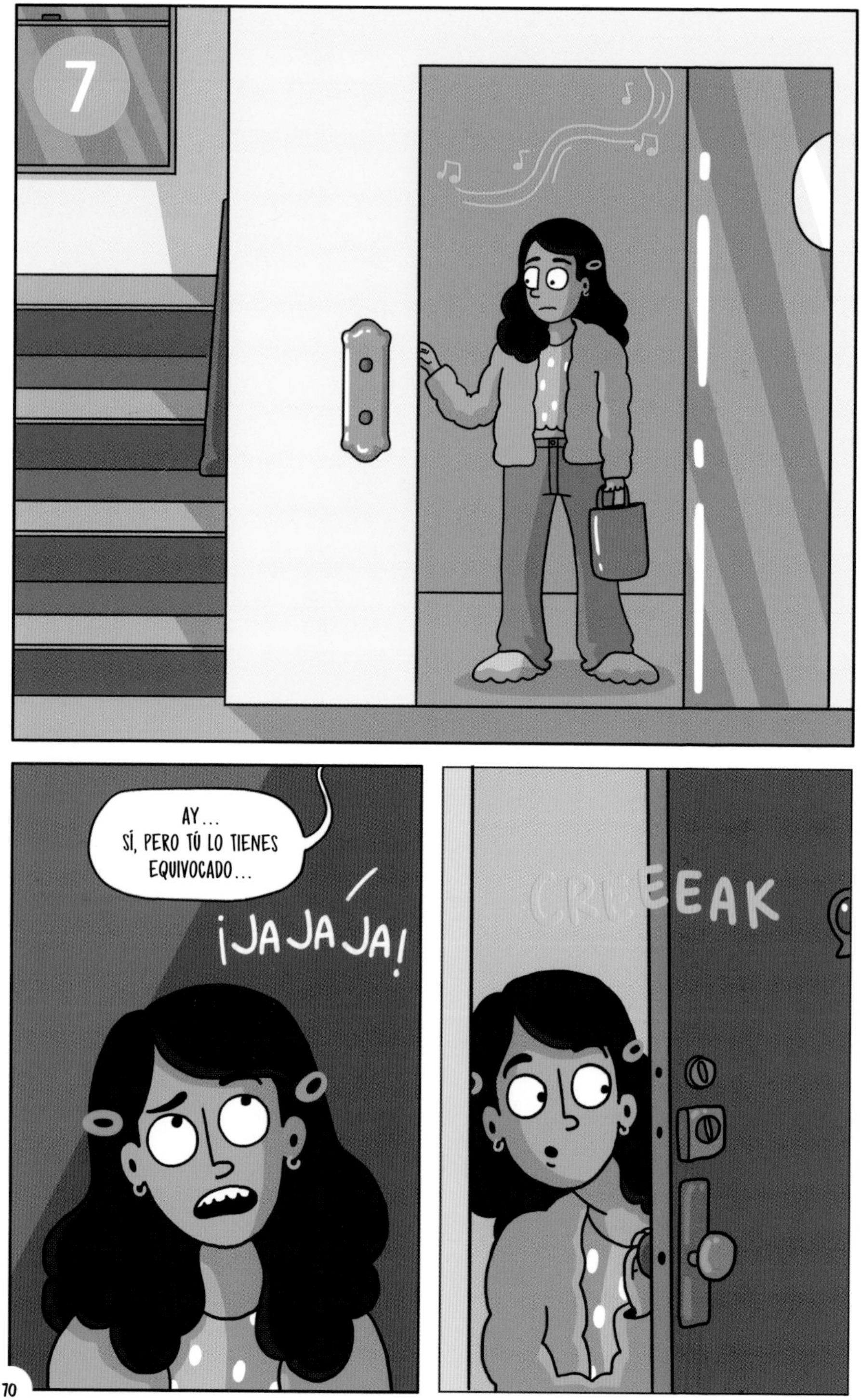
7
AY...
SÍ, PERO TÚ LO TIENES EQUIVOCADO...
¡JAJAJÁ!
CREEEAK

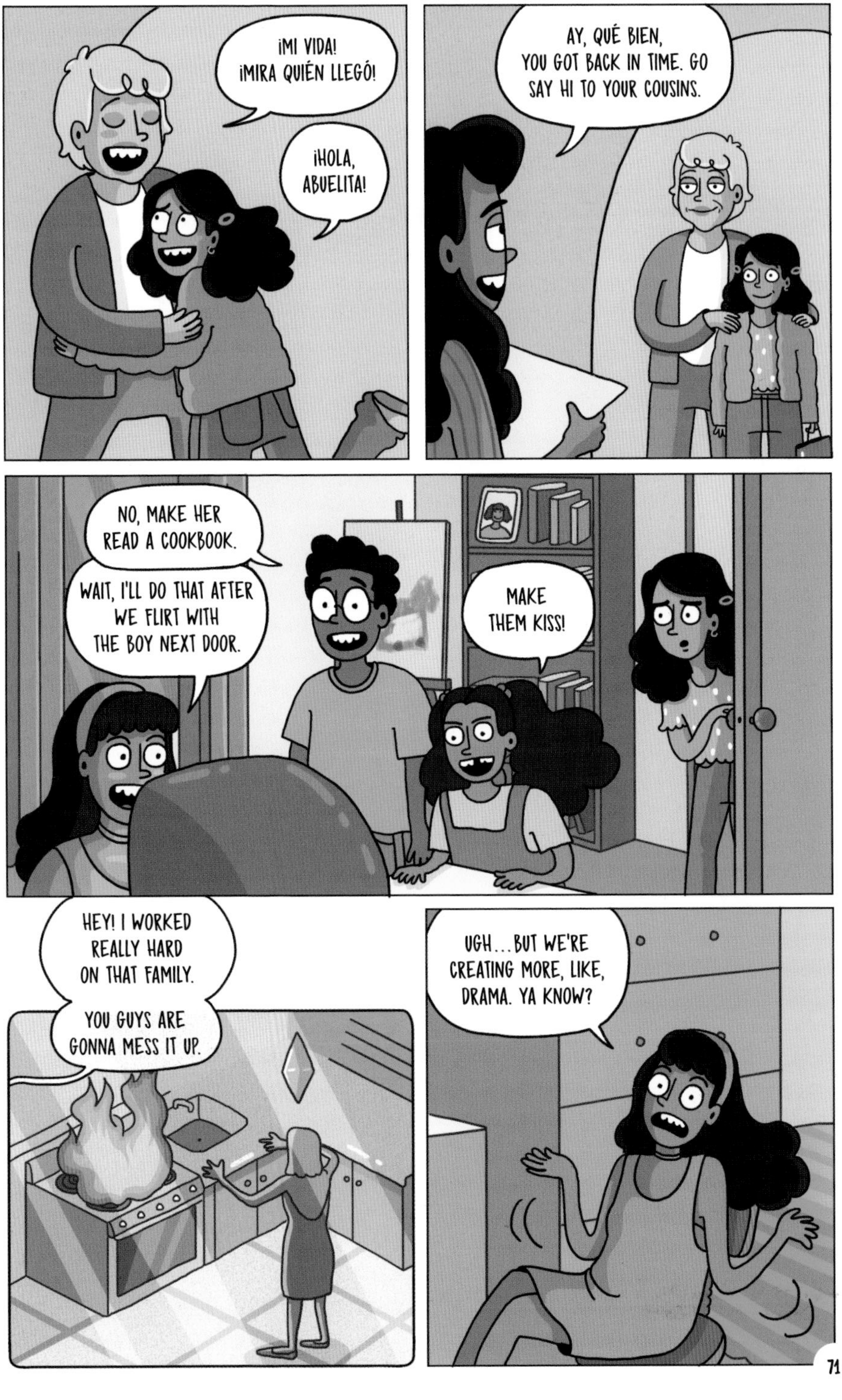
¡MI VIDA!
¡MIRA QUIÉN LLEGÓ!
¡HOLA, ABUELITA!
AY, QUÉ BIEN, YOU GOT BACK IN TIME. GO SAY HI TO YOUR COUSINS.
NO, MAKE HER READ A COOKBOOK.
WAIT, I'LL DO THAT AFTER WE FLIRT WITH THE BOY NEXT DOOR.
MAKE THEM KISS!
HEY! I WORKED REALLY HARD ON THAT FAMILY.
YOU GUYS ARE GONNA MESS IT UP.
UGH...BUT WE'RE CREATING MORE, LIKE, DRAMA. YA KNOW?

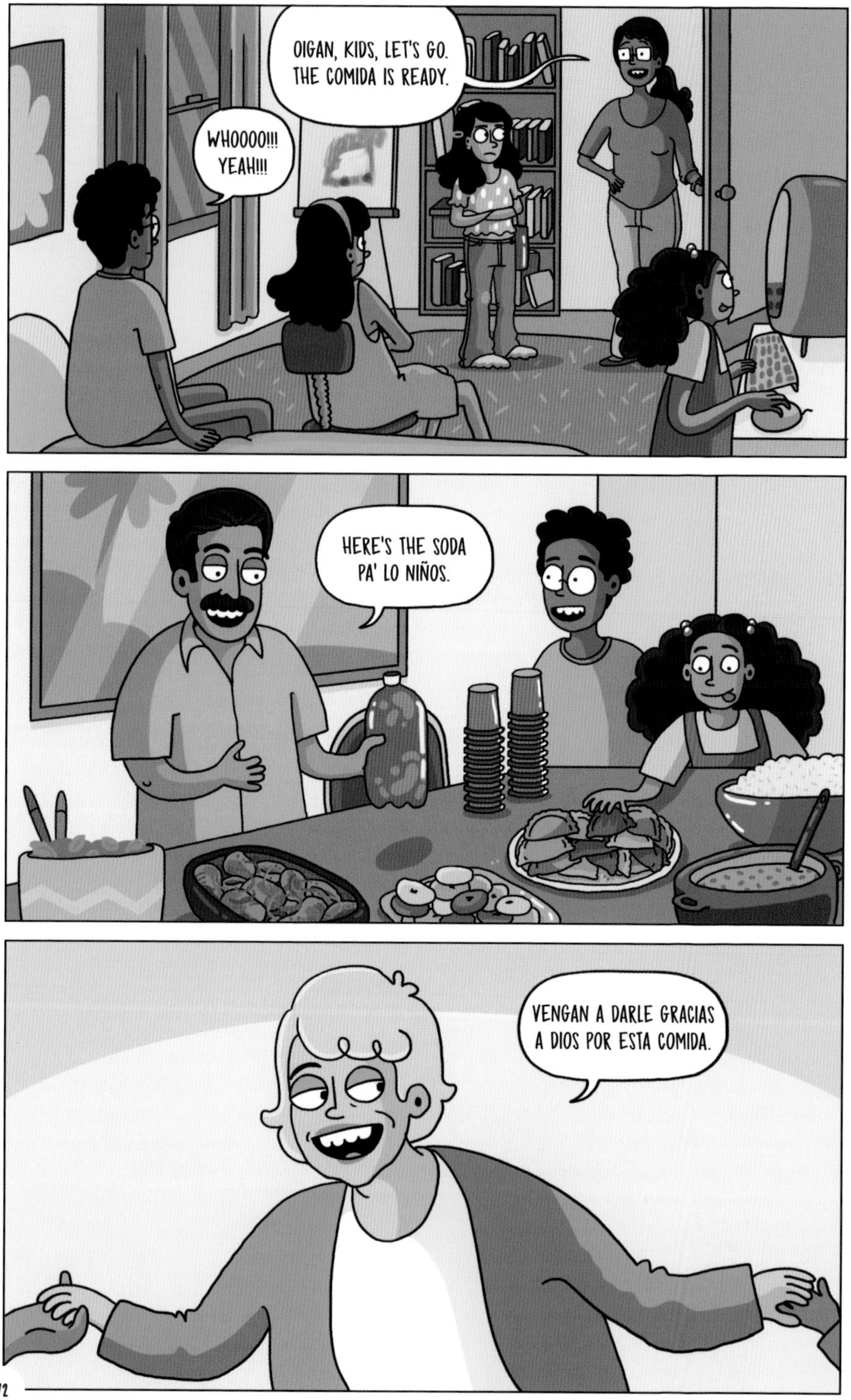
OIGAN, KIDS, LET'S GO. THE COMIDA IS READY.
WHOOOO!!! YEAH!!!
HERE'S THE SODA PA' LO NIÑOS.
VENGAN A DARLE GRACIAS A DIOS POR ESTA COMIDA.

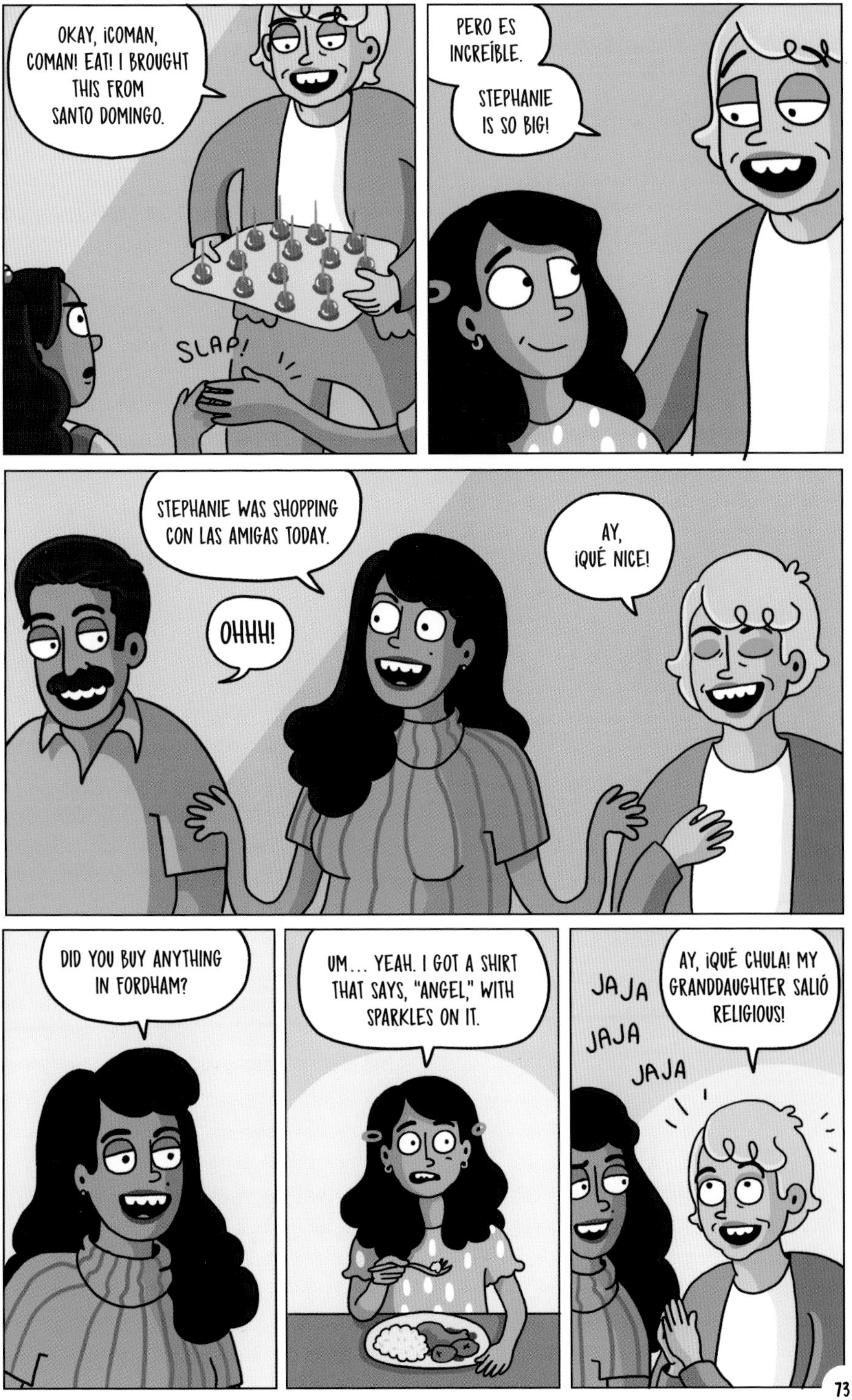
OKAY, ¡COMAN, COMAN! EAT! I BROUGHT THIS FROM SANTO DOMINGO.
SLAP!
PERO ES INCREÍBLE.
STEPHANIE IS SO BIG!
STEPHANIE WAS SHOPPING CON LAS AMIGAS TODAY.
OHHH!
AY, ¡QUÉ NICE!
DID YOU BUY ANYTHING IN FORDHAM?
UM… YEAH. I GOT A SHIRT THAT SAYS, "ANGEL," WITH SPARKLES ON IT.
JAJA
JAJA
JAJA
AY, ¡QUÉ CHULA! MY GRANDDAUGHTER SALIÓ RELIGIOUS!

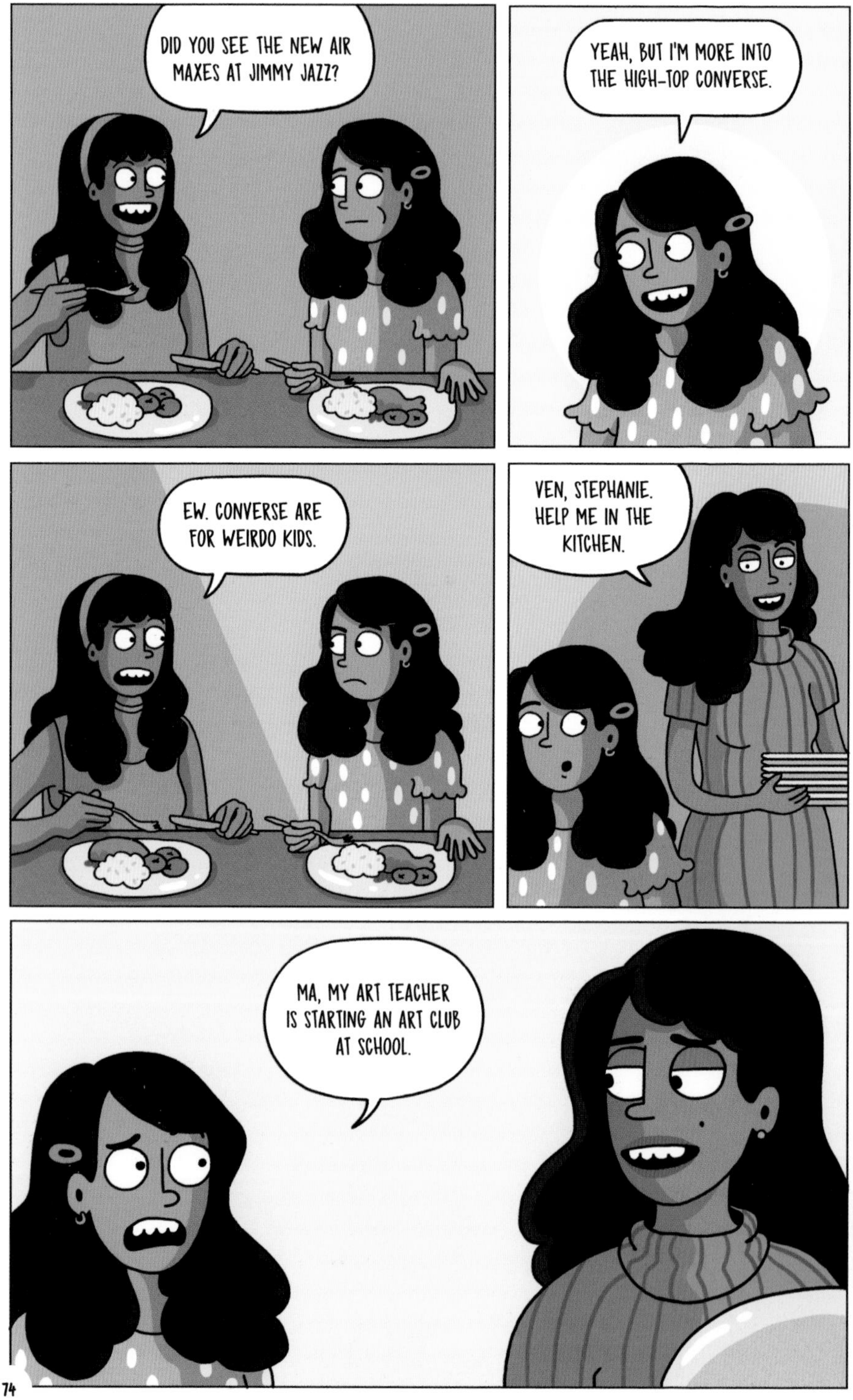
DID YOU SEE THE NEW AIR MAXES AT JIMMY JAZZ?
YEAH, BUT I'M MORE INTO THE HIGH-TOP CONVERSE.
EW. CONVERSE ARE FOR WEIRDO KIDS.
VEN, STEPHANIE. HELP ME IN THE KITCHEN.
MA, MY ART TEACHER IS STARTING AN ART CLUB AT SCHOOL.

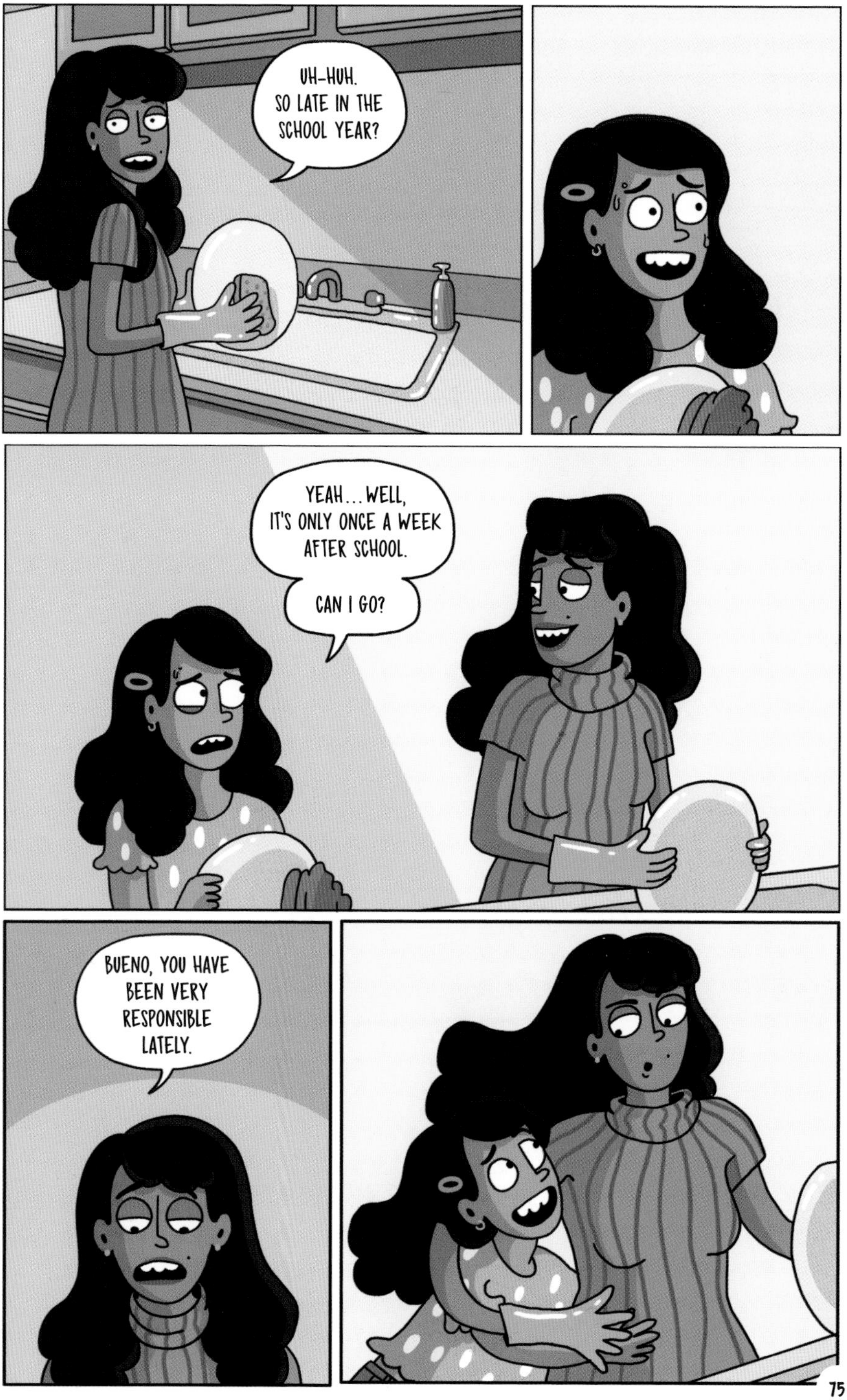
UH-HUH. SO LATE IN THE SCHOOL YEAR?
YEAH...WELL, IT'S ONLY ONCE A WEEK AFTER SCHOOL.
CAN I GO?
BUENO, YOU HAVE BEEN VERY RESPONSIBLE LATELY.

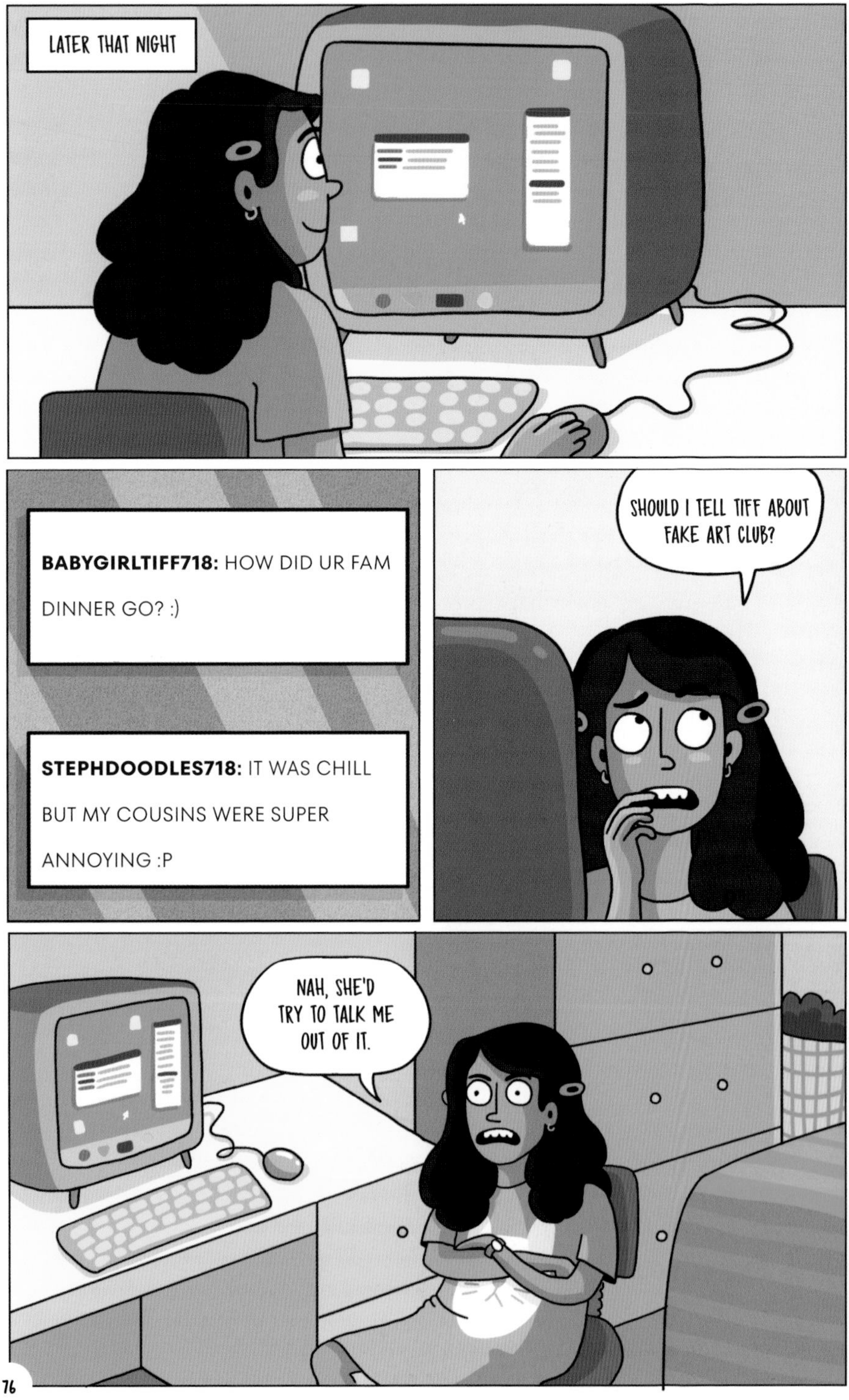
LATER THAT NIGHT
BABYGIRLTIFF718: HOW DID UR FAM DINNER GO? :)
STEPHDOODLES718: IT WAS CHILL BUT MY COUSINS WERE SUPER ANNOYING :P
SHOULD I TELL TIFF ABOUT FAKE ART CLUB?
NAH, SHE'D TRY TO TALK ME OUT OF IT.

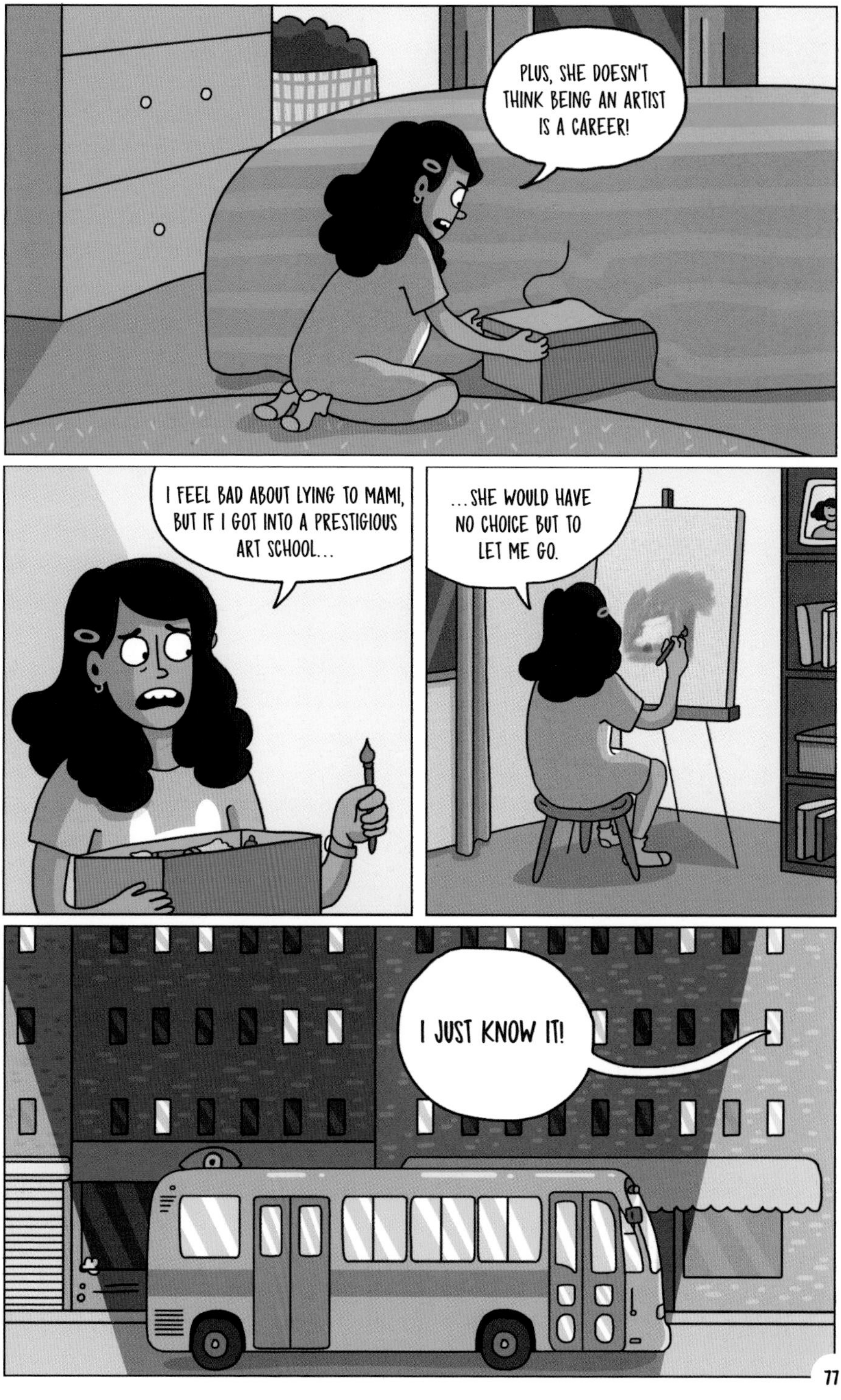
PLUS, SHE DOESN'T THINK BEING AN ARTIST IS A CAREER!
I FEEL BAD ABOUT LYING TO MAMI, BUT IF I GOT INTO A PRESTIGIOUS ART SCHOOL...
...SHE WOULD HAVE NO CHOICE BUT TO LET ME GO.
I JUST KNOW IT!

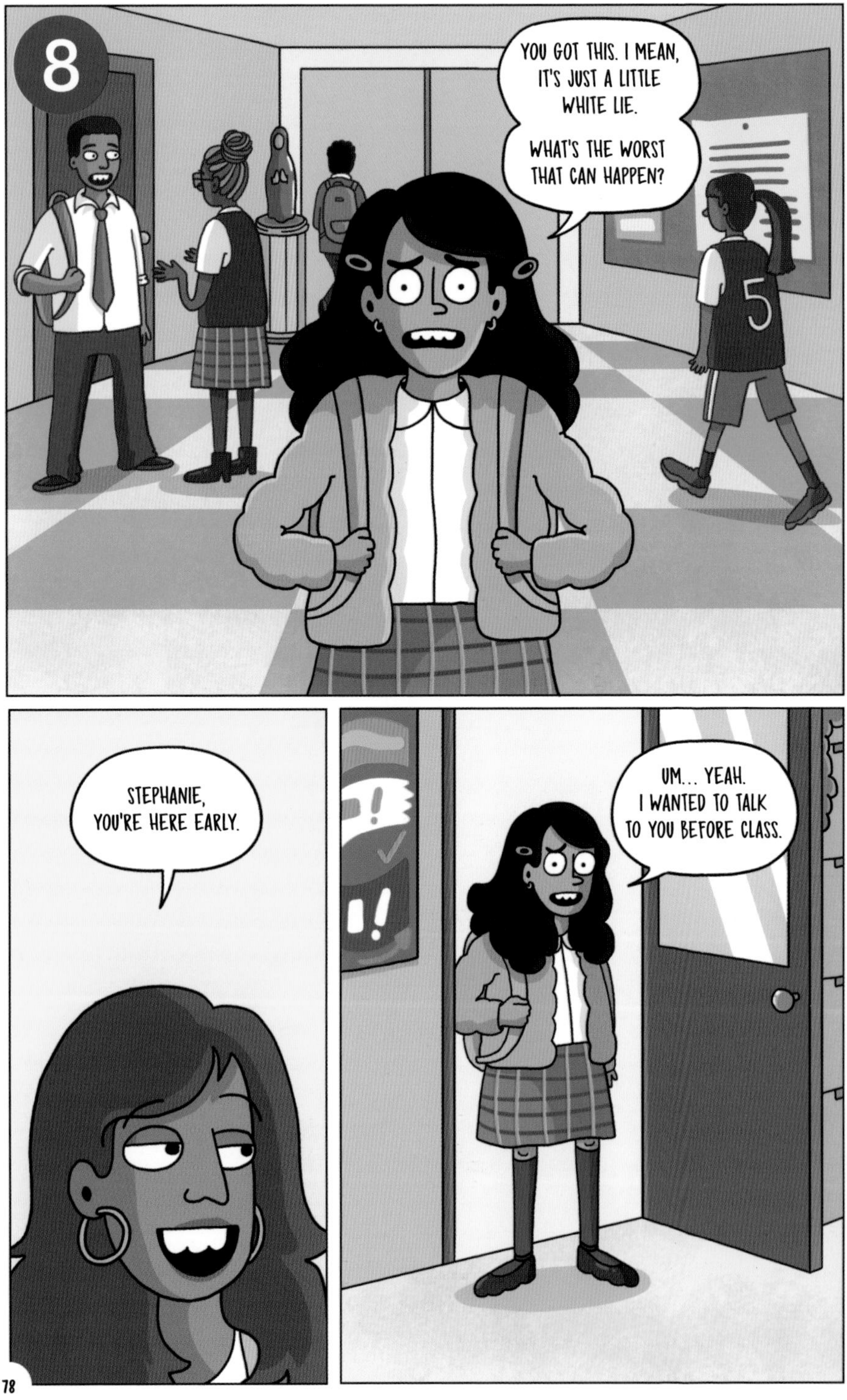
8
YOU GOT THIS. I MEAN, IT'S JUST A LITTLE WHITE LIE.
WHAT'S THE WORST THAT CAN HAPPEN?
5
STEPHANIE, YOU'RE HERE EARLY.
UM... YEAH. I WANTED TO TALK TO YOU BEFORE CLASS.

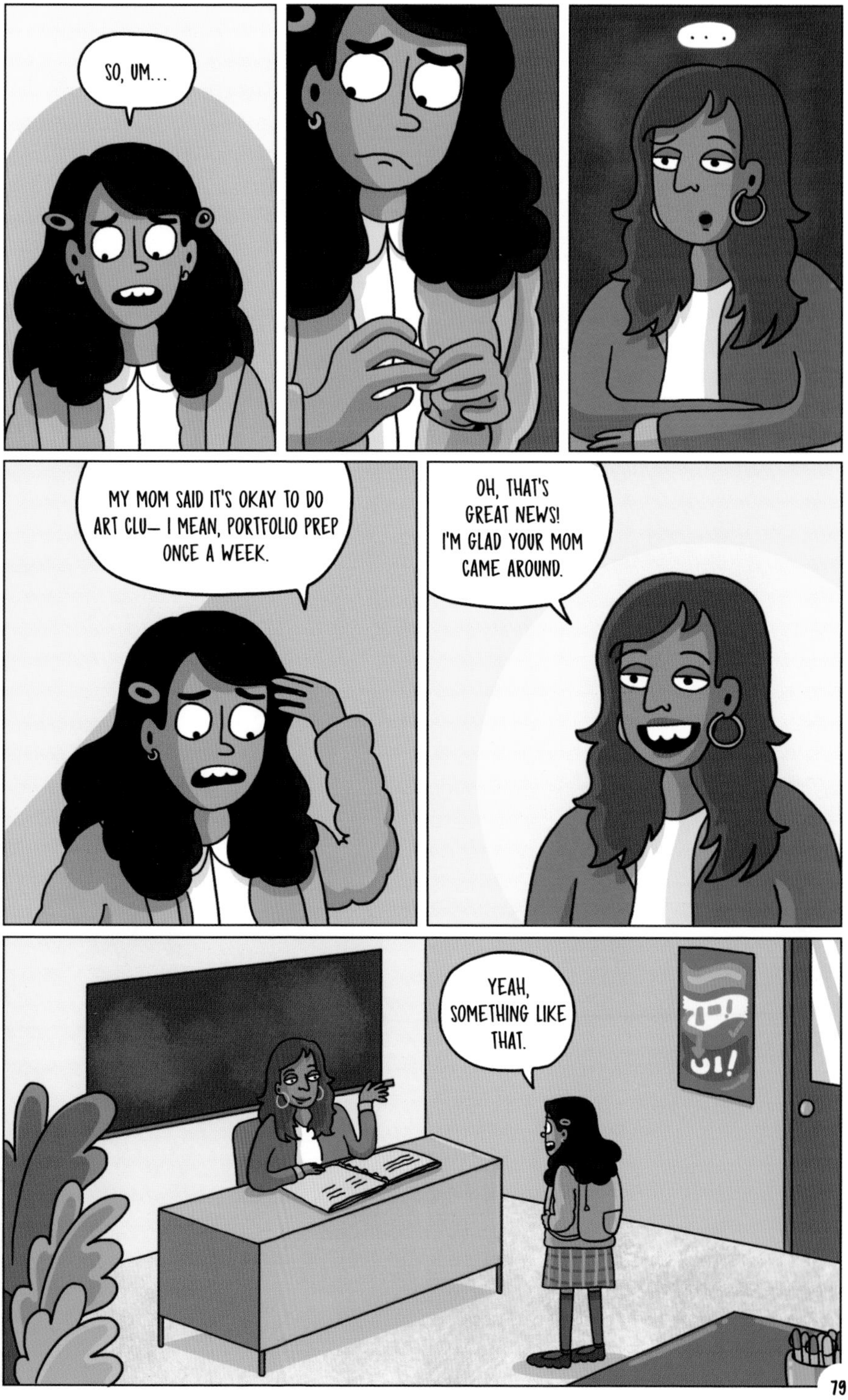
SO, UM...
...
MY MOM SAID IT'S OKAY TO DO ART CLU— I MEAN, PORTFOLIO PREP ONCE A WEEK.
OH, THAT'S GREAT NEWS! I'M GLAD YOUR MOM CAME AROUND.
YEAH, SOMETHING LIKE THAT.

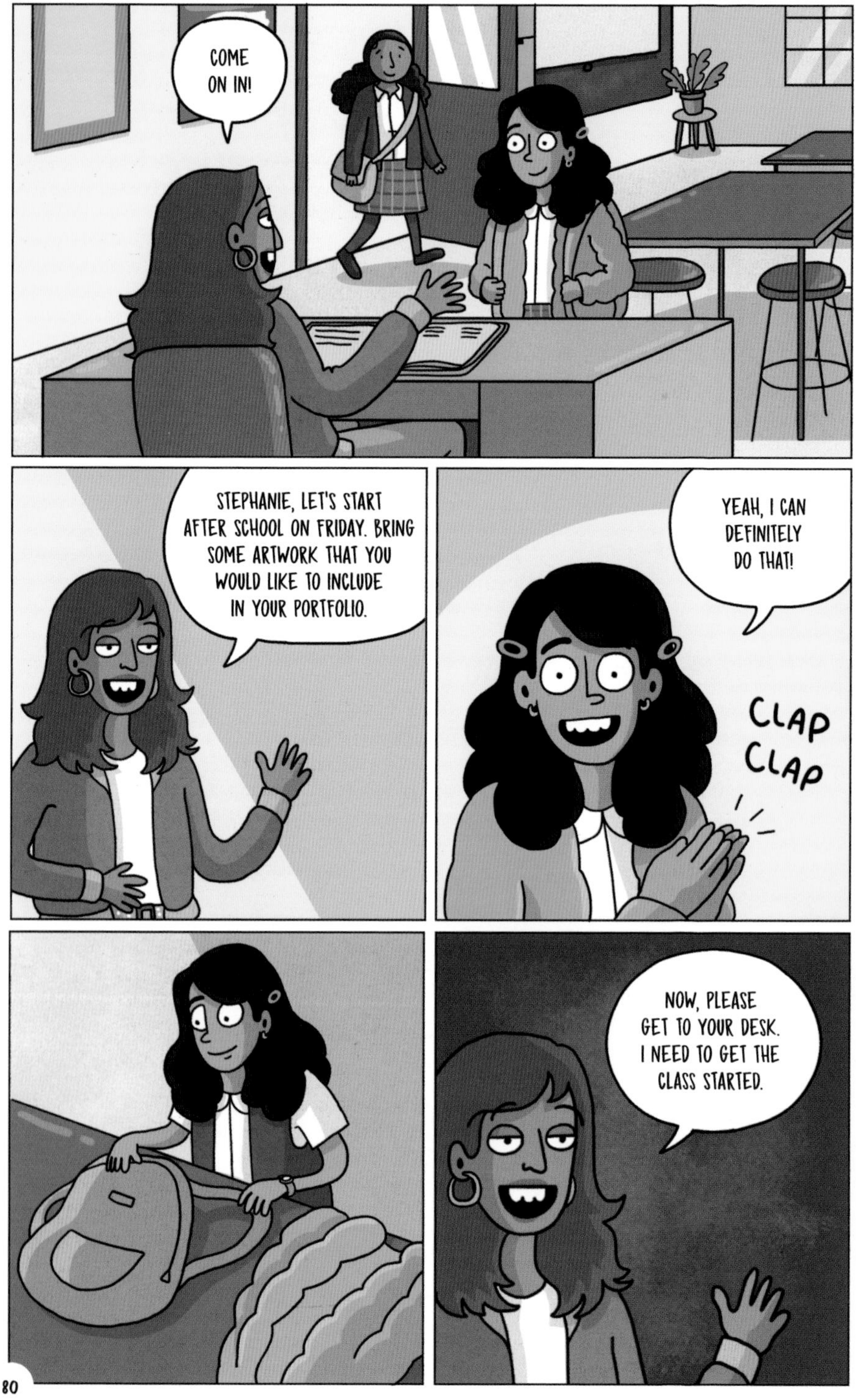
COME ON IN!
STEPHANIE, LET'S START AFTER SCHOOL ON FRIDAY. BRING SOME ARTWORK THAT YOU WOULD LIKE TO INCLUDE IN YOUR PORTFOLIO.
YEAH, I CAN DEFINITELY DO THAT!
CLAP CLAP
NOW, PLEASE GET TO YOUR DESK. I NEED TO GET THE CLASS STARTED.

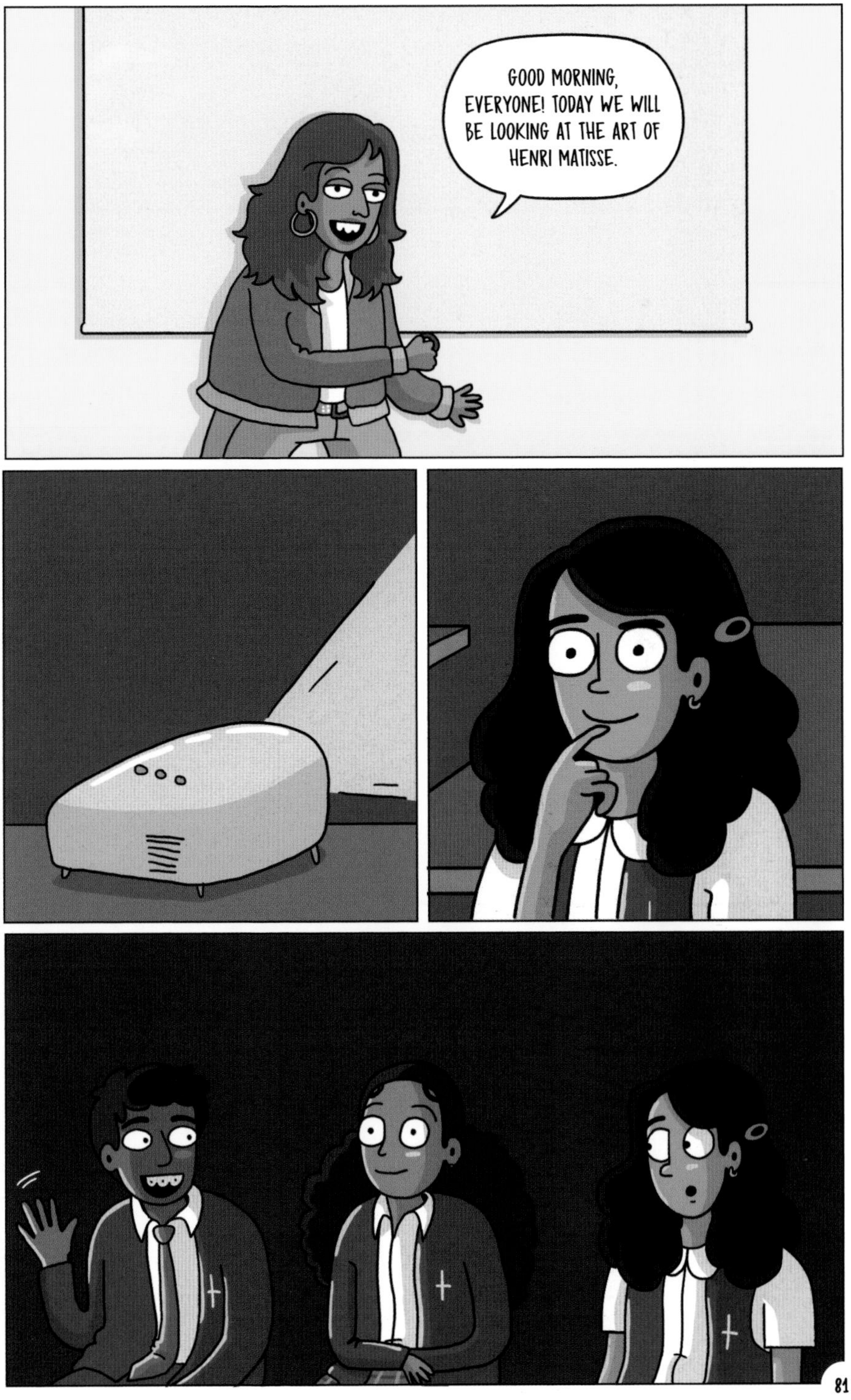
GOOD MORNING, EVERYONE! TODAY WE WILL BE LOOKING AT THE ART OF HENRI MATISSE.

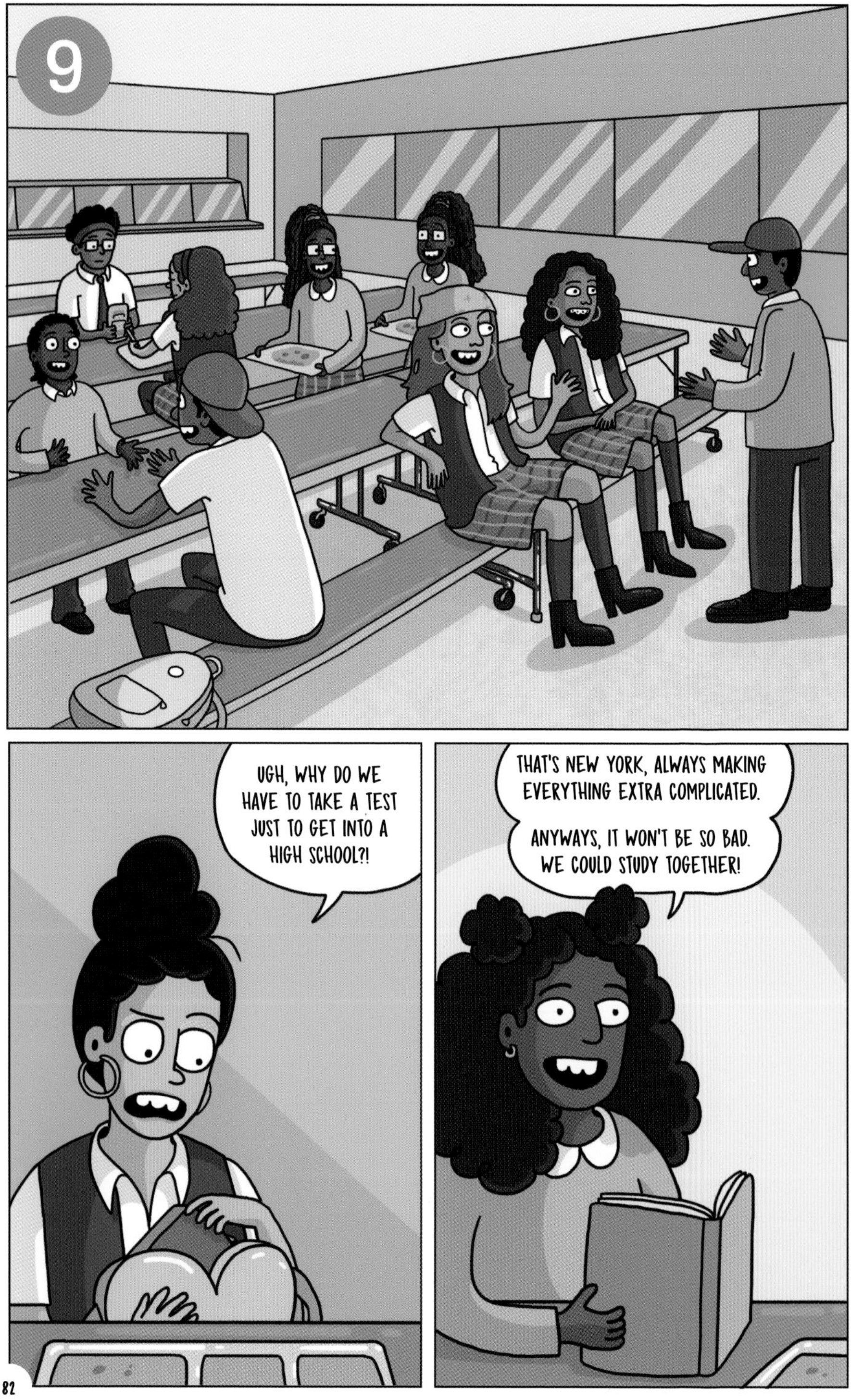
9
UGH, WHY DO WE HAVE TO TAKE A TEST JUST TO GET INTO A HIGH SCHOOL?!
THAT'S NEW YORK, ALWAYS MAKING EVERYTHING EXTRA COMPLICATED.
ANYWAYS, IT WON'T BE SO BAD. WE COULD STUDY TOGETHER!

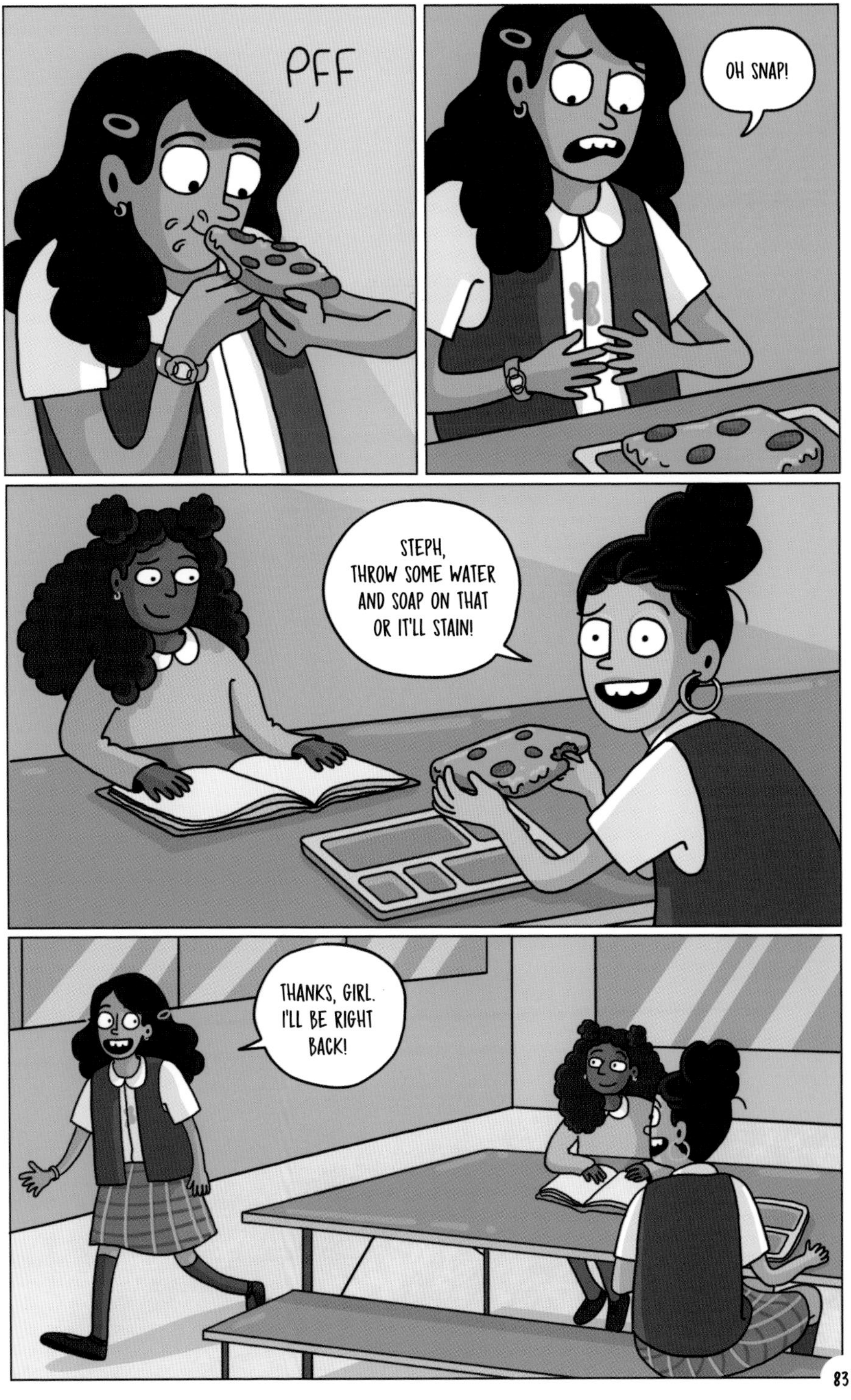
PFF
OH SNAP!
STEPH, THROW SOME WATER AND SOAP ON THAT OR IT'LL STAIN!
THANKS, GIRL. I'LL BE RIGHT BACK!

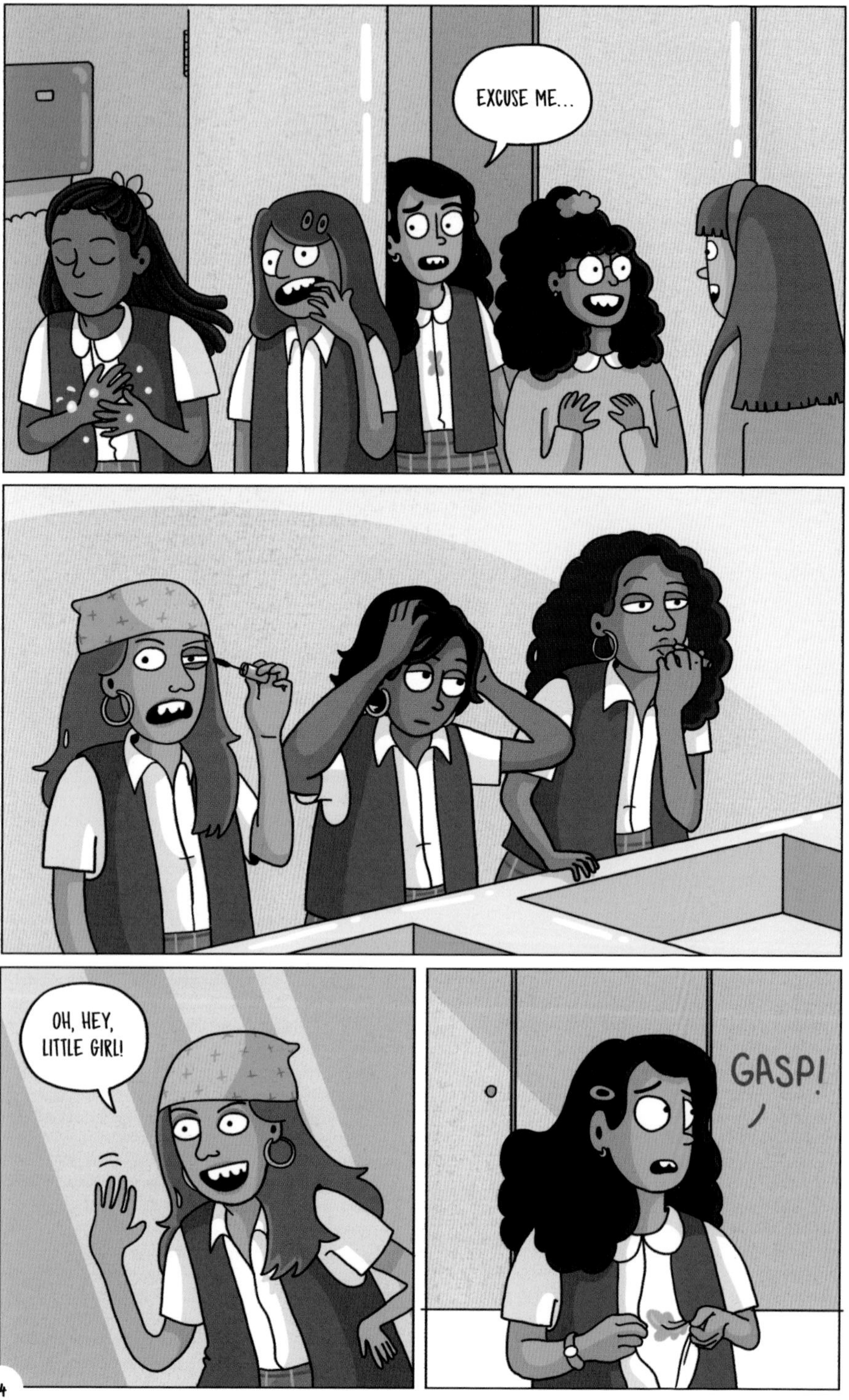
EXCUSE ME...
OH, HEY, LITTLE GIRL!
GASP!

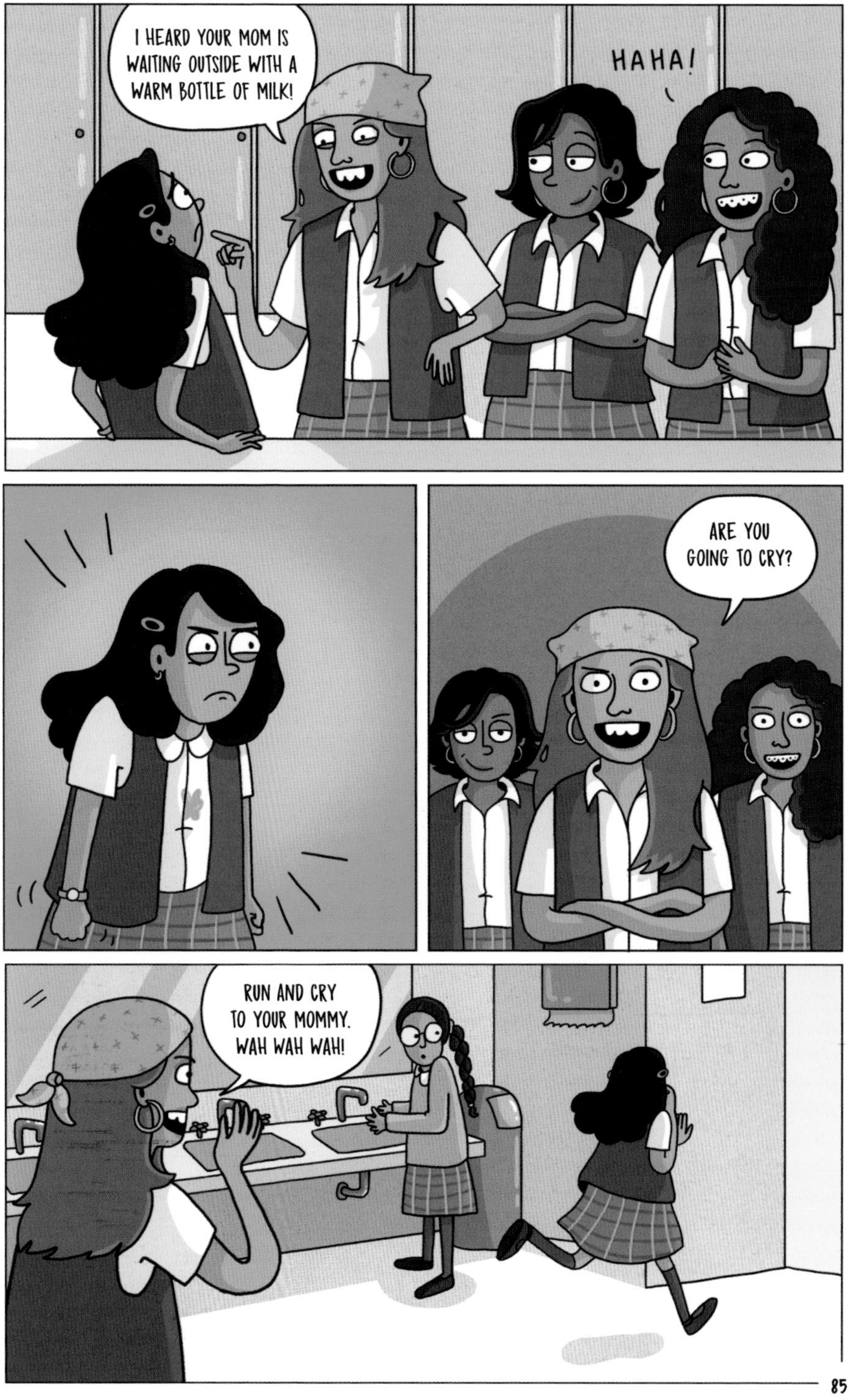
I HEARD YOUR MOM IS WAITING OUTSIDE WITH A WARM BOTTLE OF MILK!
HAHA!
ARE YOU GOING TO CRY?
RUN AND CRY TO YOUR MOMMY. WAH WAH WAH!

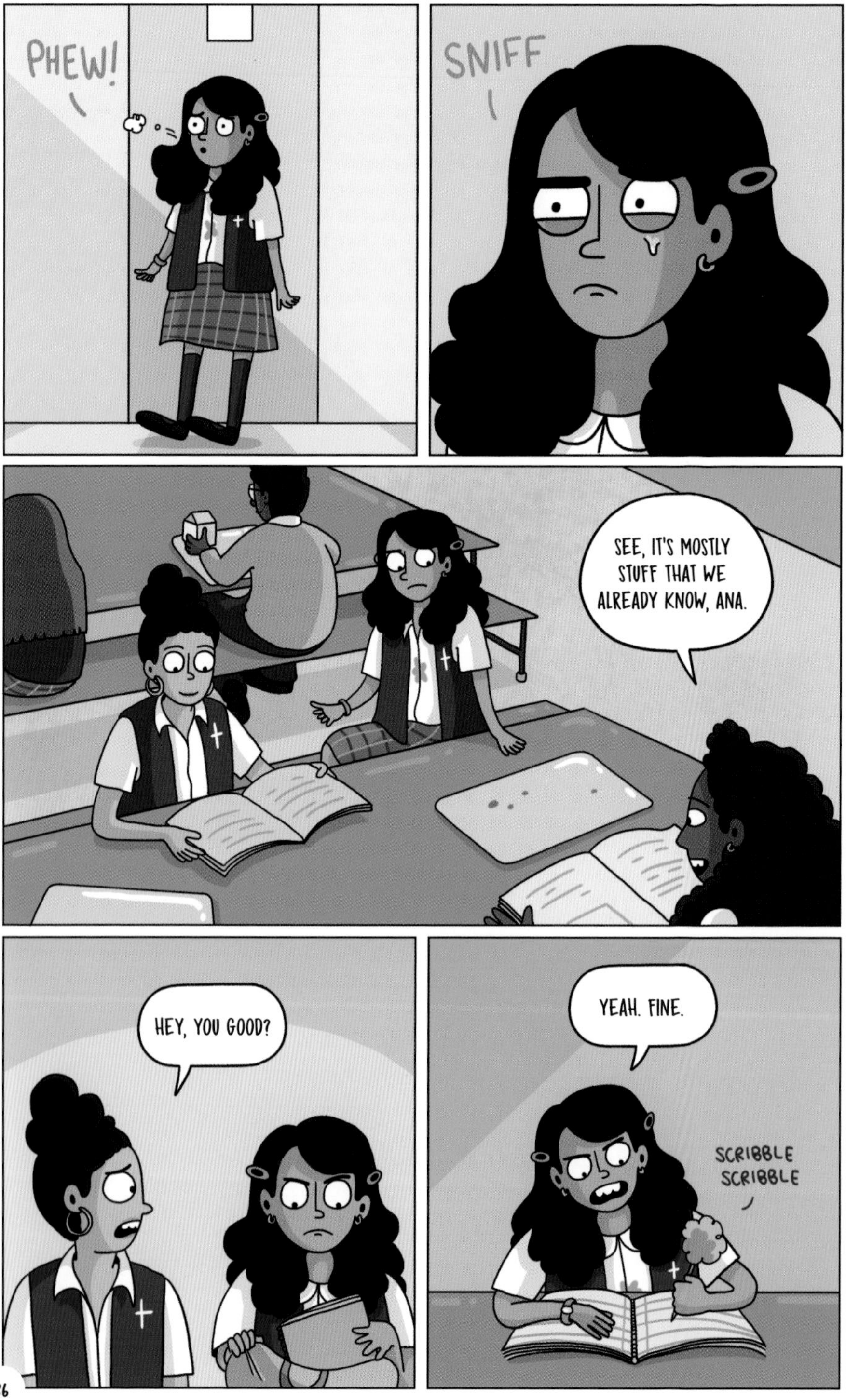
PHEW!
SNIFF
SEE, IT'S MOSTLY STUFF THAT WE ALREADY KNOW, ANA.
HEY, YOU GOOD?
YEAH. FINE.
SCRIBBLE SCRIBBLE

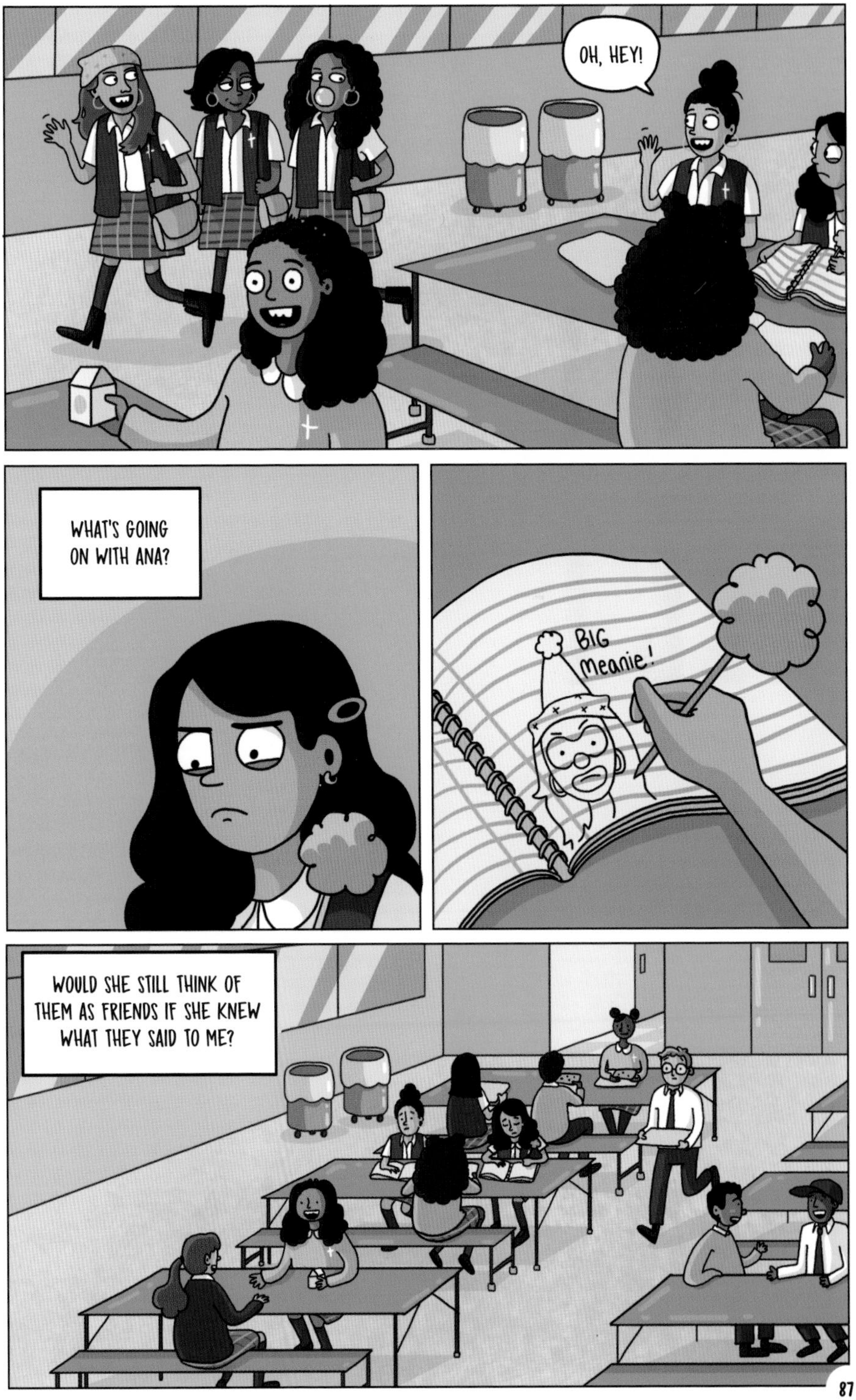
OH, HEY!
WHAT'S GOING ON WITH ANA?
BIG Meanie!
WOULD SHE STILL THINK OF THEM AS FRIENDS IF SHE KNEW WHAT THEY SAID TO ME?

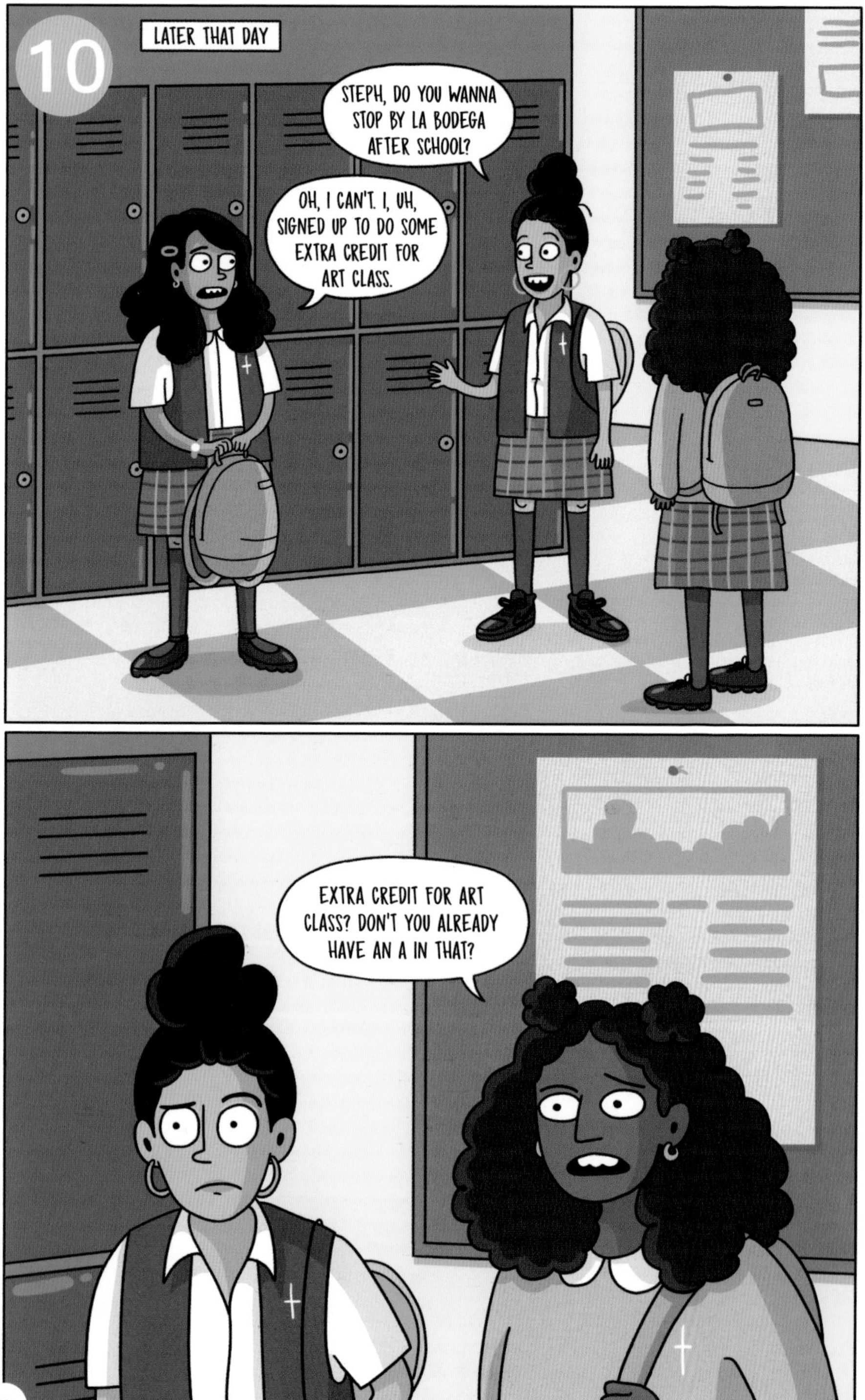
10
LATER THAT DAY
STEPH, DO YOU WANNA STOP BY LA BODEGA AFTER SCHOOL?
OH, I CAN'T. I, UH, SIGNED UP TO DO SOME EXTRA CREDIT FOR ART CLASS.
EXTRA CREDIT FOR ART CLASS? DON'T YOU ALREADY HAVE AN A IN THAT?

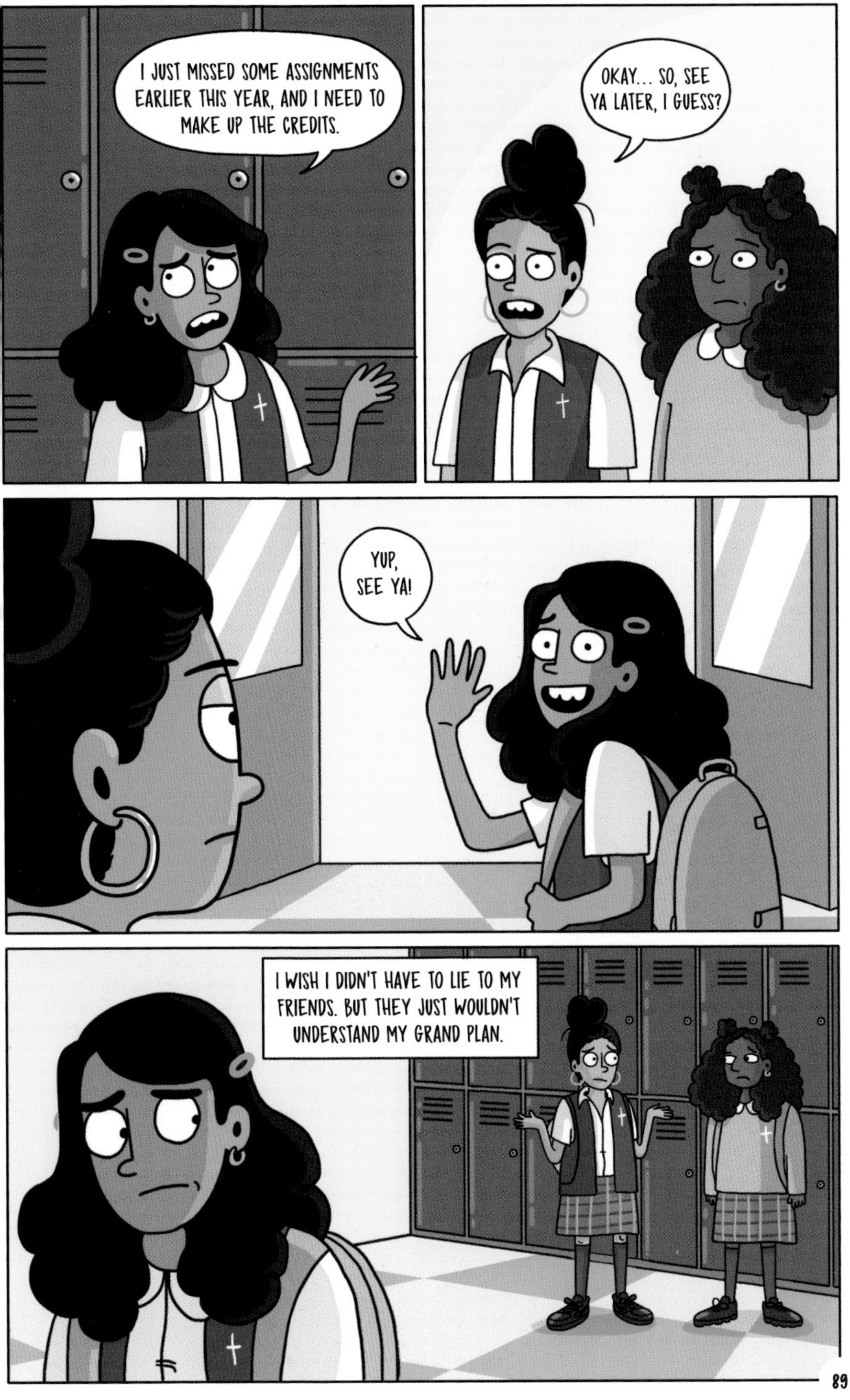
I JUST MISSED SOME ASSIGNMENTS EARLIER THIS YEAR, AND I NEED TO MAKE UP THE CREDITS.
OKAY... SO, SEE YA LATER, I GUESS?
YUP, SEE YA!
I WISH I DIDN'T HAVE TO LIE TO MY FRIENDS. BUT THEY JUST WOULDN'T UNDERSTAND MY GRAND PLAN.

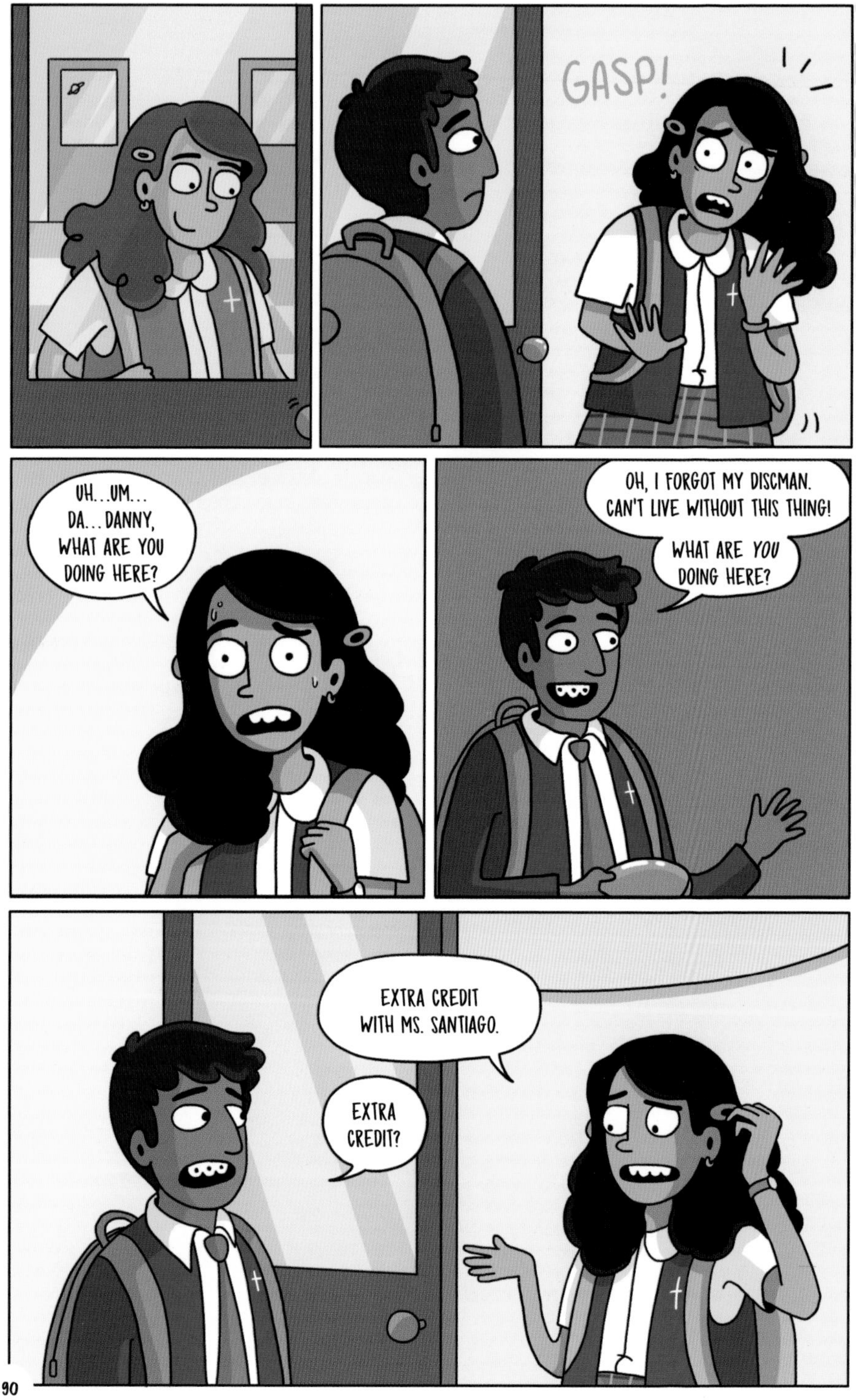
GASP!
UH...UM... DA...DANNY, WHAT ARE YOU DOING HERE?
OH, I FORGOT MY DISCMAN. CAN'T LIVE WITHOUT THIS THING!
WHAT ARE *YOU* DOING HERE?
EXTRA CREDIT WITH MS. SANTIAGO.
EXTRA CREDIT?

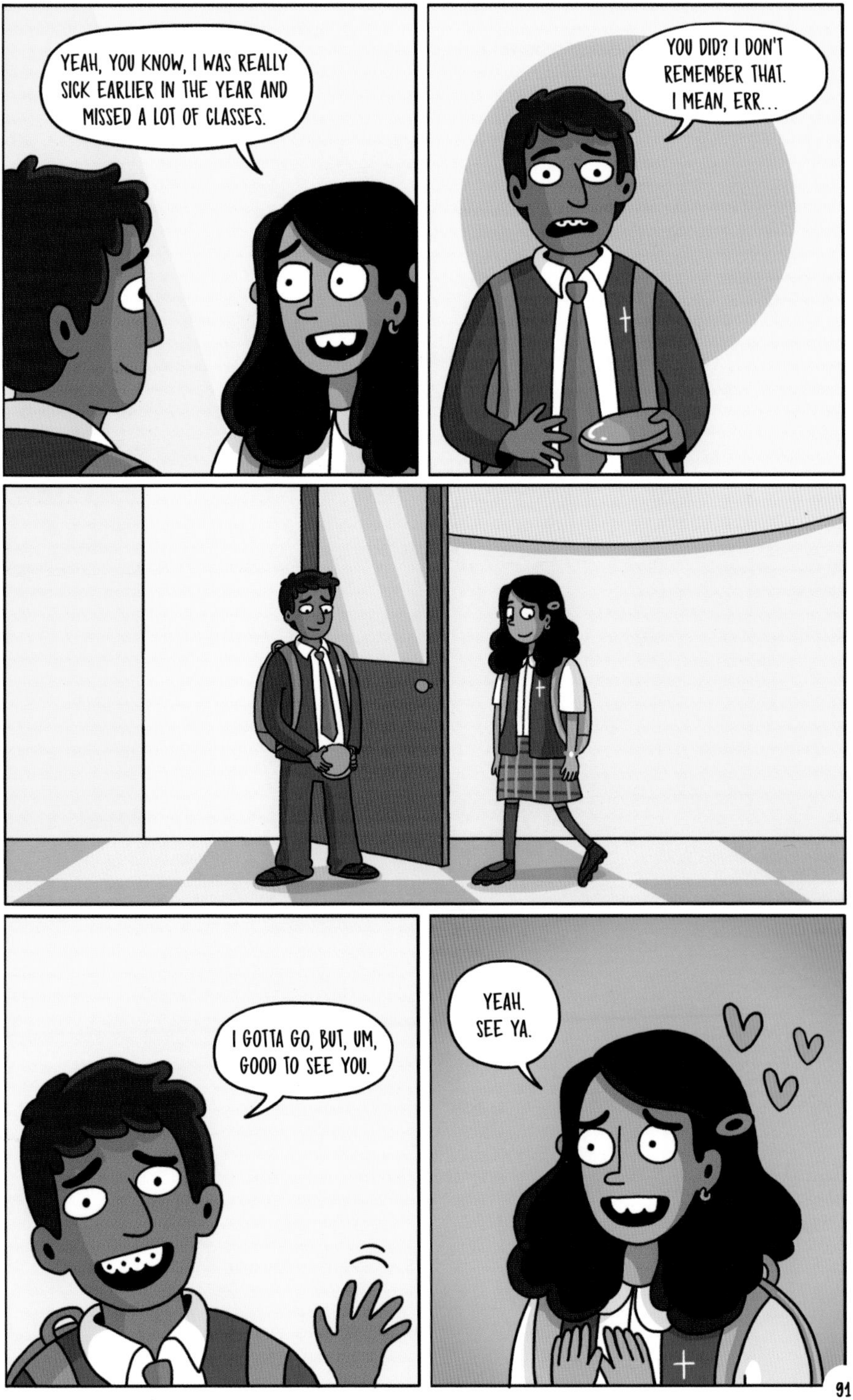
YEAH, YOU KNOW, I WAS REALLY SICK EARLIER IN THE YEAR AND MISSED A LOT OF CLASSES.
YOU DID? I DON'T REMEMBER THAT. I MEAN, ERR...
I GOTTA GO, BUT, UM, GOOD TO SEE YOU.
YEAH. SEE YA.

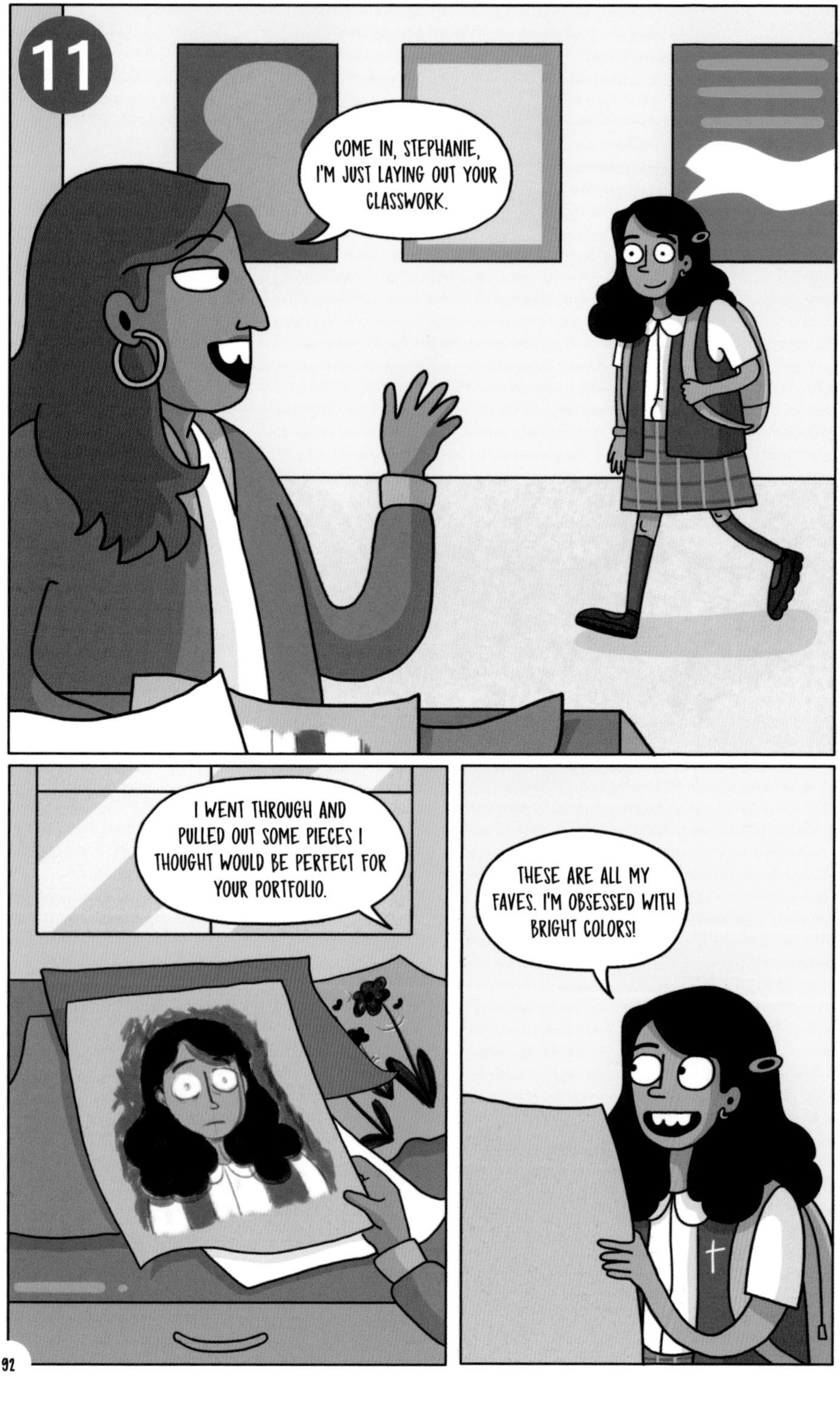
11
COME IN, STEPHANIE, I'M JUST LAYING OUT YOUR CLASSWORK.
I WENT THROUGH AND PULLED OUT SOME PIECES I THOUGHT WOULD BE PERFECT FOR YOUR PORTFOLIO.
THESE ARE ALL MY FAVES. I'M OBSESSED WITH BRIGHT COLORS!

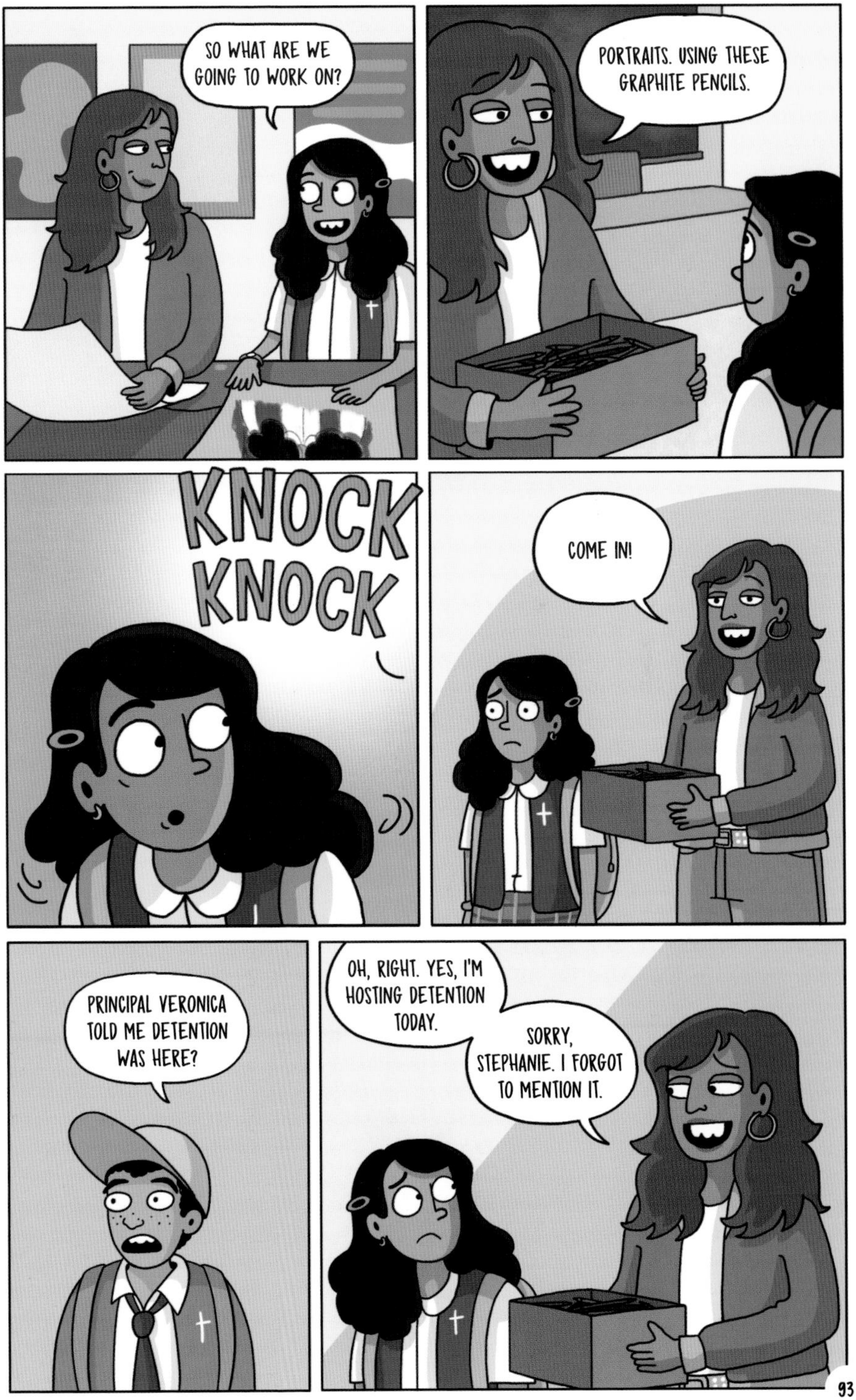
SO WHAT ARE WE GOING TO WORK ON?
PORTRAITS. USING THESE GRAPHITE PENCILS.
KNOCK KNOCK
COME IN!
PRINCIPAL VERONICA TOLD ME DETENTION WAS HERE?
OH, RIGHT. YES, I'M HOSTING DETENTION TODAY.
SORRY, STEPHANIE. I FORGOT TO MENTION IT.

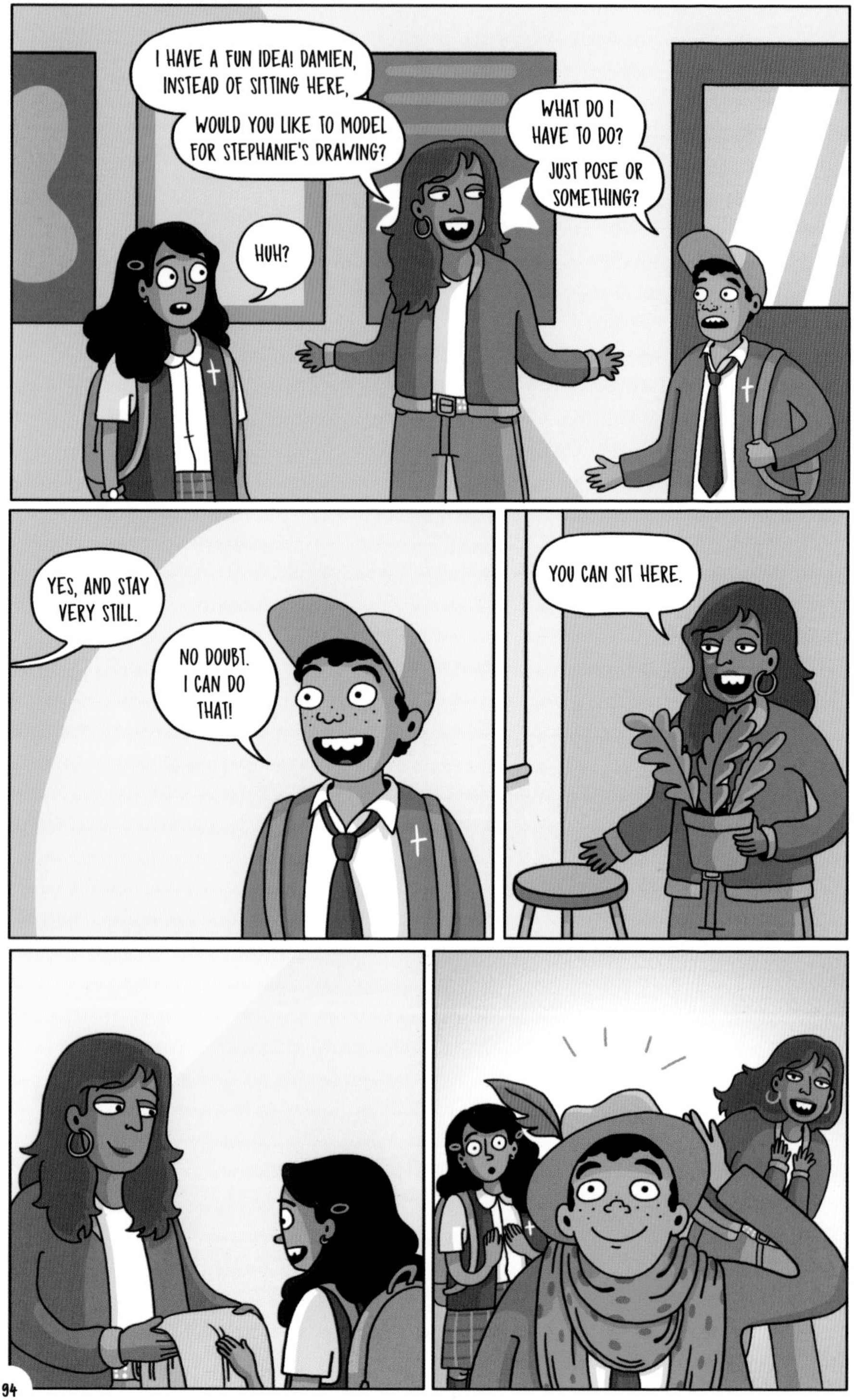
I HAVE A FUN IDEA! DAMIEN, INSTEAD OF SITTING HERE,
WOULD YOU LIKE TO MODEL FOR STEPHANIE'S DRAWING?
HUH?
WHAT DO I HAVE TO DO?
JUST POSE OR SOMETHING?
YES, AND STAY VERY STILL.
NO DOUBT. I CAN DO THAT!
YOU CAN SIT HERE.

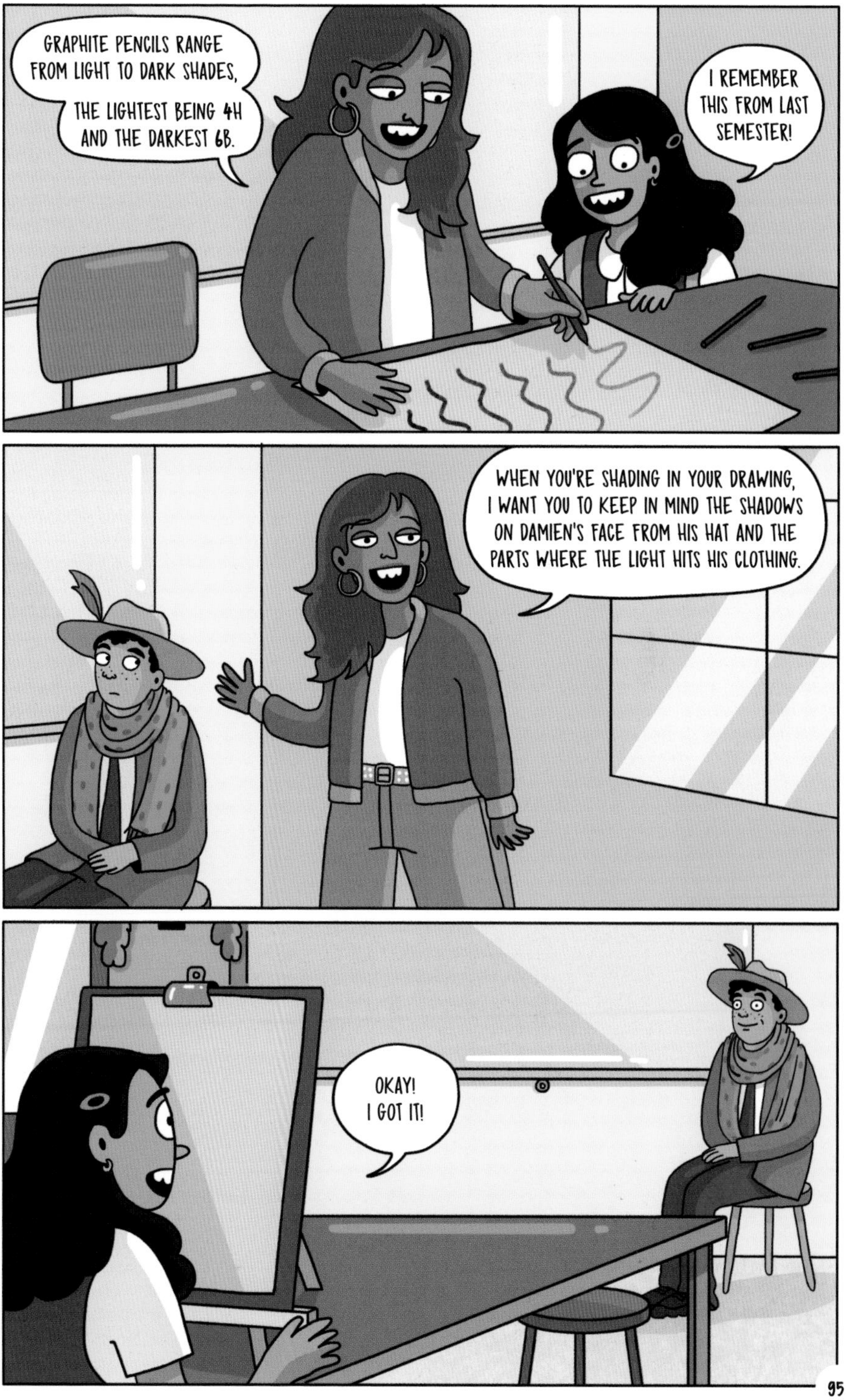
GRAPHITE PENCILS RANGE FROM LIGHT TO DARK SHADES,
THE LIGHTEST BEING 4H AND THE DARKEST 6B.
I REMEMBER THIS FROM LAST SEMESTER!
WHEN YOU'RE SHADING IN YOUR DRAWING, I WANT YOU TO KEEP IN MIND THE SHADOWS ON DAMIEN'S FACE FROM HIS HAT AND THE PARTS WHERE THE LIGHT HITS HIS CLOTHING.
OKAY! I GOT IT!

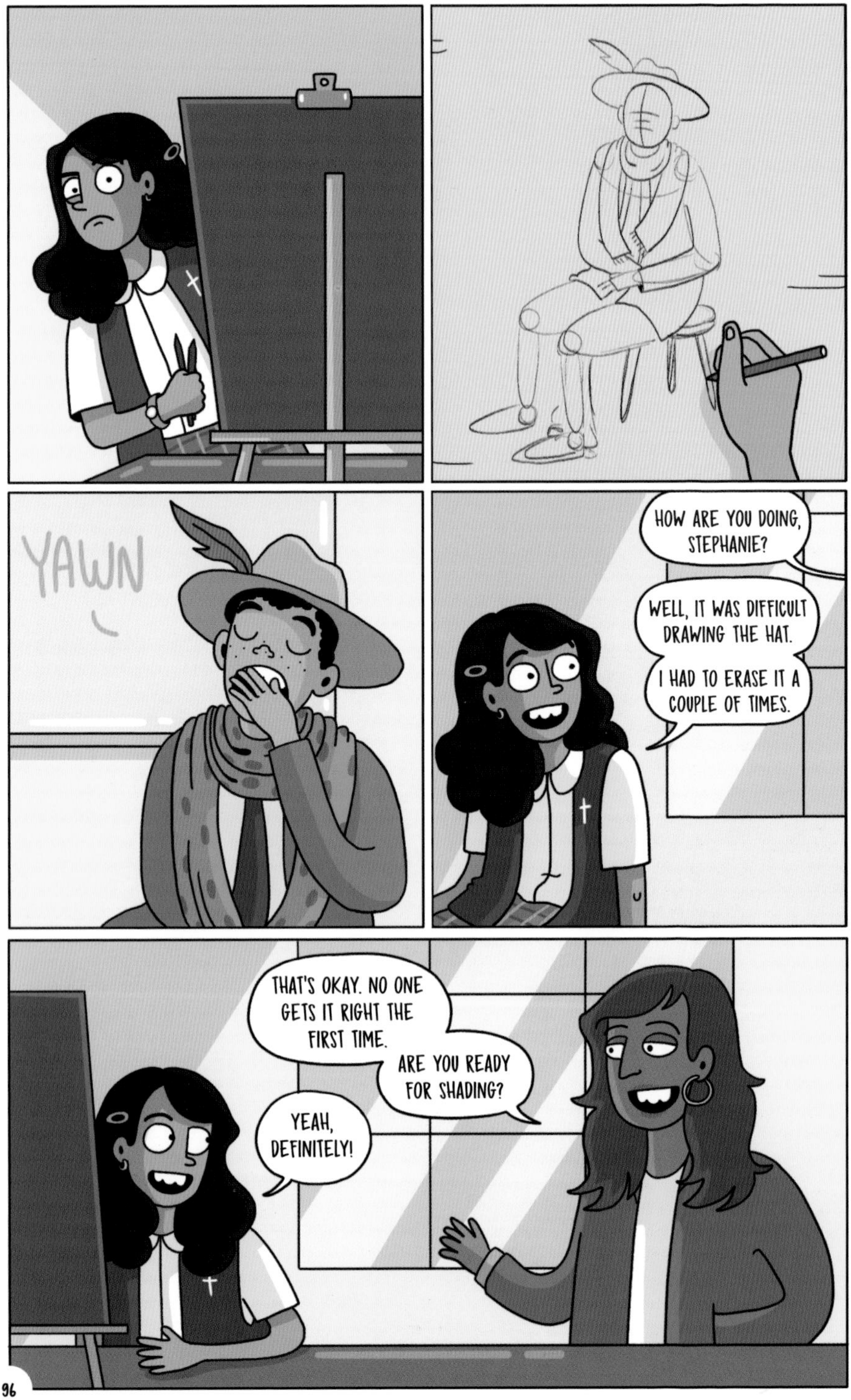
YAWN
HOW ARE YOU DOING, STEPHANIE?
WELL, IT WAS DIFFICULT DRAWING THE HAT.
I HAD TO ERASE IT A COUPLE OF TIMES.
THAT'S OKAY. NO ONE GETS IT RIGHT THE FIRST TIME.
ARE YOU READY FOR SHADING?
YEAH, DEFINITELY!

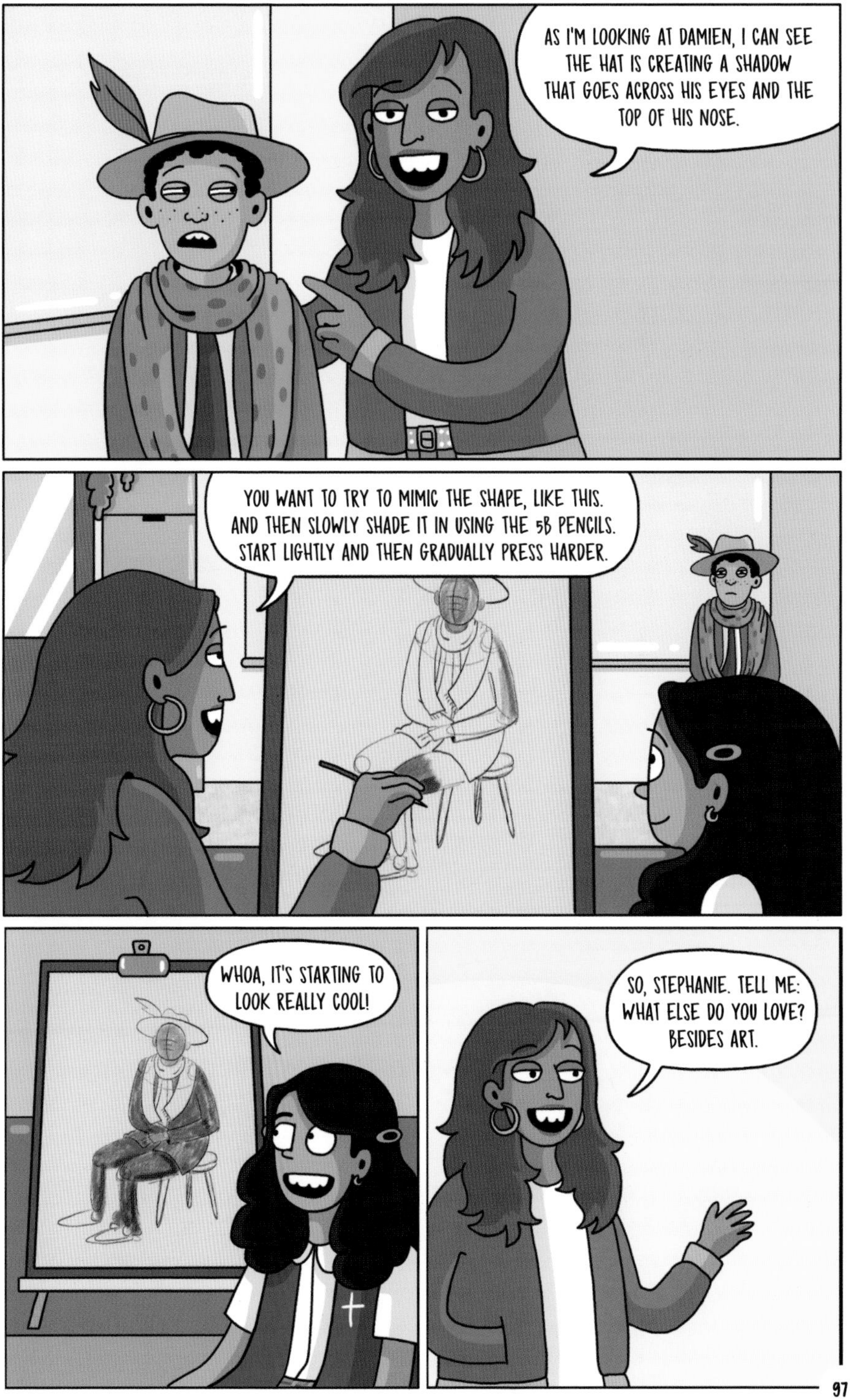
AS I'M LOOKING AT DAMIEN, I CAN SEE THE HAT IS CREATING A SHADOW THAT GOES ACROSS HIS EYES AND THE TOP OF HIS NOSE.
YOU WANT TO TRY TO MIMIC THE SHAPE, LIKE THIS. AND THEN SLOWLY SHADE IT IN USING THE 5B PENCILS. START LIGHTLY AND THEN GRADUALLY PRESS HARDER.
WHOA, IT'S STARTING TO LOOK REALLY COOL!
SO, STEPHANIE. TELL ME: WHAT ELSE DO YOU LOVE? BESIDES ART.

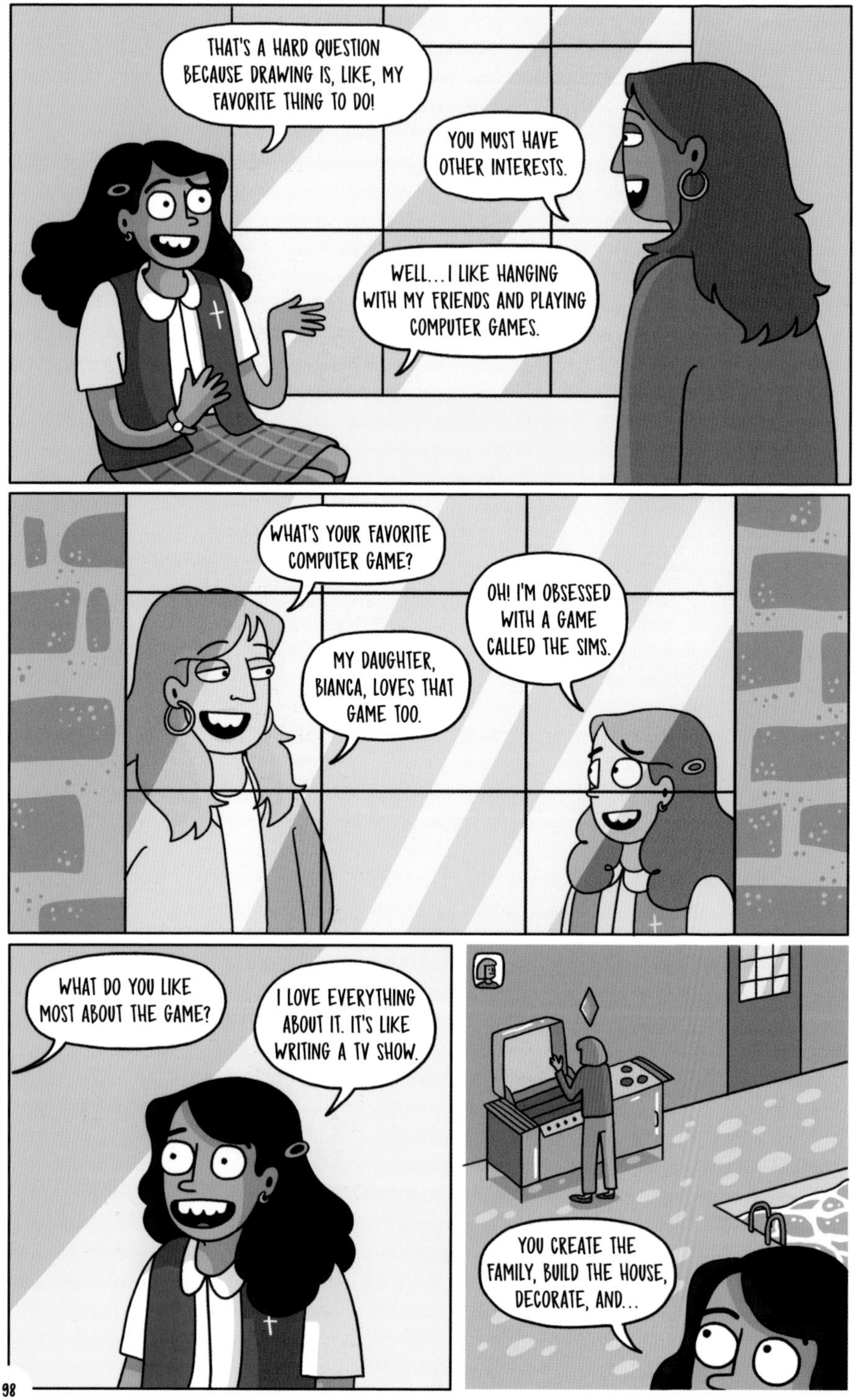
THAT'S A HARD QUESTION BECAUSE DRAWING IS, LIKE, MY FAVORITE THING TO DO!
YOU MUST HAVE OTHER INTERESTS.
WELL... I LIKE HANGING WITH MY FRIENDS AND PLAYING COMPUTER GAMES.
WHAT'S YOUR FAVORITE COMPUTER GAME?
OH! I'M OBSESSED WITH A GAME CALLED THE SIMS.
MY DAUGHTER, BIANCA, LOVES THAT GAME TOO.
WHAT DO YOU LIKE MOST ABOUT THE GAME?
I LOVE EVERYTHING ABOUT IT. IT'S LIKE WRITING A TV SHOW.
YOU CREATE THE FAMILY, BUILD THE HOUSE, DECORATE, AND...

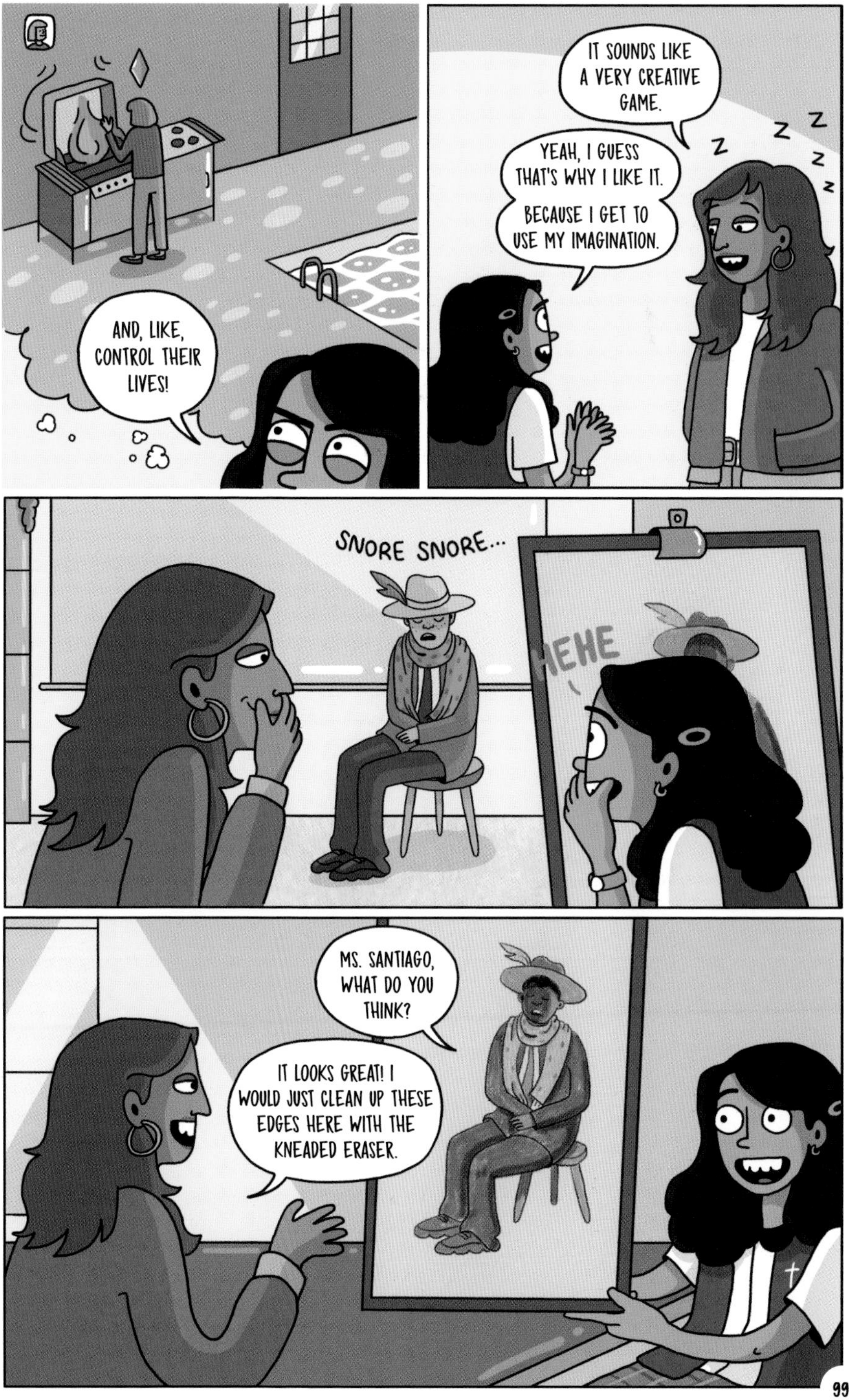
AND, LIKE, CONTROL THEIR LIVES!
IT SOUNDS LIKE A VERY CREATIVE GAME.
Z Z Z Z Z
YEAH, I GUESS THAT'S WHY I LIKE IT.
BECAUSE I GET TO USE MY IMAGINATION.
SNORE SNORE...
HEHE
MS. SANTIAGO, WHAT DO YOU THINK?
IT LOOKS GREAT! I WOULD JUST CLEAN UP THESE EDGES HERE WITH THE KNEADED ERASER.

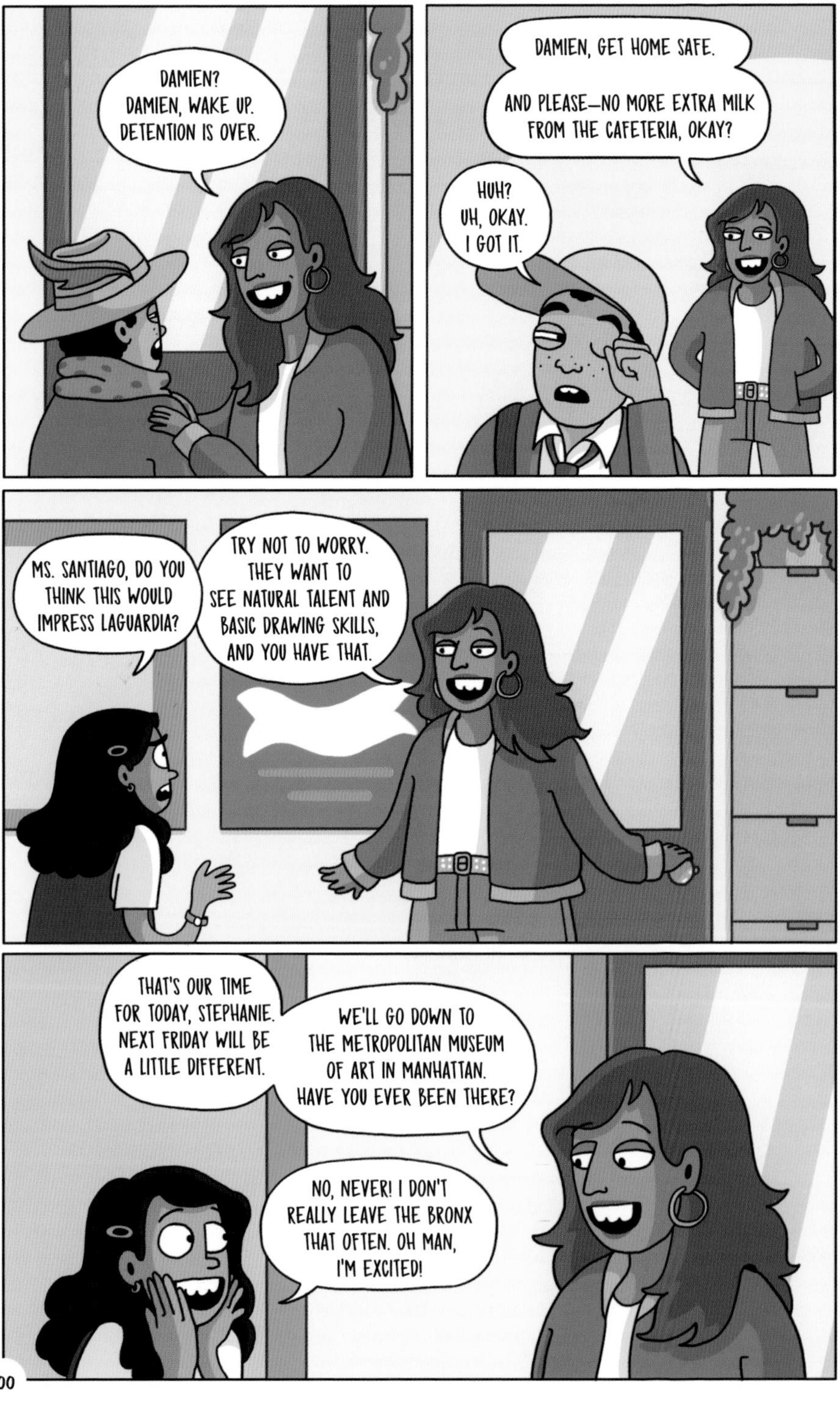
DAMIEN? DAMIEN, WAKE UP. DETENTION IS OVER.
DAMIEN, GET HOME SAFE.
AND PLEASE—NO MORE EXTRA MILK FROM THE CAFETERIA, OKAY?
HUH? UH, OKAY. I GOT IT.
MS. SANTIAGO, DO YOU THINK THIS WOULD IMPRESS LAGUARDIA?
TRY NOT TO WORRY. THEY WANT TO SEE NATURAL TALENT AND BASIC DRAWING SKILLS, AND YOU HAVE THAT.
THAT'S OUR TIME FOR TODAY, STEPHANIE. NEXT FRIDAY WILL BE A LITTLE DIFFERENT.
WE'LL GO DOWN TO THE METROPOLITAN MUSEUM OF ART IN MANHATTAN. HAVE YOU EVER BEEN THERE?
NO, NEVER! I DON'T REALLY LEAVE THE BRONX THAT OFTEN. OH MAN, I'M EXCITED!

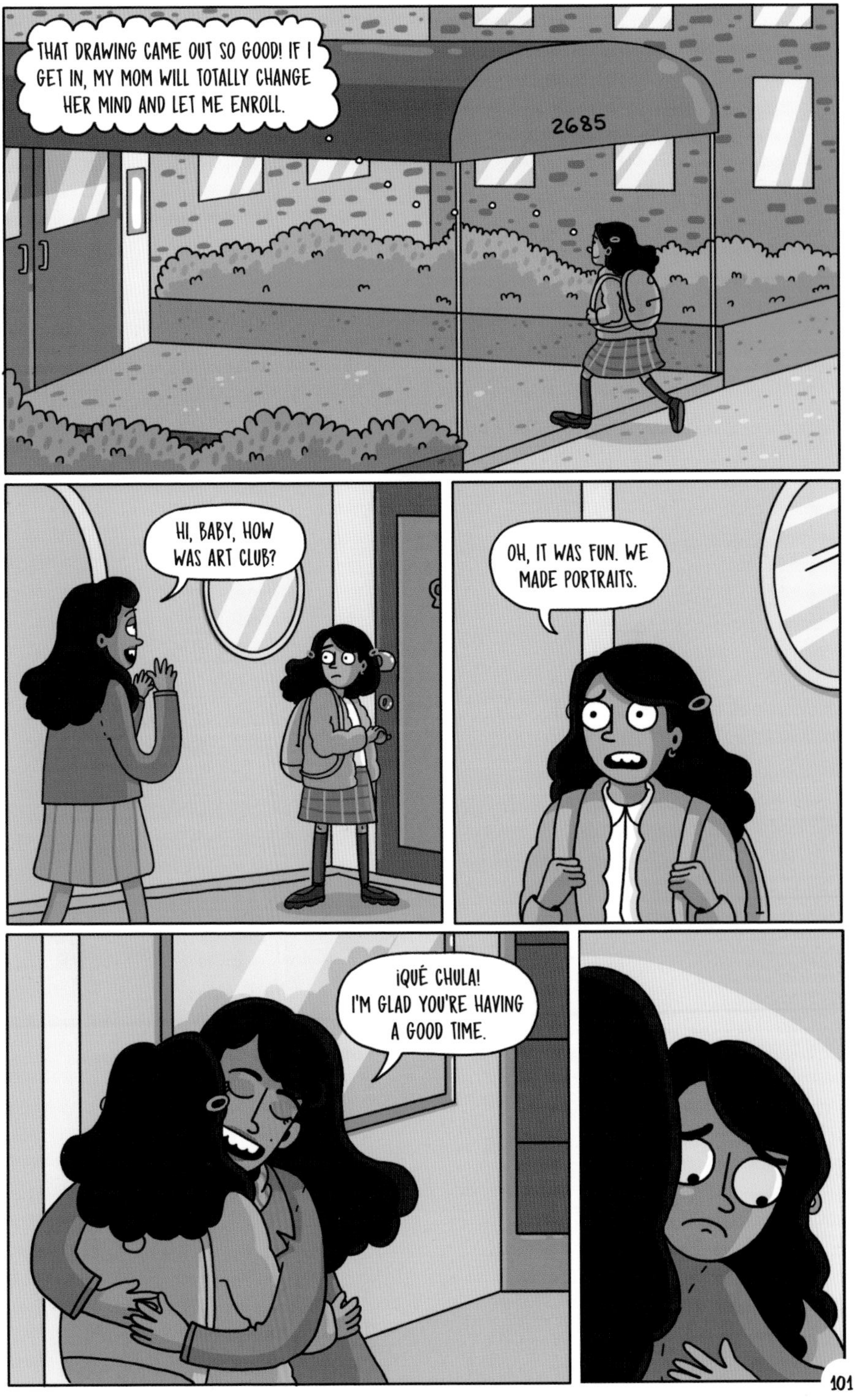
THAT DRAWING CAME OUT SO GOOD! IF I GET IN, MY MOM WILL TOTALLY CHANGE HER MIND AND LET ME ENROLL.
2685
HI, BABY, HOW WAS ART CLUB?
OH, IT WAS FUN. WE MADE PORTRAITS.
¡QUÉ CHULA! I'M GLAD YOU'RE HAVING A GOOD TIME.

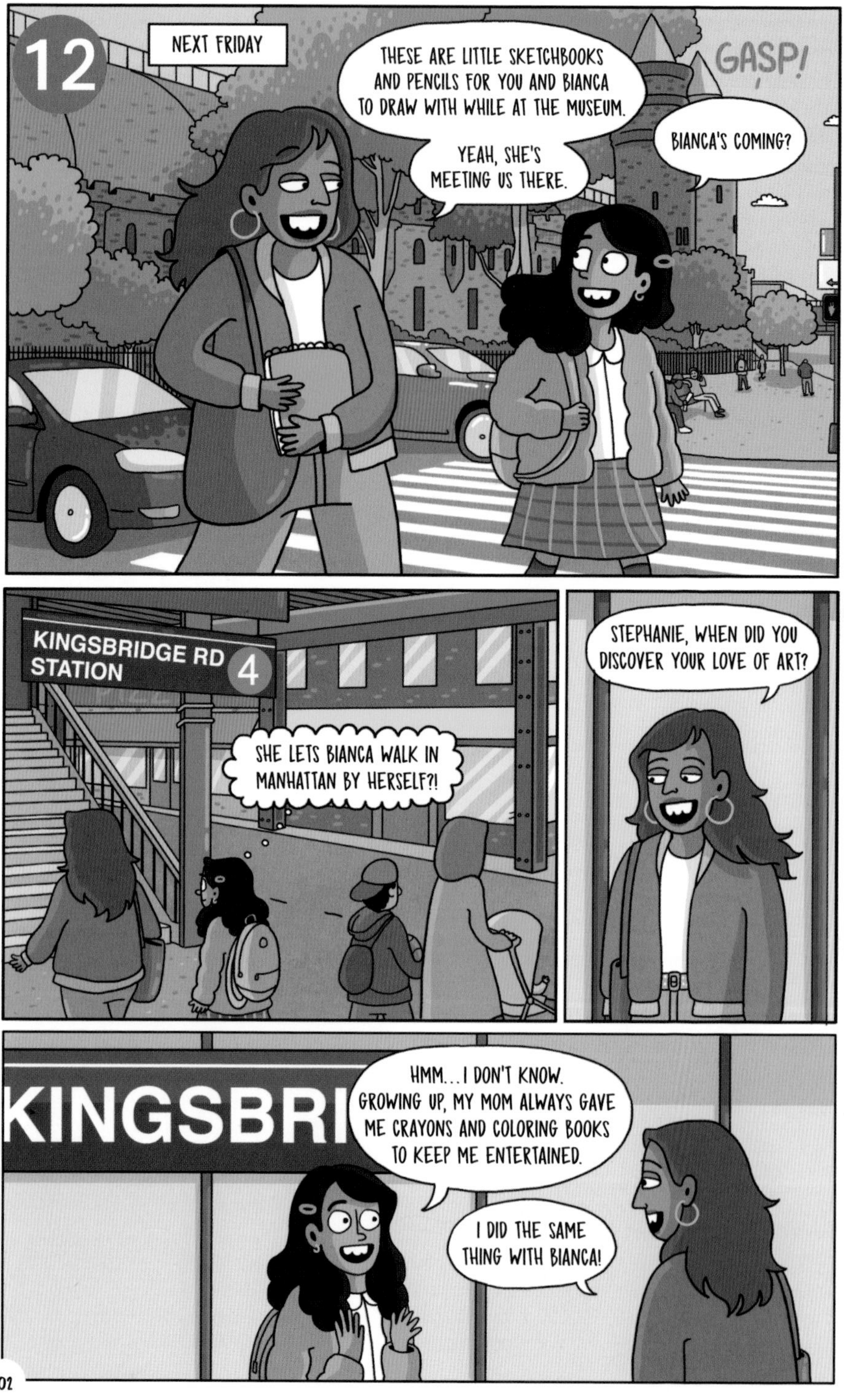
12
NEXT FRIDAY
THESE ARE LITTLE SKETCHBOOKS AND PENCILS FOR YOU AND BIANCA TO DRAW WITH WHILE AT THE MUSEUM.
YEAH, SHE'S MEETING US THERE.
GASP!
BIANCA'S COMING?
KINGSBRIDGE RD STATION 4
SHE LETS BIANCA WALK IN MANHATTAN BY HERSELF?!
STEPHANIE, WHEN DID YOU DISCOVER YOUR LOVE OF ART?
KINGSBRI
HMM...I DON'T KNOW. GROWING UP, MY MOM ALWAYS GAVE ME CRAYONS AND COLORING BOOKS TO KEEP ME ENTERTAINED.
I DID THE SAME THING WITH BIANCA!

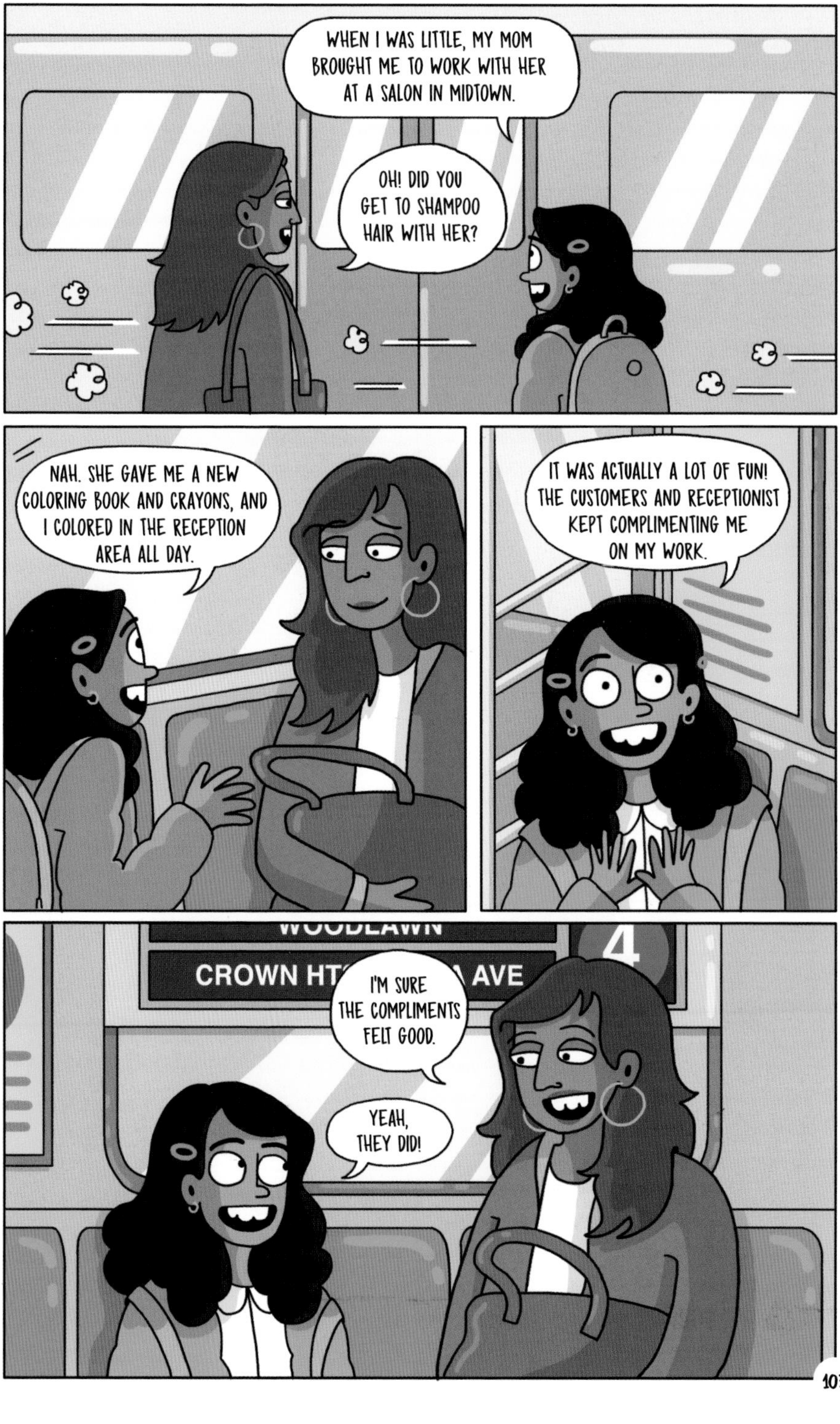
WHEN I WAS LITTLE, MY MOM BROUGHT ME TO WORK WITH HER AT A SALON IN MIDTOWN.
OH! DID YOU GET TO SHAMPOO HAIR WITH HER?
NAH. SHE GAVE ME A NEW COLORING BOOK AND CRAYONS, AND I COLORED IN THE RECEPTION AREA ALL DAY.
IT WAS ACTUALLY A LOT OF FUN! THE CUSTOMERS AND RECEPTIONIST KEPT COMPLIMENTING ME ON MY WORK.
I'M SURE THE COMPLIMENTS FELT GOOD.
YEAH, THEY DID!

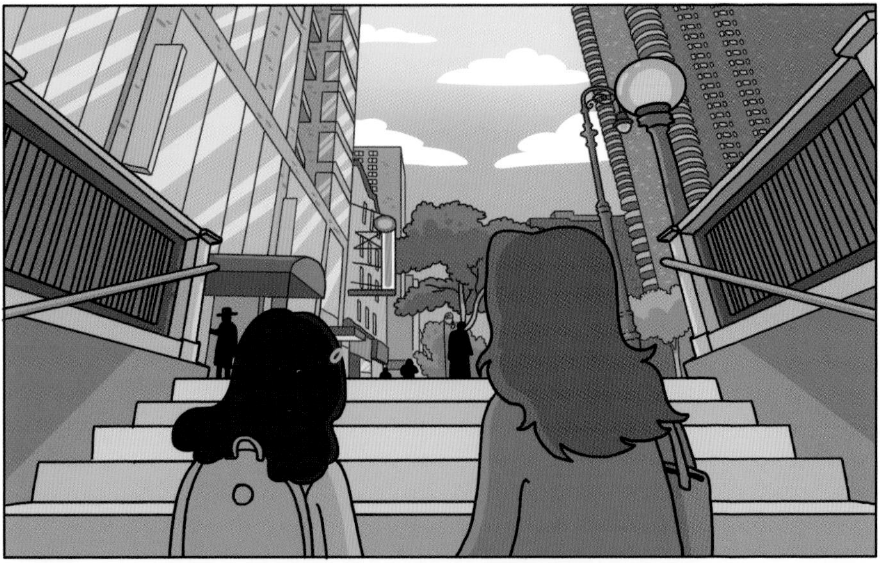

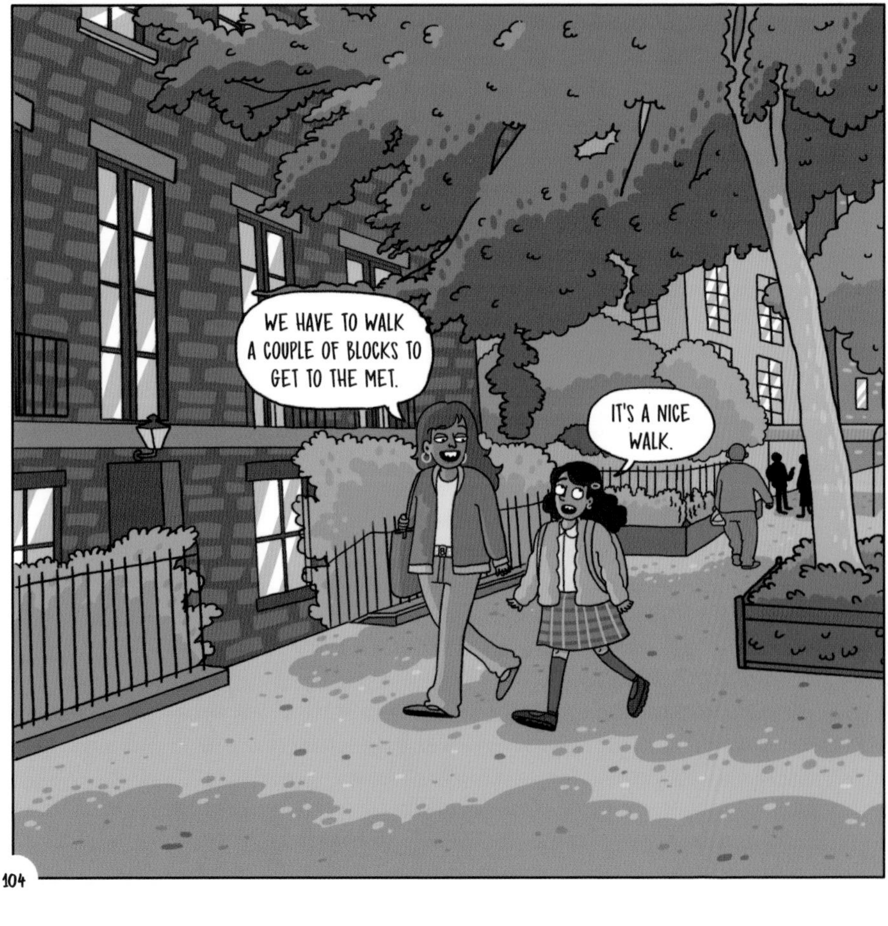
WE HAVE TO WALK A COUPLE OF BLOCKS TO GET TO THE MET.
IT'S A NICE WALK.

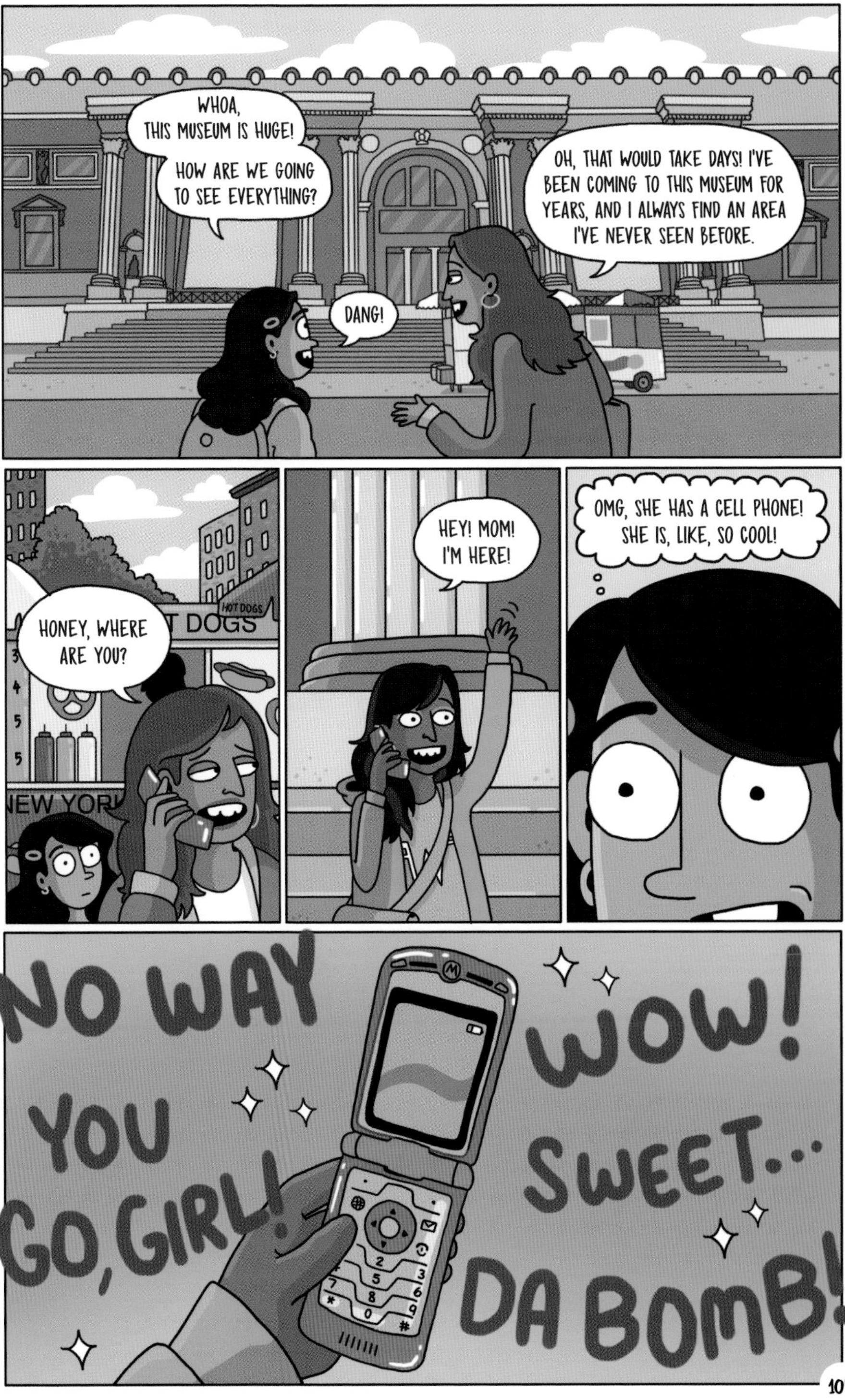
WHOA, THIS MUSEUM IS HUGE!
HOW ARE WE GOING TO SEE EVERYTHING?
OH, THAT WOULD TAKE DAYS! I'VE BEEN COMING TO THIS MUSEUM FOR YEARS, AND I ALWAYS FIND AN AREA I'VE NEVER SEEN BEFORE.
DANG!
HOT DOGS
HONEY, WHERE ARE YOU?
NEW YORK
HEY! MOM! I'M HERE!
OMG, SHE HAS A CELL PHONE! SHE IS, LIKE, SO COOL!
NO WAY
YOU GO, GIRL!
WOW!
SWEET...
DA BOMB!

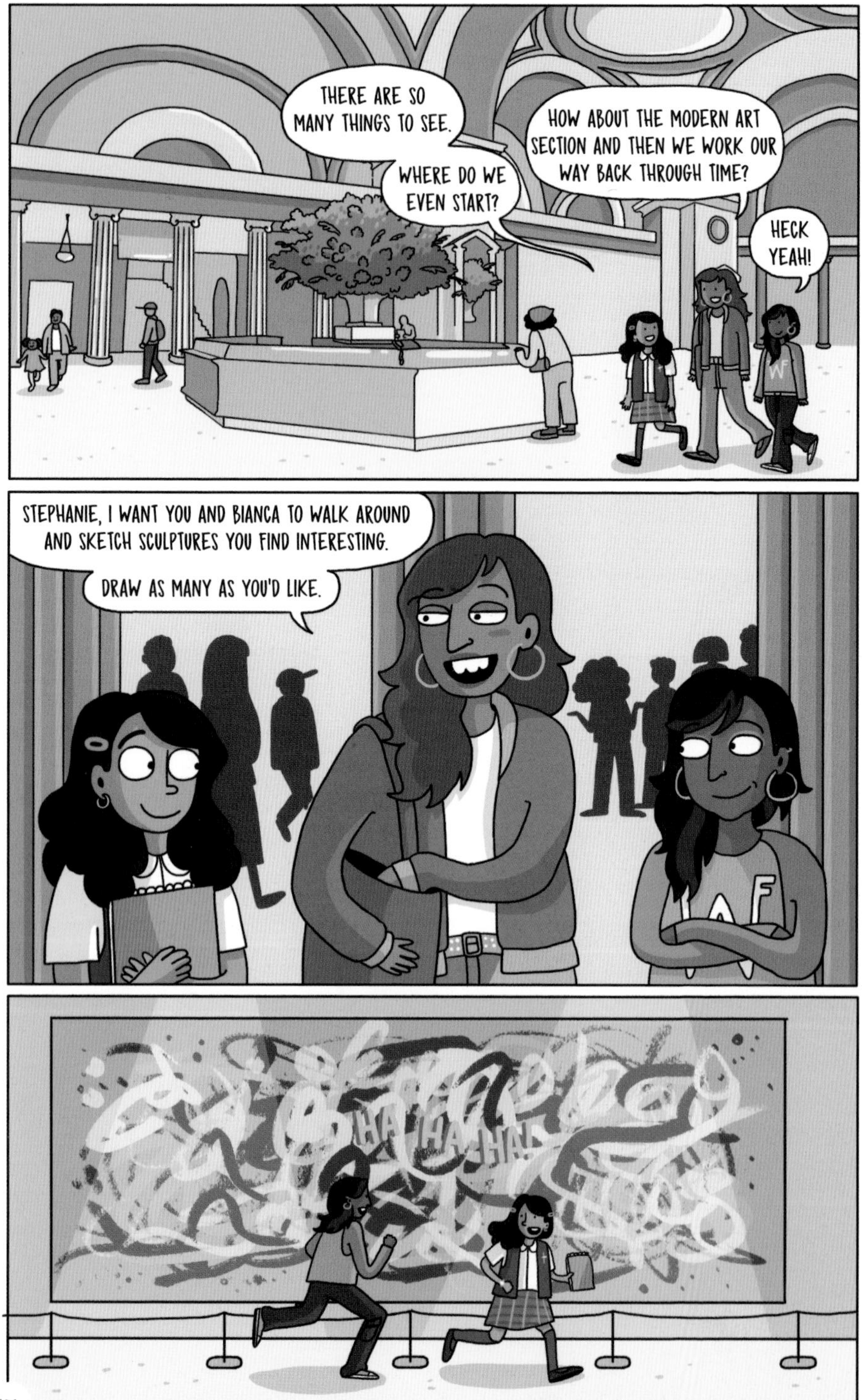
THERE ARE SO MANY THINGS TO SEE.
WHERE DO WE EVEN START?
HOW ABOUT THE MODERN ART SECTION AND THEN WE WORK OUR WAY BACK THROUGH TIME?
HECK YEAH!
STEPHANIE, I WANT YOU AND BIANCA TO WALK AROUND AND SKETCH SCULPTURES YOU FIND INTERESTING.
DRAW AS MANY AS YOU'D LIKE.
HA! HA! HA! HA!

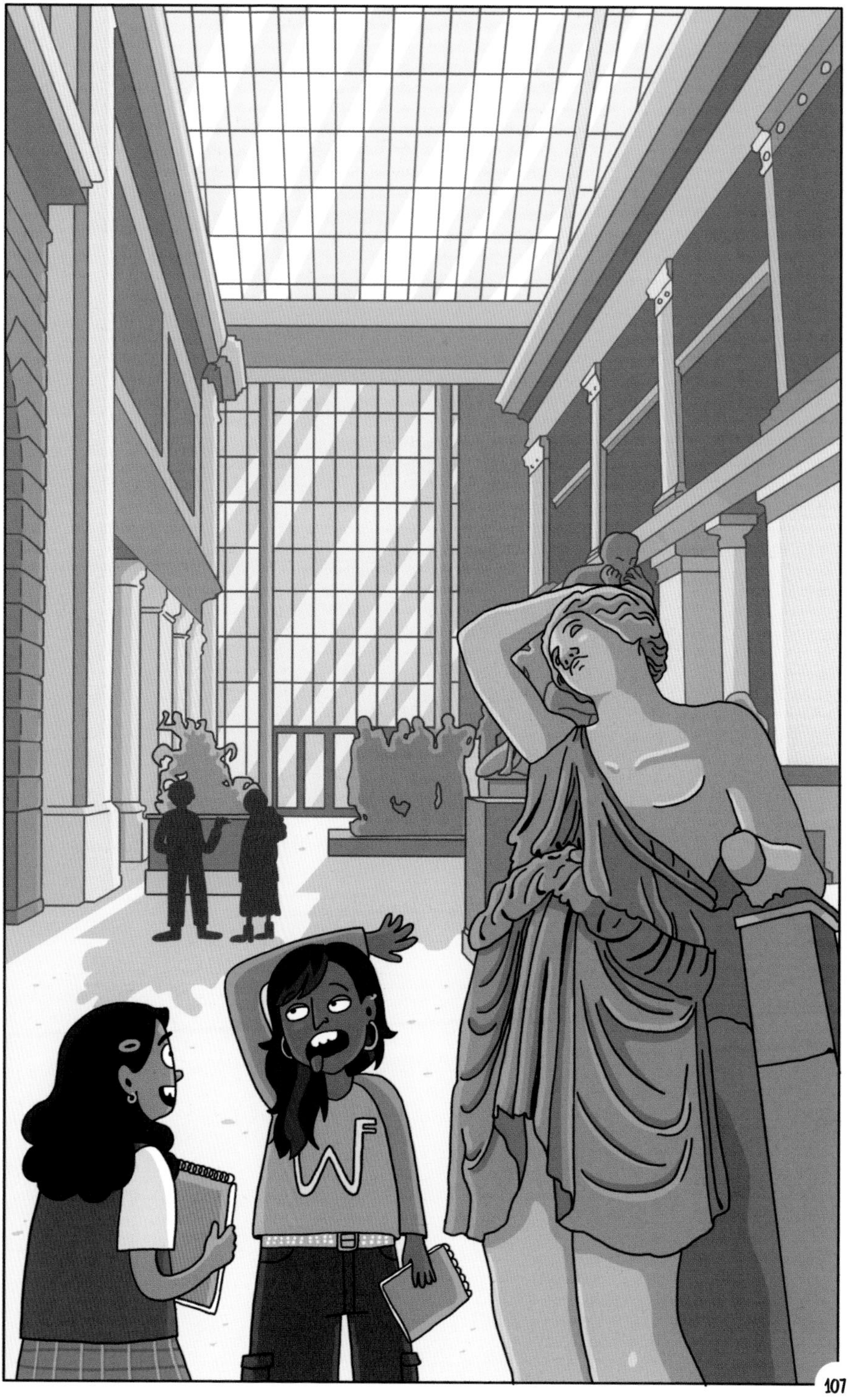
WF

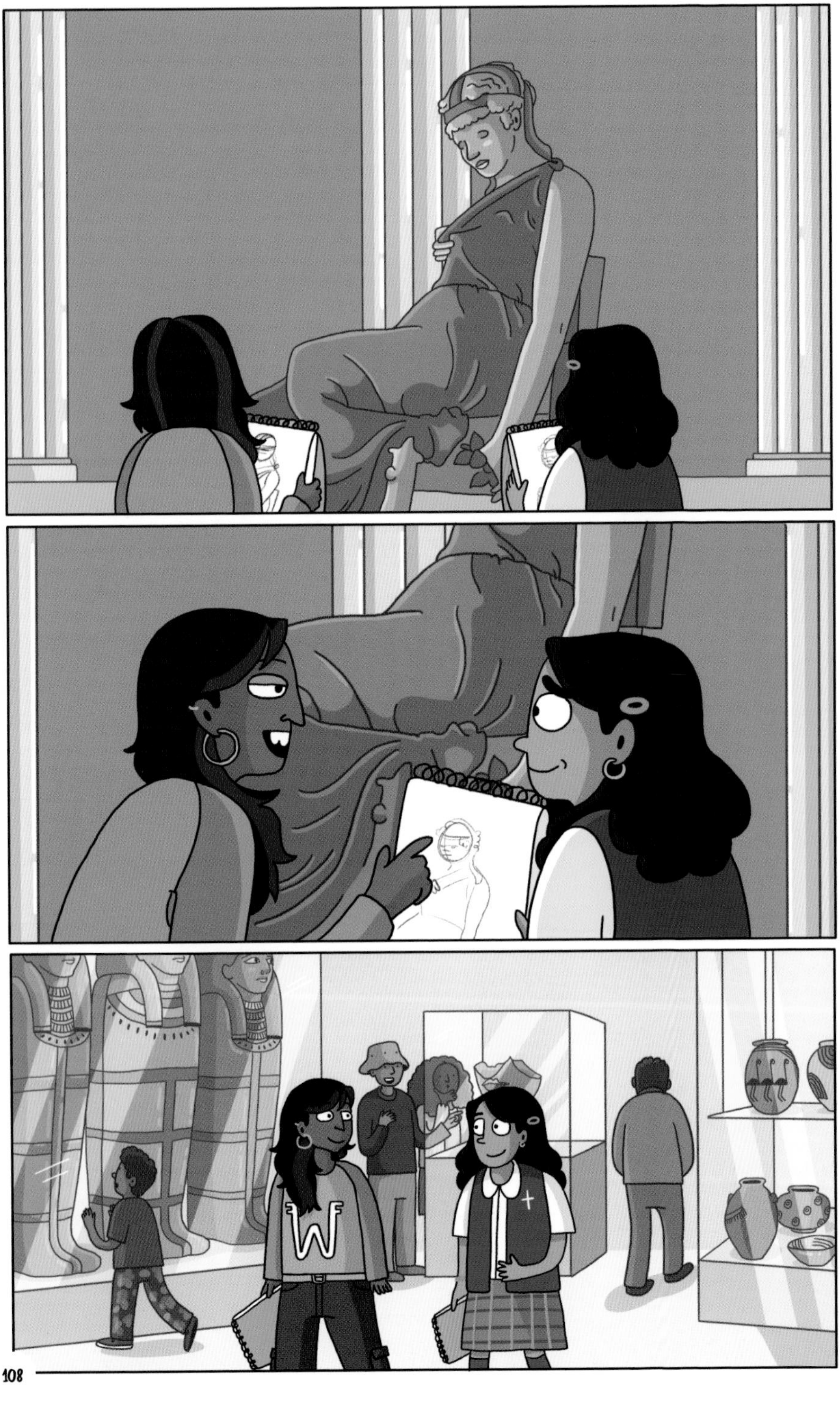

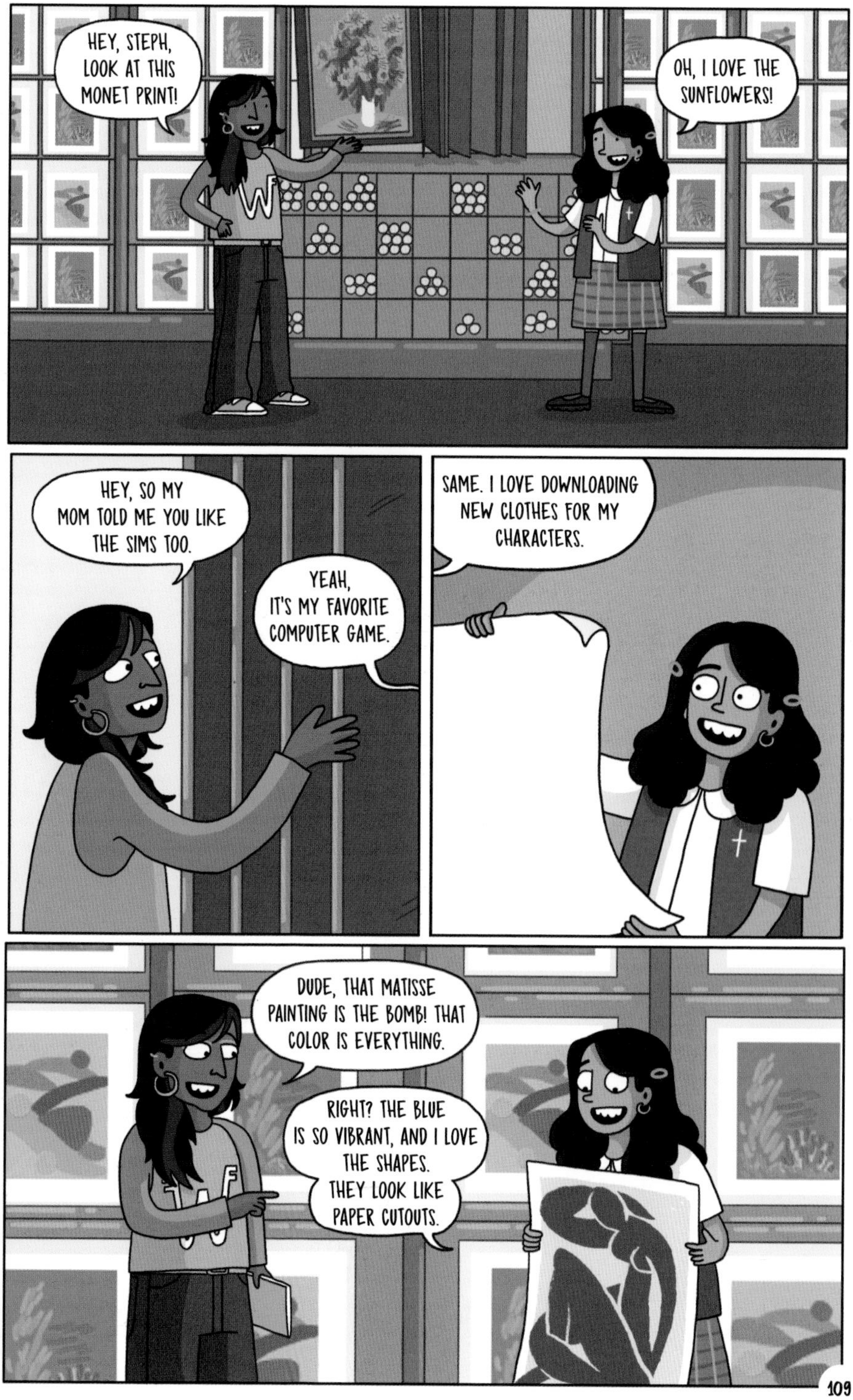
HEY, STEPH, LOOK AT THIS MONET PRINT!
OH, I LOVE THE SUNFLOWERS!
HEY, SO MY MOM TOLD ME YOU LIKE THE SIMS TOO.
YEAH, IT'S MY FAVORITE COMPUTER GAME.
SAME. I LOVE DOWNLOADING NEW CLOTHES FOR MY CHARACTERS.
DUDE, THAT MATISSE PAINTING IS THE BOMB! THAT COLOR IS EVERYTHING.
RIGHT? THE BLUE IS SO VIBRANT, AND I LOVE THE SHAPES. THEY LOOK LIKE PAPER CUTOUTS.

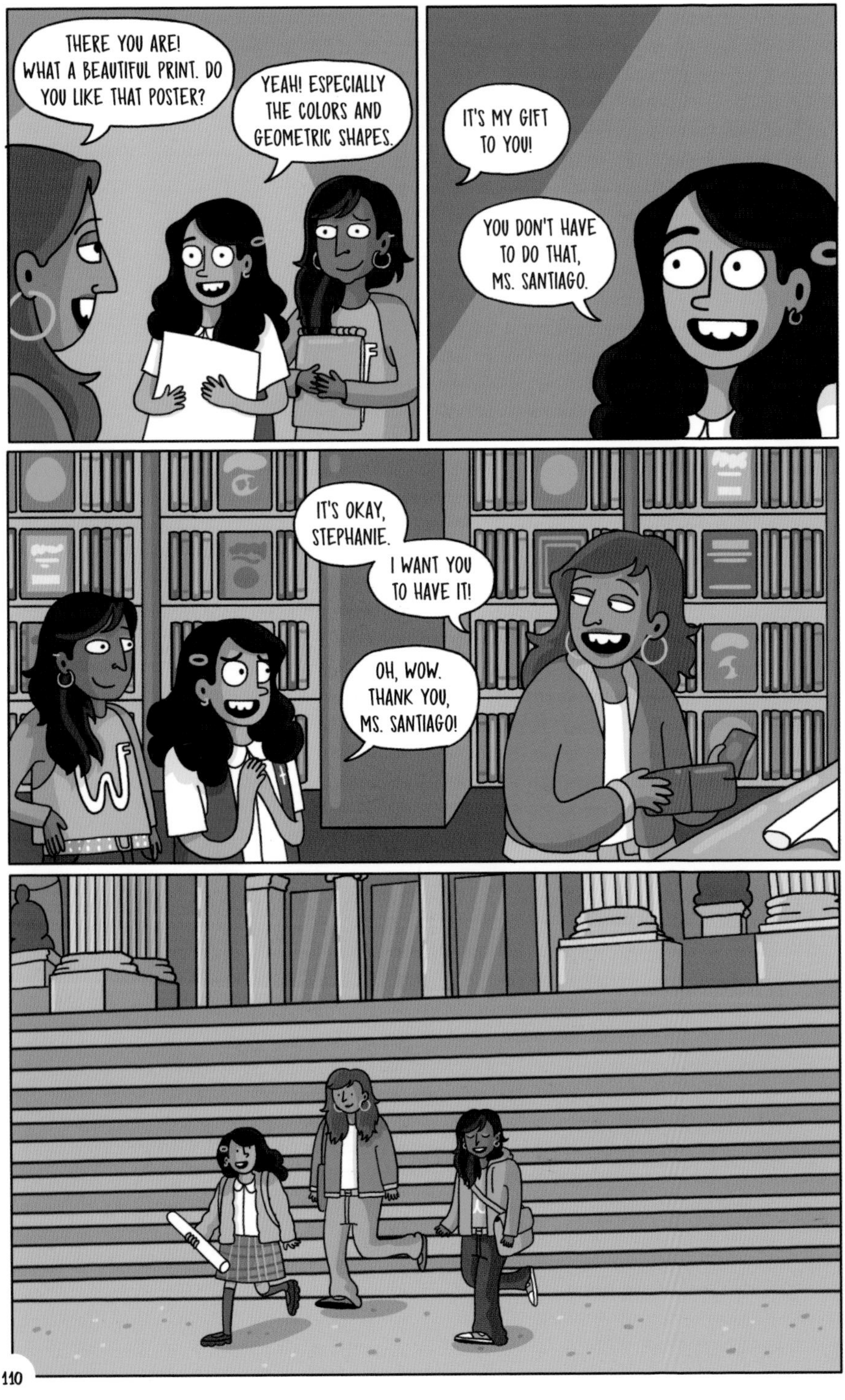
THERE YOU ARE! WHAT A BEAUTIFUL PRINT. DO YOU LIKE THAT POSTER?
YEAH! ESPECIALLY THE COLORS AND GEOMETRIC SHAPES.
IT'S MY GIFT TO YOU!
YOU DON'T HAVE TO DO THAT, MS. SANTIAGO.
IT'S OKAY, STEPHANIE.
I WANT YOU TO HAVE IT!
OH, WOW. THANK YOU, MS. SANTIAGO!

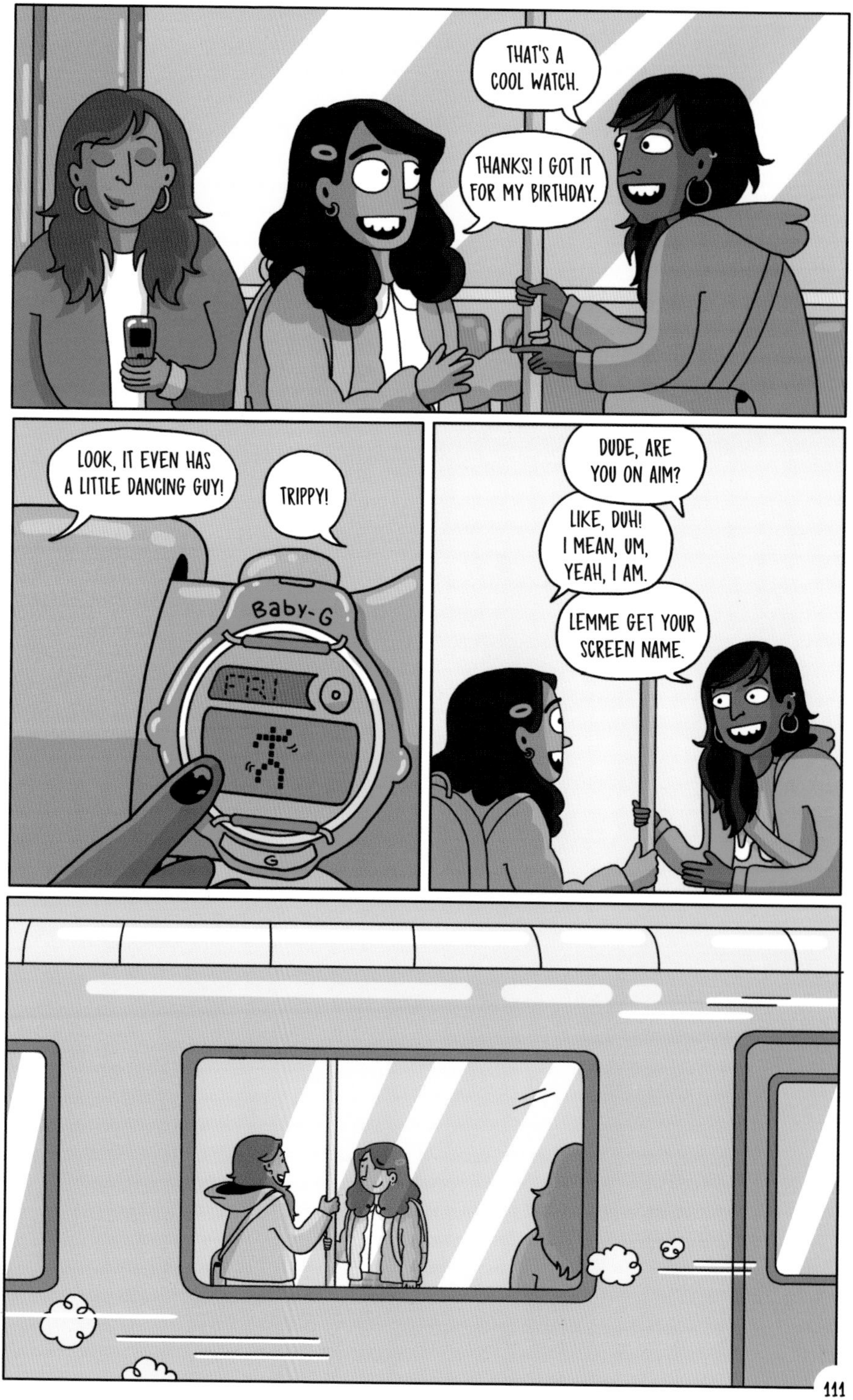
THAT'S A COOL WATCH.
THANKS! I GOT IT FOR MY BIRTHDAY.
LOOK, IT EVEN HAS A LITTLE DANCING GUY!
TRIPPY!
Baby-G
FRI
G
DUDE, ARE YOU ON AIM?
LIKE, DUH! I MEAN, UM, YEAH, I AM.
LEMME GET YOUR SCREEN NAME.

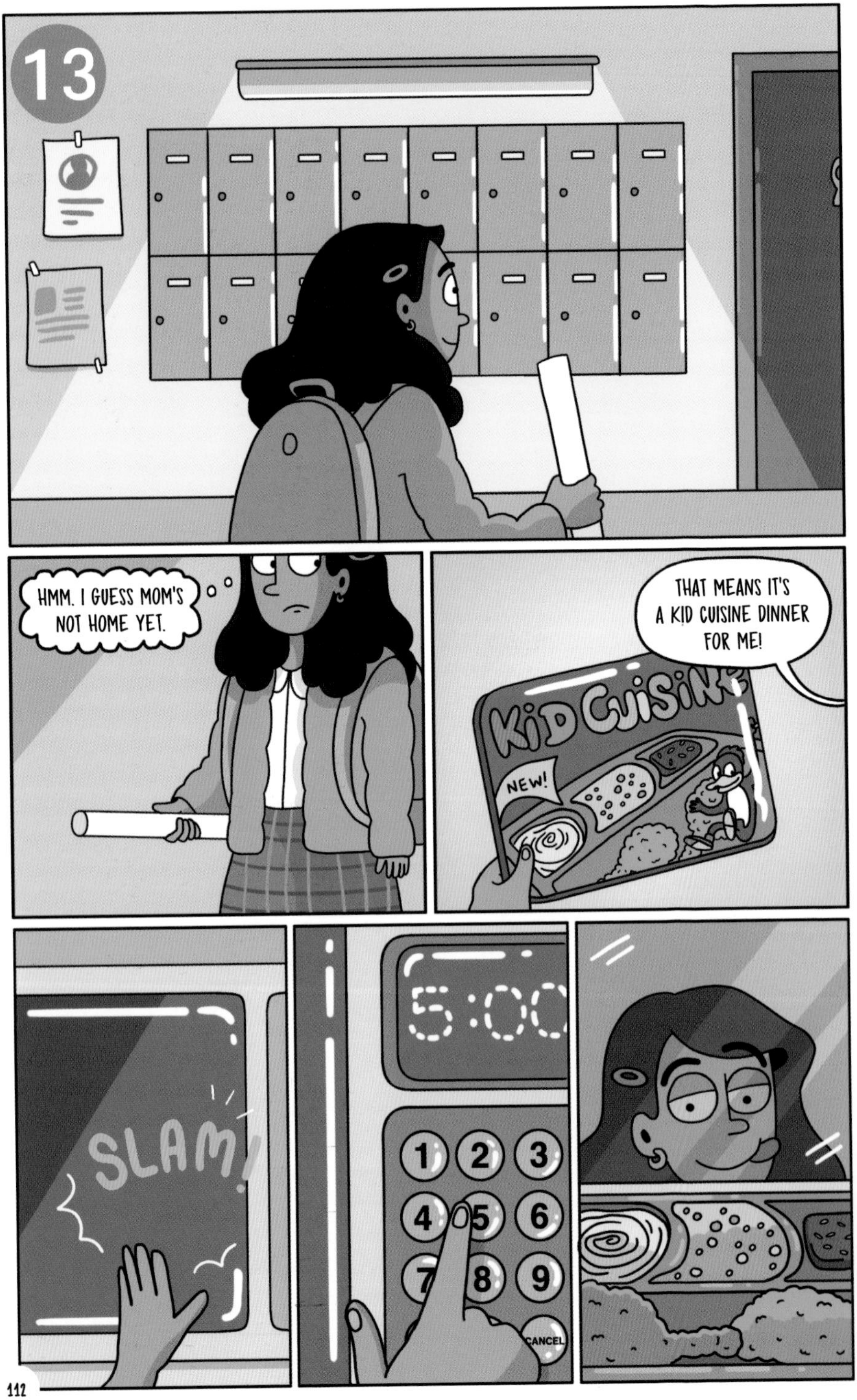
13
HMM. I GUESS MOM'S NOT HOME YET.
THAT MEANS IT'S A KID CUISINE DINNER FOR ME!
KID CUISINE
NEW!
SLAM!
5:00
1 2 3
4 5 6
7 8 9
CANCEL

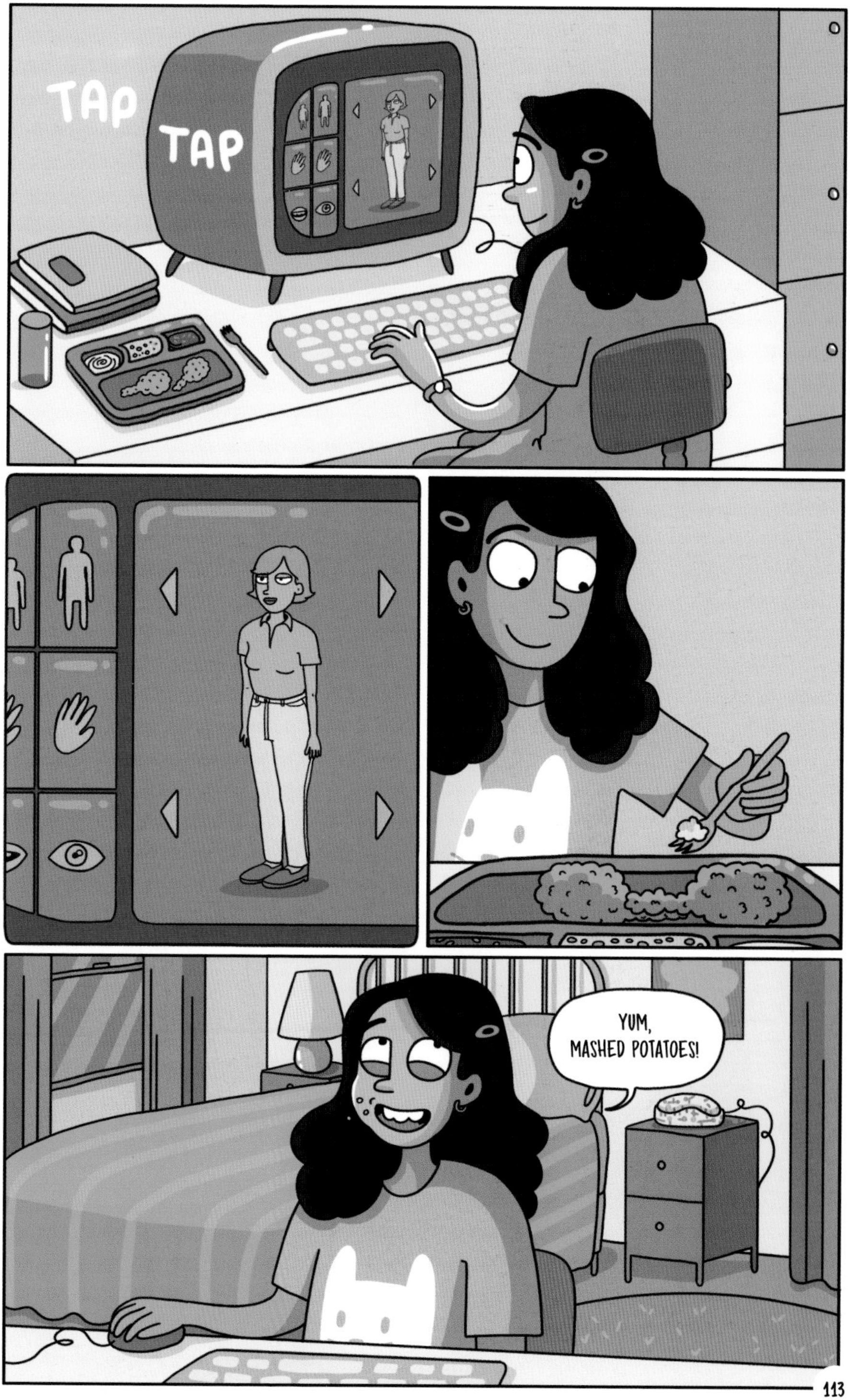
TAP
TAP
YUM,
MASHED POTATOES!

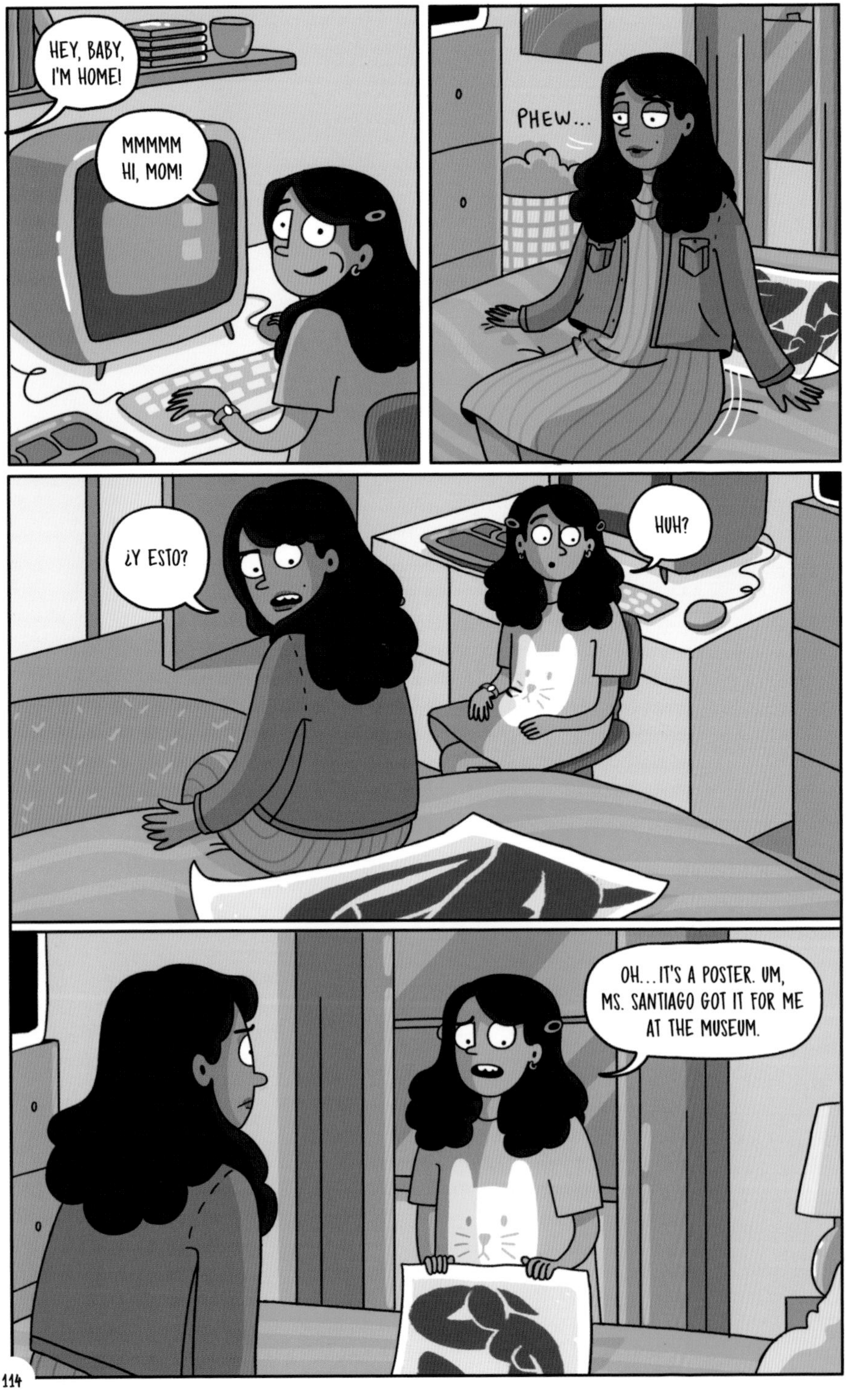
HEY, BABY, I'M HOME!
MMMMM HI, MOM!
PHEW...
¿Y ESTO?
HUH?
OH...IT'S A POSTER. UM, MS. SANTIAGO GOT IT FOR ME AT THE MUSEUM.

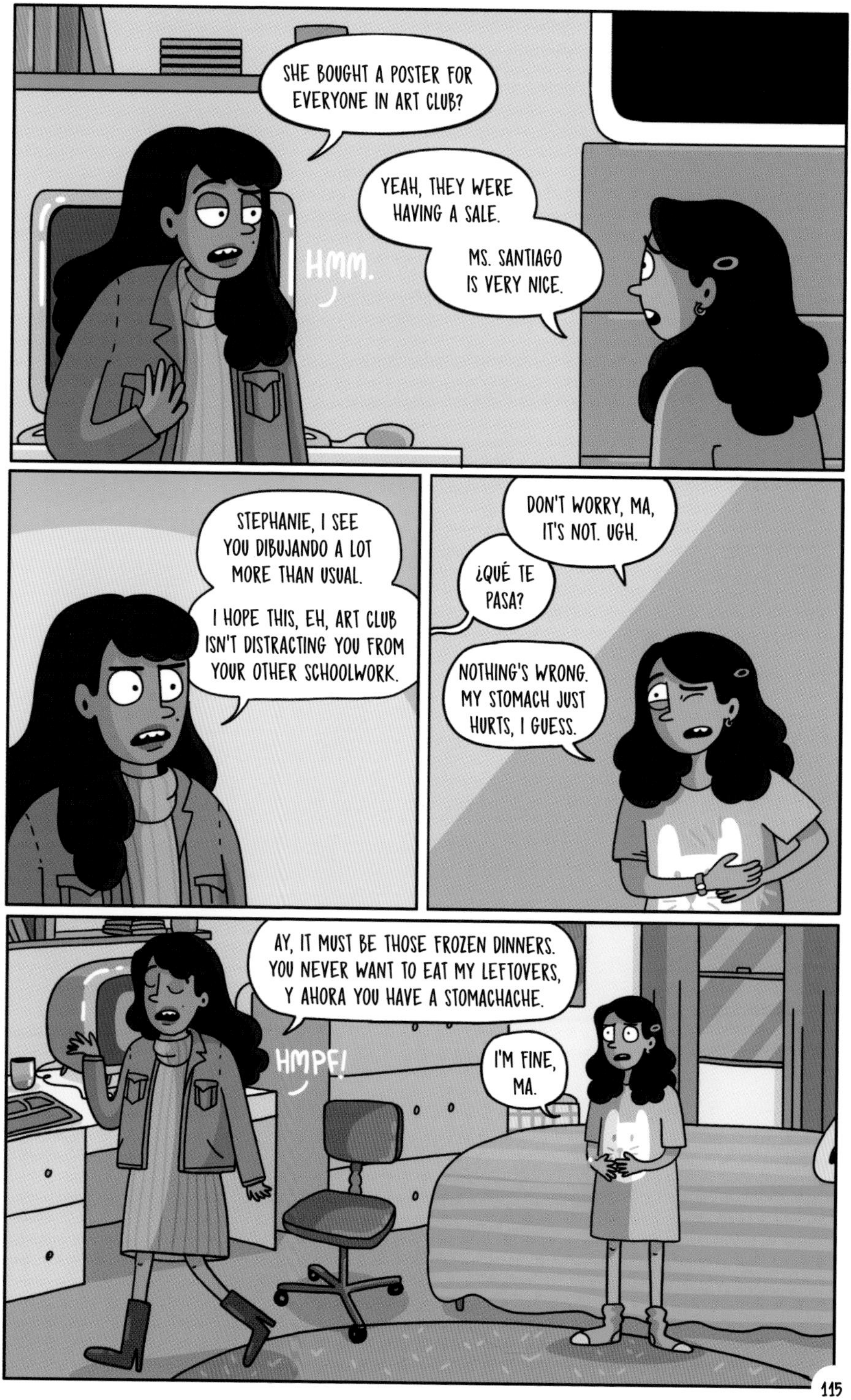
SHE BOUGHT A POSTER FOR EVERYONE IN ART CLUB?
YEAH, THEY WERE HAVING A SALE.
MS. SANTIAGO IS VERY NICE.
HMM.
STEPHANIE, I SEE YOU DIBUJANDO A LOT MORE THAN USUAL.
I HOPE THIS, EH, ART CLUB ISN'T DISTRACTING YOU FROM YOUR OTHER SCHOOLWORK.
¿QUÉ TE PASA?
DON'T WORRY, MA, IT'S NOT. UGH.
NOTHING'S WRONG. MY STOMACH JUST HURTS, I GUESS.
AY, IT MUST BE THOSE FROZEN DINNERS. YOU NEVER WANT TO EAT MY LEFTOVERS, Y AHORA YOU HAVE A STOMACHACHE.
HMPF!
I'M FINE, MA.

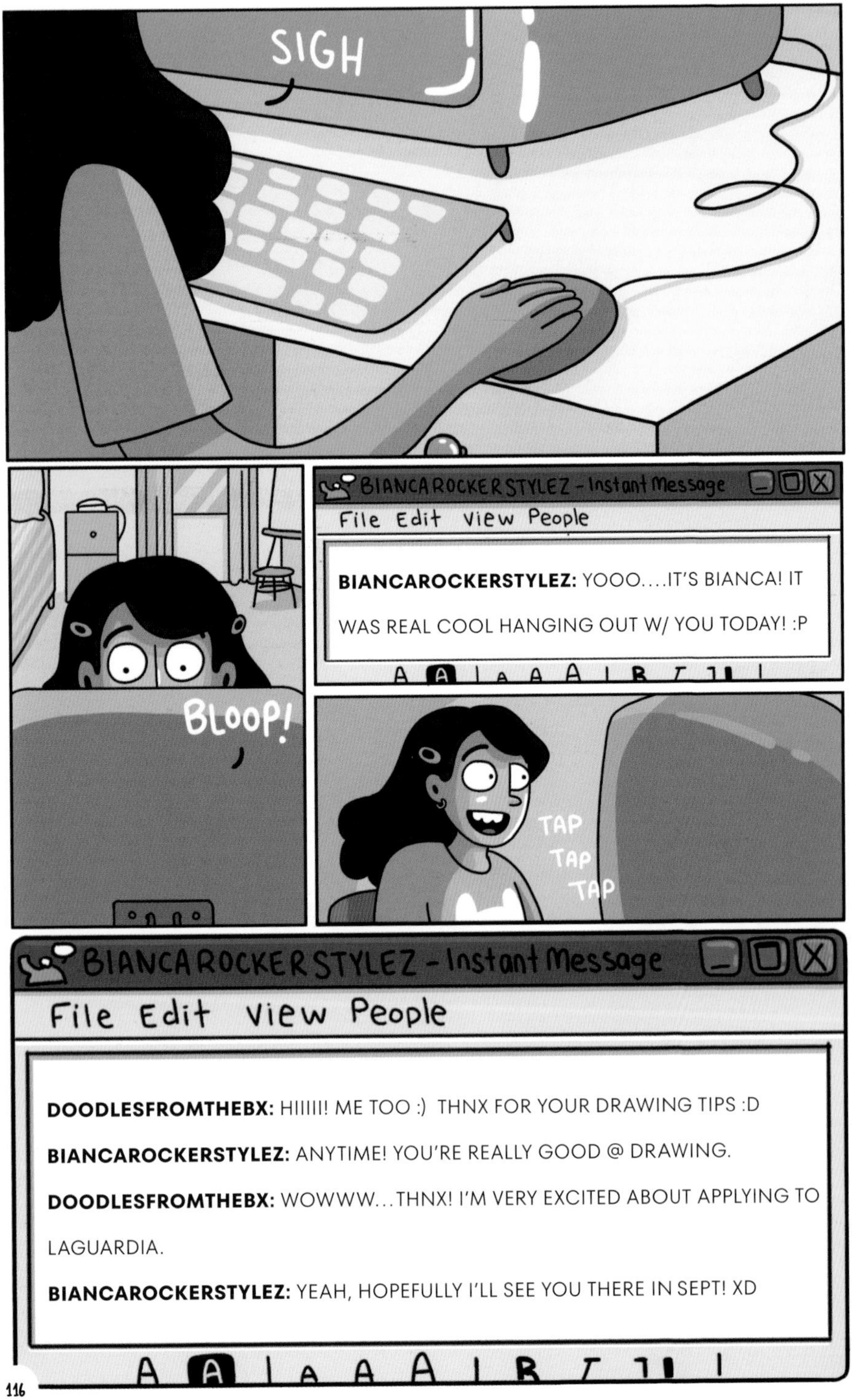
SIGH
BLOOP!
BIANCAROCKERSTYLEZ - Instant Message
File Edit View People
BIANCAROCKERSTYLEZ: YOOO....IT'S BIANCA! IT WAS REAL COOL HANGING OUT W/ YOU TODAY! :P
TAP TAP TAP
BIANCAROCKERSTYLEZ - Instant Message
File Edit View People
DOODLESFROMTHEBX: HIIIII! ME TOO :) THNX FOR YOUR DRAWING TIPS :D
BIANCAROCKERSTYLEZ: ANYTIME! YOU'RE REALLY GOOD @ DRAWING.
DOODLESFROMTHEBX: WOWWW...THNX! I'M VERY EXCITED ABOUT APPLYING TO LAGUARDIA.
BIANCAROCKERSTYLEZ: YEAH, HOPEFULLY I'LL SEE YOU THERE IN SEPT! XD

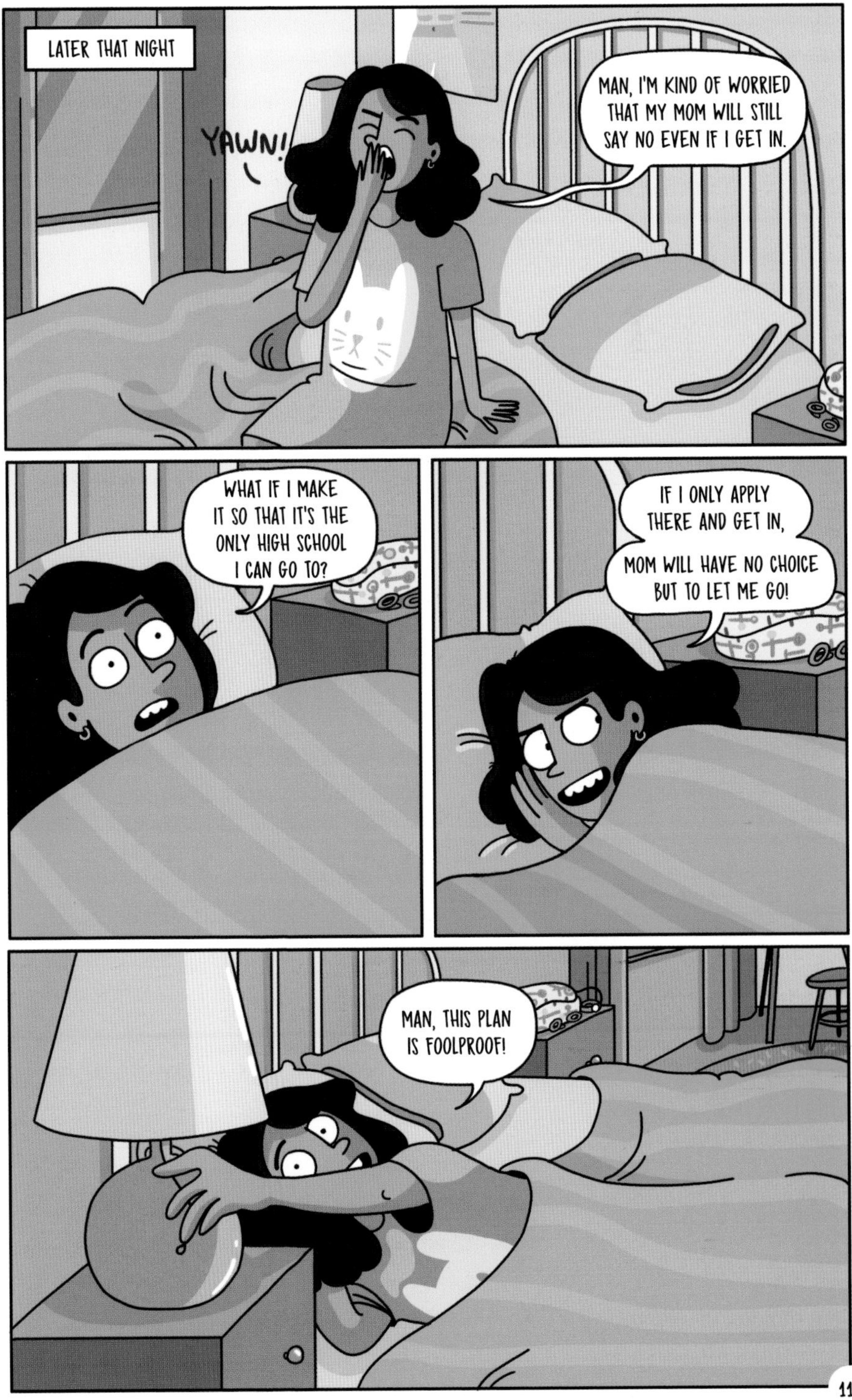
LATER THAT NIGHT
YAWN!
MAN, I'M KIND OF WORRIED THAT MY MOM WILL STILL SAY NO EVEN IF I GET IN.
WHAT IF I MAKE IT SO THAT IT'S THE ONLY HIGH SCHOOL I CAN GO TO?
IF I ONLY APPLY THERE AND GET IN,
MOM WILL HAVE NO CHOICE BUT TO LET ME GO!
MAN, THIS PLAN IS FOOLPROOF!

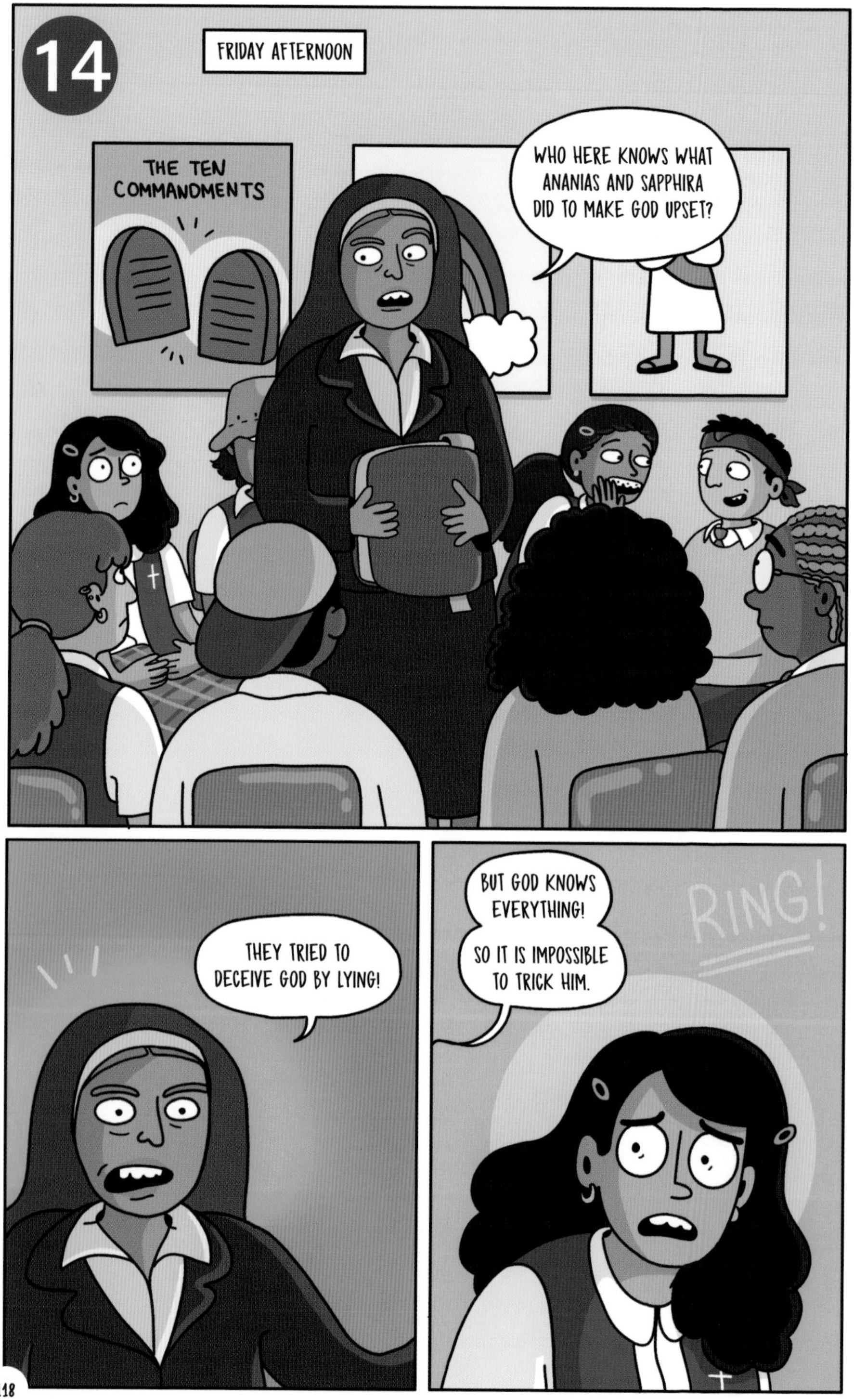
14
FRIDAY AFTERNOON
THE TEN COMMANDMENTS
WHO HERE KNOWS WHAT ANANIAS AND SAPPHIRA DID TO MAKE GOD UPSET?
THEY TRIED TO DECEIVE GOD BY LYING!
BUT GOD KNOWS EVERYTHING!
SO IT IS IMPOSSIBLE TO TRICK HIM.
RING!

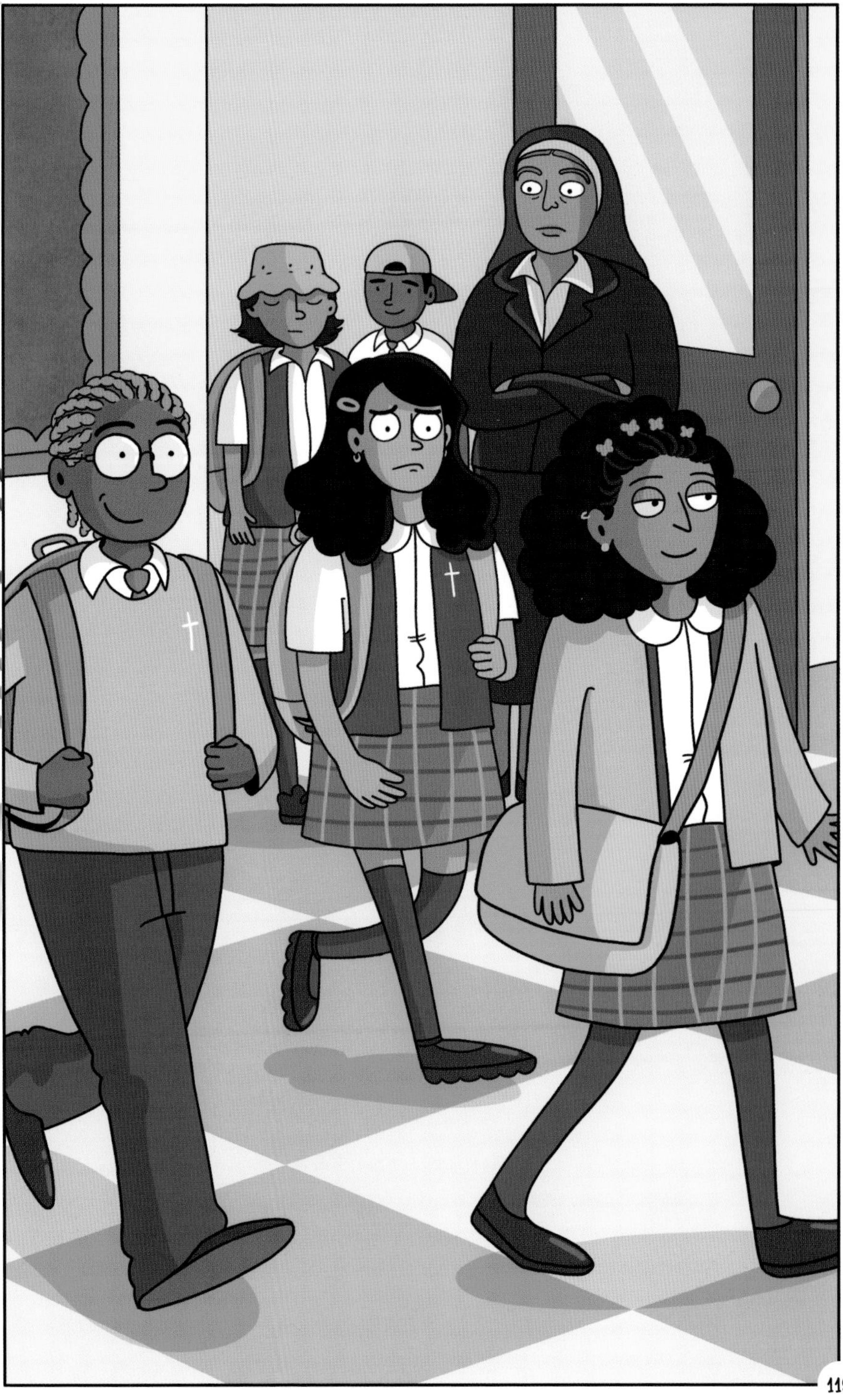

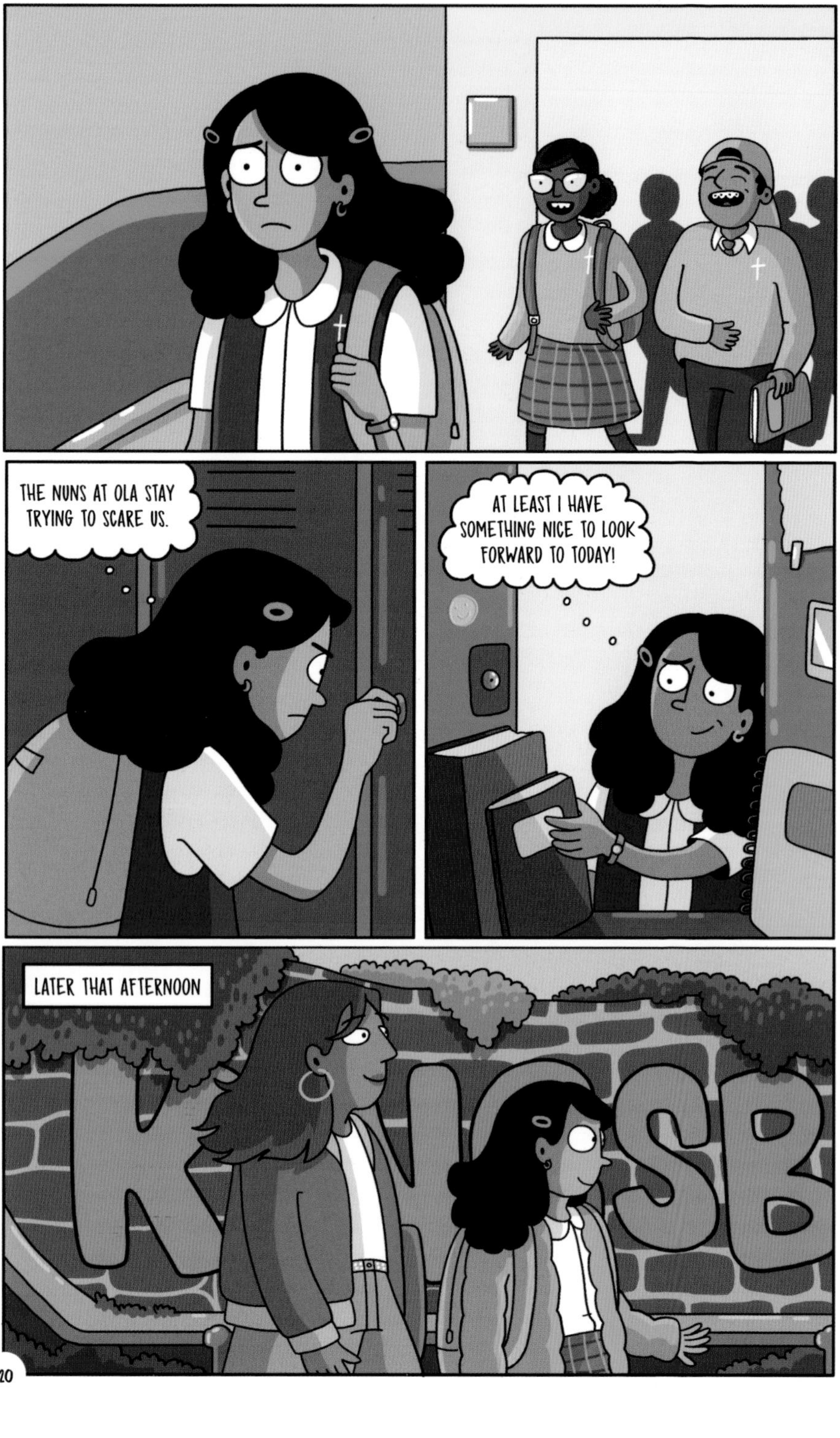

THE NUNS AT OLA STAY TRYING TO SCARE US.
AT LEAST I HAVE SOMETHING NICE TO LOOK FORWARD TO TODAY!
LATER THAT AFTERNOON

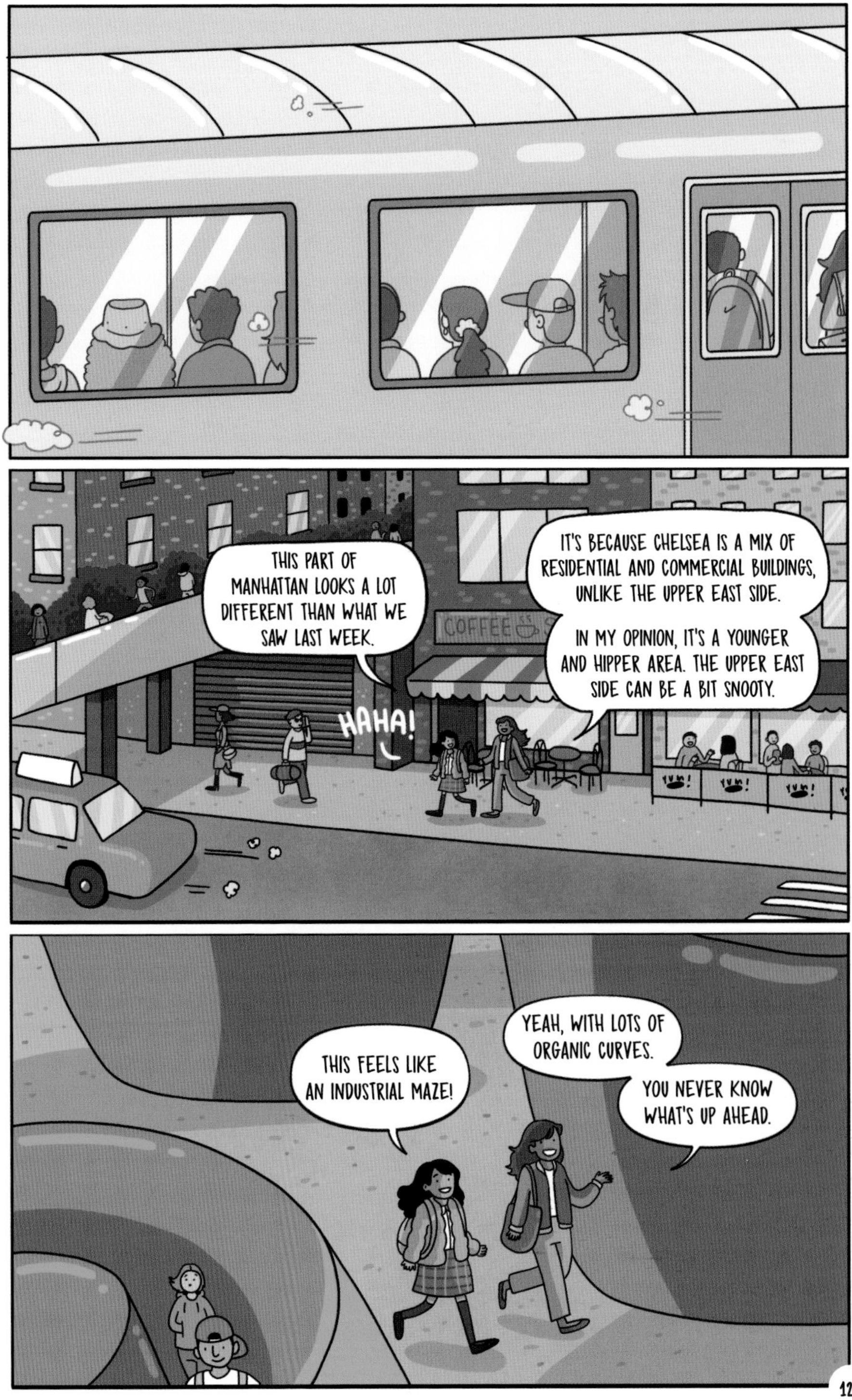
THIS PART OF MANHATTAN LOOKS A LOT DIFFERENT THAN WHAT WE SAW LAST WEEK.
IT'S BECAUSE CHELSEA IS A MIX OF RESIDENTIAL AND COMMERCIAL BUILDINGS, UNLIKE THE UPPER EAST SIDE.
IN MY OPINION, IT'S A YOUNGER AND HIPPER AREA. THE UPPER EAST SIDE CAN BE A BIT SNOOTY.
HAHA!
COFFEE
YUM!
THIS FEELS LIKE AN INDUSTRIAL MAZE!
YEAH, WITH LOTS OF ORGANIC CURVES.
YOU NEVER KNOW WHAT'S UP AHEAD.

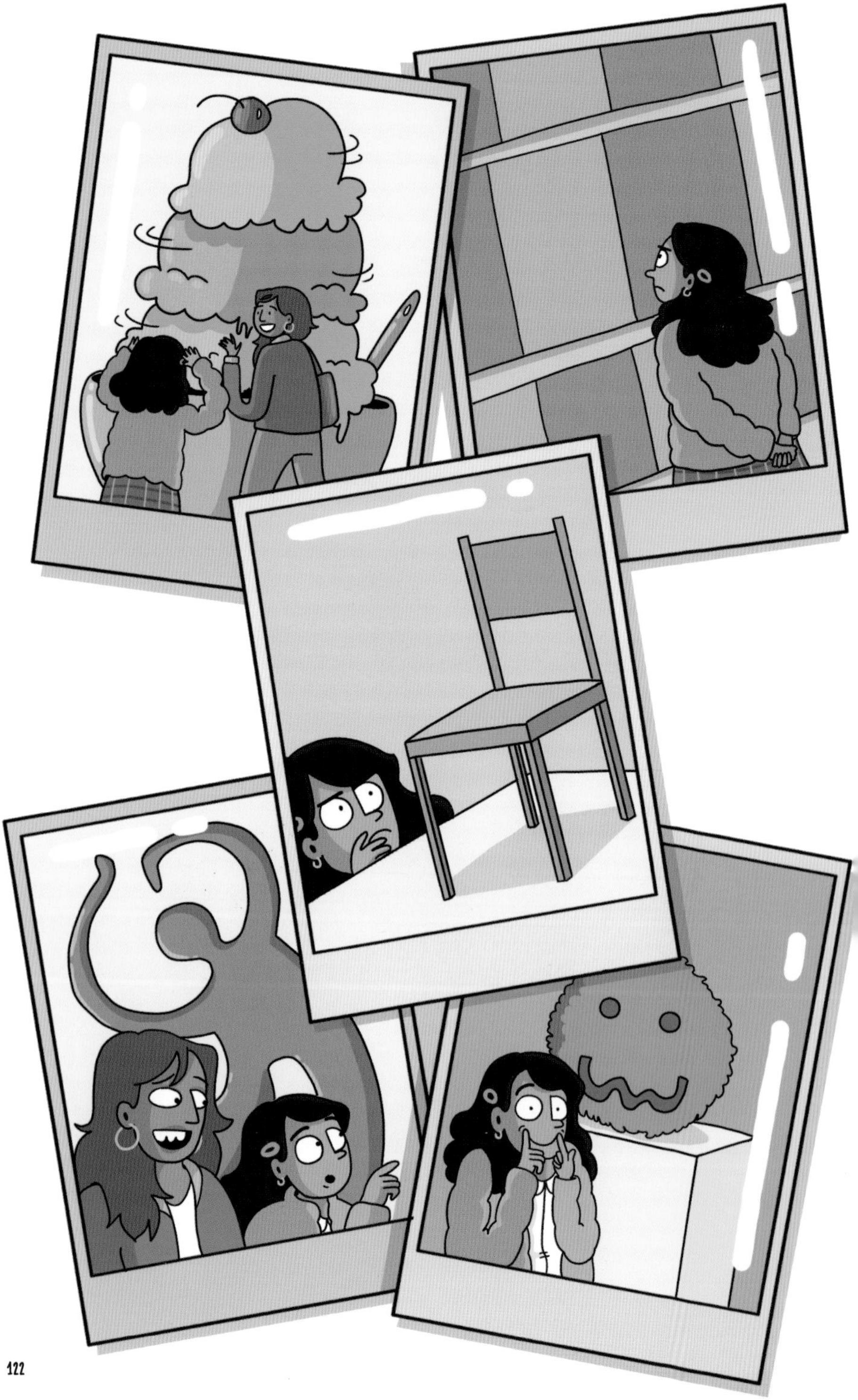

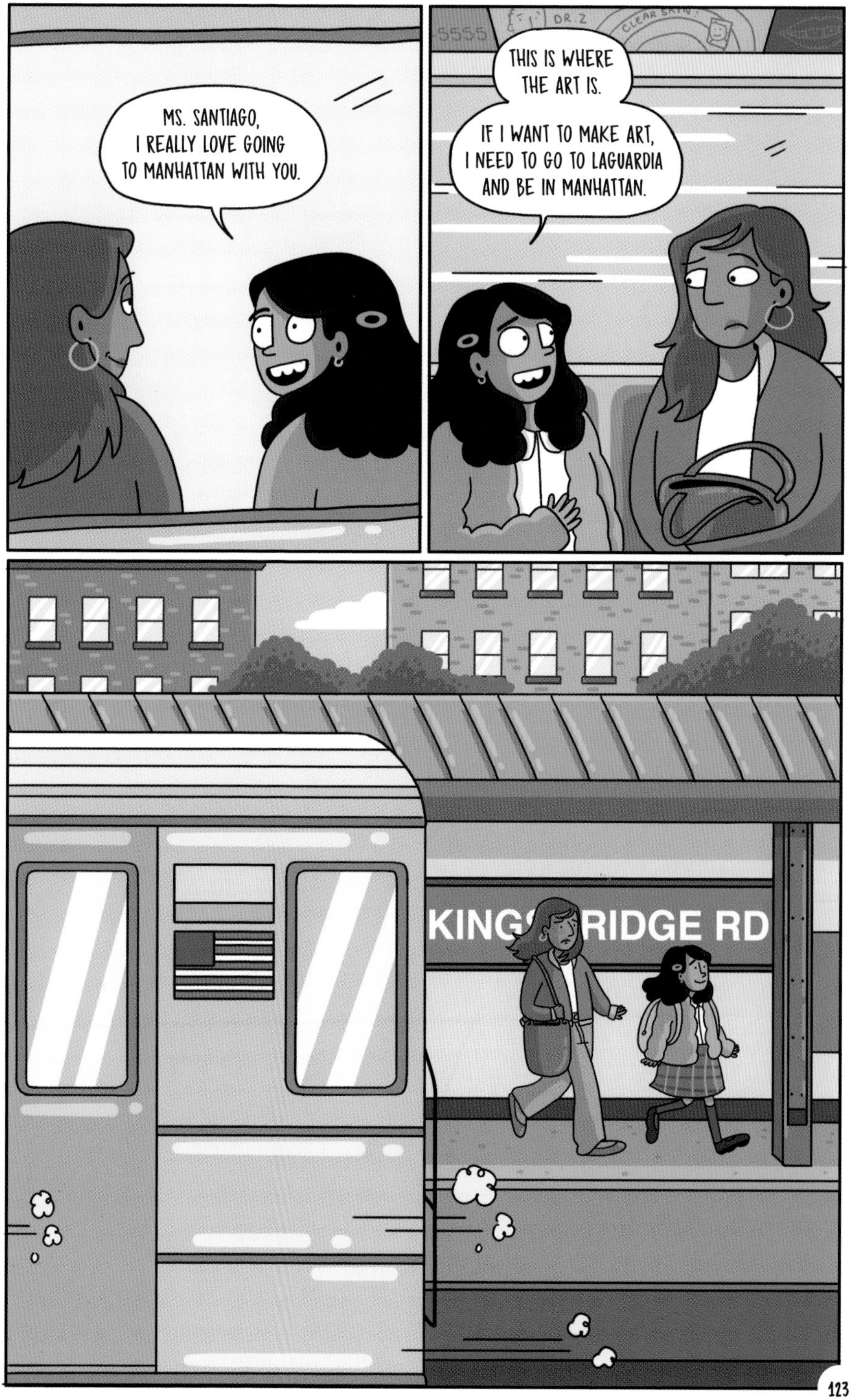

MS. SANTIAGO, I REALLY LOVE GOING TO MANHATTAN WITH YOU.
THIS IS WHERE THE ART IS.
IF I WANT TO MAKE ART, I NEED TO GO TO LAGUARDIA AND BE IN MANHATTAN.

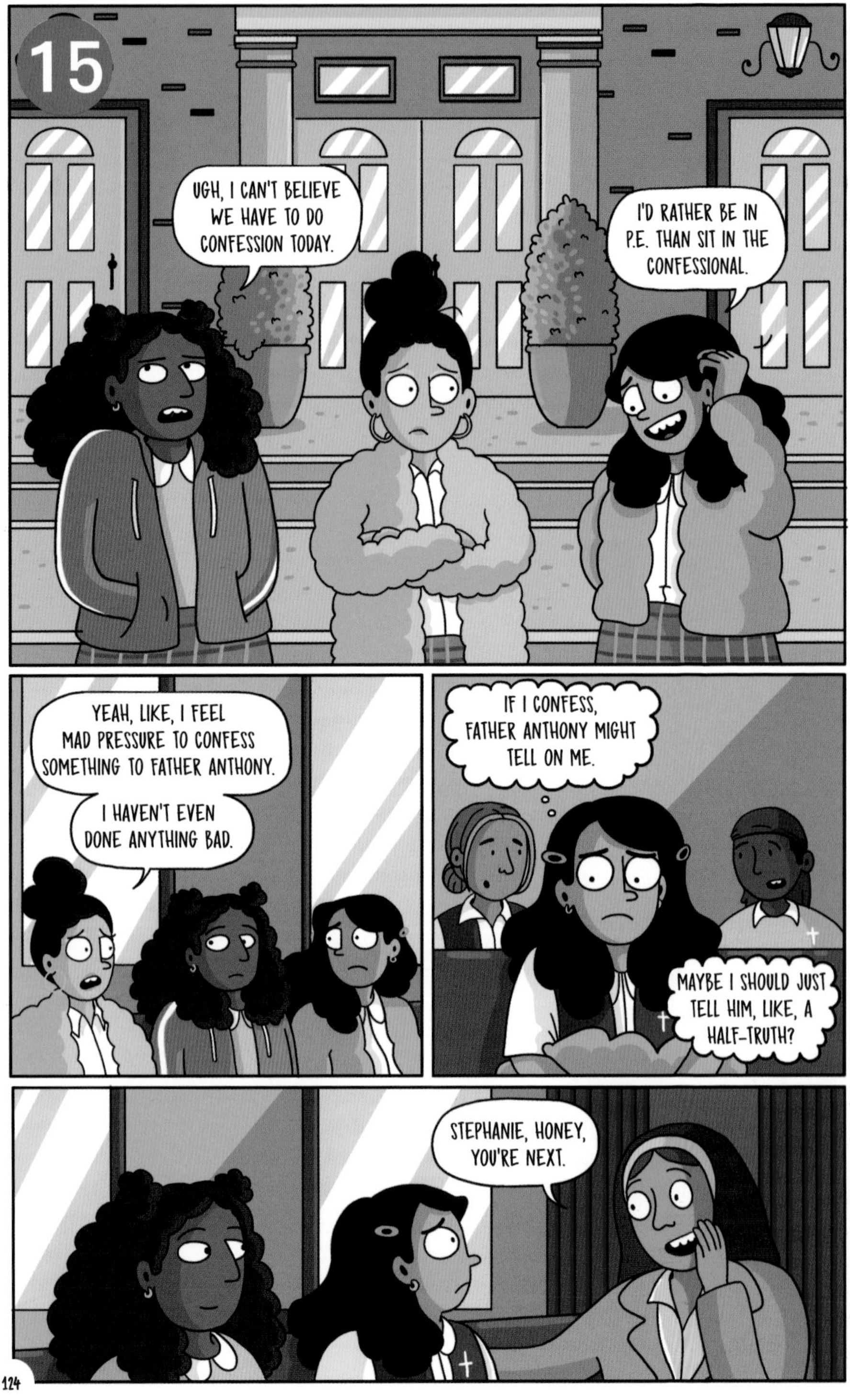
15
UGH, I CAN'T BELIEVE WE HAVE TO DO CONFESSION TODAY.
I'D RATHER BE IN P.E. THAN SIT IN THE CONFESSIONAL.
YEAH, LIKE, I FEEL MAD PRESSURE TO CONFESS SOMETHING TO FATHER ANTHONY.
I HAVEN'T EVEN DONE ANYTHING BAD.
IF I CONFESS, FATHER ANTHONY MIGHT TELL ON ME.
MAYBE I SHOULD JUST TELL HIM, LIKE, A HALF-TRUTH?
STEPHANIE, HONEY, YOU'RE NEXT.

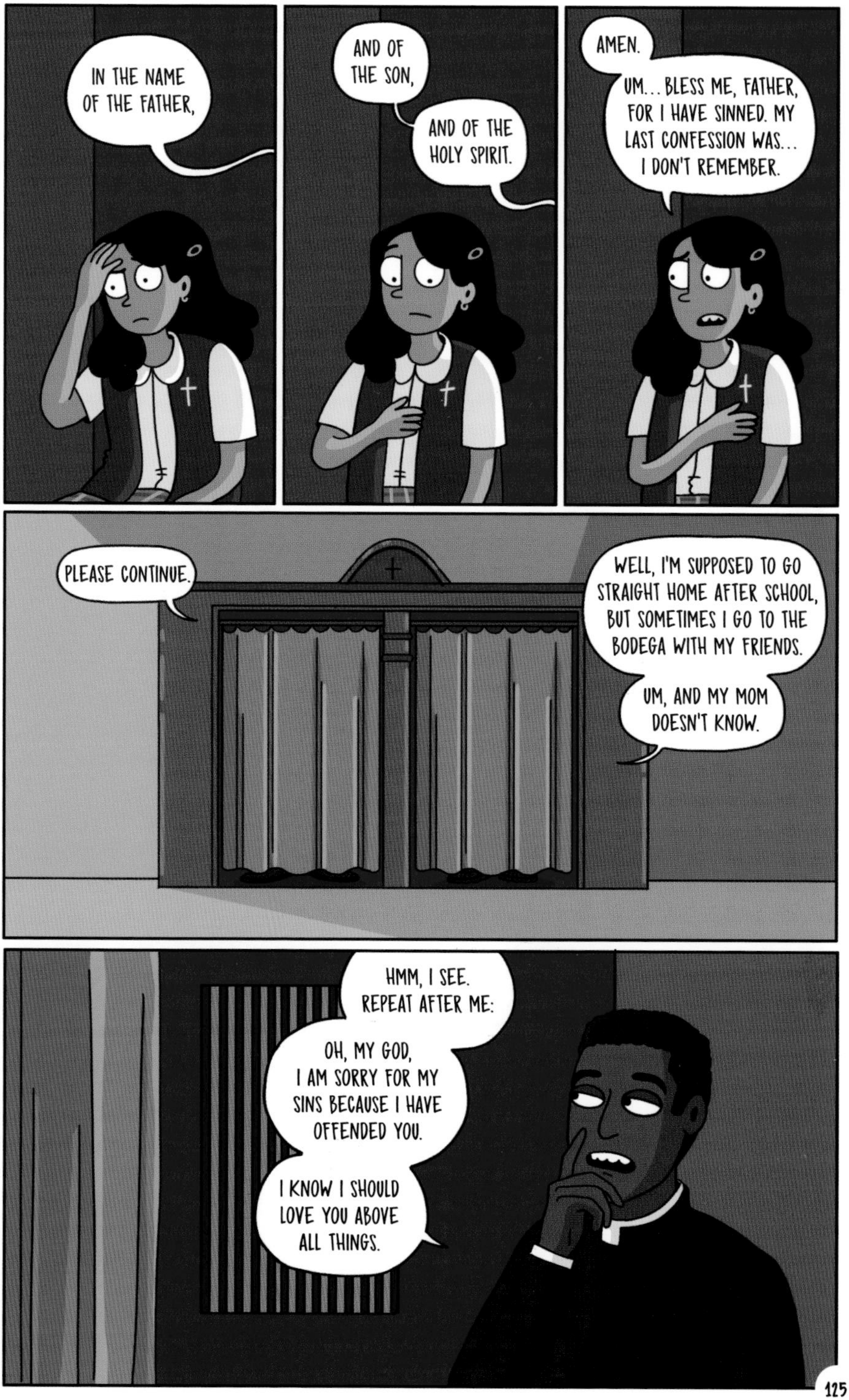
IN THE NAME OF THE FATHER,
AND OF THE SON,
AND OF THE HOLY SPIRIT.
AMEN.
UM... BLESS ME, FATHER, FOR I HAVE SINNED. MY LAST CONFESSION WAS... I DON'T REMEMBER.
PLEASE CONTINUE.
WELL, I'M SUPPOSED TO GO STRAIGHT HOME AFTER SCHOOL, BUT SOMETIMES I GO TO THE BODEGA WITH MY FRIENDS.
UM, AND MY MOM DOESN'T KNOW.
HMM, I SEE. REPEAT AFTER ME:
OH, MY GOD, I AM SORRY FOR MY SINS BECAUSE I HAVE OFFENDED YOU.
I KNOW I SHOULD LOVE YOU ABOVE ALL THINGS.

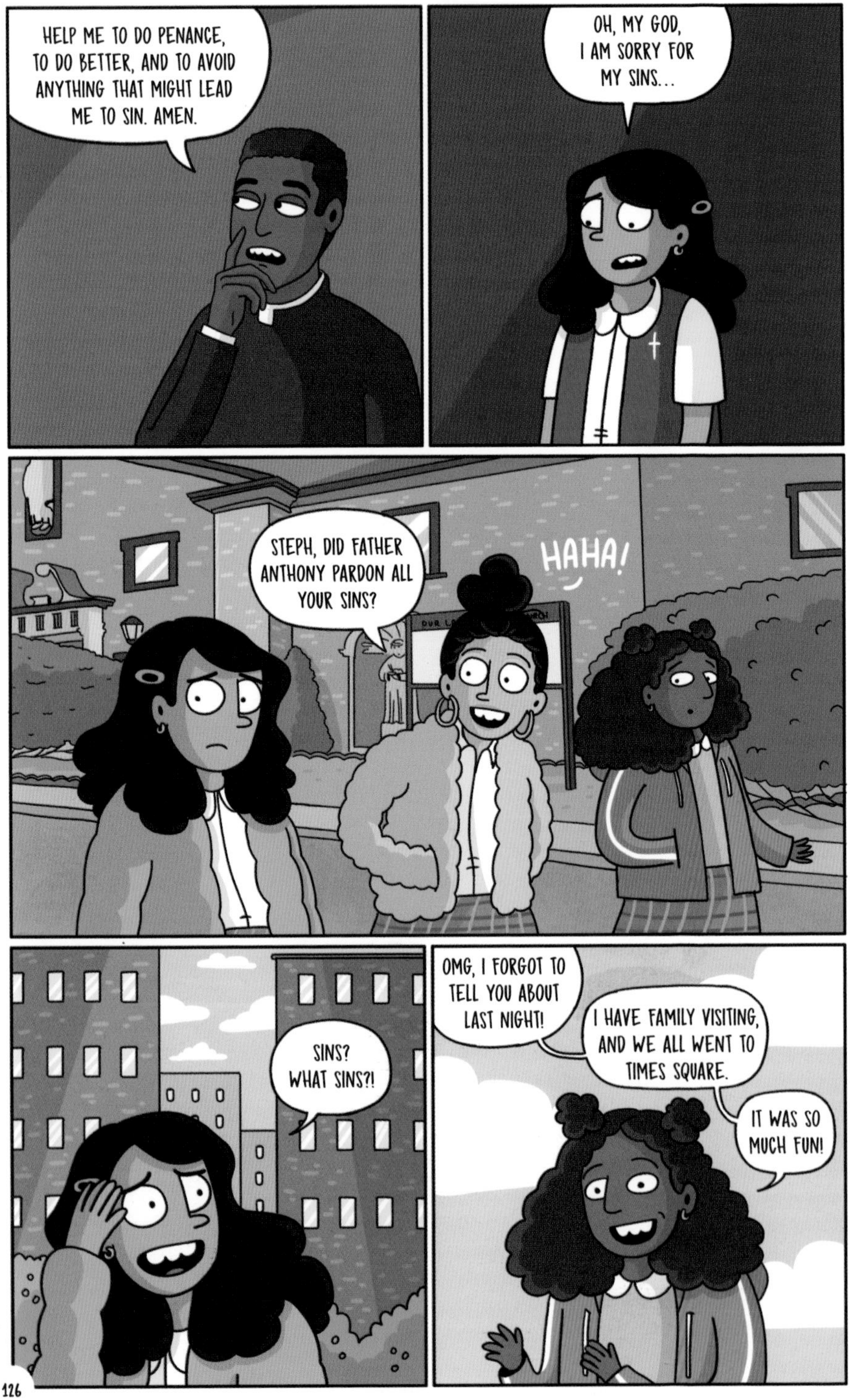
HELP ME TO DO PENANCE, TO DO BETTER, AND TO AVOID ANYTHING THAT MIGHT LEAD ME TO SIN. AMEN.
OH, MY GOD, I AM SORRY FOR MY SINS...
STEPH, DID FATHER ANTHONY PARDON ALL YOUR SINS?
HAHA!
SINS? WHAT SINS?!
OMG, I FORGOT TO TELL YOU ABOUT LAST NIGHT!
I HAVE FAMILY VISITING, AND WE ALL WENT TO TIMES SQUARE.
IT WAS SO MUCH FUN!

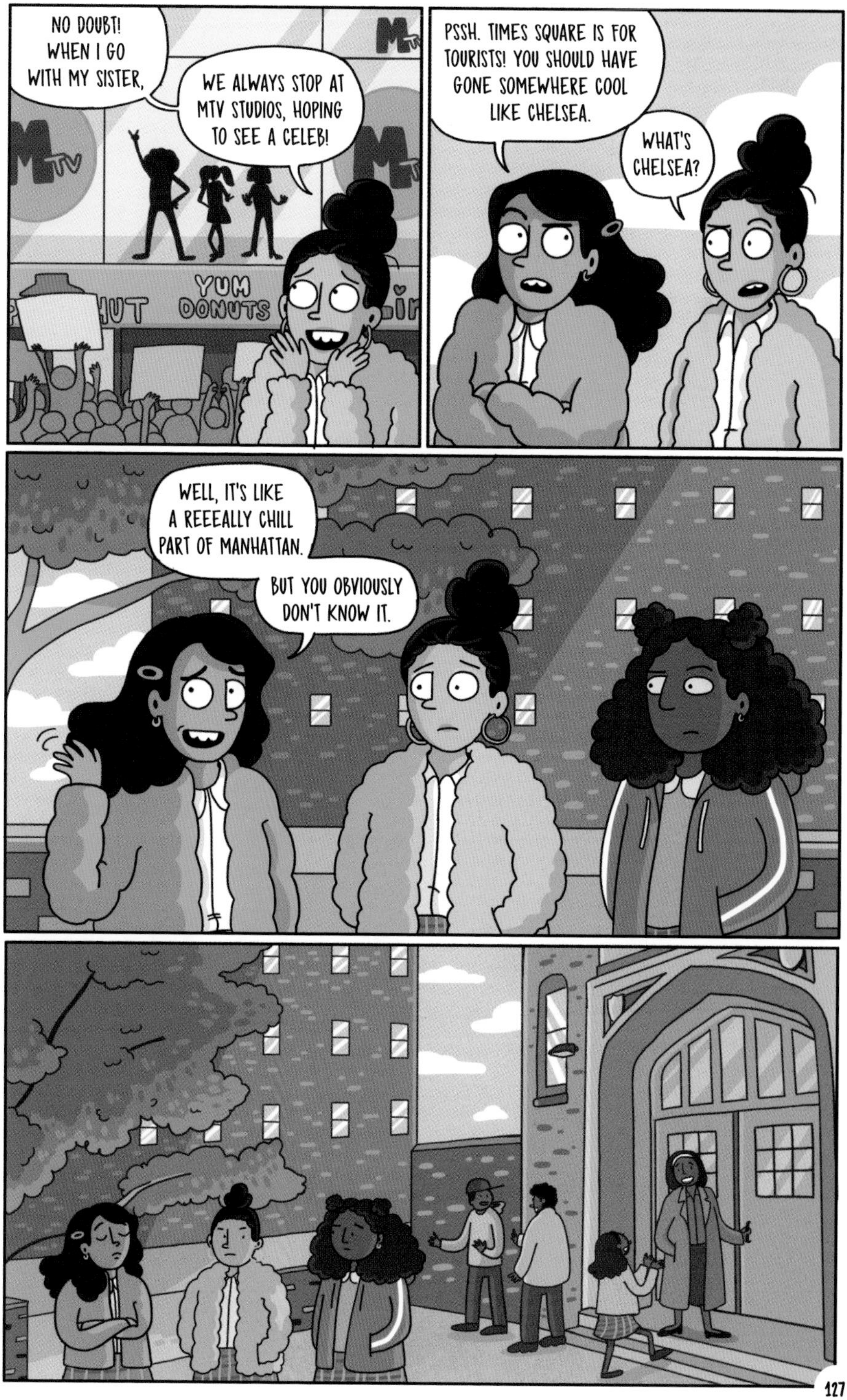
NO DOUBT! WHEN I GO WITH MY SISTER,
WE ALWAYS STOP AT MTV STUDIOS, HOPING TO SEE A CELEB!
YUM DONUTS
PSSH. TIMES SQUARE IS FOR TOURISTS! YOU SHOULD HAVE GONE SOMEWHERE COOL LIKE CHELSEA.
WHAT'S CHELSEA?
WELL, IT'S LIKE A REEEALLY CHILL PART OF MANHATTAN.
BUT YOU OBVIOUSLY DON'T KNOW IT.

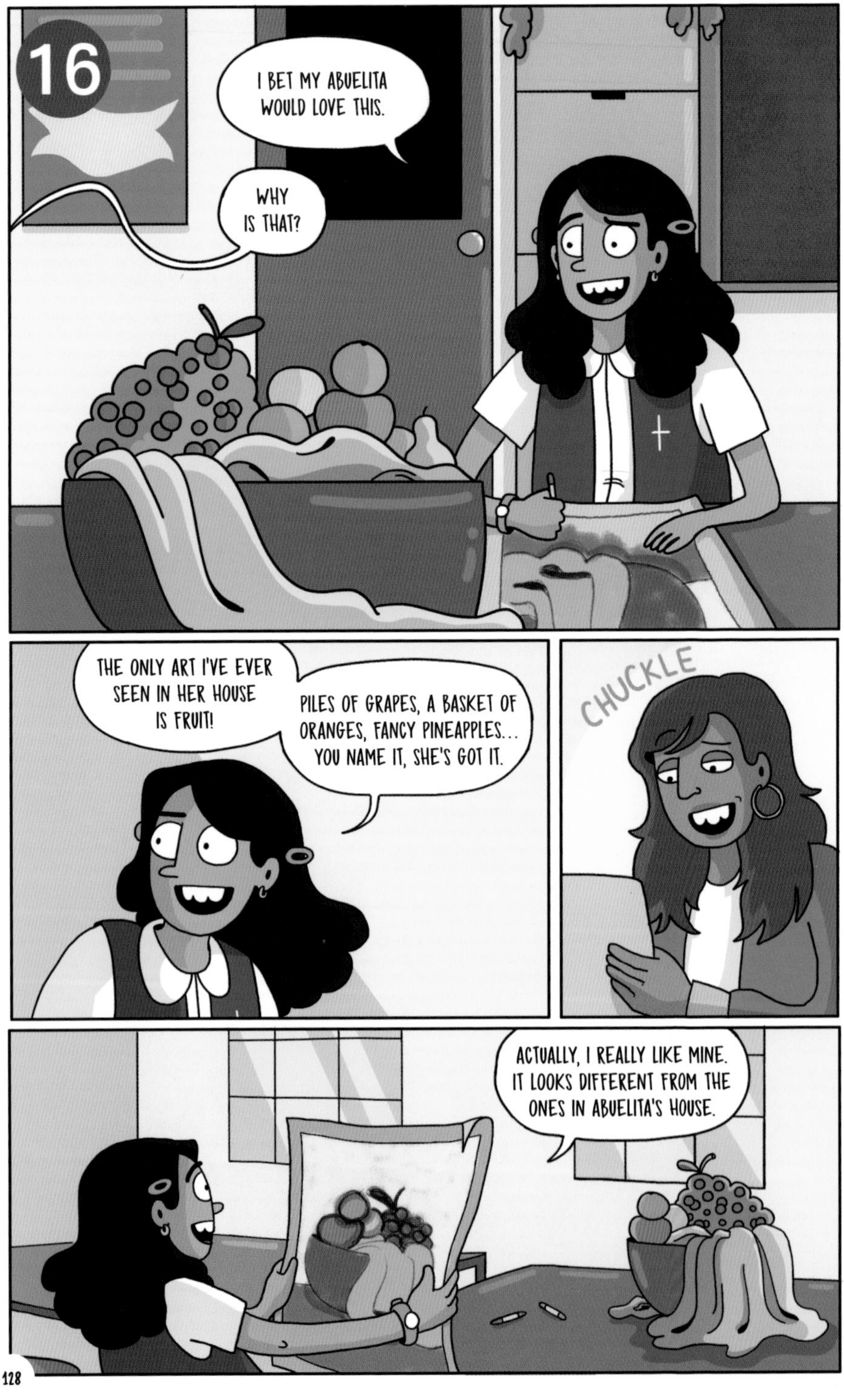
16
I BET MY ABUELITA WOULD LOVE THIS.
WHY IS THAT?
THE ONLY ART I'VE EVER SEEN IN HER HOUSE IS FRUIT!
PILES OF GRAPES, A BASKET OF ORANGES, FANCY PINEAPPLES... YOU NAME IT, SHE'S GOT IT.
CHUCKLE
ACTUALLY, I REALLY LIKE MINE. IT LOOKS DIFFERENT FROM THE ONES IN ABUELITA'S HOUSE.

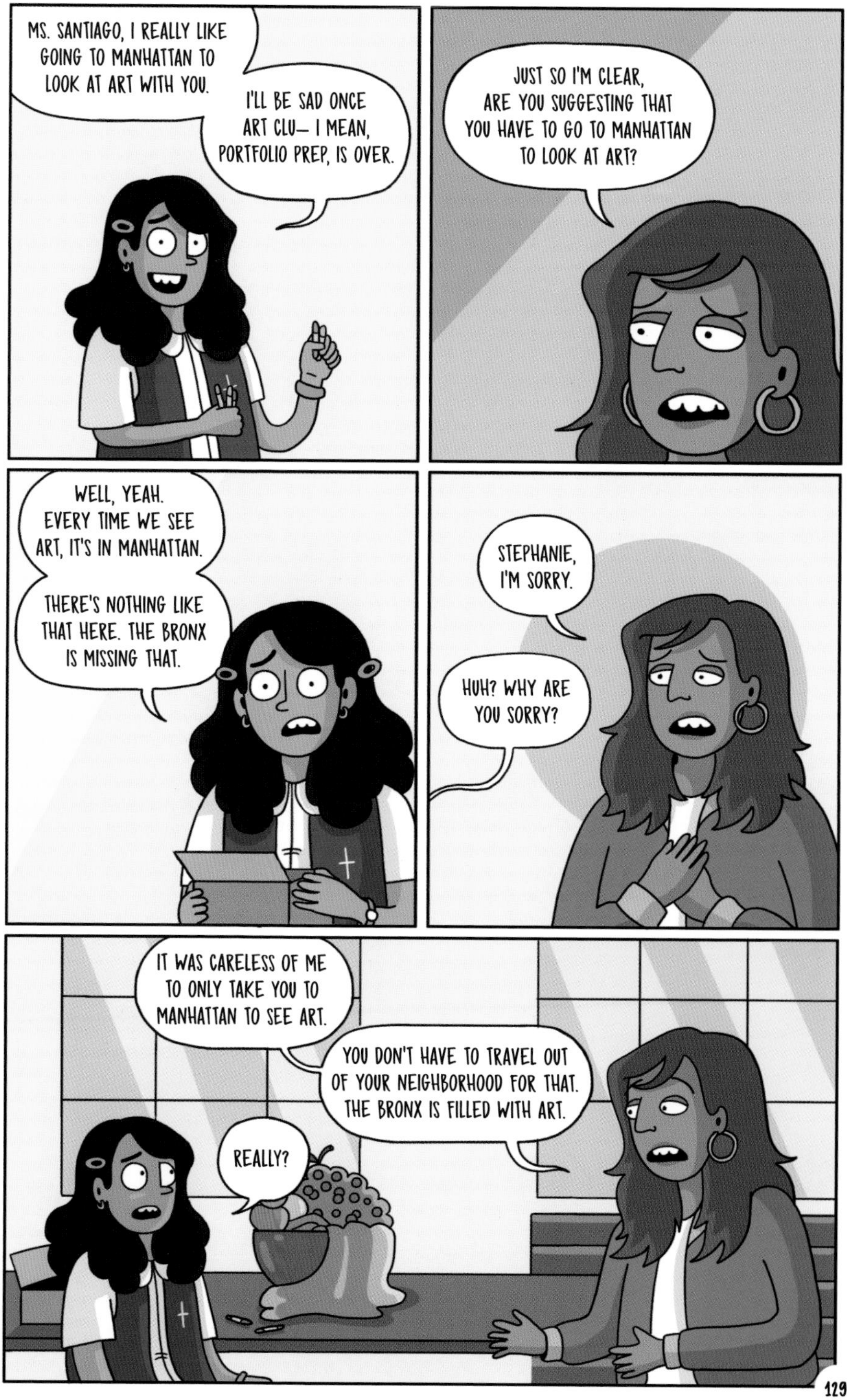
MS. SANTIAGO, I REALLY LIKE GOING TO MANHATTAN TO LOOK AT ART WITH YOU.
I'LL BE SAD ONCE ART CLU— I MEAN, PORTFOLIO PREP, IS OVER.
JUST SO I'M CLEAR, ARE YOU SUGGESTING THAT YOU HAVE TO GO TO MANHATTAN TO LOOK AT ART?
WELL, YEAH. EVERY TIME WE SEE ART, IT'S IN MANHATTAN.
THERE'S NOTHING LIKE THAT HERE. THE BRONX IS MISSING THAT.
STEPHANIE, I'M SORRY.
HUH? WHY ARE YOU SORRY?
IT WAS CARELESS OF ME TO ONLY TAKE YOU TO MANHATTAN TO SEE ART.
YOU DON'T HAVE TO TRAVEL OUT OF YOUR NEIGHBORHOOD FOR THAT. THE BRONX IS FILLED WITH ART.
REALLY?

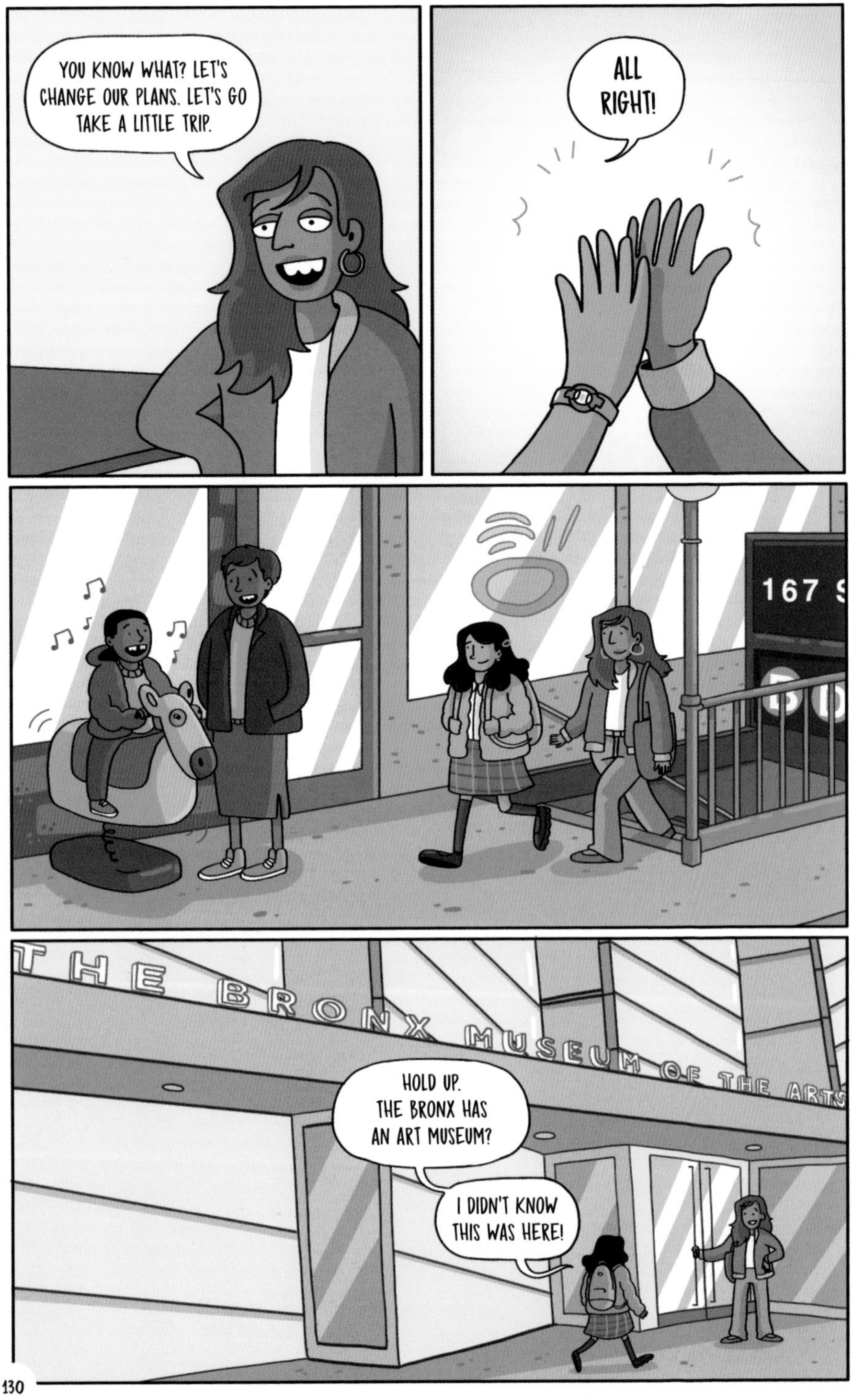
YOU KNOW WHAT? LET'S CHANGE OUR PLANS. LET'S GO TAKE A LITTLE TRIP.
ALL RIGHT!
167 S
THE BRONX MUSEUM OF THE ARTS
HOLD UP. THE BRONX HAS AN ART MUSEUM?
I DIDN'T KNOW THIS WAS HERE!

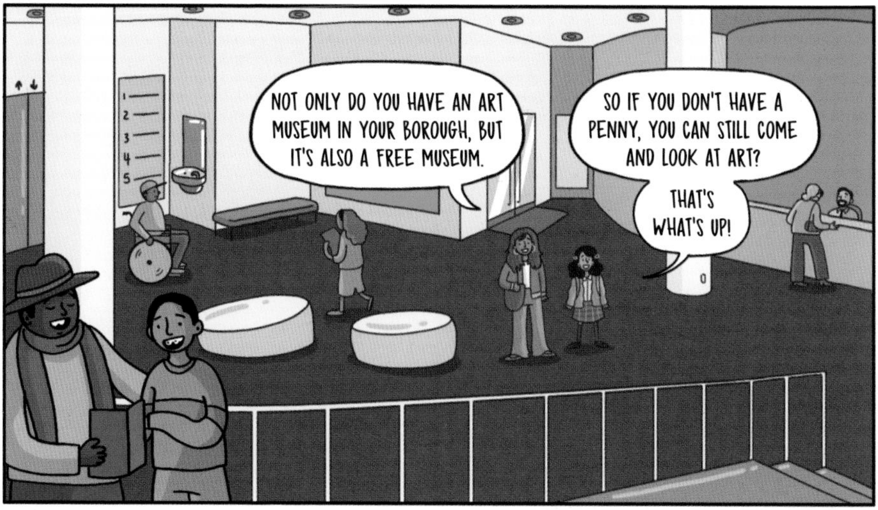
NOT ONLY DO YOU HAVE AN ART MUSEUM IN YOUR BOROUGH, BUT IT'S ALSO A FREE MUSEUM.
SO IF YOU DON'T HAVE A PENNY, YOU CAN STILL COME AND LOOK AT ART?
THAT'S WHAT'S UP!

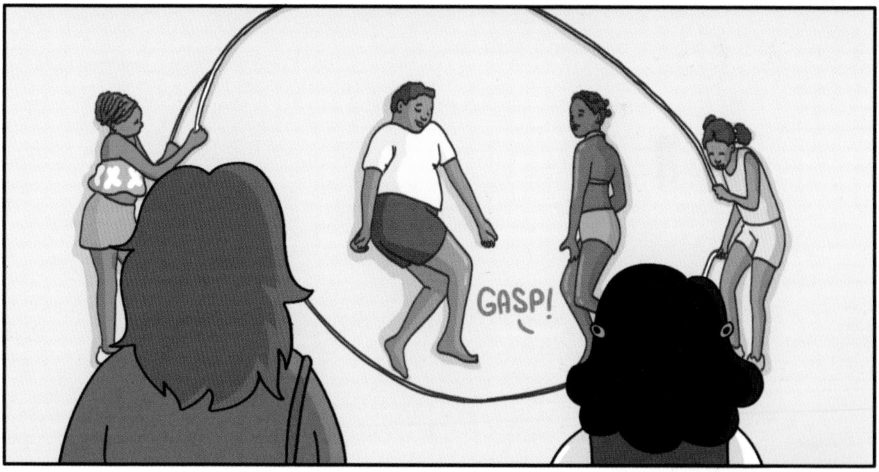
GASP!

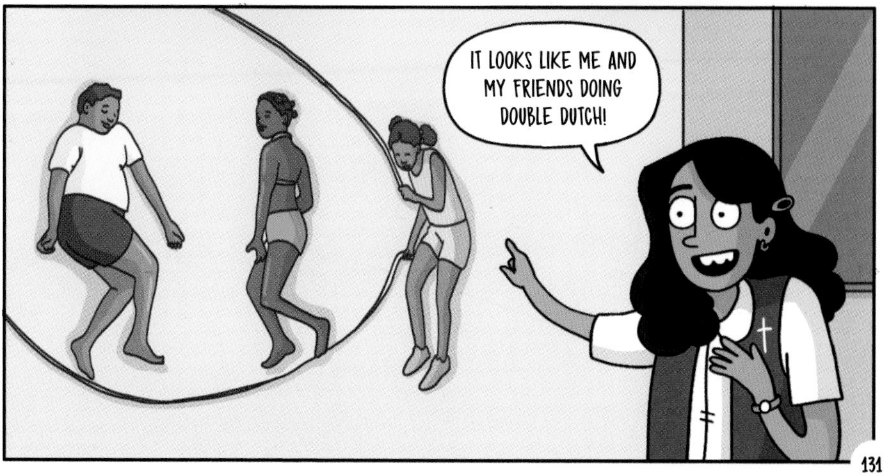
IT LOOKS LIKE ME AND MY FRIENDS DOING DOUBLE DUTCH!

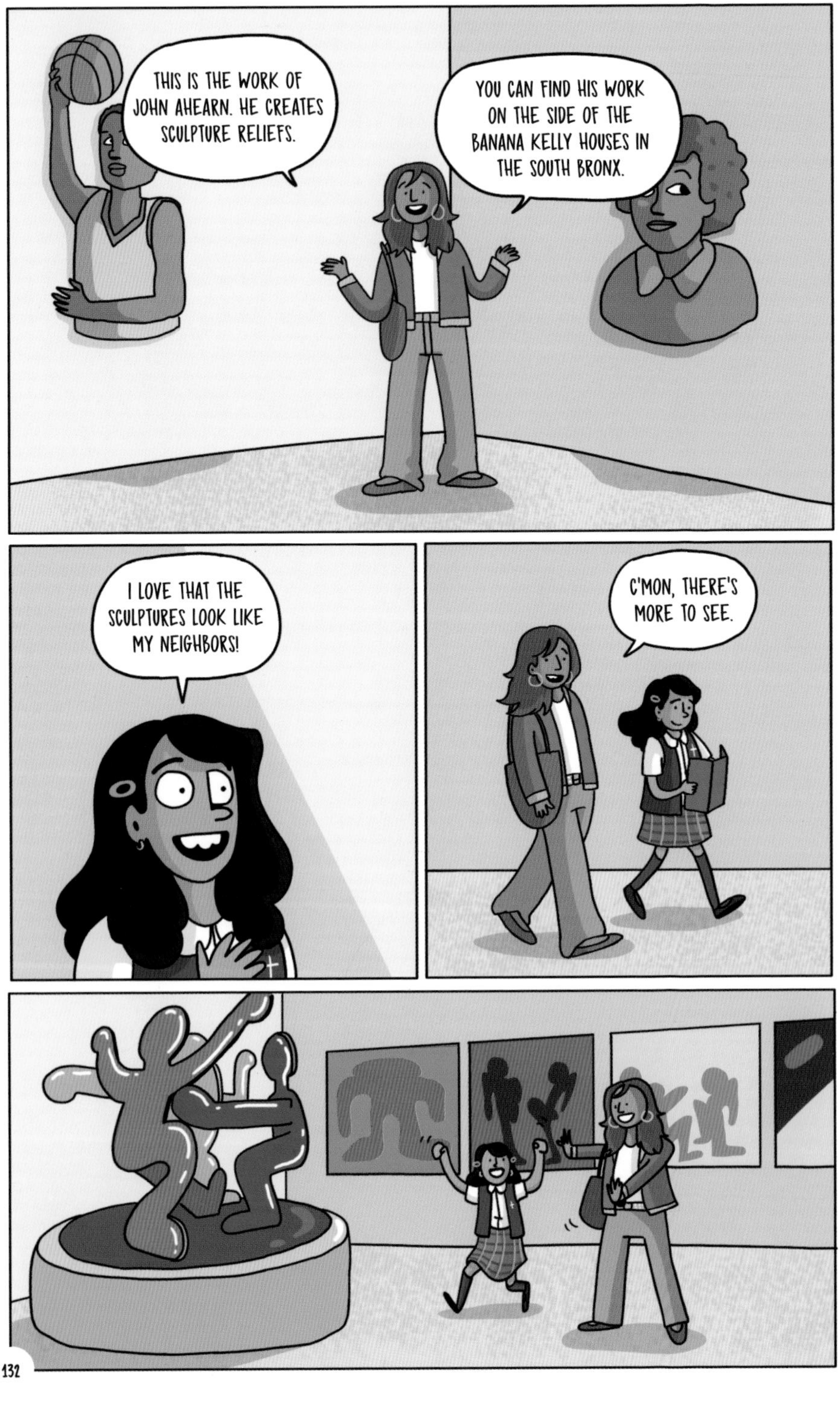
THIS IS THE WORK OF JOHN AHEARN. HE CREATES SCULPTURE RELIEFS.
YOU CAN FIND HIS WORK ON THE SIDE OF THE BANANA KELLY HOUSES IN THE SOUTH BRONX.
I LOVE THAT THE SCULPTURES LOOK LIKE MY NEIGHBORS!
C'MON, THERE'S MORE TO SEE.

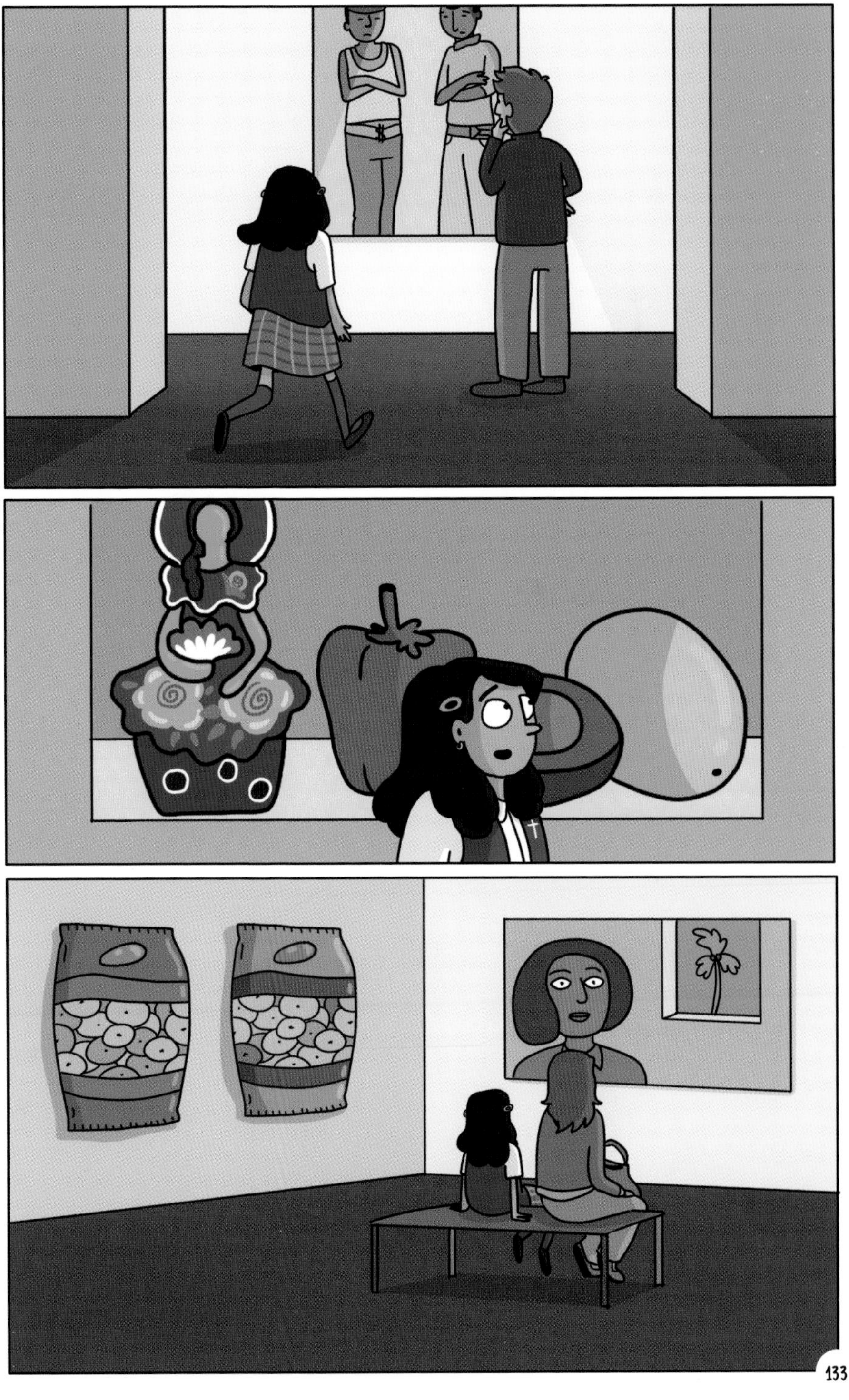

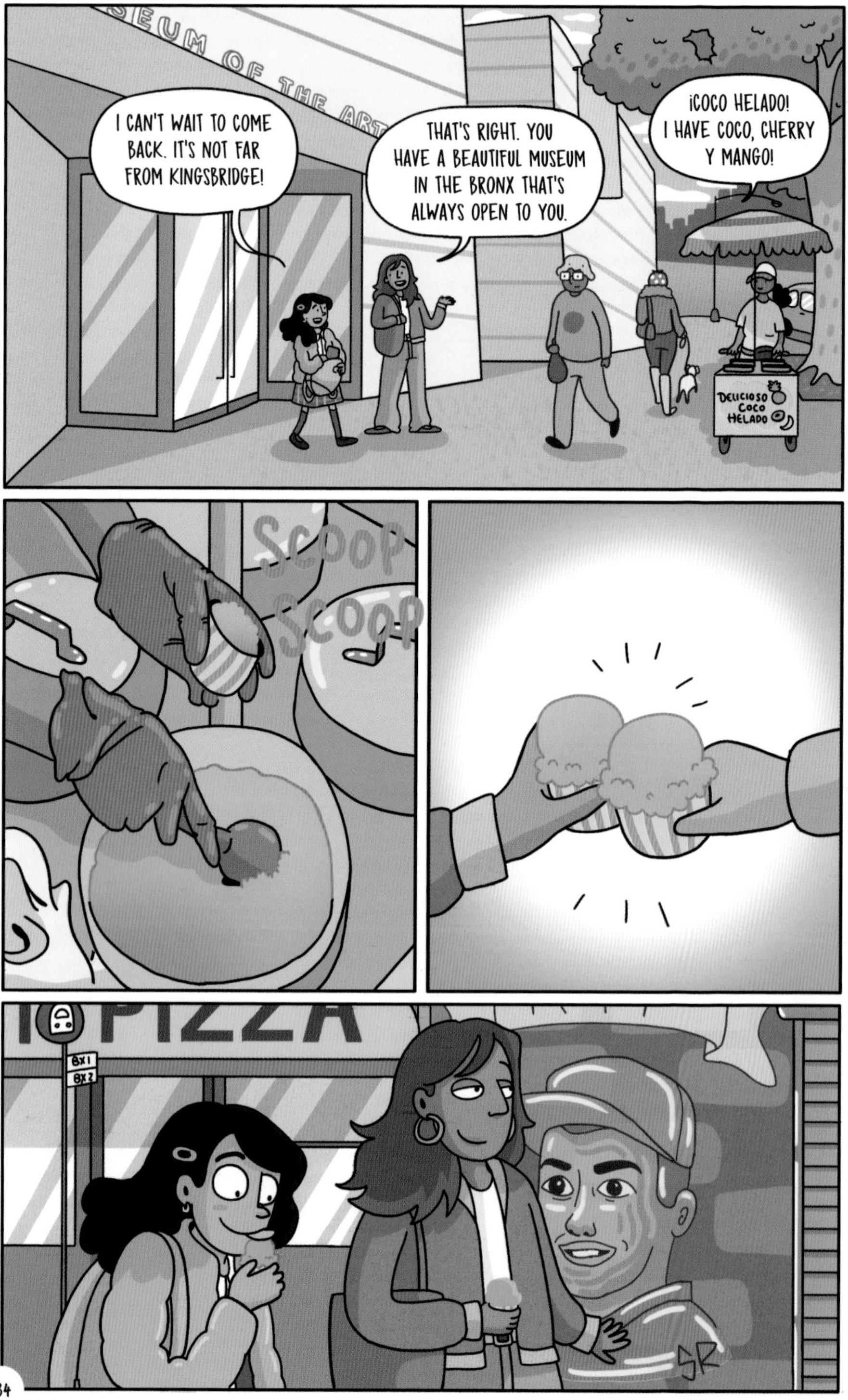
SEUM OF THE ART
I CAN'T WAIT TO COME BACK. IT'S NOT FAR FROM KINGSBRIDGE!
THAT'S RIGHT. YOU HAVE A BEAUTIFUL MUSEUM IN THE BRONX THAT'S ALWAYS OPEN TO YOU.
¡COCO HELADO! I HAVE COCO, CHERRY Y MANGO!
DELICIOSO COCO HELADO
SCOOP SCOOP
PIZZA
BX1
BX2

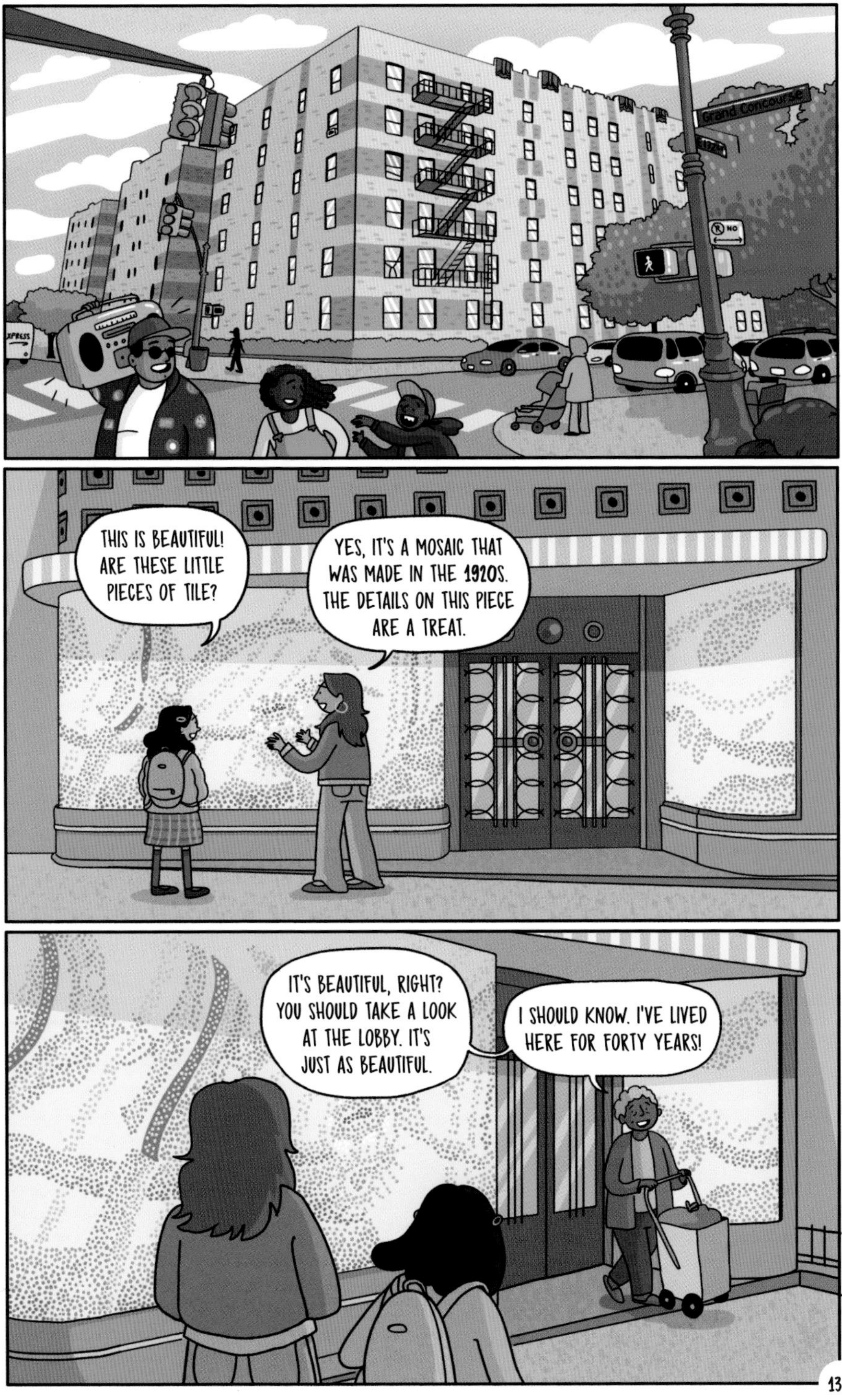
Grand Concourse
THIS IS BEAUTIFUL! ARE THESE LITTLE PIECES OF TILE?
YES, IT'S A MOSAIC THAT WAS MADE IN THE 1920S. THE DETAILS ON THIS PIECE ARE A TREAT.
IT'S BEAUTIFUL, RIGHT? YOU SHOULD TAKE A LOOK AT THE LOBBY. IT'S JUST AS BEAUTIFUL.
I SHOULD KNOW. I'VE LIVED HERE FOR FORTY YEARS!

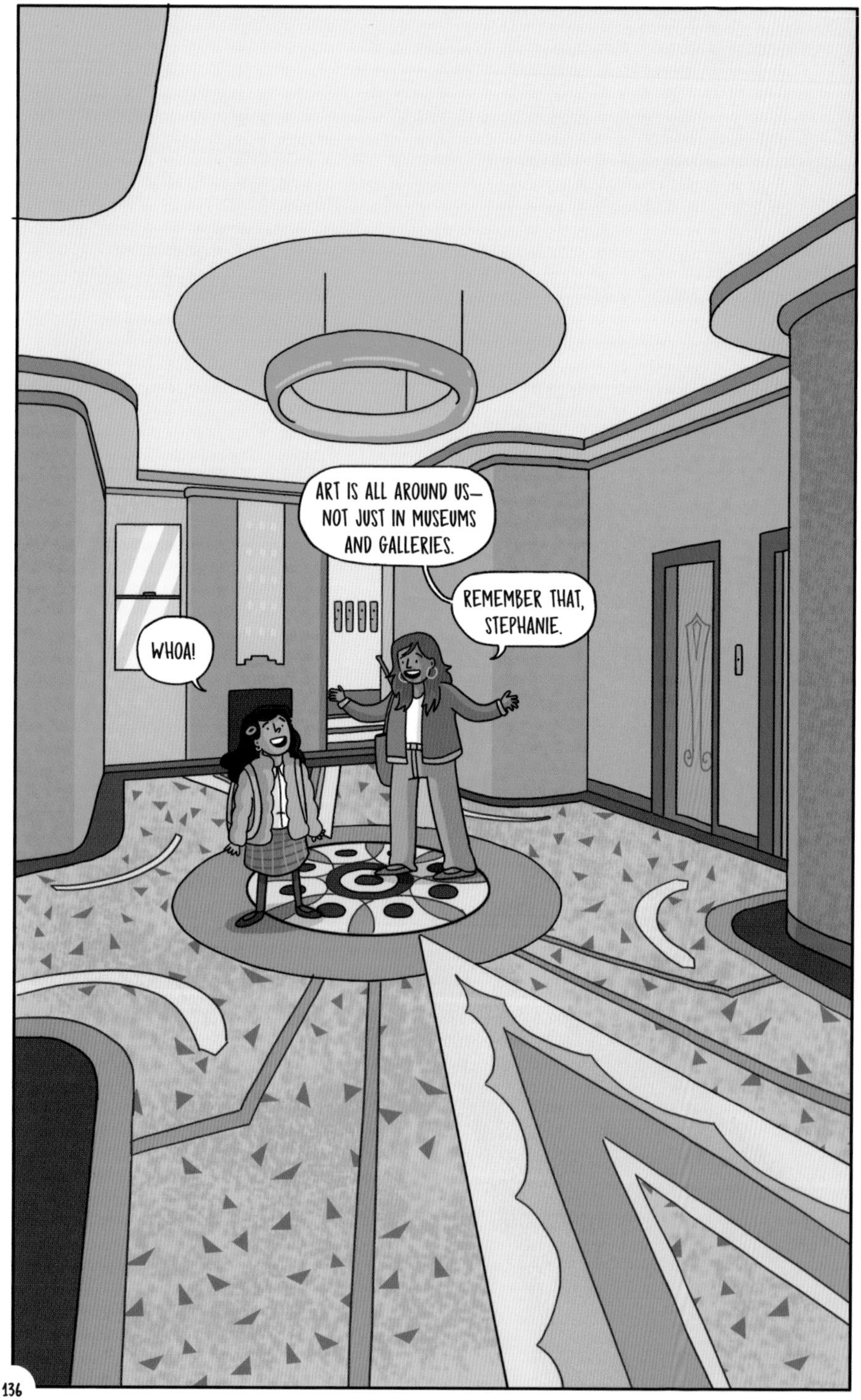
ART IS ALL AROUND US—
NOT JUST IN MUSEUMS AND GALLERIES.
REMEMBER THAT, STEPHANIE.
WHOA!

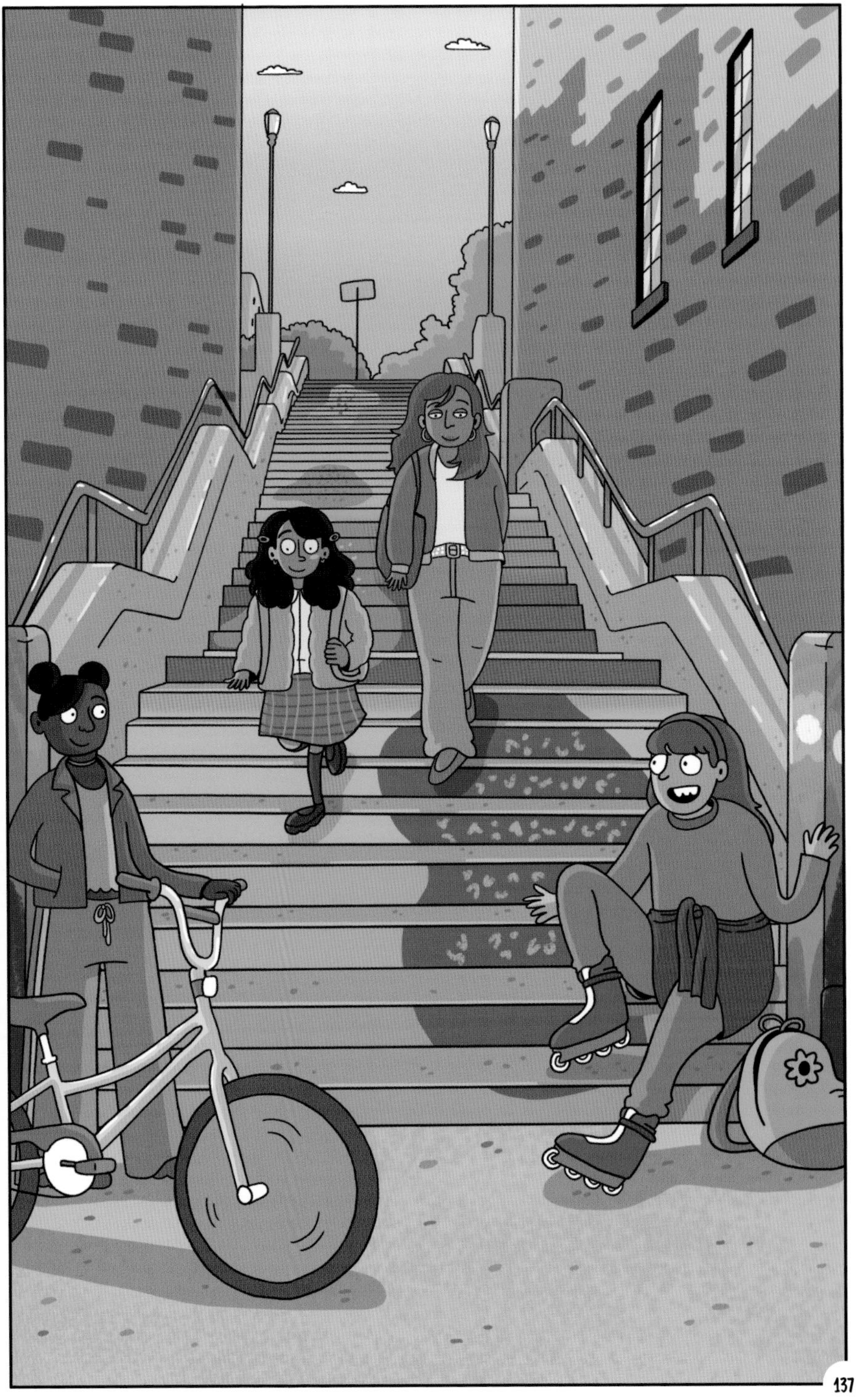

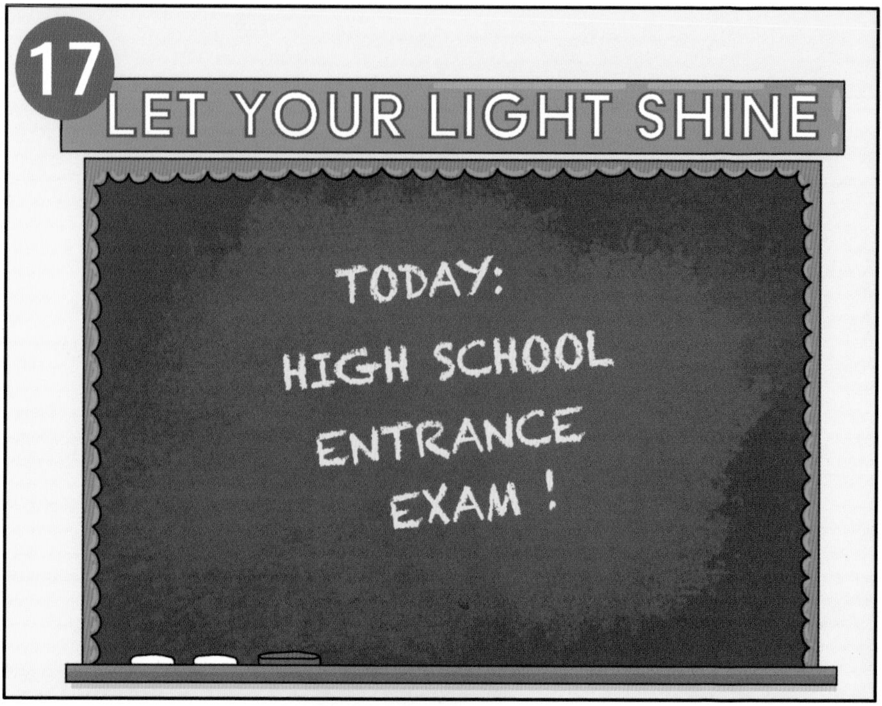
17
LET YOUR LIGHT SHINE
TODAY:
HIGH SCHOOL
ENTRANCE
EXAM !

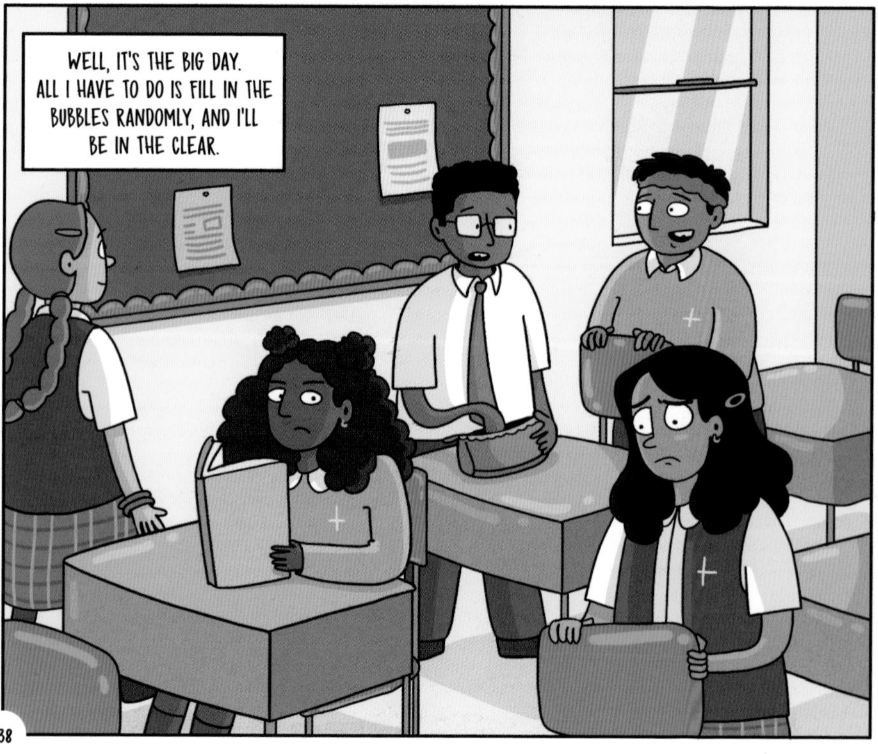
WELL, IT'S THE BIG DAY.
ALL I HAVE TO DO IS FILL IN THE BUBBLES RANDOMLY, AND I'LL BE IN THE CLEAR.

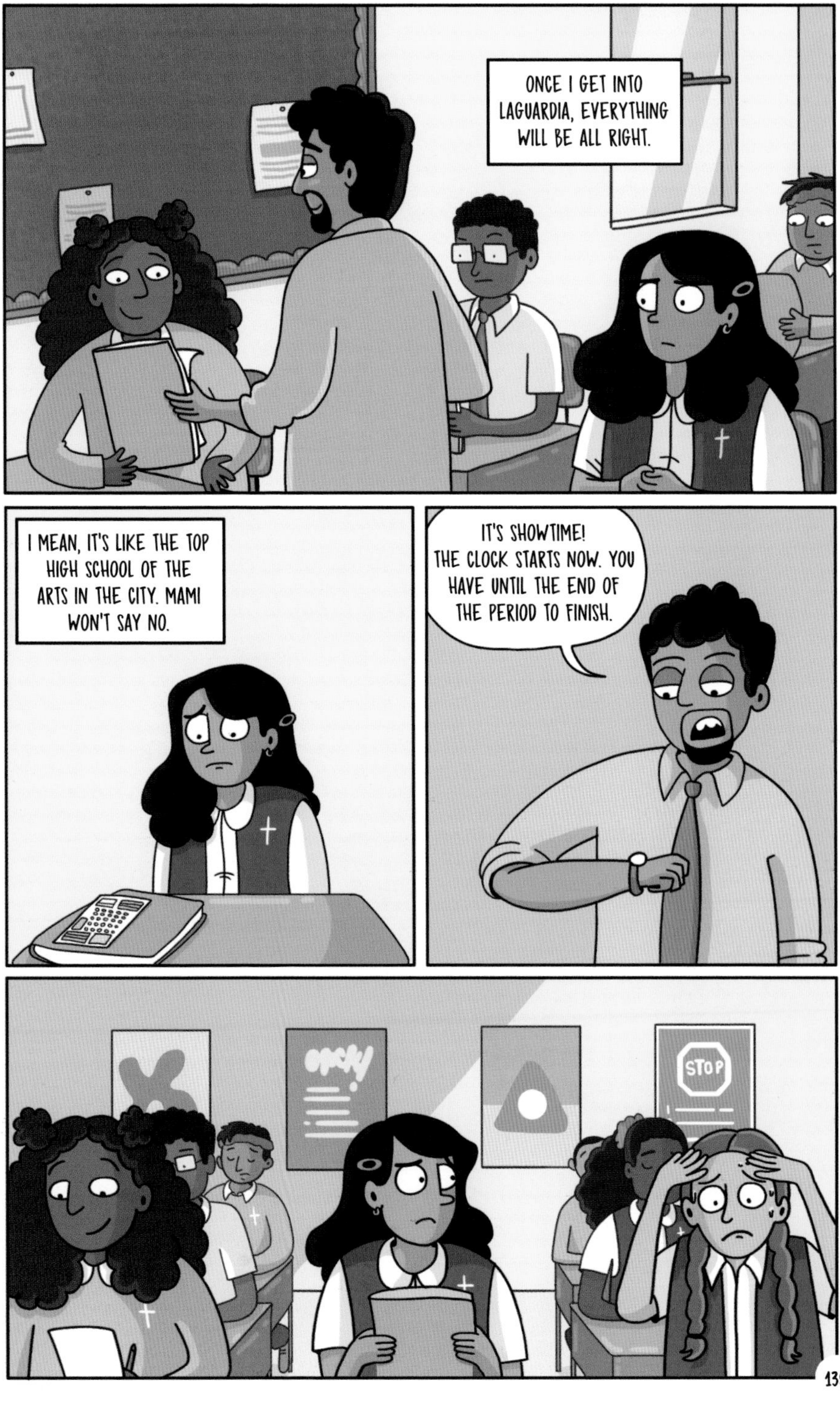
ONCE I GET INTO LAGUARDIA, EVERYTHING WILL BE ALL RIGHT.
I MEAN, IT'S LIKE THE TOP HIGH SCHOOL OF THE ARTS IN THE CITY. MAMI WON'T SAY NO.
IT'S SHOWTIME! THE CLOCK STARTS NOW. YOU HAVE UNTIL THE END OF THE PERIOD TO FINISH.
STOP

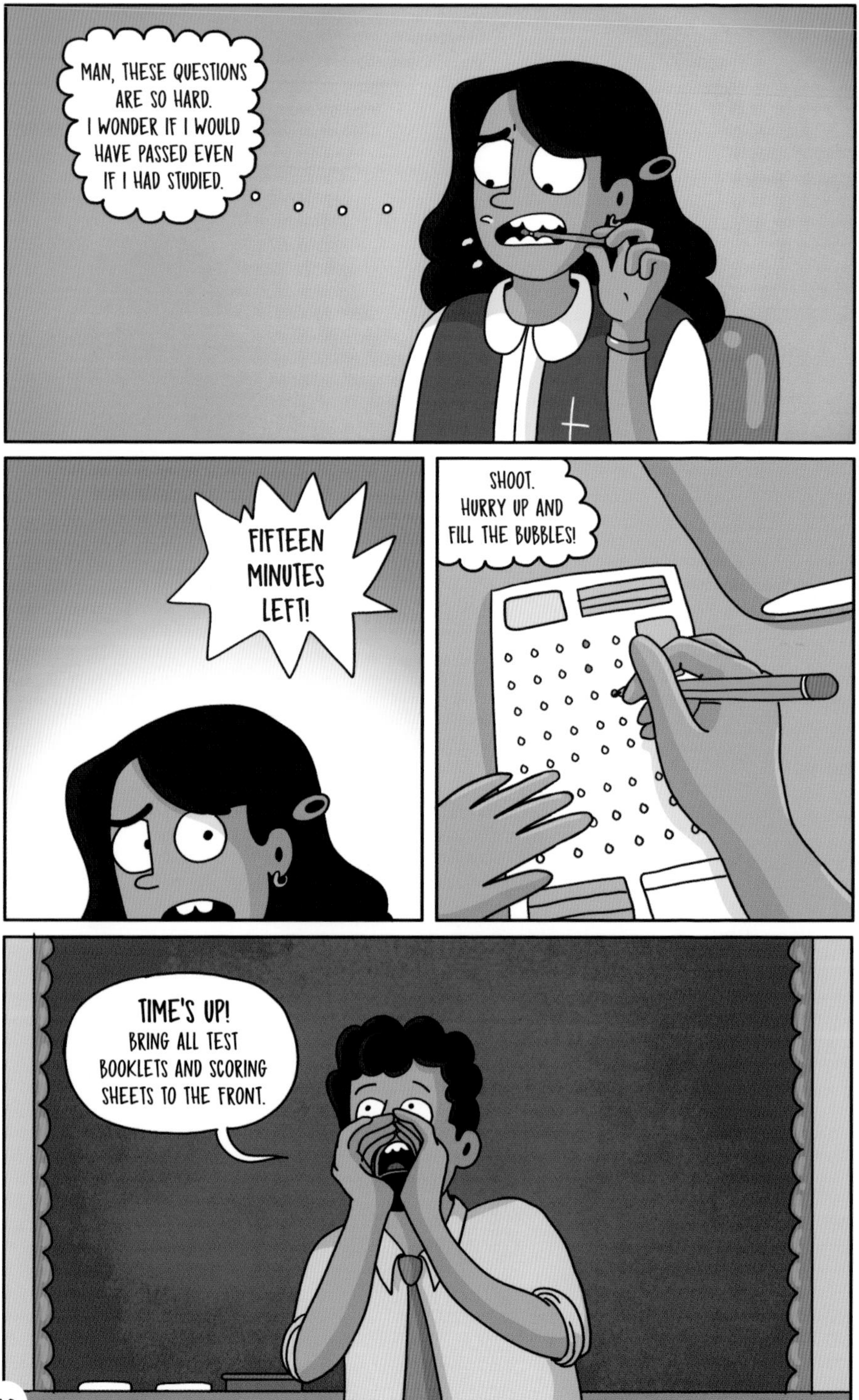
MAN, THESE QUESTIONS ARE SO HARD. I WONDER IF I WOULD HAVE PASSED EVEN IF I HAD STUDIED.
FIFTEEN MINUTES LEFT!
SHOOT. HURRY UP AND FILL THE BUBBLES!
TIME'S UP! BRING ALL TEST BOOKLETS AND SCORING SHEETS TO THE FRONT.

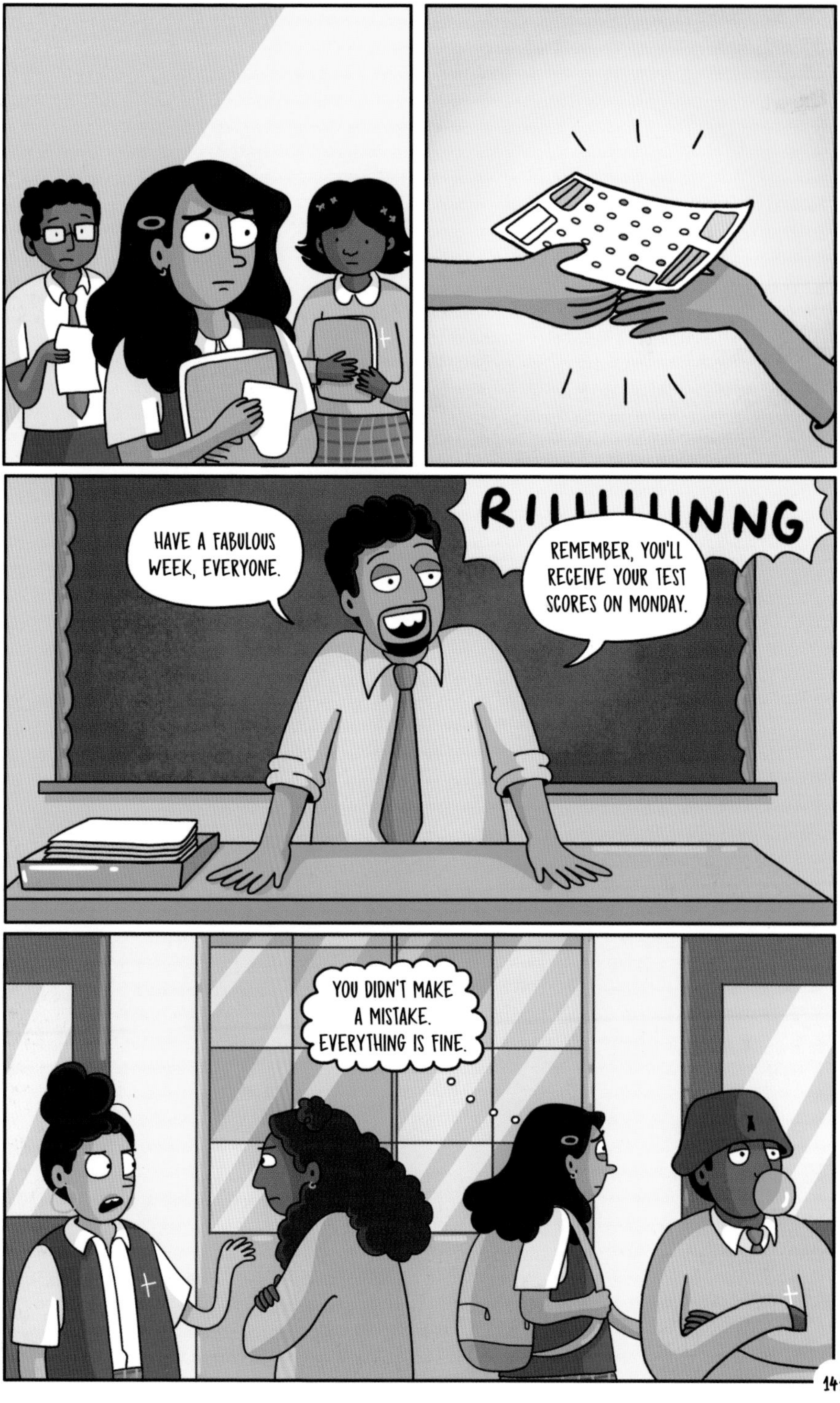
HAVE A FABULOUS WEEK, EVERYONE.
RIIIIIIINNG
REMEMBER, YOU'LL RECEIVE YOUR TEST SCORES ON MONDAY.
YOU DIDN'T MAKE A MISTAKE. EVERYTHING IS FINE.

18

STEPHANIE, I'M JUST TAKING PHOTOS OF YOUR PORTFOLIO.

OH, SUPER DOPE.

HOW DID THE EXAM GO? WORD ON THE STREET IS IT WAS A HARD ONE.

OH, UM, YOU KNOW, IT WAS PRETTY DIFFICULT...

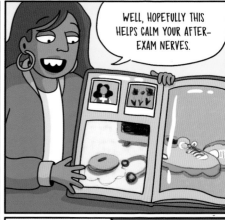

WELL, HOPEFULLY THIS HELPS CALM YOUR AFTER-EXAM NERVES.

WOW! IT'S SO COOL TO SEE MY ART ALL TOGETHER LIKE THIS.

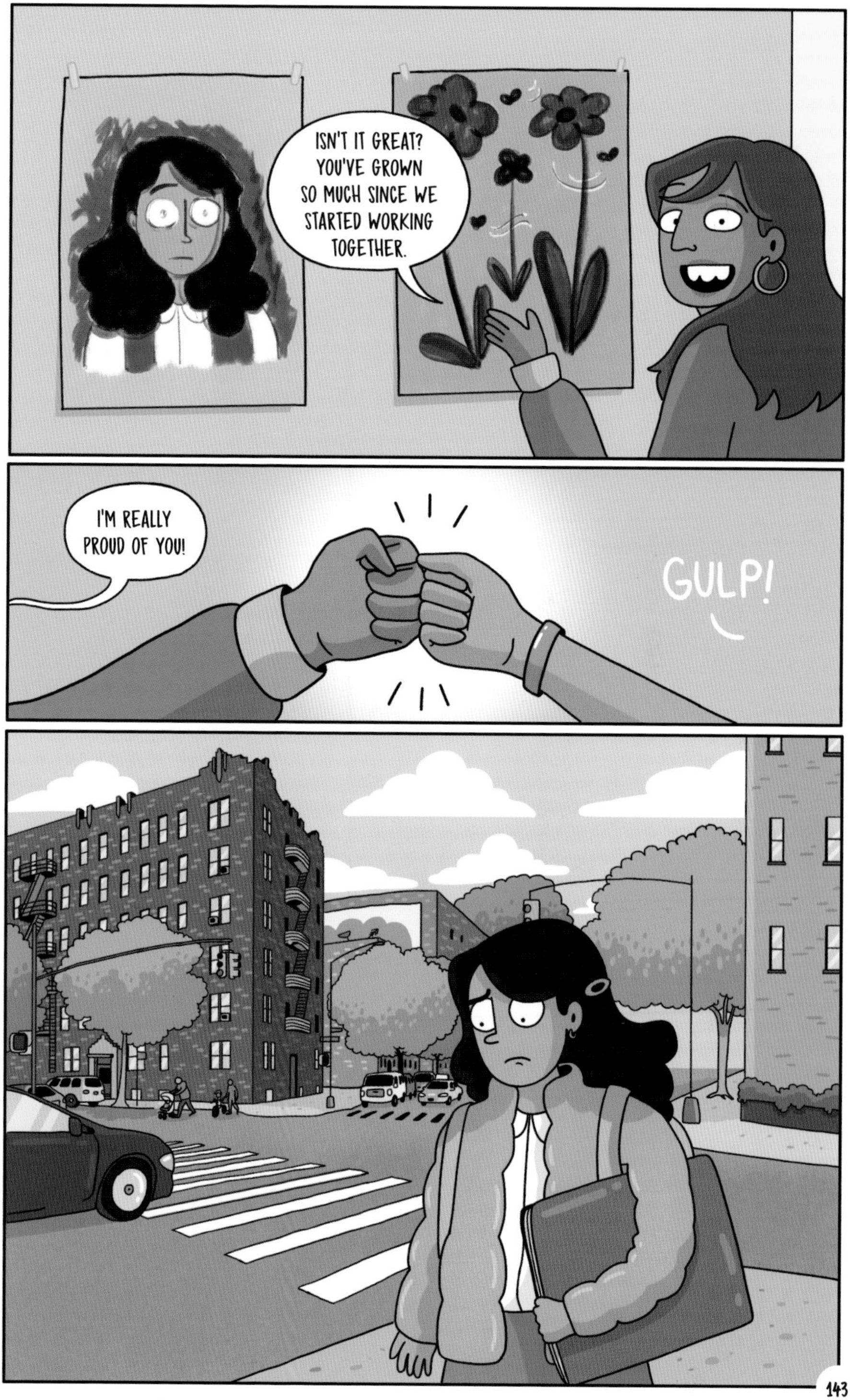
ISN'T IT GREAT? YOU'VE GROWN SO MUCH SINCE WE STARTED WORKING TOGETHER.
I'M REALLY PROUD OF YOU!
GULP!

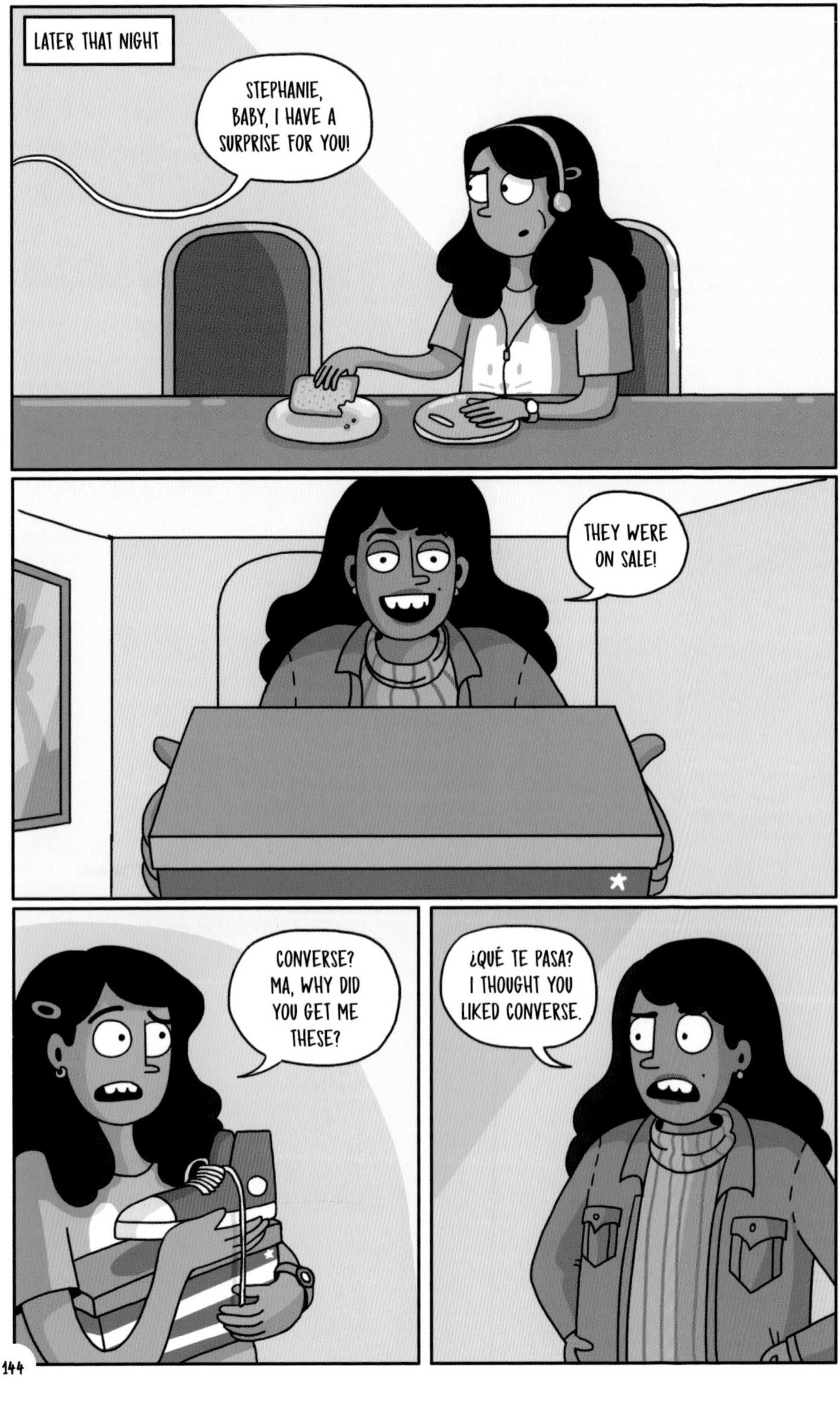
LATER THAT NIGHT
STEPHANIE, BABY, I HAVE A SURPRISE FOR YOU!
THEY WERE ON SALE!
CONVERSE? MA, WHY DID YOU GET ME THESE?
¿QUÉ TE PASA? I THOUGHT YOU LIKED CONVERSE.

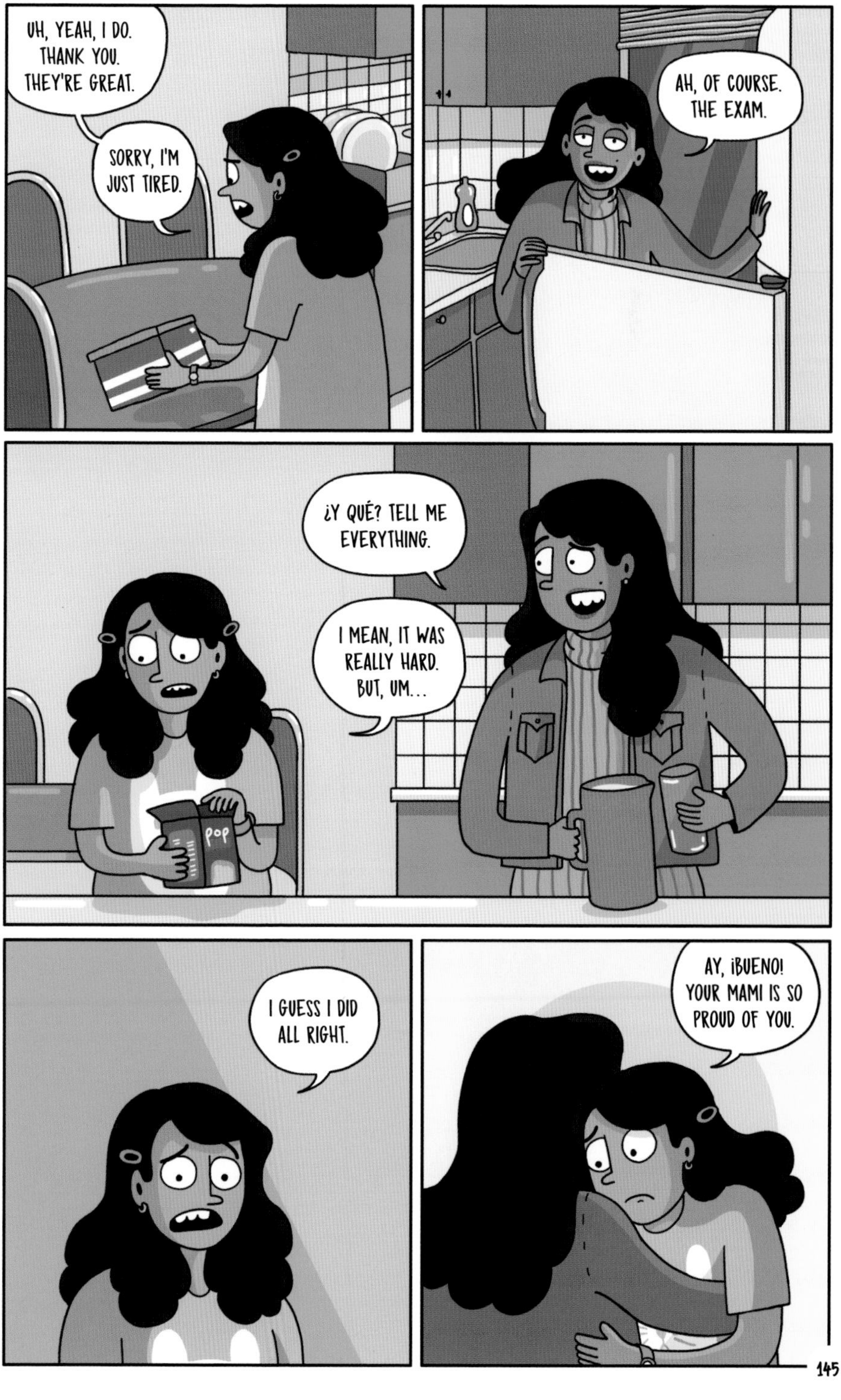
UH, YEAH, I DO. THANK YOU. THEY'RE GREAT.
SORRY, I'M JUST TIRED.
AH, OF COURSE. THE EXAM.
¿Y QUÉ? TELL ME EVERYTHING.
I MEAN, IT WAS REALLY HARD. BUT, UM...
pop
I GUESS I DID ALL RIGHT.
AY, ¡BUENO! YOUR MAMI IS SO PROUD OF YOU.

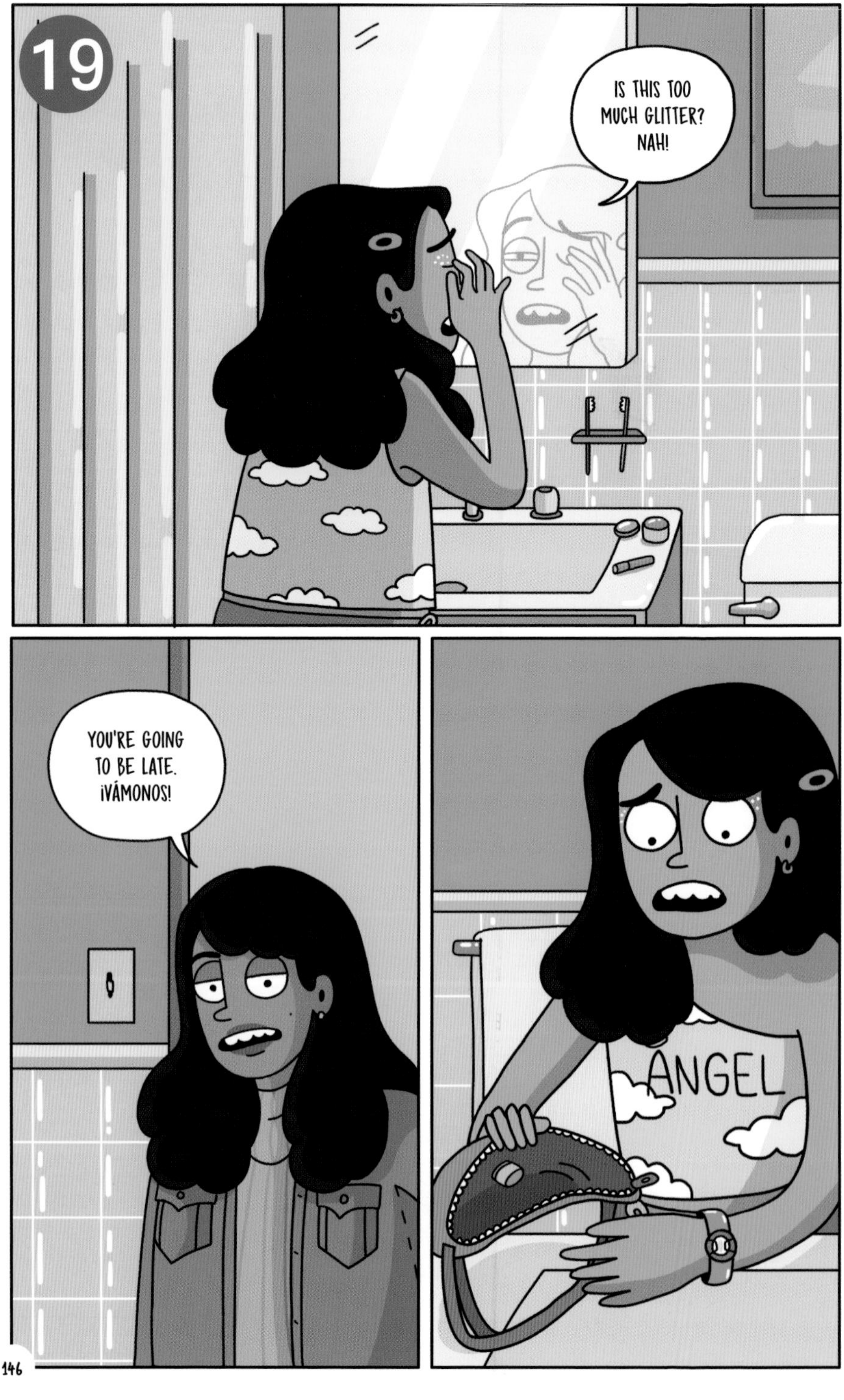
19
IS THIS TOO MUCH GLITTER? NAH!
YOU'RE GOING TO BE LATE. ¡VÁMONOS!
ANGEL

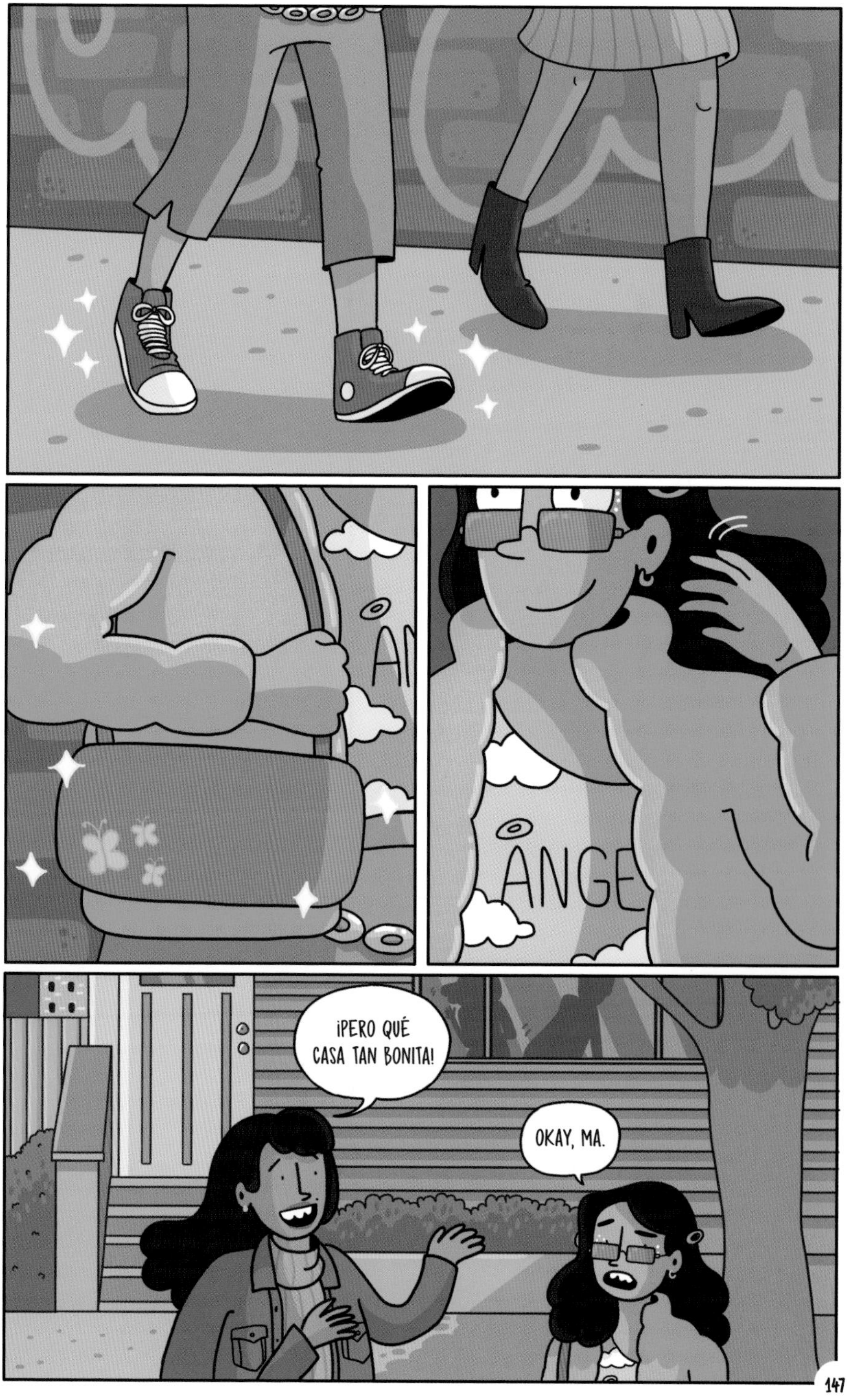
¡PERO QUÉ CASA TAN BONITA!
OKAY, MA.

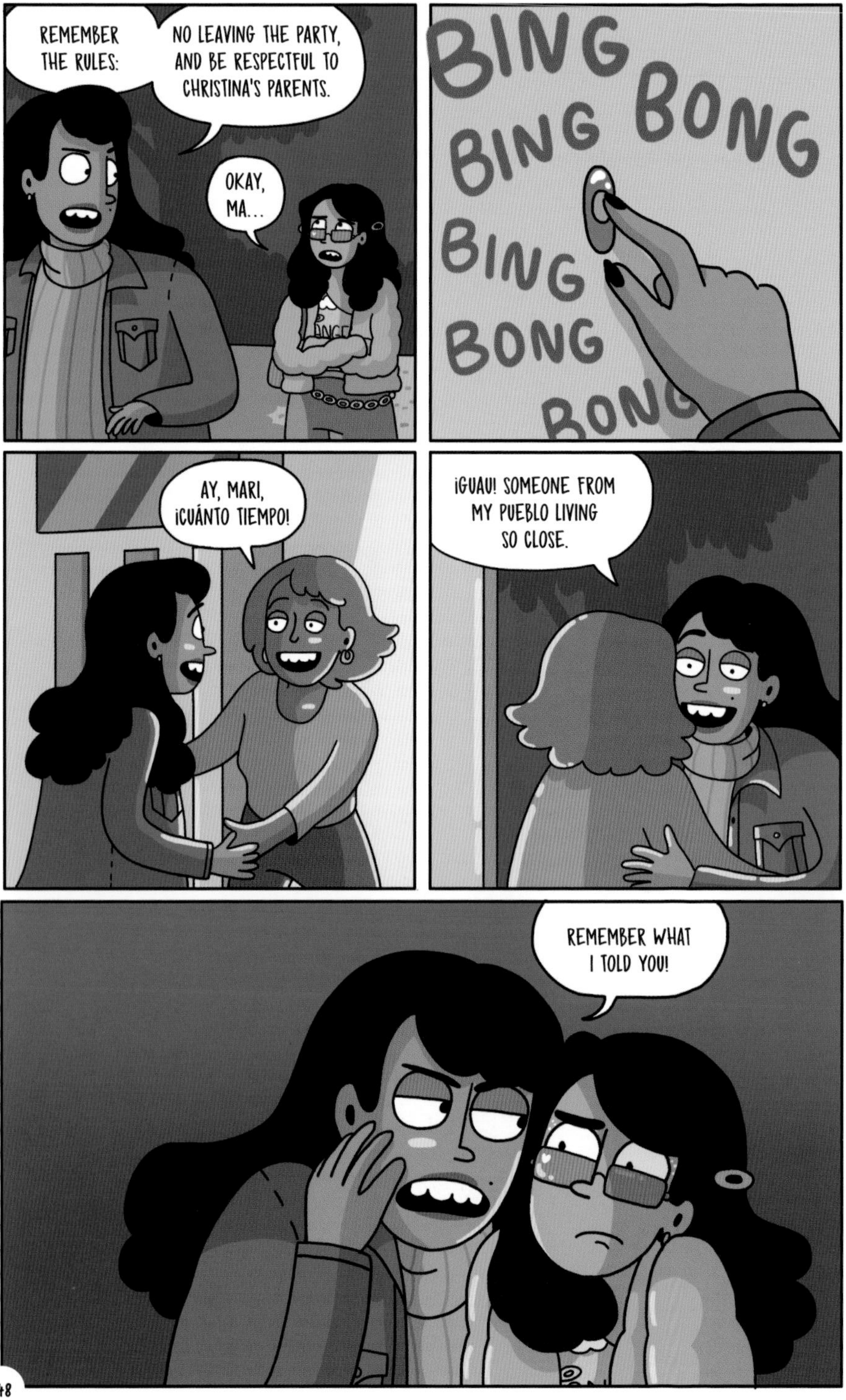

REMEMBER THE RULES:
NO LEAVING THE PARTY, AND BE RESPECTFUL TO CHRISTINA'S PARENTS.
OKAY, MA...
BING
BING BONG
BING
BONG
BONG
AY, MARI, ¡CUÁNTO TIEMPO!
¡GUAU! SOMEONE FROM MY PUEBLO LIVING SO CLOSE.
REMEMBER WHAT I TOLD YOU!

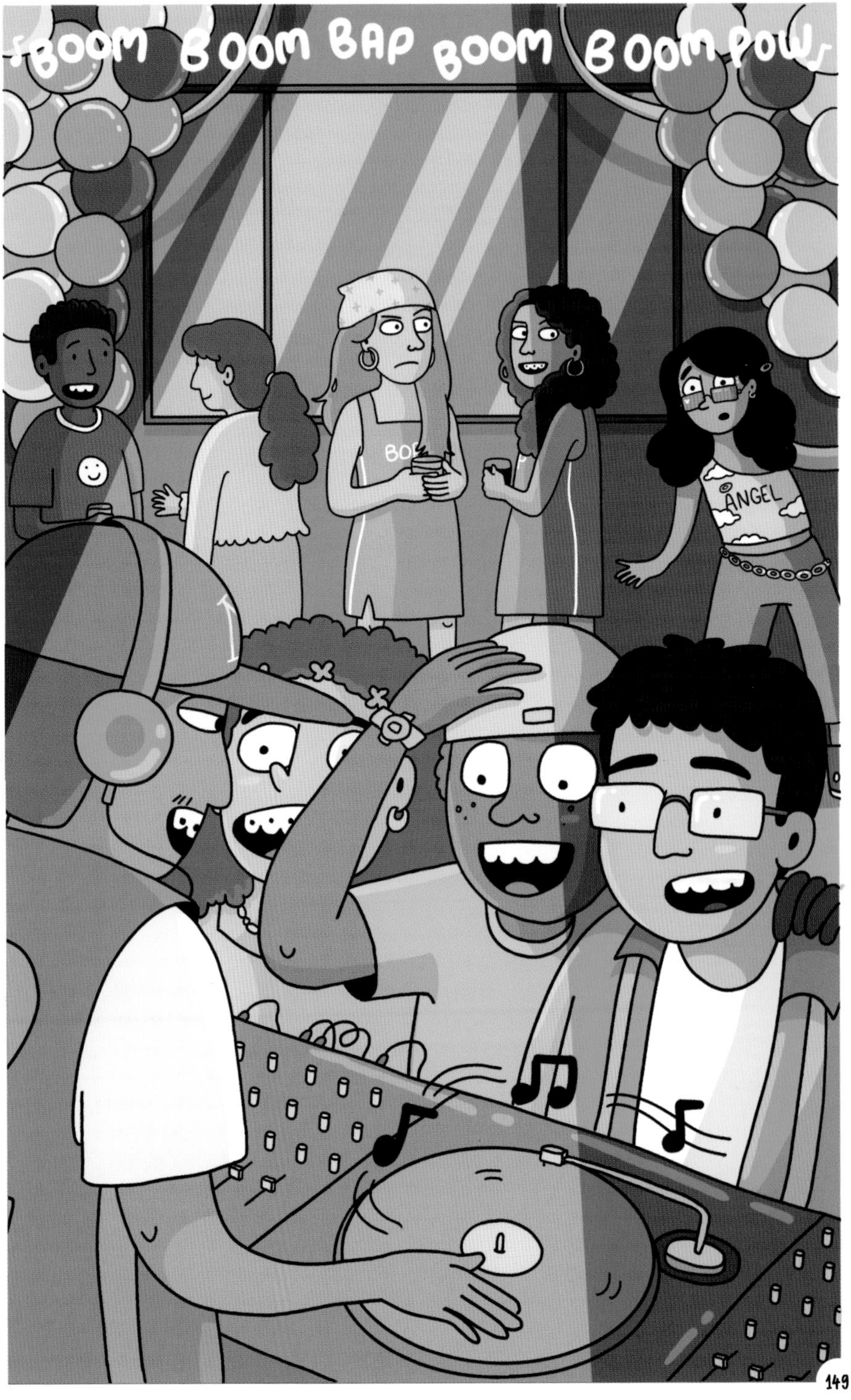
BOOM BOOM BAP BOOM BOOM POW
BOP
ANGEL

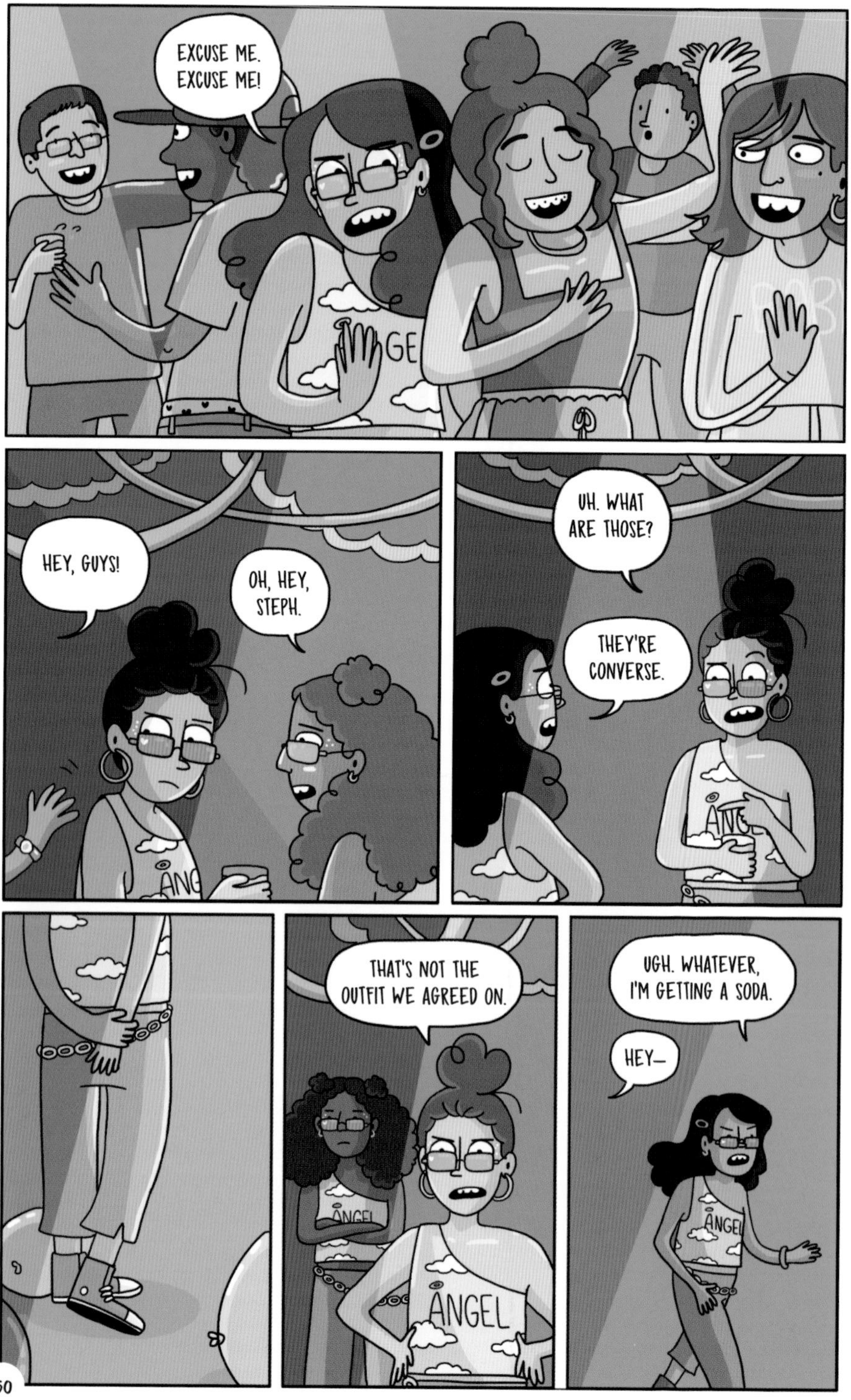
EXCUSE ME. EXCUSE ME!
ANGEL
HEY, GUYS!
OH, HEY, STEPH.
ANGEL
UH. WHAT ARE THOSE?
THEY'RE CONVERSE.
ANGEL
THAT'S NOT THE OUTFIT WE AGREED ON.
ANGEL
ANGEL
UGH. WHATEVER, I'M GETTING A SODA.
HEY—
ANGEL

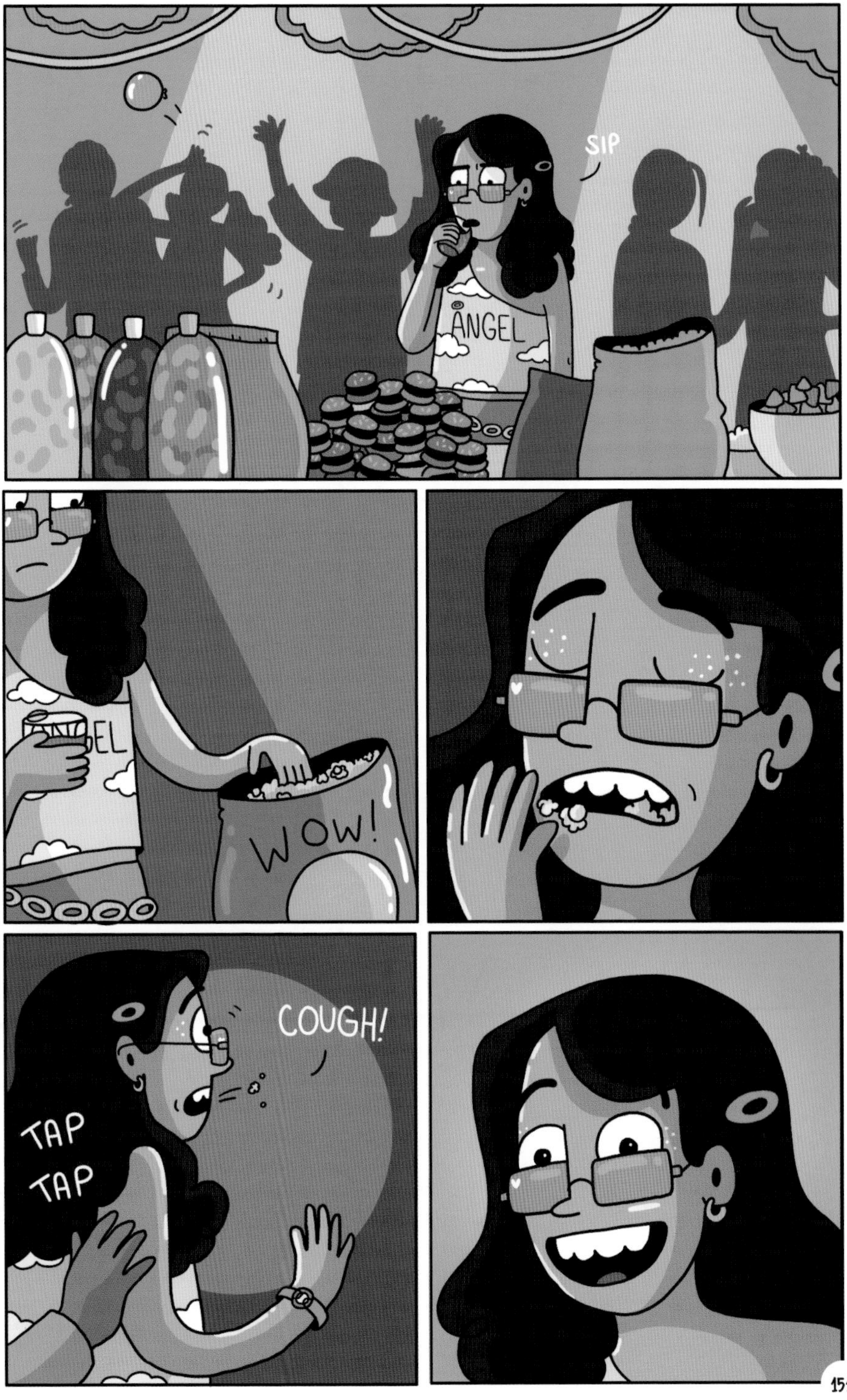
SIP
ANGEL
WOW!
COUGH!
TAP
TAP

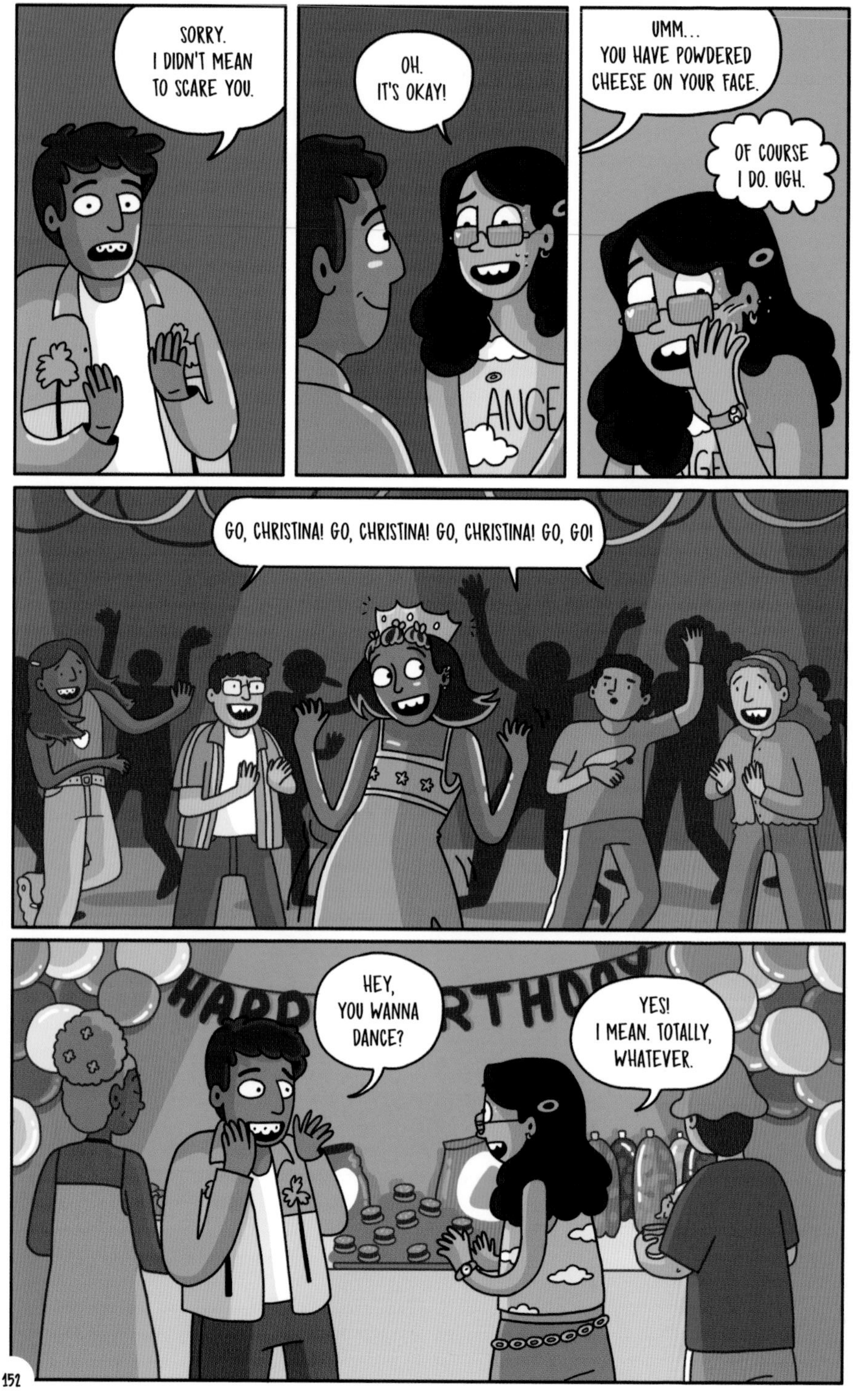
SORRY.
I DIDN'T MEAN
TO SCARE YOU.
OH.
IT'S OKAY!
UMM...
YOU HAVE POWDERED
CHEESE ON YOUR FACE.
OF COURSE
I DO. UGH.
ANGE
GO, CHRISTINA! GO, CHRISTINA! GO, CHRISTINA! GO, GO!
HEY,
YOU WANNA
DANCE?
YES!
I MEAN. TOTALLY,
WHATEVER.

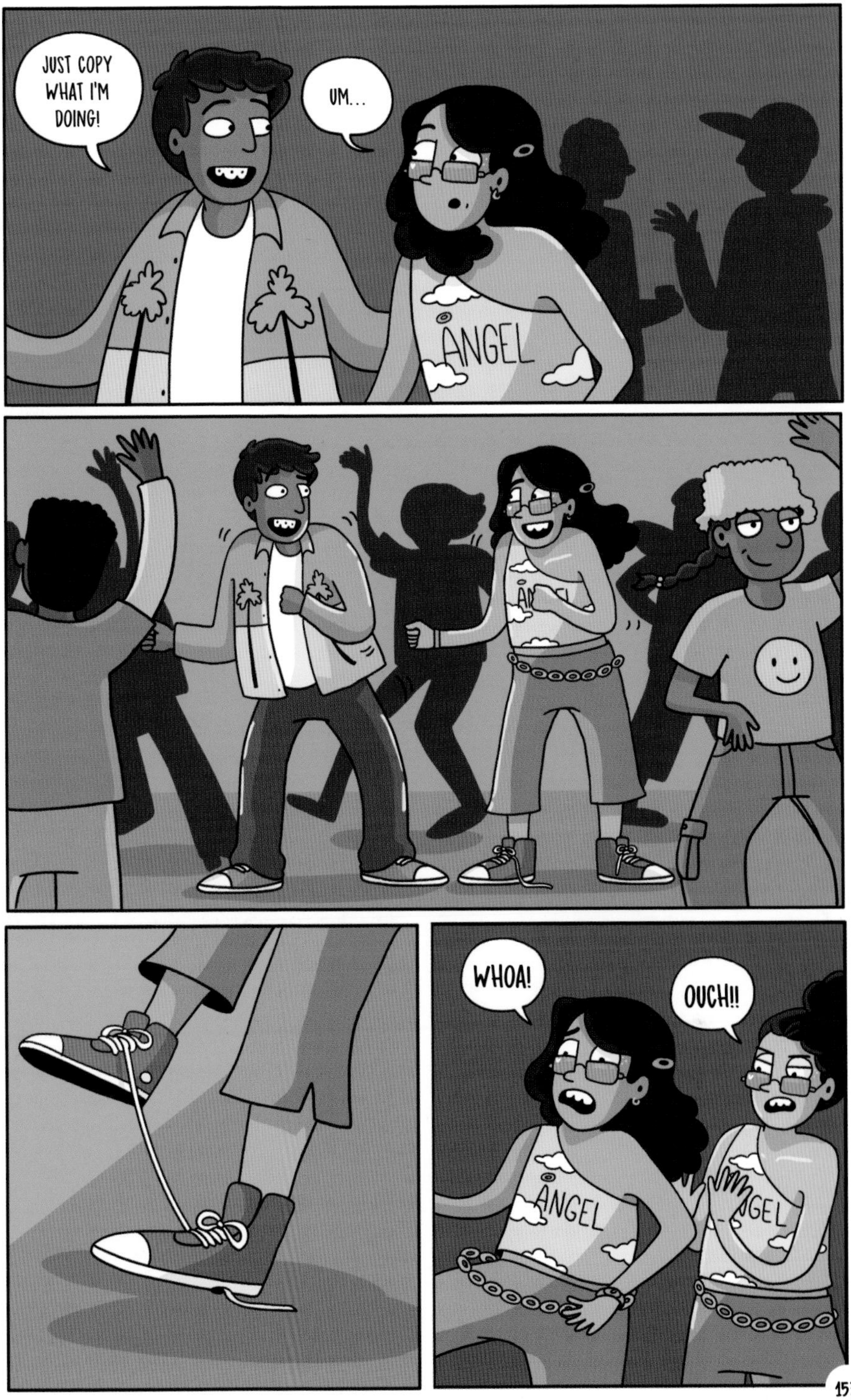
JUST COPY WHAT I'M DOING!
UM...
ANGEL
ANGEL
WHOA!
OUCH!!
ANGEL
ANGEL

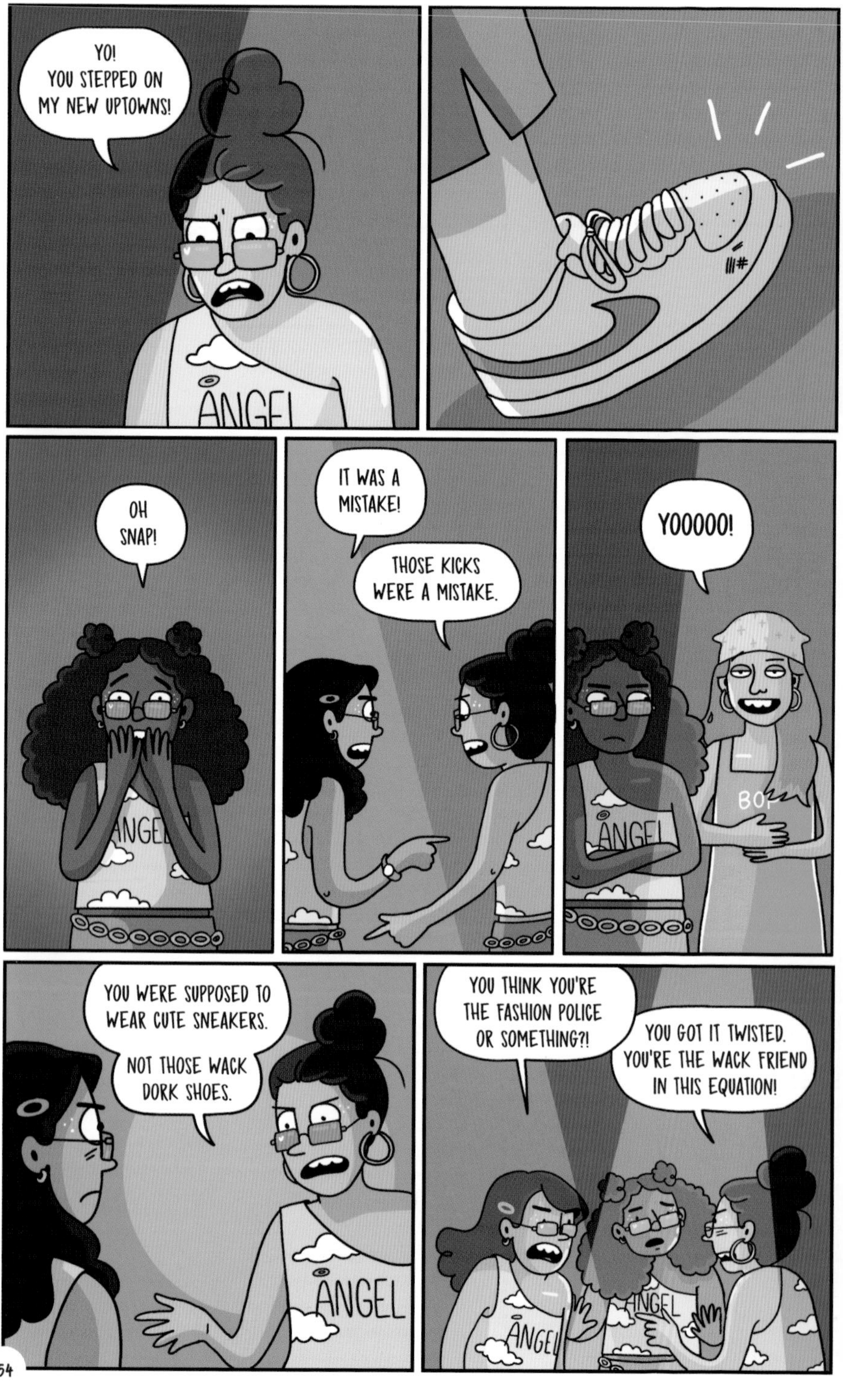
YO!
YOU STEPPED ON MY NEW UPTOWNS!
ANGEL
OH SNAP!
ANGEL
IT WAS A MISTAKE!
THOSE KICKS WERE A MISTAKE.
YOOOOO!
ANGEL
BOI
YOU WERE SUPPOSED TO WEAR CUTE SNEAKERS.
NOT THOSE WACK DORK SHOES.
ANGEL
YOU THINK YOU'RE THE FASHION POLICE OR SOMETHING?!
YOU GOT IT TWISTED. YOU'RE THE WACK FRIEND IN THIS EQUATION!
ANGEL
ANGEL

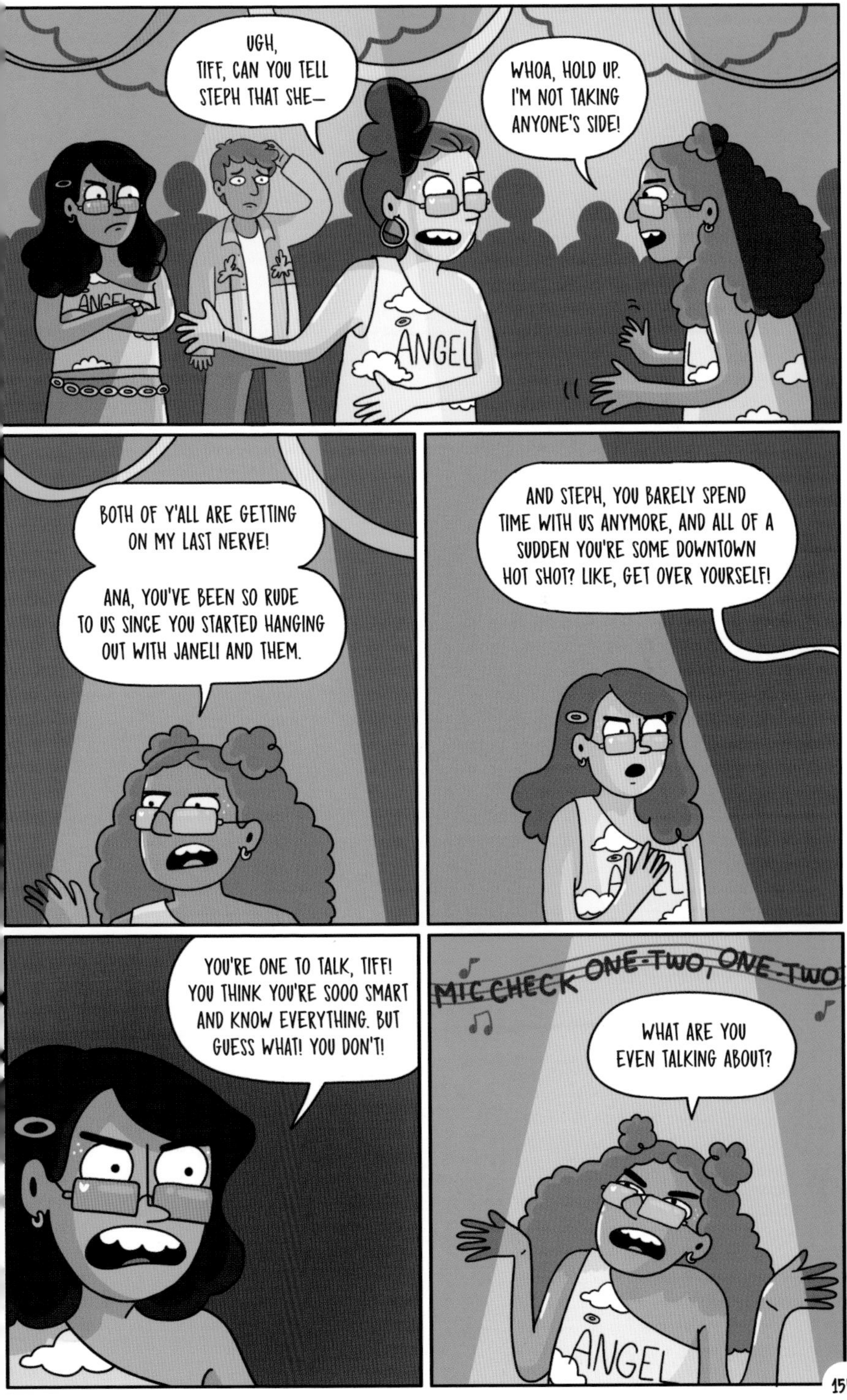
UGH, TIFF, CAN YOU TELL STEPH THAT SHE—
WHOA, HOLD UP. I'M NOT TAKING ANYONE'S SIDE!
ANGEL
ANGEL
BOTH OF Y'ALL ARE GETTING ON MY LAST NERVE!
ANA, YOU'VE BEEN SO RUDE TO US SINCE YOU STARTED HANGING OUT WITH JANELI AND THEM.
AND STEPH, YOU BARELY SPEND TIME WITH US ANYMORE, AND ALL OF A SUDDEN YOU'RE SOME DOWNTOWN HOT SHOT? LIKE, GET OVER YOURSELF!
YOU'RE ONE TO TALK, TIFF! YOU THINK YOU'RE SOOO SMART AND KNOW EVERYTHING. BUT GUESS WHAT! YOU DON'T!
MIC CHECK ONE-TWO, ONE-TWO
WHAT ARE YOU EVEN TALKING ABOUT?
ANGEL

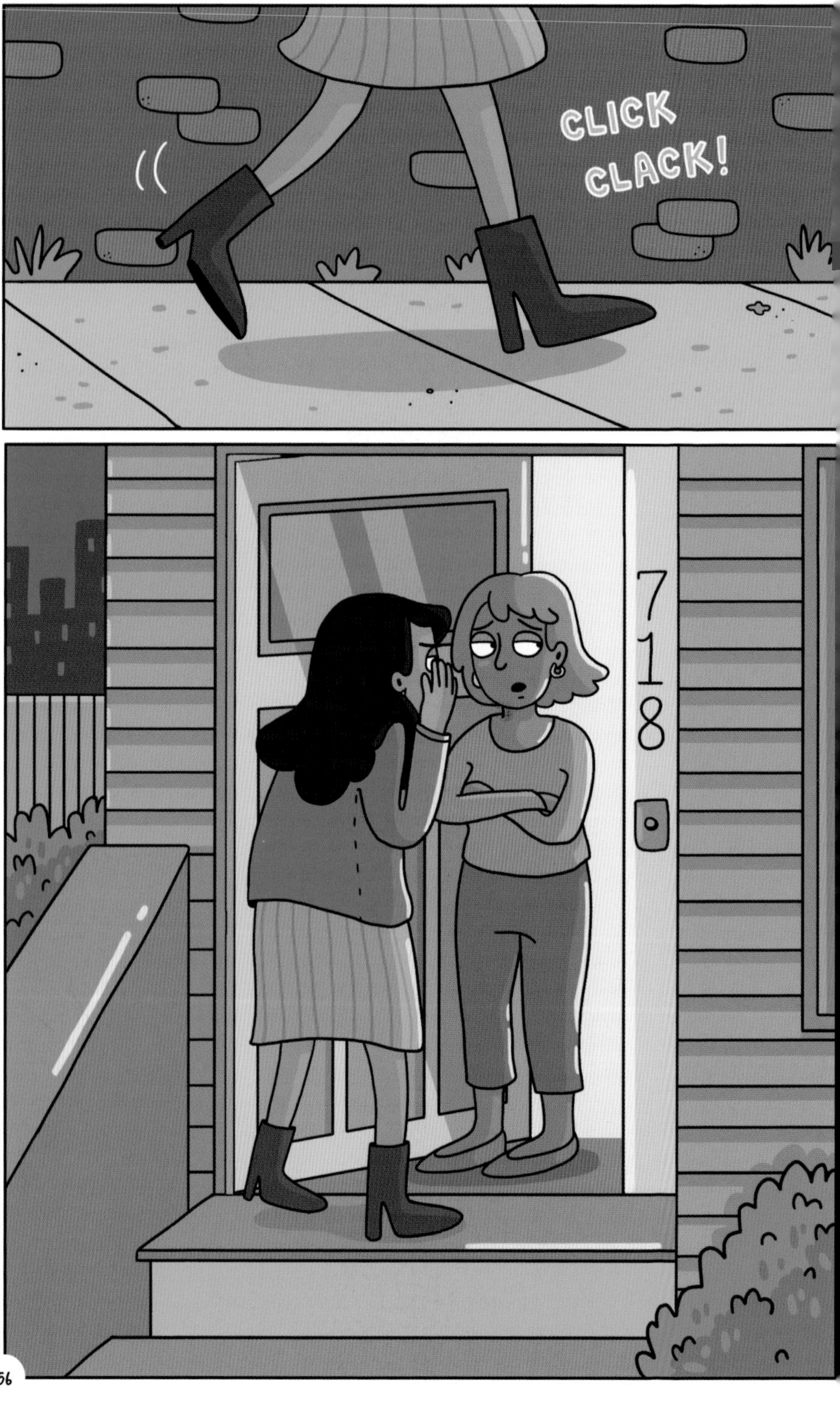
CLICK
CLACK!
718

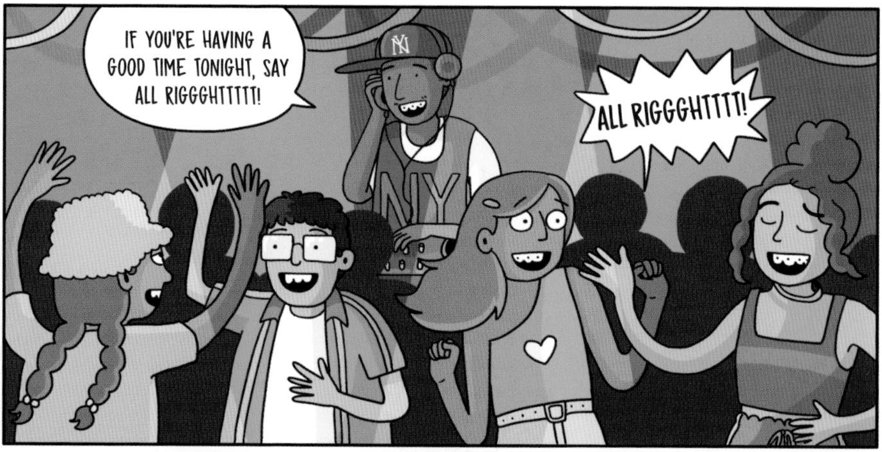
IF YOU'RE HAVING A GOOD TIME TONIGHT, SAY ALL RIGGGHTTTTT!
ALL RIGGGHTTTTT!

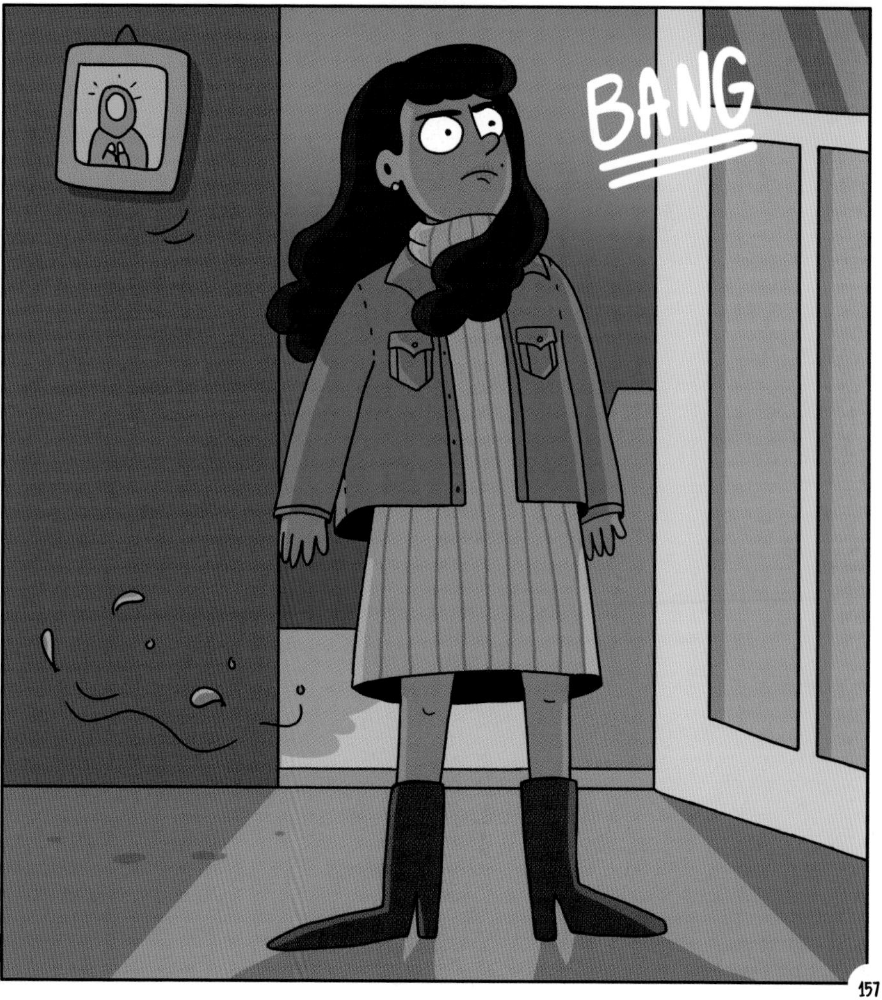
BANG

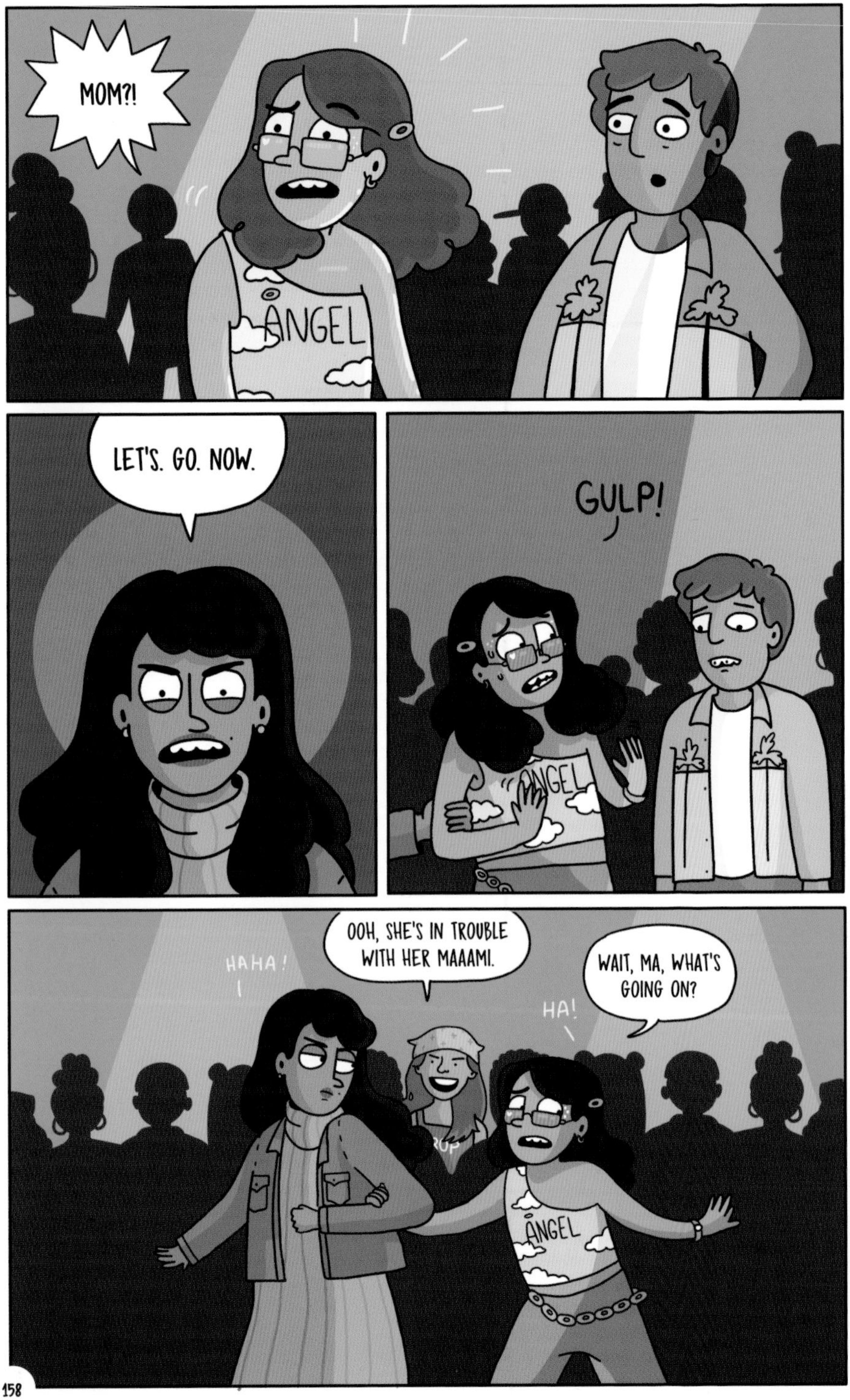
MOM?!
ANGEL
LET'S. GO. NOW.
GULP!
ANGEL
HAHA!
OOH, SHE'S IN TROUBLE WITH HER MAAAMI.
HA!
WAIT, MA, WHAT'S GOING ON?
ANGEL

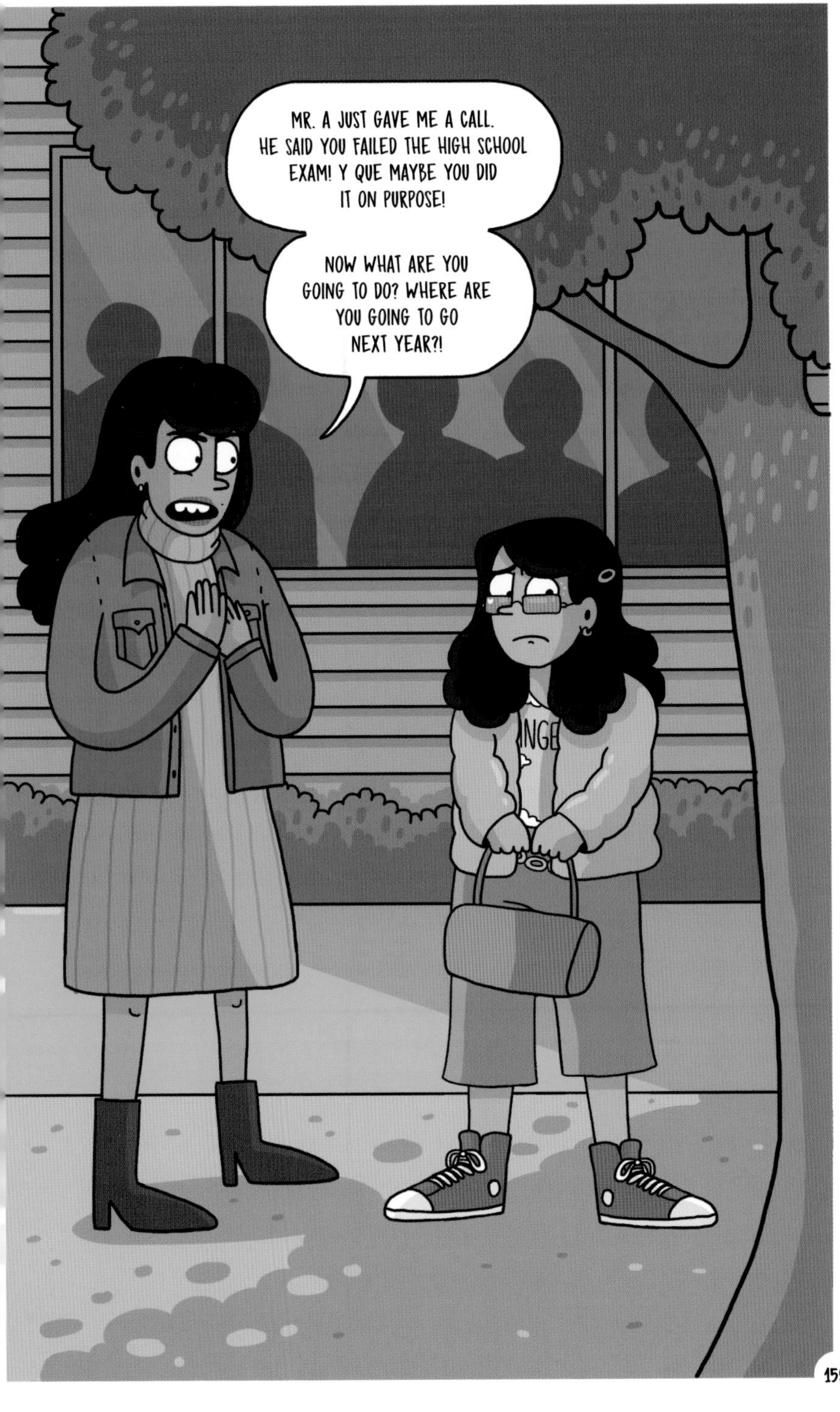
MR. A JUST GAVE ME A CALL. HE SAID YOU FAILED THE HIGH SCHOOL EXAM! Y QUE MAYBE YOU DID IT ON PURPOSE!
NOW WHAT ARE YOU GOING TO DO? WHERE ARE YOU GOING TO GO NEXT YEAR?!
INGE

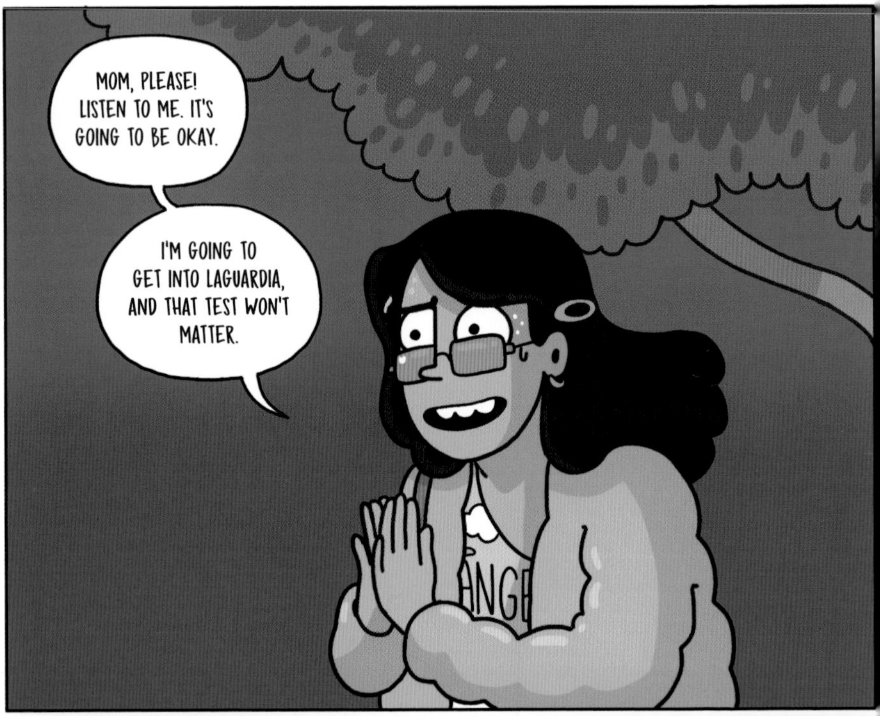
MOM, PLEASE! LISTEN TO ME. IT'S GOING TO BE OKAY.
I'M GOING TO GET INTO LAGUARDIA, AND THAT TEST WON'T MATTER.

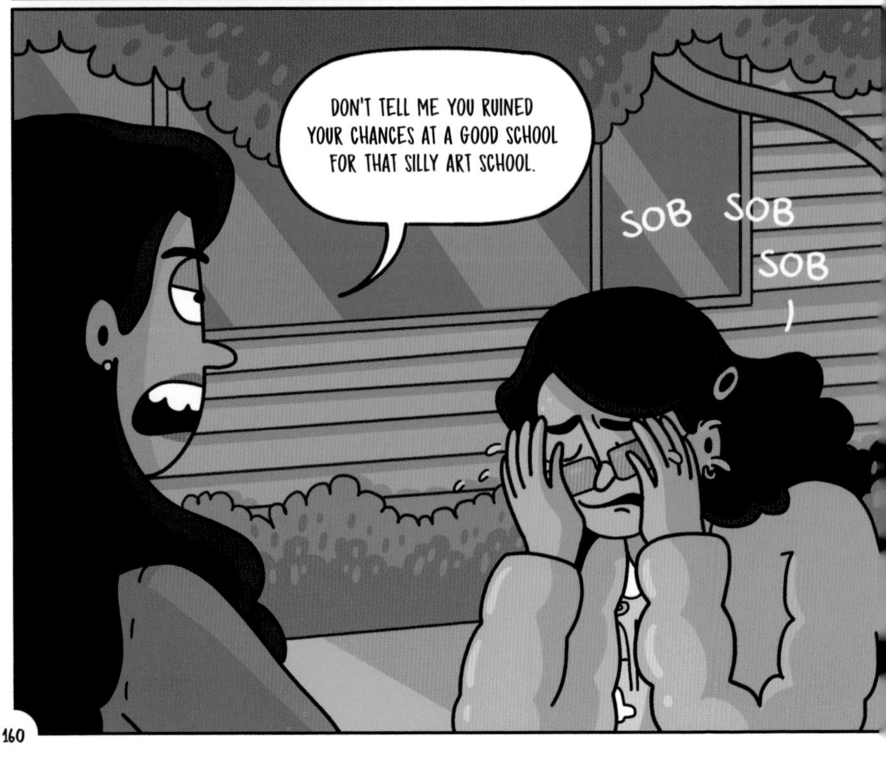
DON'T TELL ME YOU RUINED YOUR CHANCES AT A GOOD SCHOOL FOR THAT SILLY ART SCHOOL.
SOB SOB SOB

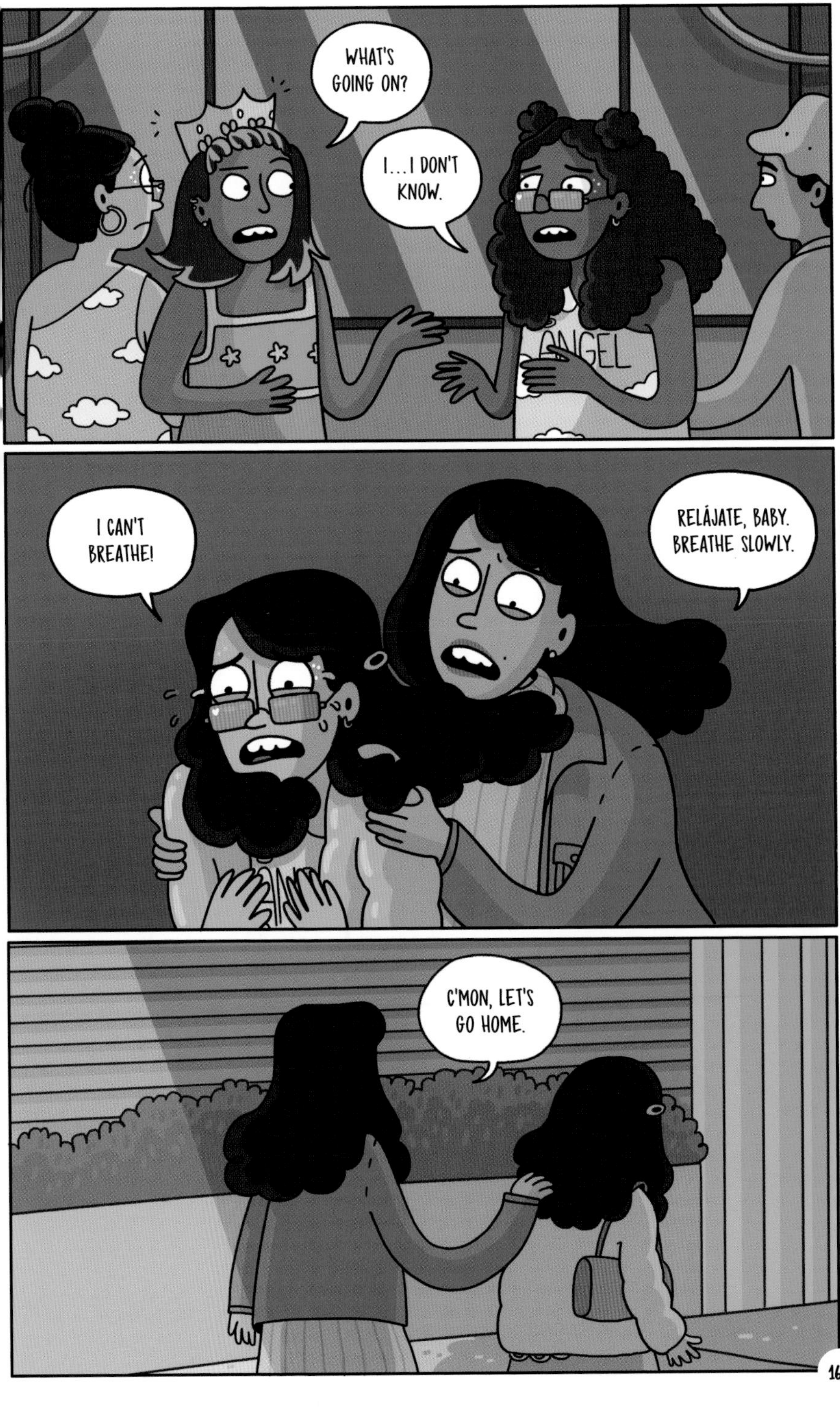
WHAT'S GOING ON?
I... I DON'T KNOW.
ANGEL
I CAN'T BREATHE!
RELÁJATE, BABY. BREATHE SLOWLY.
C'MON, LET'S GO HOME.

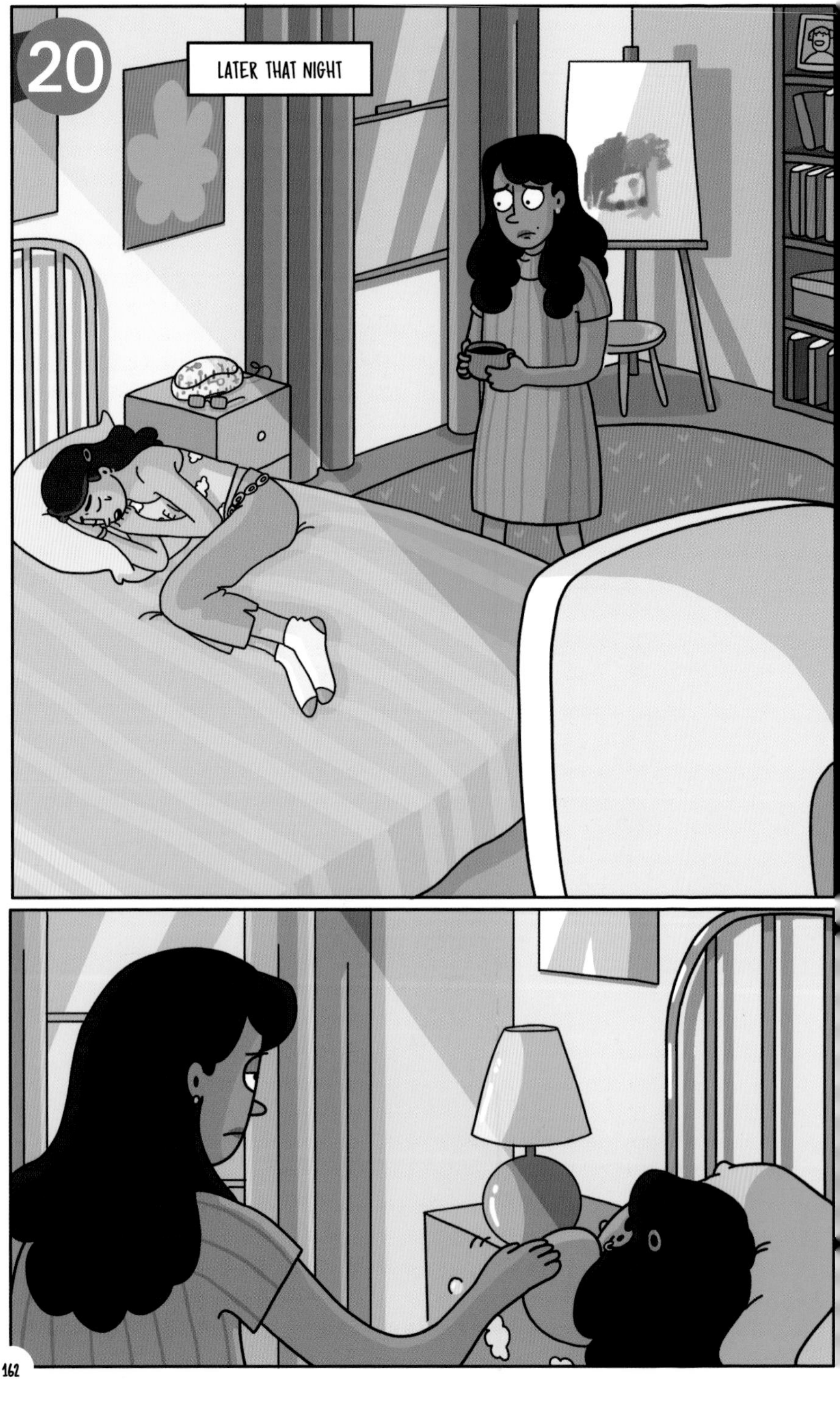
20
LATER THAT NIGHT

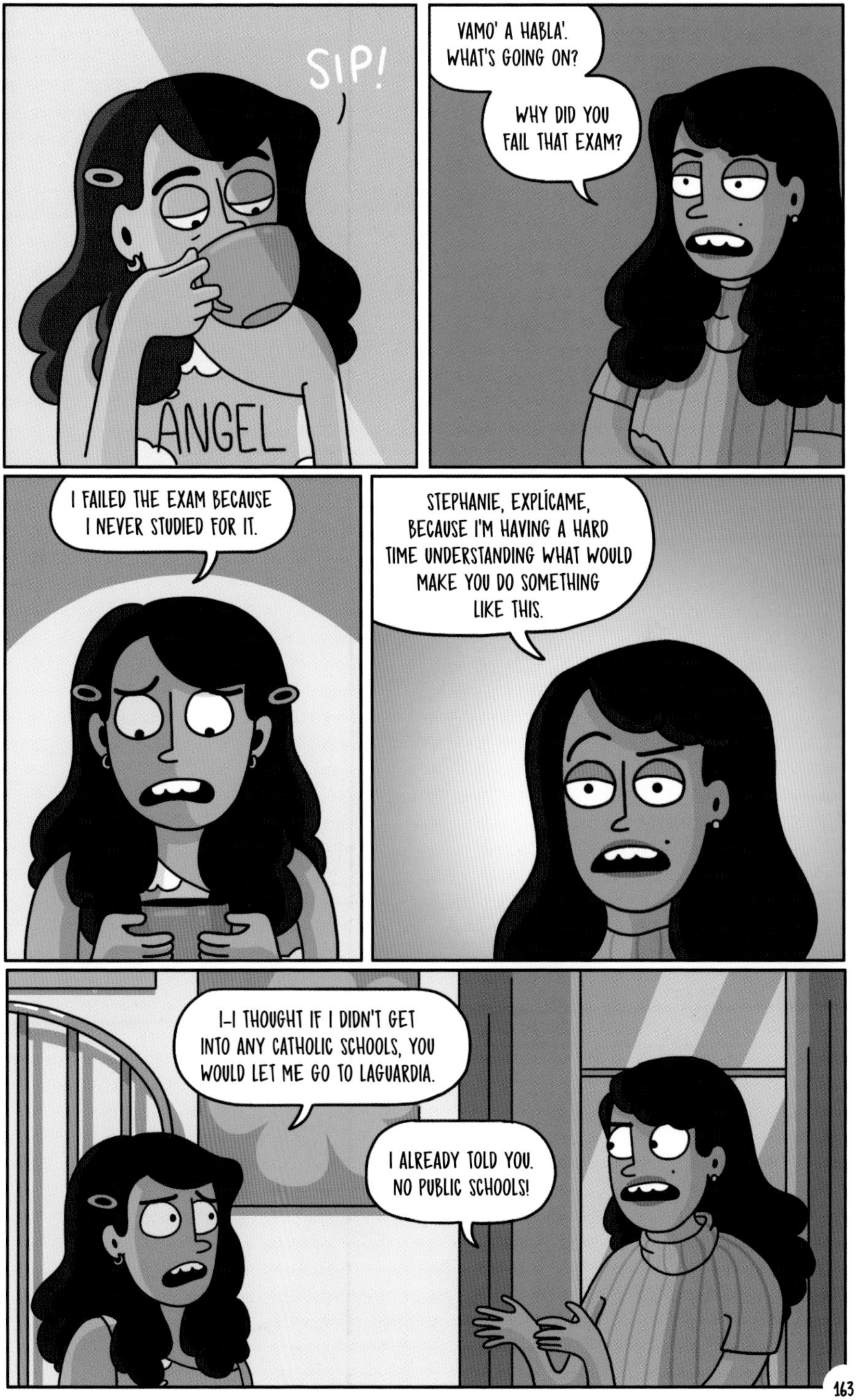
SIP!
ANGEL
VAMO' A HABLA'. WHAT'S GOING ON?
WHY DID YOU FAIL THAT EXAM?
I FAILED THE EXAM BECAUSE I NEVER STUDIED FOR IT.
STEPHANIE, EXPLÍCAME, BECAUSE I'M HAVING A HARD TIME UNDERSTANDING WHAT WOULD MAKE YOU DO SOMETHING LIKE THIS.
I-I THOUGHT IF I DIDN'T GET INTO ANY CATHOLIC SCHOOLS, YOU WOULD LET ME GO TO LAGUARDIA.
I ALREADY TOLD YOU. NO PUBLIC SCHOOLS!

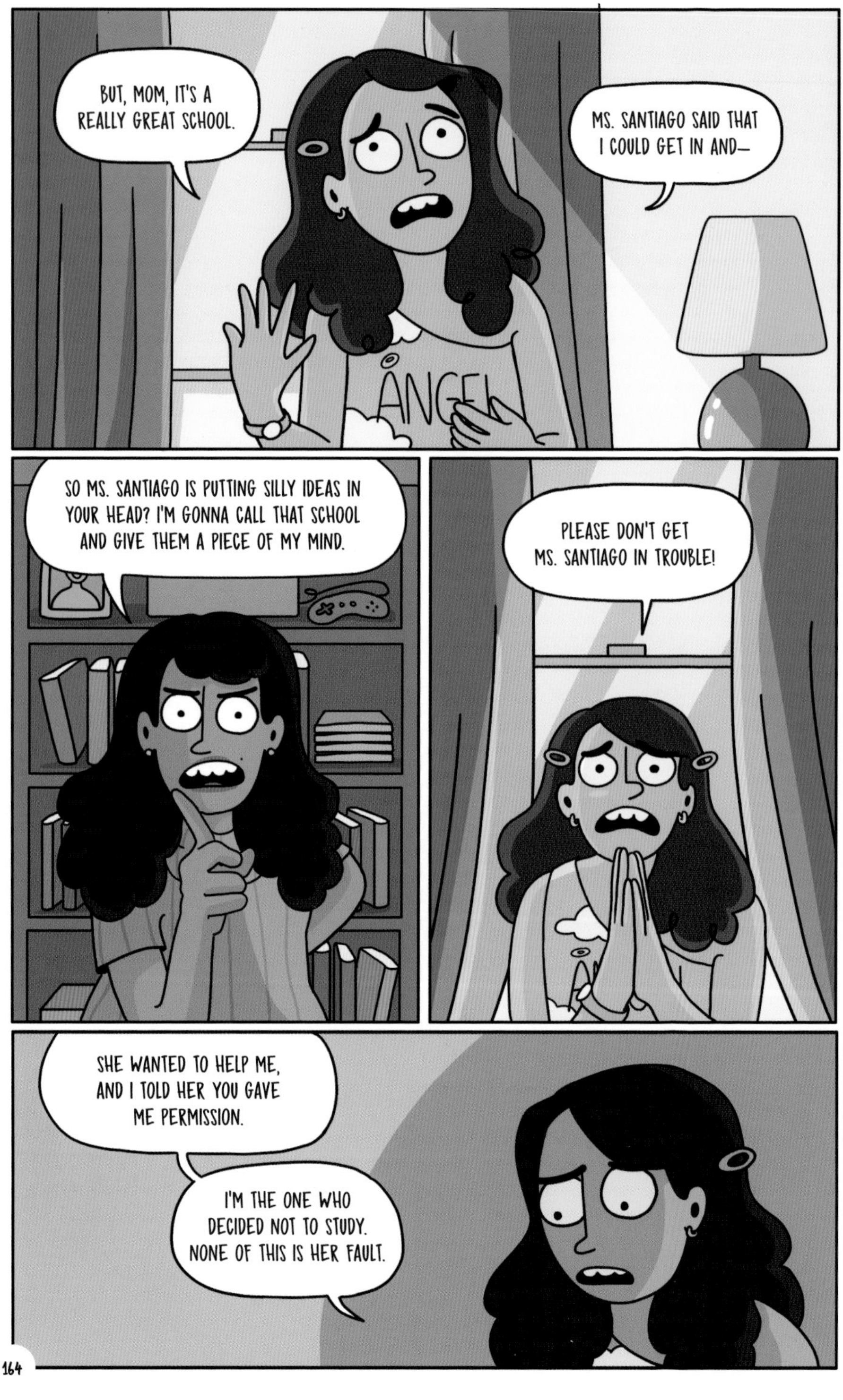
BUT, MOM, IT'S A REALLY GREAT SCHOOL.
MS. SANTIAGO SAID THAT I COULD GET IN AND—
ANGEL
SO MS. SANTIAGO IS PUTTING SILLY IDEAS IN YOUR HEAD? I'M GONNA CALL THAT SCHOOL AND GIVE THEM A PIECE OF MY MIND.
PLEASE DON'T GET MS. SANTIAGO IN TROUBLE!
SHE WANTED TO HELP ME, AND I TOLD HER YOU GAVE ME PERMISSION.
I'M THE ONE WHO DECIDED NOT TO STUDY. NONE OF THIS IS HER FAULT.

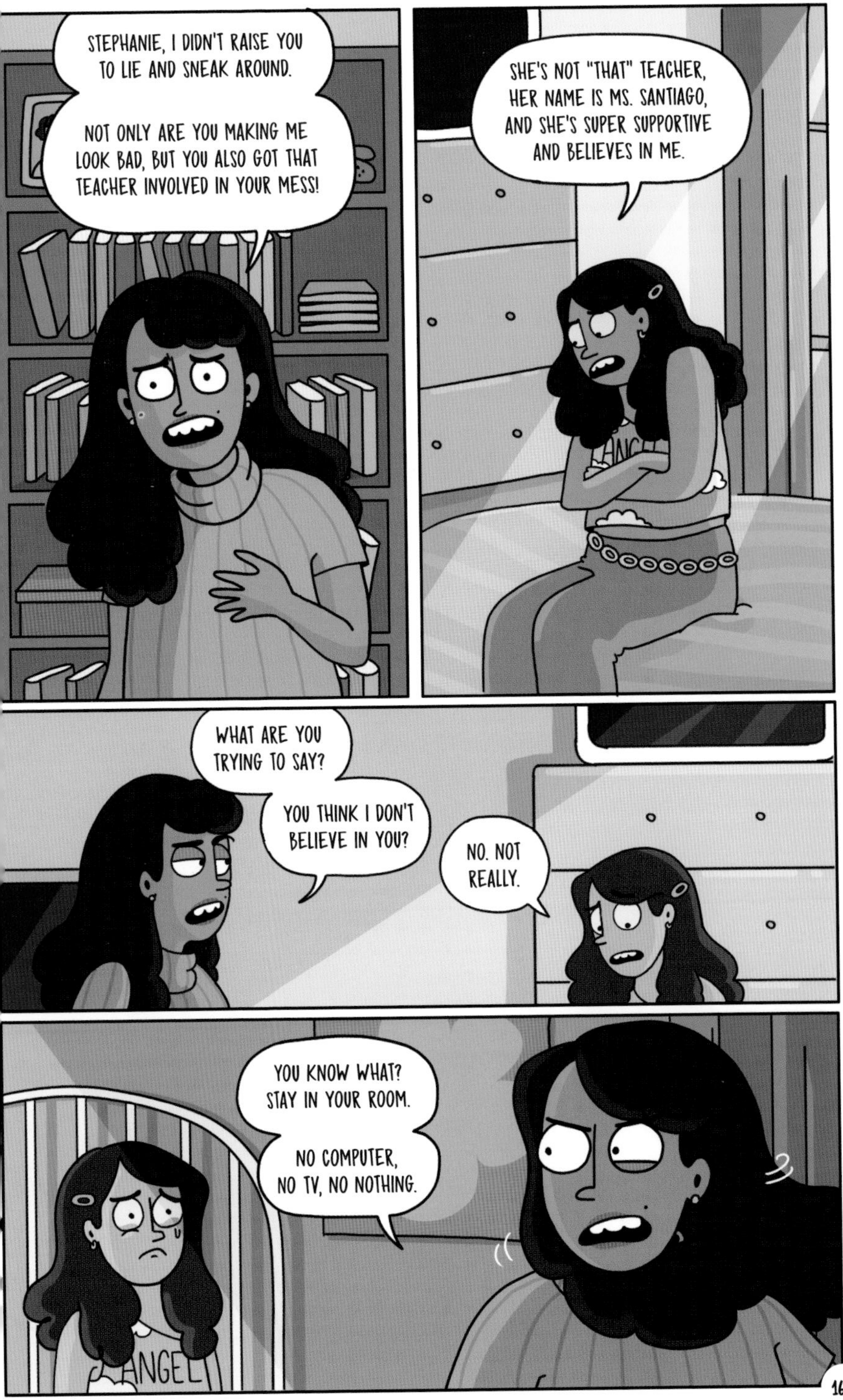
STEPHANIE, I DIDN'T RAISE YOU TO LIE AND SNEAK AROUND.
NOT ONLY ARE YOU MAKING ME LOOK BAD, BUT YOU ALSO GOT THAT TEACHER INVOLVED IN YOUR MESS!
SHE'S NOT "THAT" TEACHER, HER NAME IS MS. SANTIAGO, AND SHE'S SUPER SUPPORTIVE AND BELIEVES IN ME.
ANGEL
WHAT ARE YOU TRYING TO SAY?
YOU THINK I DON'T BELIEVE IN YOU?
NO. NOT REALLY.
YOU KNOW WHAT? STAY IN YOUR ROOM.
NO COMPUTER, NO TV, NO NOTHING.
ANGEL

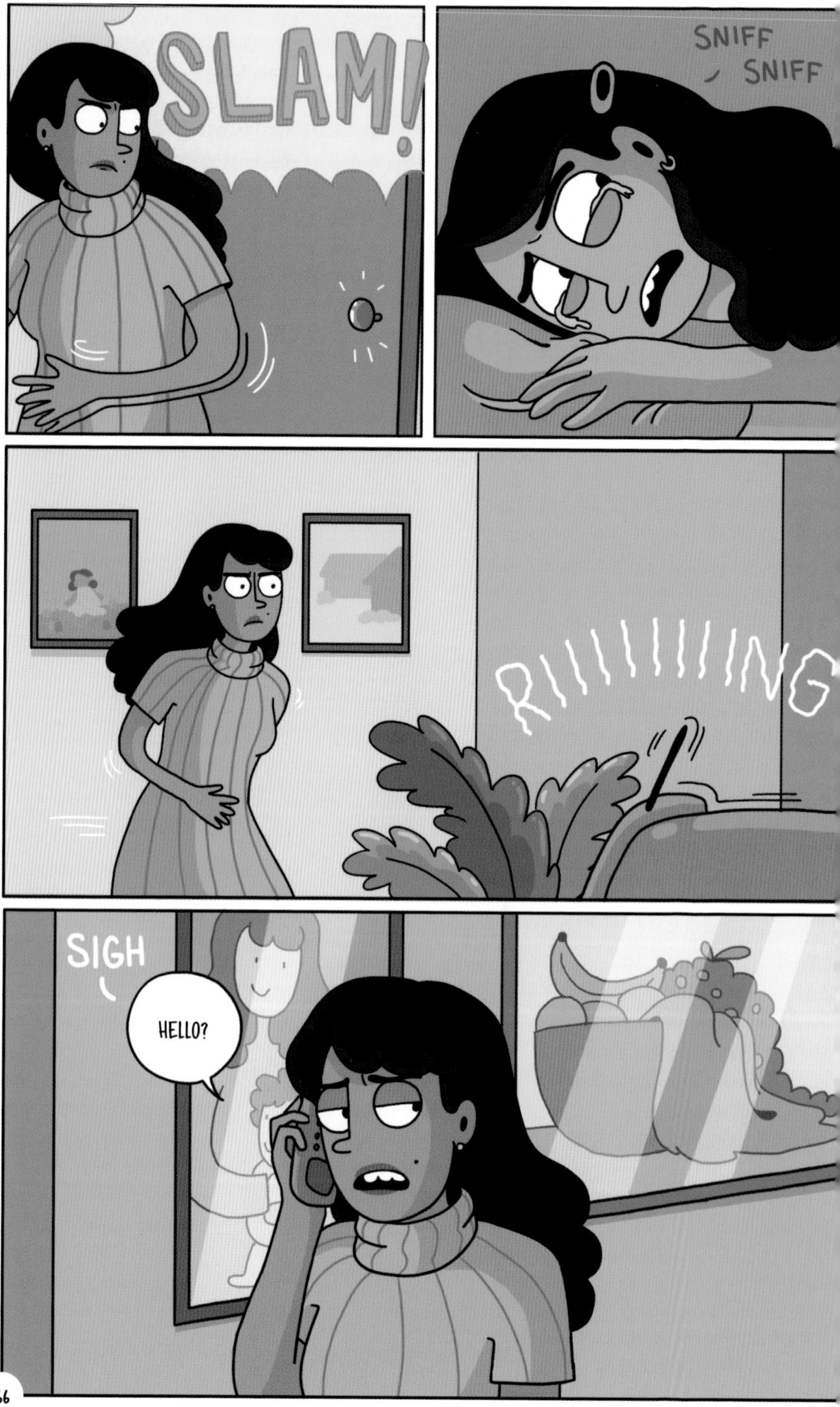
SLAM!
SNIFF
SNIFF
RIIIIIIING
SIGH
HELLO?

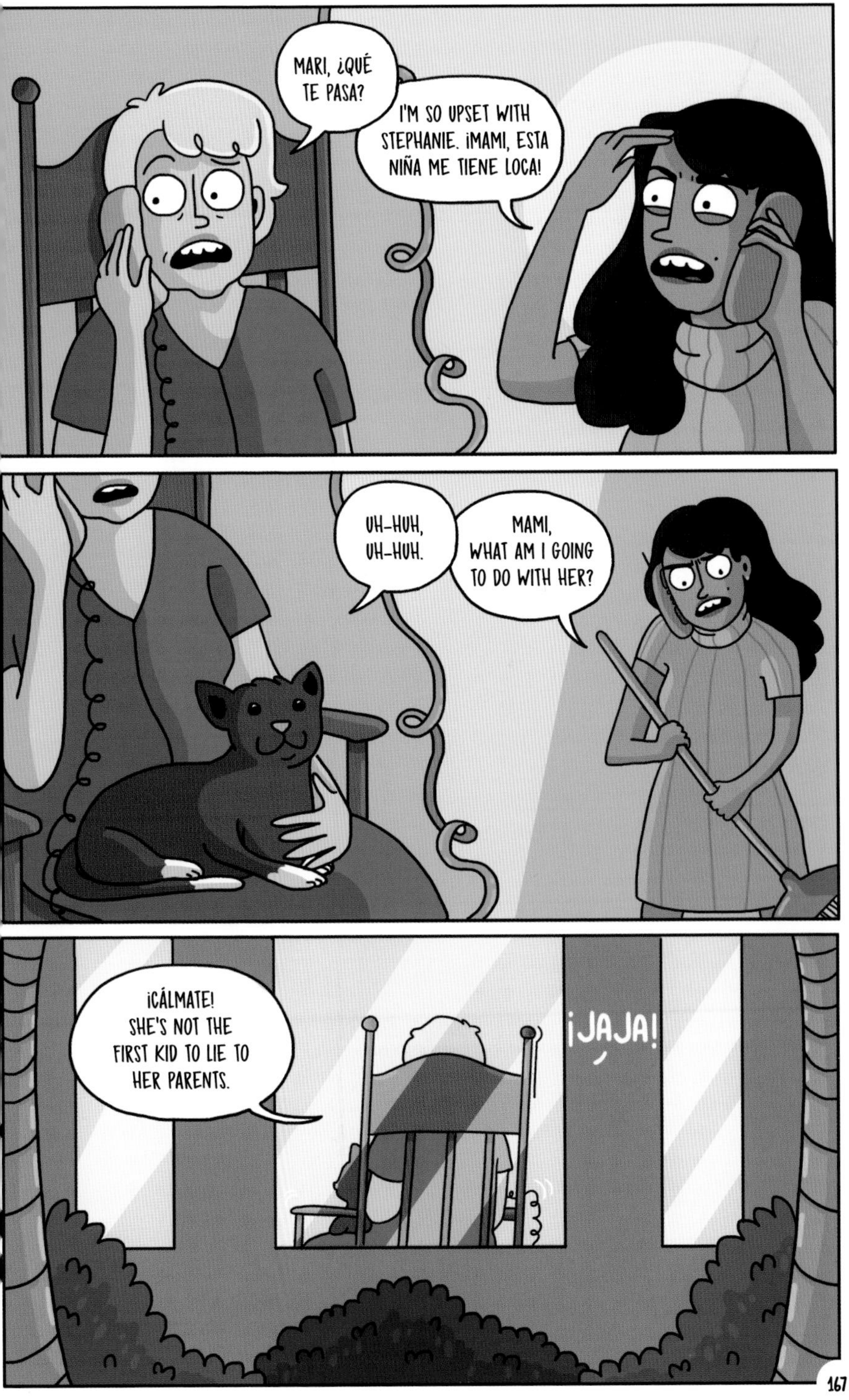
MARI, ¿QUÉ TE PASA?
I'M SO UPSET WITH STEPHANIE. ¡MAMI, ESTA NIÑA ME TIENE LOCA!
UH-HUH, UH-HUH.
MAMI, WHAT AM I GOING TO DO WITH HER?
¡CÁLMATE! SHE'S NOT THE FIRST KID TO LIE TO HER PARENTS.
¡JAJA!

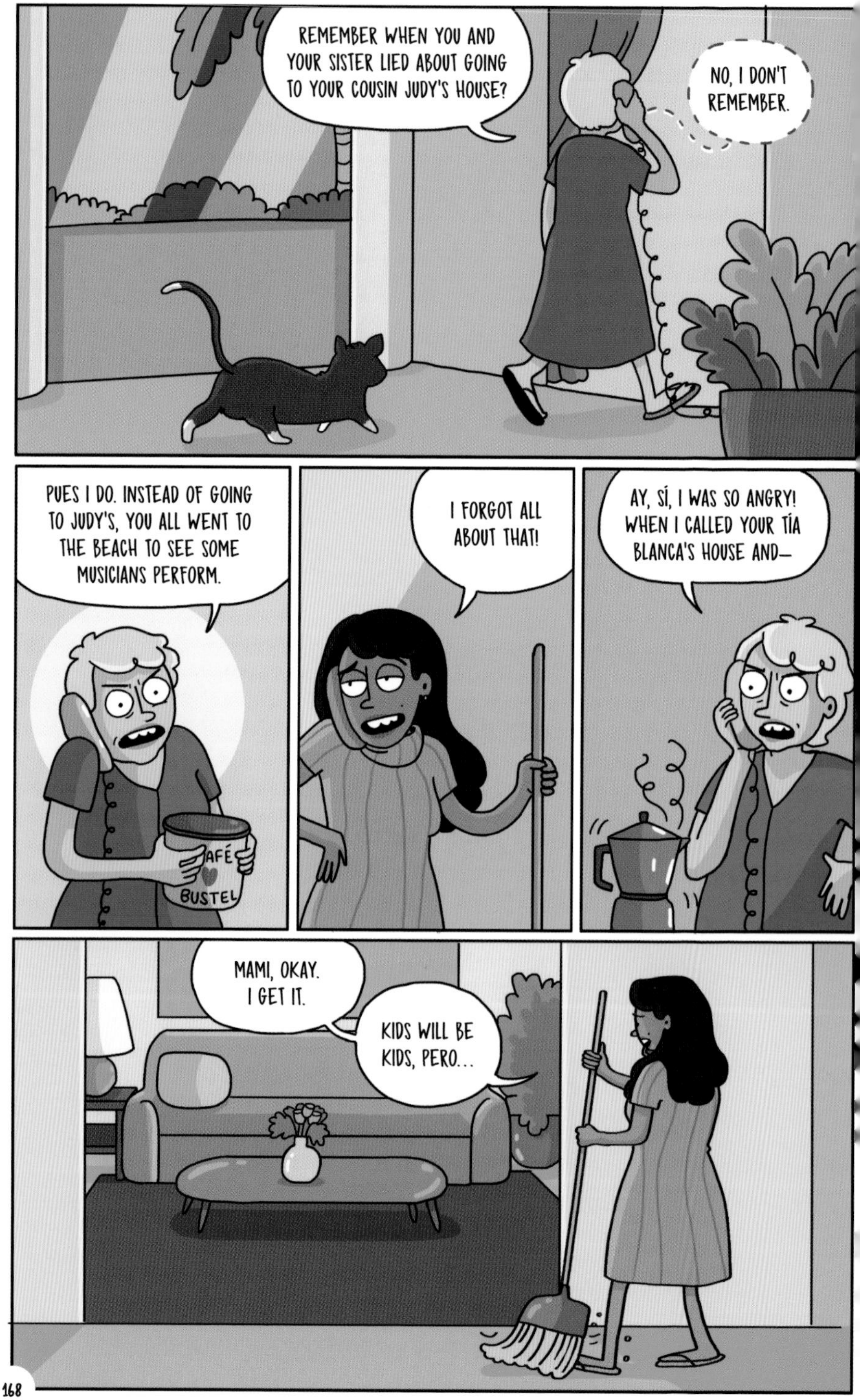

REMEMBER WHEN YOU AND YOUR SISTER LIED ABOUT GOING TO YOUR COUSIN JUDY'S HOUSE?
NO, I DON'T REMEMBER.
PUES I DO. INSTEAD OF GOING TO JUDY'S, YOU ALL WENT TO THE BEACH TO SEE SOME MUSICIANS PERFORM.
AFÉ BUSTEL
I FORGOT ALL ABOUT THAT!
AY, SÍ, I WAS SO ANGRY! WHEN I CALLED YOUR TÍA BLANCA'S HOUSE AND—
MAMI, OKAY. I GET IT.
KIDS WILL BE KIDS, PERO...

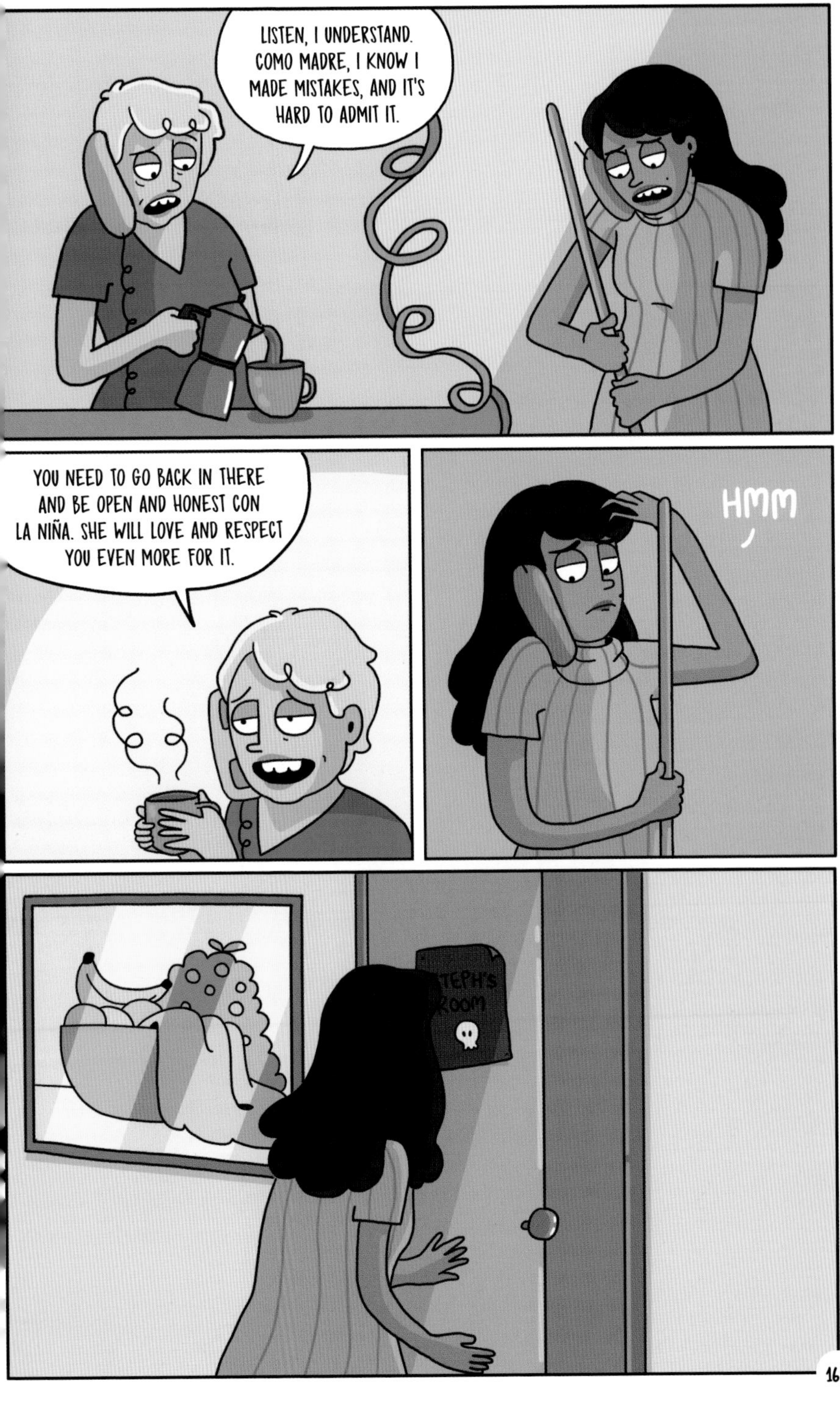
LISTEN, I UNDERSTAND. COMO MADRE, I KNOW I MADE MISTAKES, AND IT'S HARD TO ADMIT IT.
YOU NEED TO GO BACK IN THERE AND BE OPEN AND HONEST CON LA NIÑA. SHE WILL LOVE AND RESPECT YOU EVEN MORE FOR IT.
HMM
STEPH'S ROOM

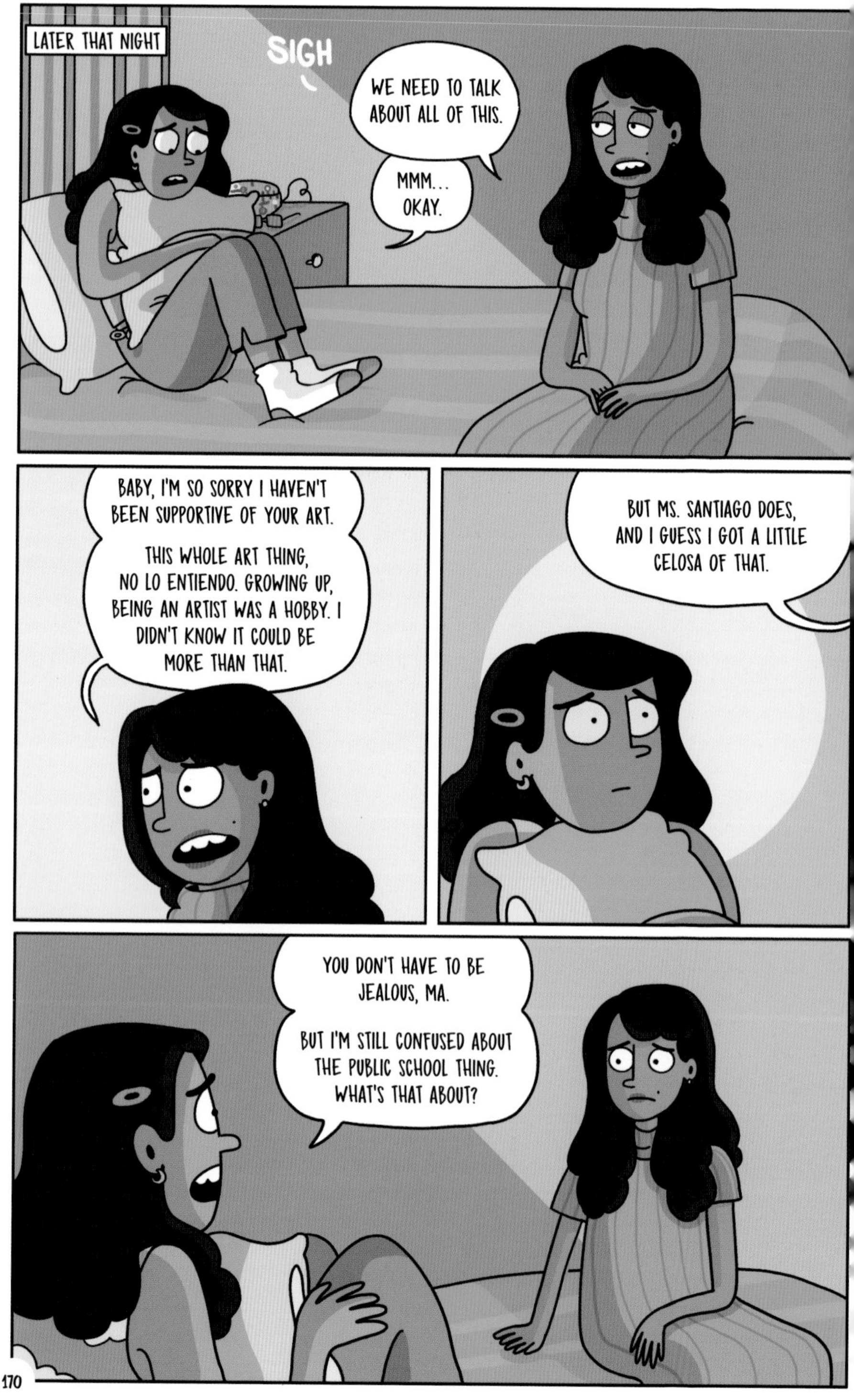
LATER THAT NIGHT
SIGH
WE NEED TO TALK ABOUT ALL OF THIS.
MMM... OKAY.
BABY, I'M SO SORRY I HAVEN'T BEEN SUPPORTIVE OF YOUR ART.
THIS WHOLE ART THING, NO LO ENTIENDO. GROWING UP, BEING AN ARTIST WAS A HOBBY. I DIDN'T KNOW IT COULD BE MORE THAN THAT.
BUT MS. SANTIAGO DOES, AND I GUESS I GOT A LITTLE CELOSA OF THAT.
YOU DON'T HAVE TO BE JEALOUS, MA.
BUT I'M STILL CONFUSED ABOUT THE PUBLIC SCHOOL THING. WHAT'S THAT ABOUT?

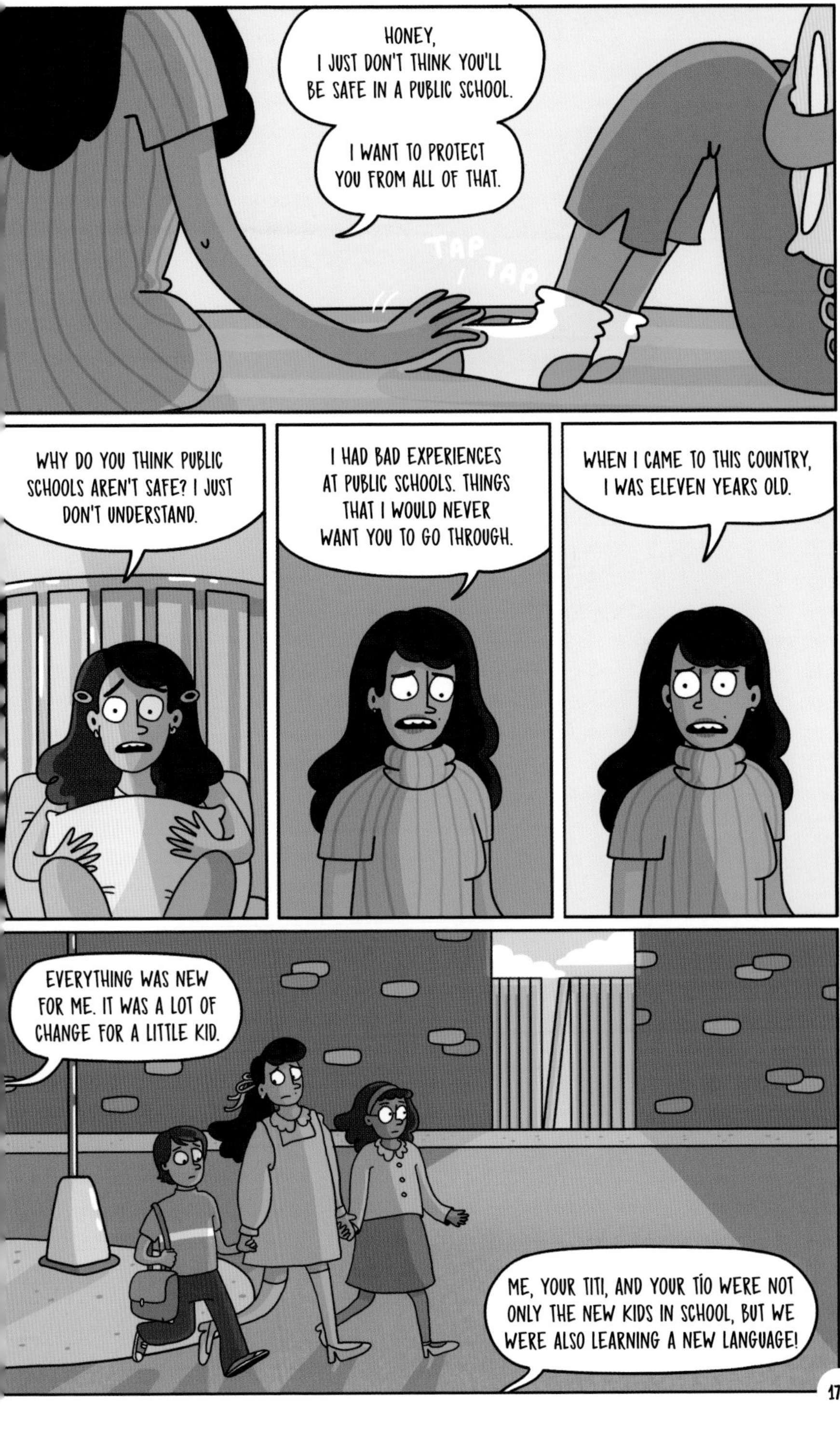
HONEY, I JUST DON'T THINK YOU'LL BE SAFE IN A PUBLIC SCHOOL.
I WANT TO PROTECT YOU FROM ALL OF THAT.
TAP TAP
WHY DO YOU THINK PUBLIC SCHOOLS AREN'T SAFE? I JUST DON'T UNDERSTAND.
I HAD BAD EXPERIENCES AT PUBLIC SCHOOLS. THINGS THAT I WOULD NEVER WANT YOU TO GO THROUGH.
WHEN I CAME TO THIS COUNTRY, I WAS ELEVEN YEARS OLD.
EVERYTHING WAS NEW FOR ME. IT WAS A LOT OF CHANGE FOR A LITTLE KID.
ME, YOUR TITI, AND YOUR TÍO WERE NOT ONLY THE NEW KIDS IN SCHOOL, BUT WE WERE ALSO LEARNING A NEW LANGUAGE!

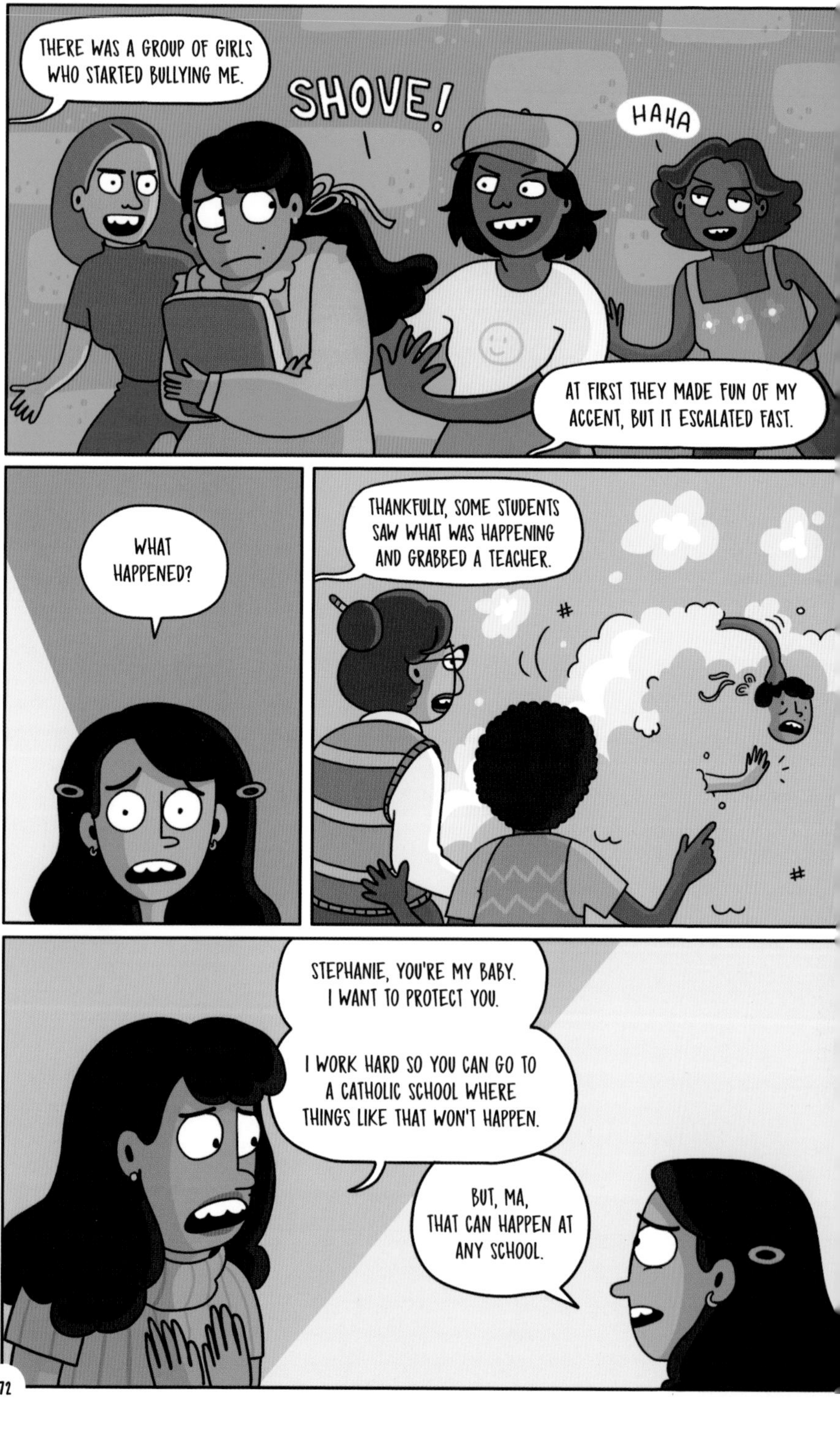
THERE WAS A GROUP OF GIRLS WHO STARTED BULLYING ME.
SHOVE!
HAHA
AT FIRST THEY MADE FUN OF MY ACCENT, BUT IT ESCALATED FAST.
WHAT HAPPENED?
THANKFULLY, SOME STUDENTS SAW WHAT WAS HAPPENING AND GRABBED A TEACHER.
STEPHANIE, YOU'RE MY BABY. I WANT TO PROTECT YOU.
I WORK HARD SO YOU CAN GO TO A CATHOLIC SCHOOL WHERE THINGS LIKE THAT WON'T HAPPEN.
BUT, MA, THAT CAN HAPPEN AT ANY SCHOOL.

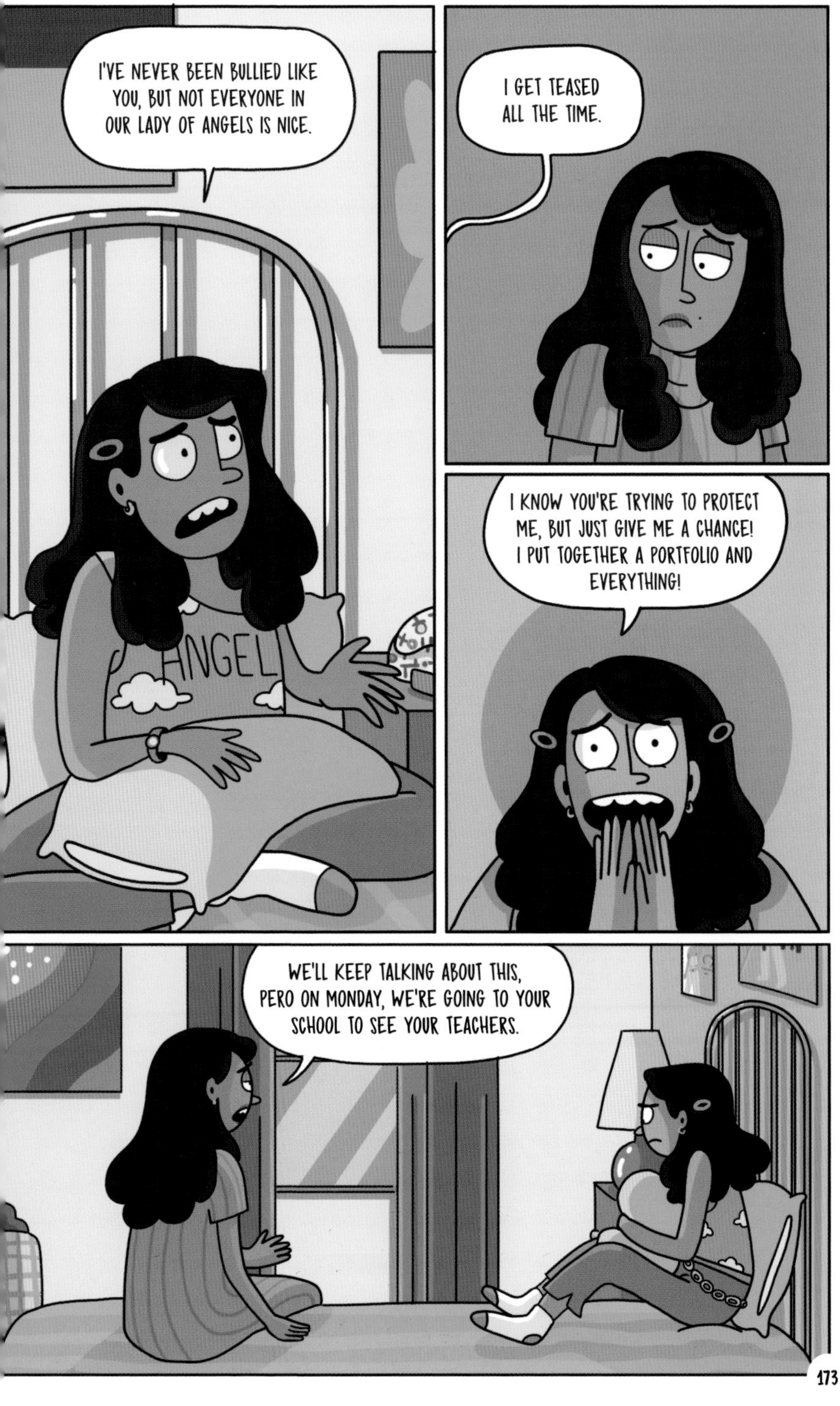
I'VE NEVER BEEN BULLIED LIKE YOU, BUT NOT EVERYONE IN OUR LADY OF ANGELS IS NICE.
ANGEL
I GET TEASED ALL THE TIME.
I KNOW YOU'RE TRYING TO PROTECT ME, BUT JUST GIVE ME A CHANCE! I PUT TOGETHER A PORTFOLIO AND EVERYTHING!
WE'LL KEEP TALKING ABOUT THIS, PERO ON MONDAY, WE'RE GOING TO YOUR SCHOOL TO SEE YOUR TEACHERS.

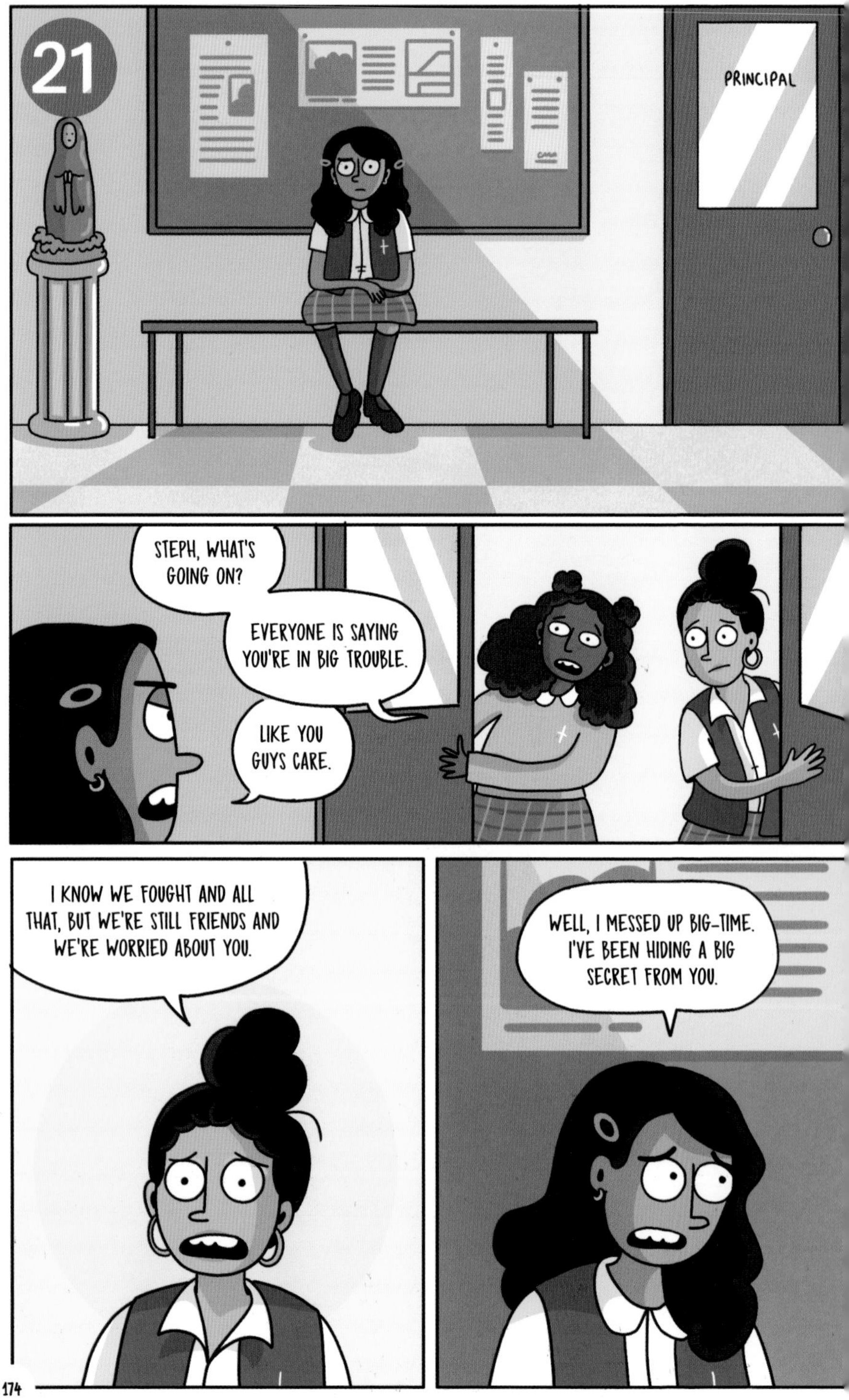
21
PRINCIPAL
STEPH, WHAT'S GOING ON?
EVERYONE IS SAYING YOU'RE IN BIG TROUBLE.
LIKE YOU GUYS CARE.
I KNOW WE FOUGHT AND ALL THAT, BUT WE'RE STILL FRIENDS AND WE'RE WORRIED ABOUT YOU.
WELL, I MESSED UP BIG-TIME. I'VE BEEN HIDING A BIG SECRET FROM YOU.

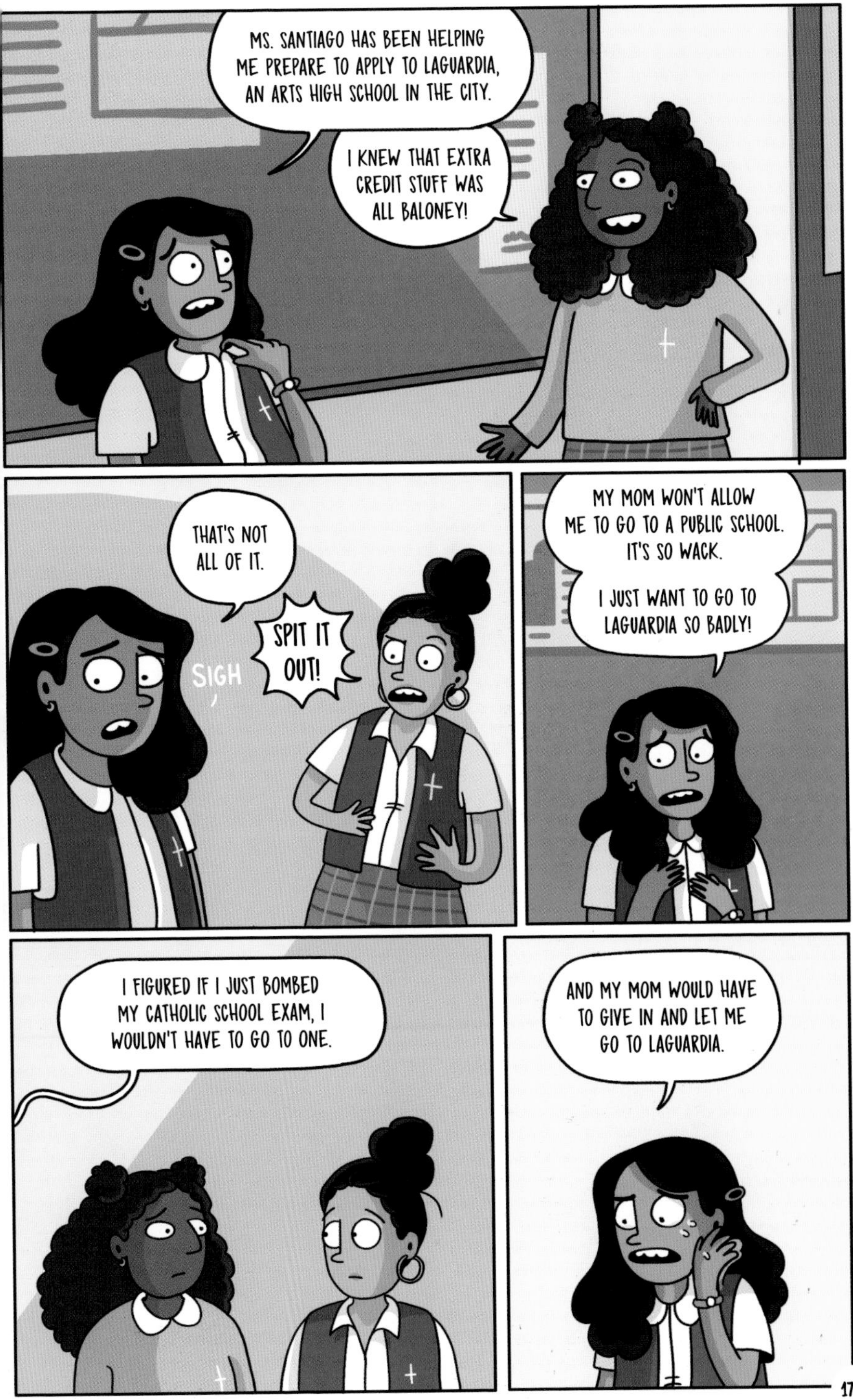
MS. SANTIAGO HAS BEEN HELPING ME PREPARE TO APPLY TO LAGUARDIA, AN ARTS HIGH SCHOOL IN THE CITY.
I KNEW THAT EXTRA CREDIT STUFF WAS ALL BALONEY!
THAT'S NOT ALL OF IT.
SIGH
SPIT IT OUT!
MY MOM WON'T ALLOW ME TO GO TO A PUBLIC SCHOOL. IT'S SO WACK.
I JUST WANT TO GO TO LAGUARDIA SO BADLY!
I FIGURED IF I JUST BOMBED MY CATHOLIC SCHOOL EXAM, I WOULDN'T HAVE TO GO TO ONE.
AND MY MOM WOULD HAVE TO GIVE IN AND LET ME GO TO LAGUARDIA.

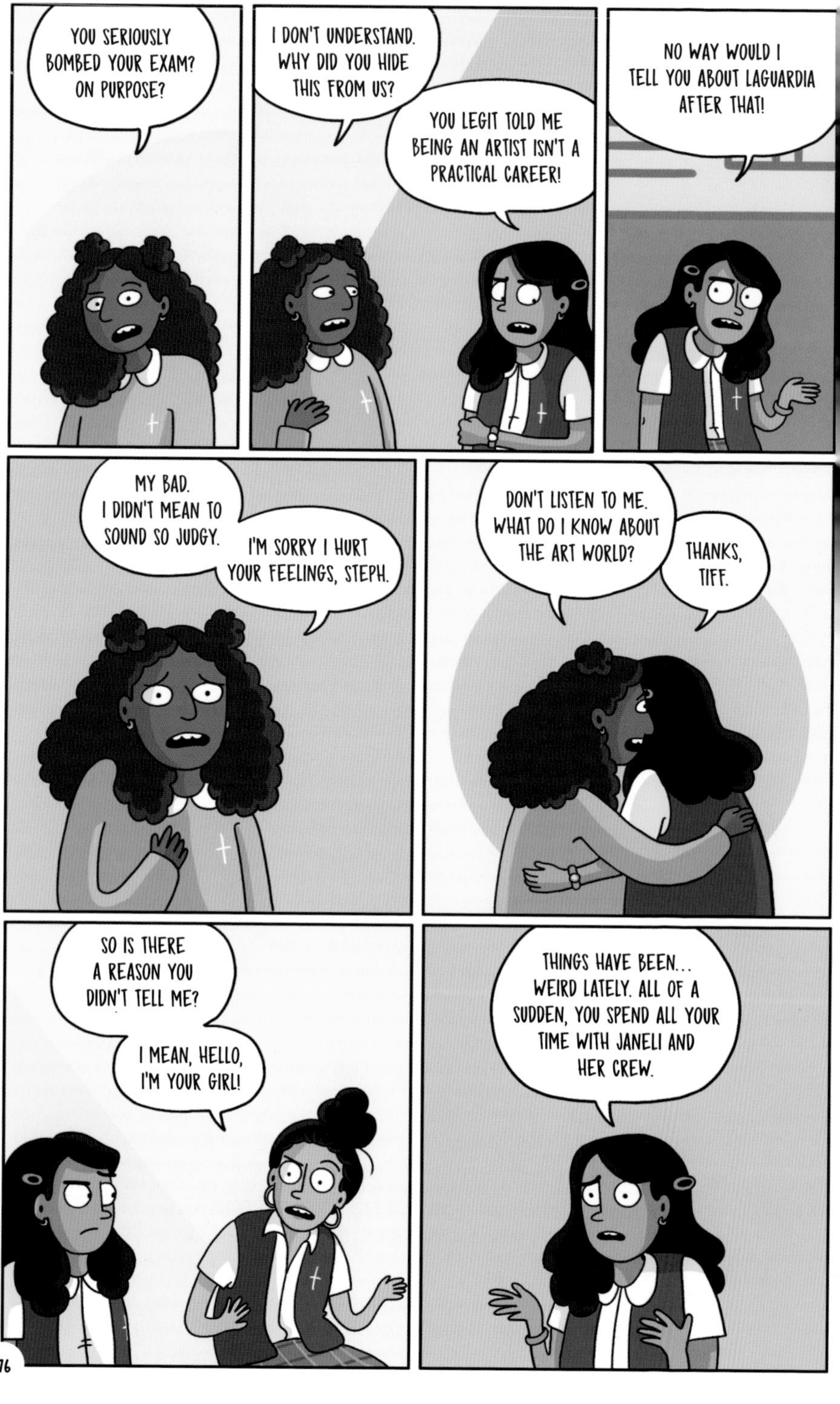
YOU SERIOUSLY BOMBED YOUR EXAM? ON PURPOSE?
I DON'T UNDERSTAND. WHY DID YOU HIDE THIS FROM US?
YOU LEGIT TOLD ME BEING AN ARTIST ISN'T A PRACTICAL CAREER!
NO WAY WOULD I TELL YOU ABOUT LAGUARDIA AFTER THAT!
MY BAD. I DIDN'T MEAN TO SOUND SO JUDGY.
I'M SORRY I HURT YOUR FEELINGS, STEPH.
DON'T LISTEN TO ME. WHAT DO I KNOW ABOUT THE ART WORLD?
THANKS, TIFF.
SO IS THERE A REASON YOU DIDN'T TELL ME?
I MEAN, HELLO, I'M YOUR GIRL!
THINGS HAVE BEEN... WEIRD LATELY. ALL OF A SUDDEN, YOU SPEND ALL YOUR TIME WITH JANELI AND HER CREW.

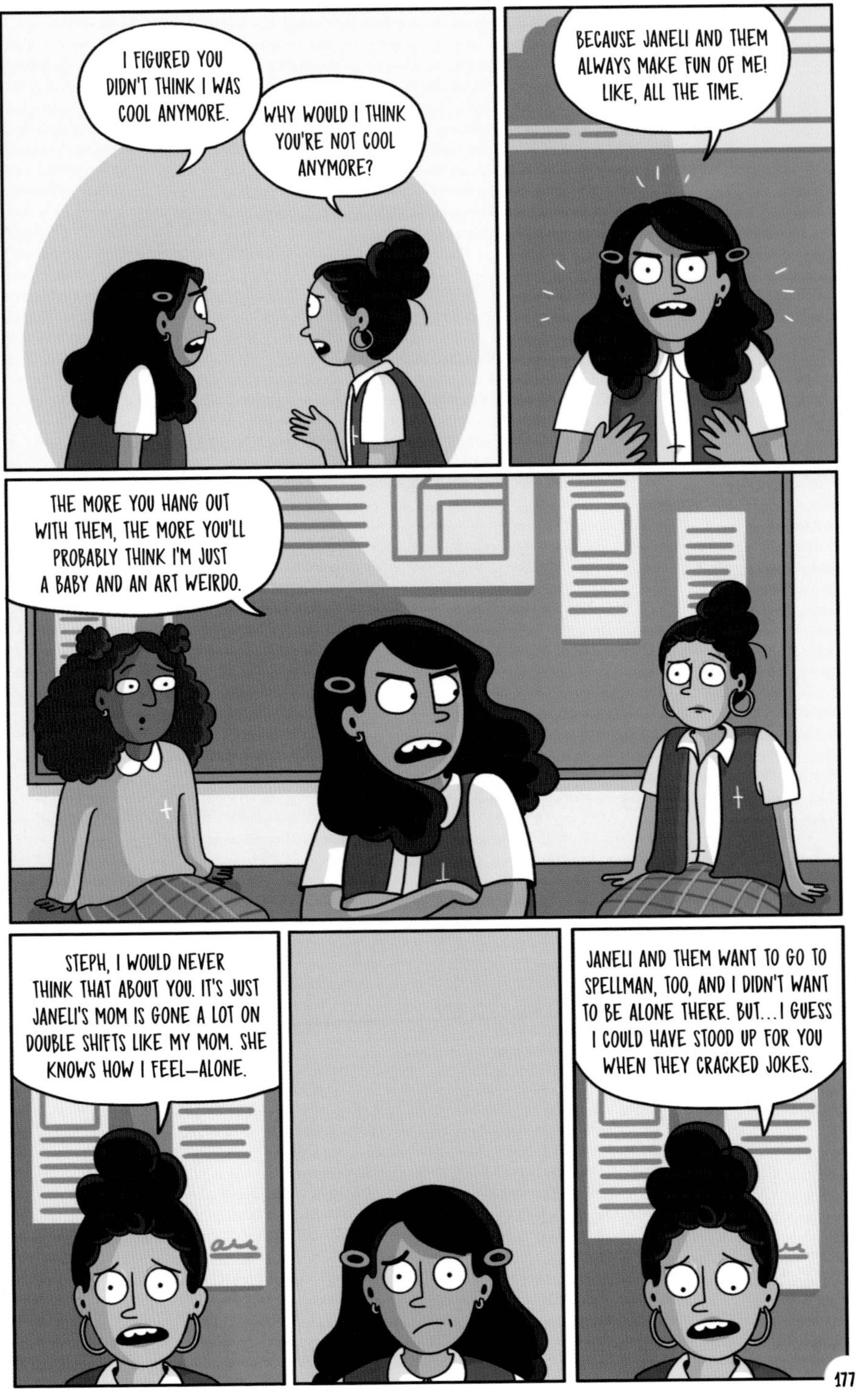

I FIGURED YOU DIDN'T THINK I WAS COOL ANYMORE.
WHY WOULD I THINK YOU'RE NOT COOL ANYMORE?
BECAUSE JANELI AND THEM ALWAYS MAKE FUN OF ME! LIKE, ALL THE TIME.
THE MORE YOU HANG OUT WITH THEM, THE MORE YOU'LL PROBABLY THINK I'M JUST A BABY AND AN ART WEIRDO.
STEPH, I WOULD NEVER THINK THAT ABOUT YOU. IT'S JUST JANELI'S MOM IS GONE A LOT ON DOUBLE SHIFTS LIKE MY MOM. SHE KNOWS HOW I FEEL—ALONE.
JANELI AND THEM WANT TO GO TO SPELLMAN, TOO, AND I DIDN'T WANT TO BE ALONE THERE. BUT... I GUESS I COULD HAVE STOOD UP FOR YOU WHEN THEY CRACKED JOKES.

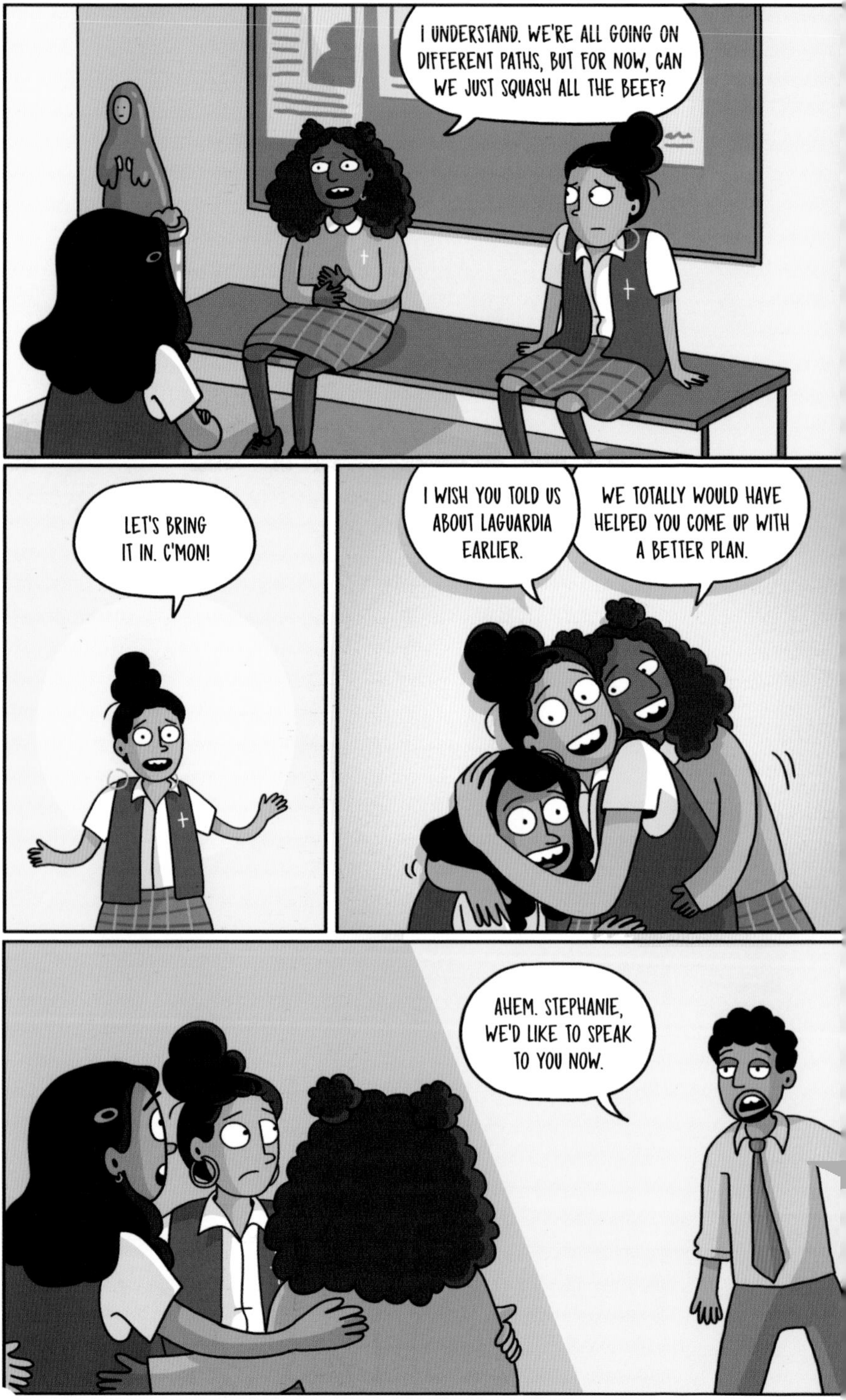
I UNDERSTAND. WE'RE ALL GOING ON DIFFERENT PATHS, BUT FOR NOW, CAN WE JUST SQUASH ALL THE BEEF?
LET'S BRING IT IN. C'MON!
I WISH YOU TOLD US ABOUT LAGUARDIA EARLIER.
WE TOTALLY WOULD HAVE HELPED YOU COME UP WITH A BETTER PLAN.
AHEM. STEPHANIE, WE'D LIKE TO SPEAK TO YOU NOW.

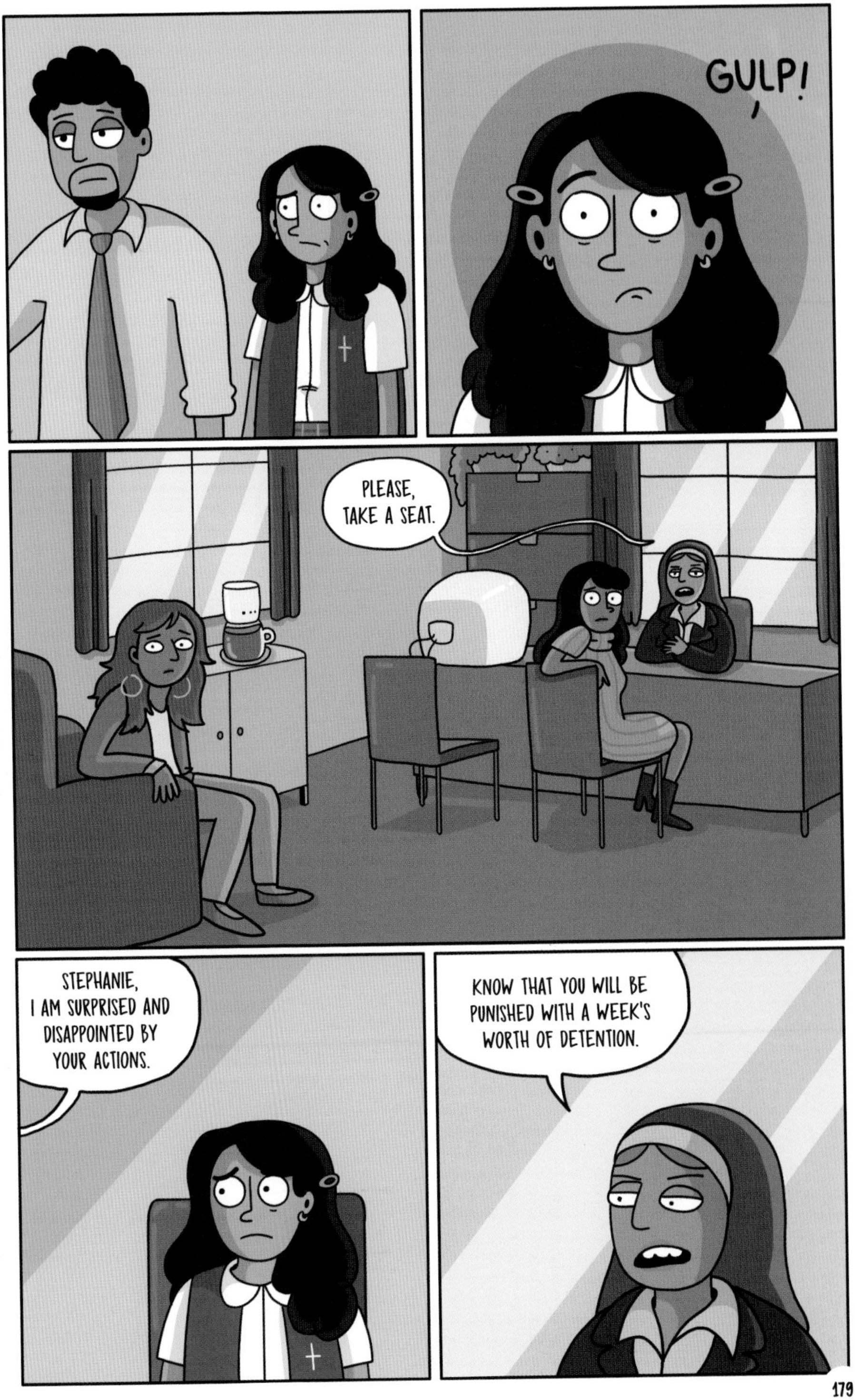
GULP!
PLEASE, TAKE A SEAT.
STEPHANIE, I AM SURPRISED AND DISAPPOINTED BY YOUR ACTIONS.
KNOW THAT YOU WILL BE PUNISHED WITH A WEEK'S WORTH OF DETENTION.

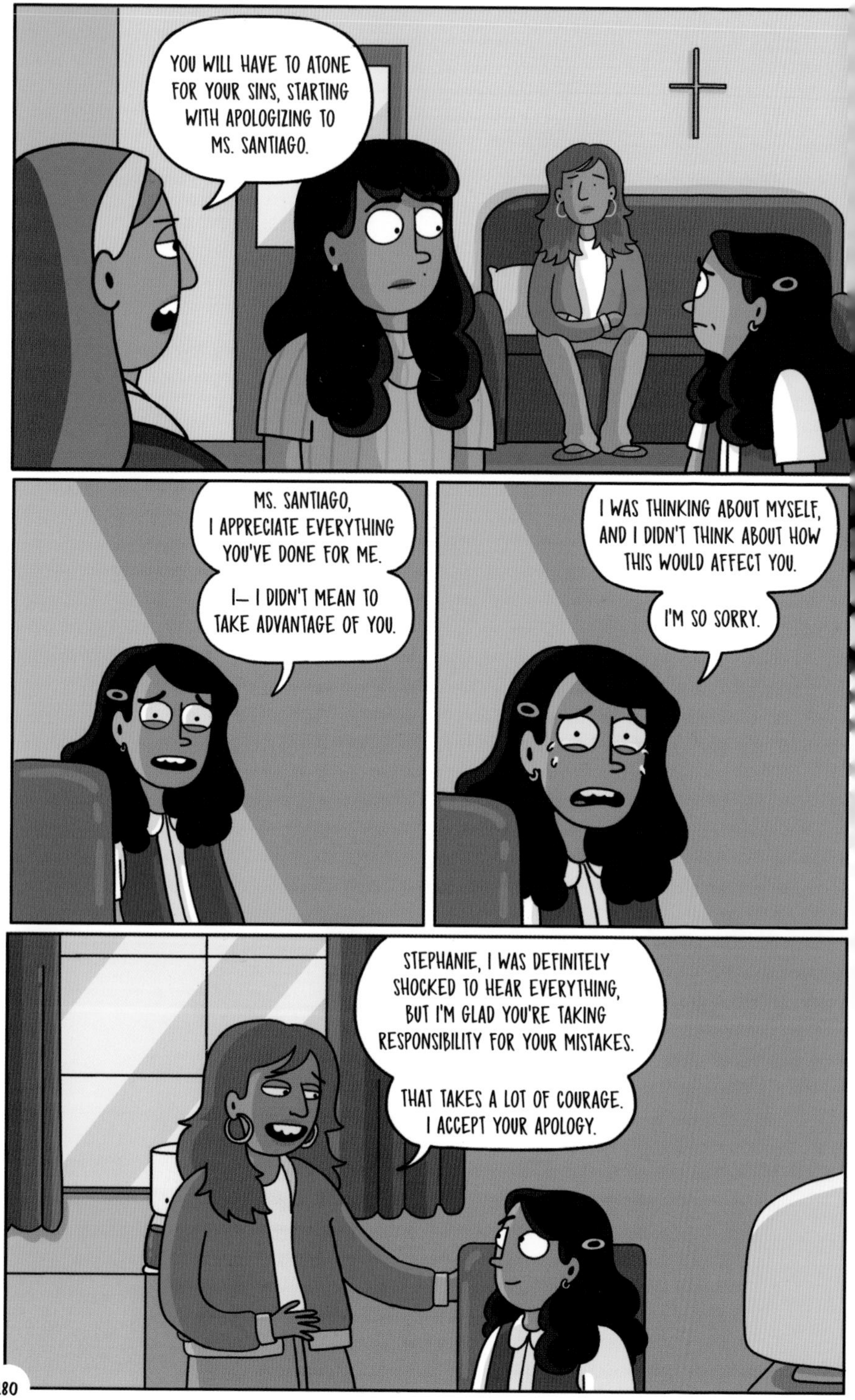
YOU WILL HAVE TO ATONE FOR YOUR SINS, STARTING WITH APOLOGIZING TO MS. SANTIAGO.
MS. SANTIAGO, I APPRECIATE EVERYTHING YOU'VE DONE FOR ME.
I— I DIDN'T MEAN TO TAKE ADVANTAGE OF YOU.
I WAS THINKING ABOUT MYSELF, AND I DIDN'T THINK ABOUT HOW THIS WOULD AFFECT YOU.
I'M SO SORRY.
STEPHANIE, I WAS DEFINITELY SHOCKED TO HEAR EVERYTHING, BUT I'M GLAD YOU'RE TAKING RESPONSIBILITY FOR YOUR MISTAKES.
THAT TAKES A LOT OF COURAGE. I ACCEPT YOUR APOLOGY.

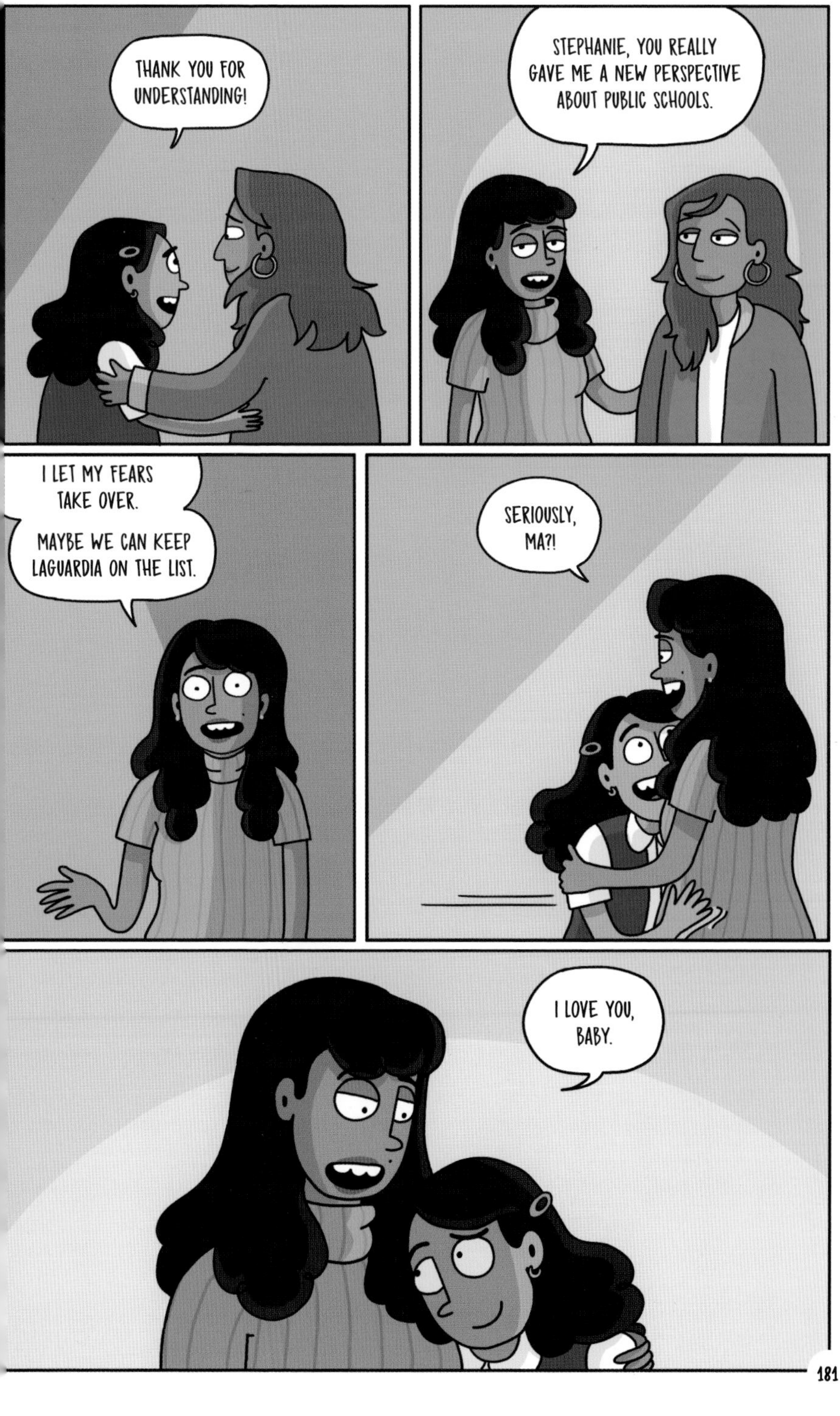
THANK YOU FOR UNDERSTANDING!
STEPHANIE, YOU REALLY GAVE ME A NEW PERSPECTIVE ABOUT PUBLIC SCHOOLS.
I LET MY FEARS TAKE OVER.
MAYBE WE CAN KEEP LAGUARDIA ON THE LIST.
SERIOUSLY, MA?!
I LOVE YOU, BABY.

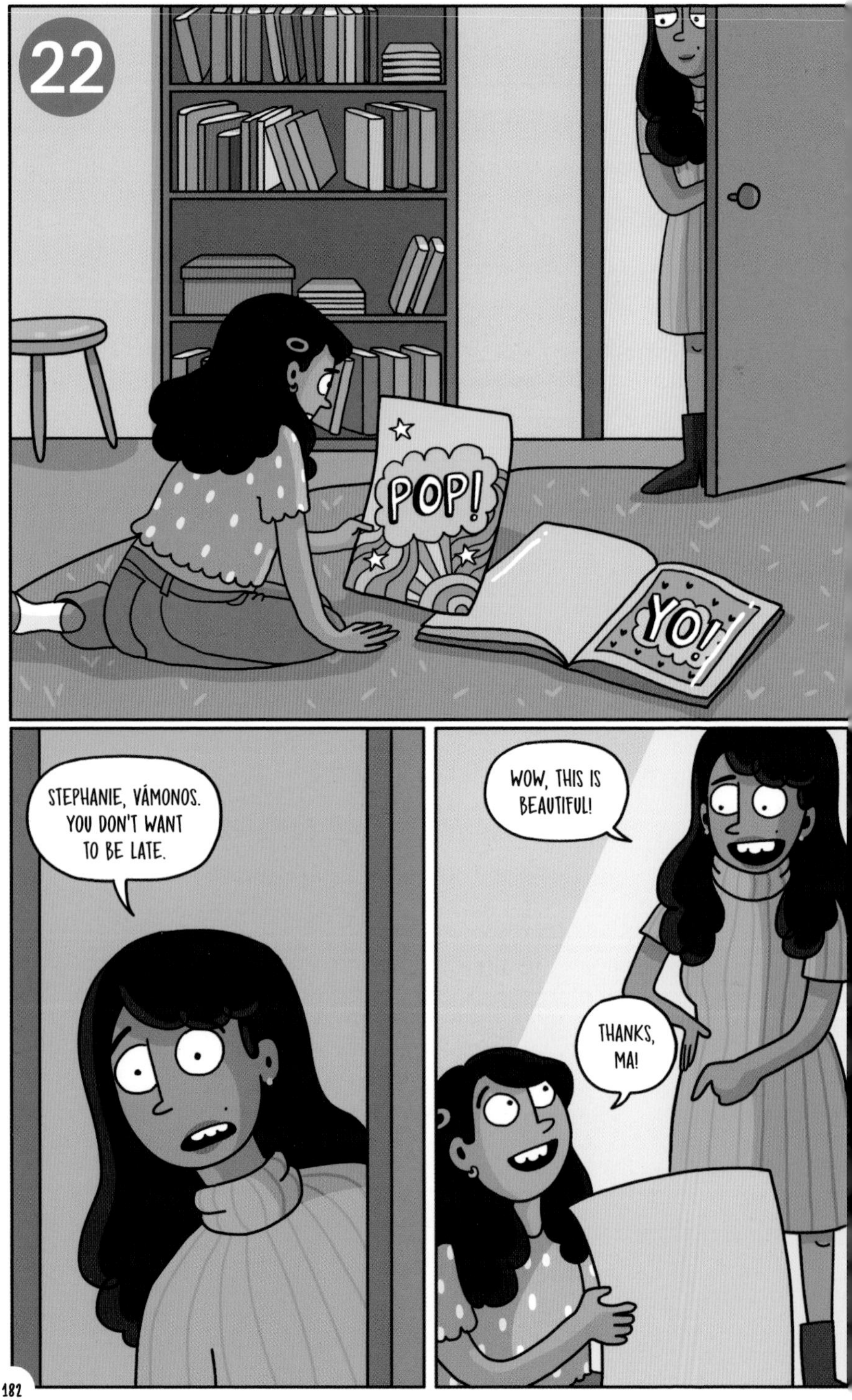
22
POP!
YO!
STEPHANIE, VÁMONOS. YOU DON'T WANT TO BE LATE.
WOW, THIS IS BEAUTIFUL!
THANKS, MA!

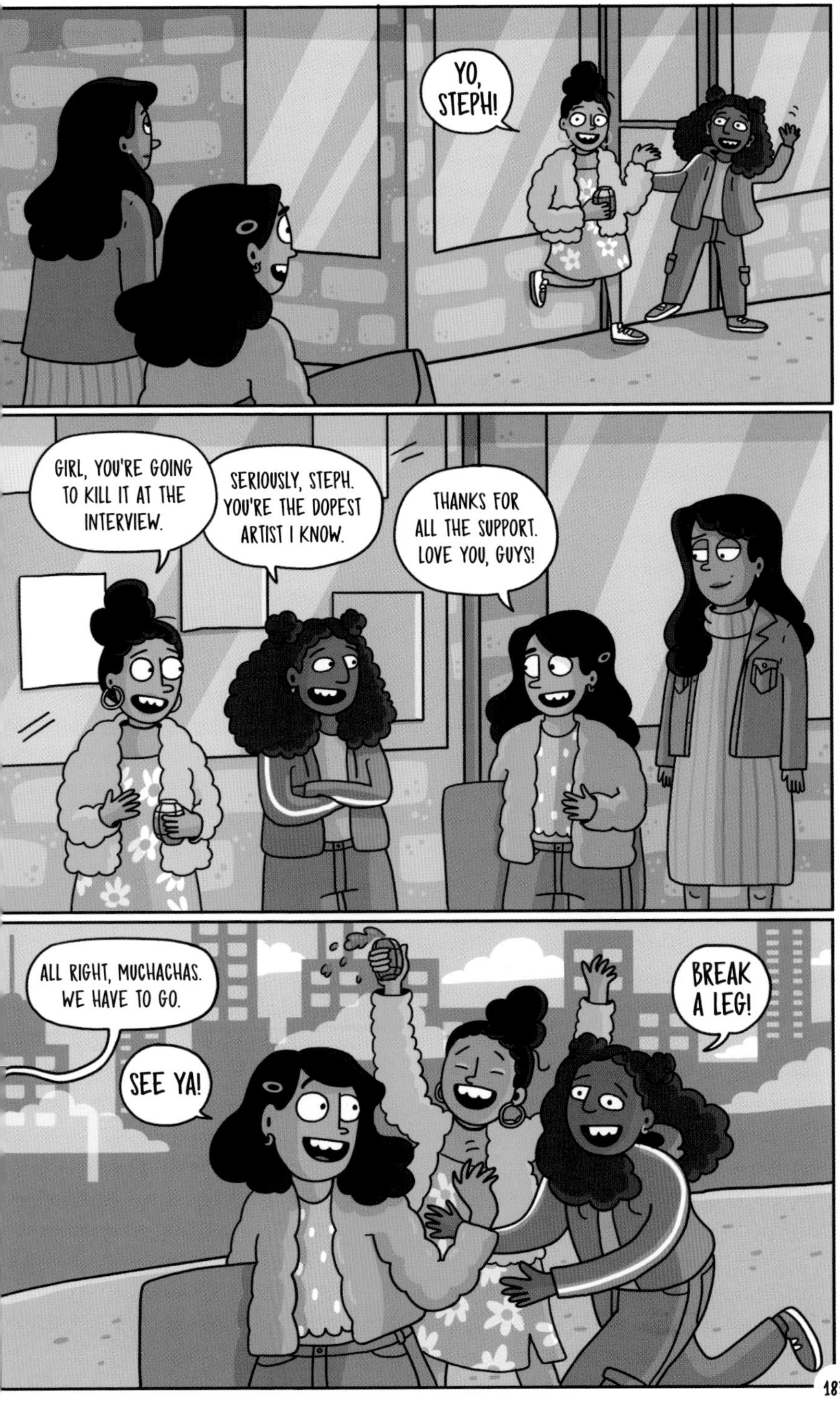

YO, STEPH!
GIRL, YOU'RE GOING TO KILL IT AT THE INTERVIEW.
SERIOUSLY, STEPH. YOU'RE THE DOPEST ARTIST I KNOW.
THANKS FOR ALL THE SUPPORT. LOVE YOU, GUYS!
ALL RIGHT, MUCHACHAS. WE HAVE TO GO.
SEE YA!
BREAK A LEG!

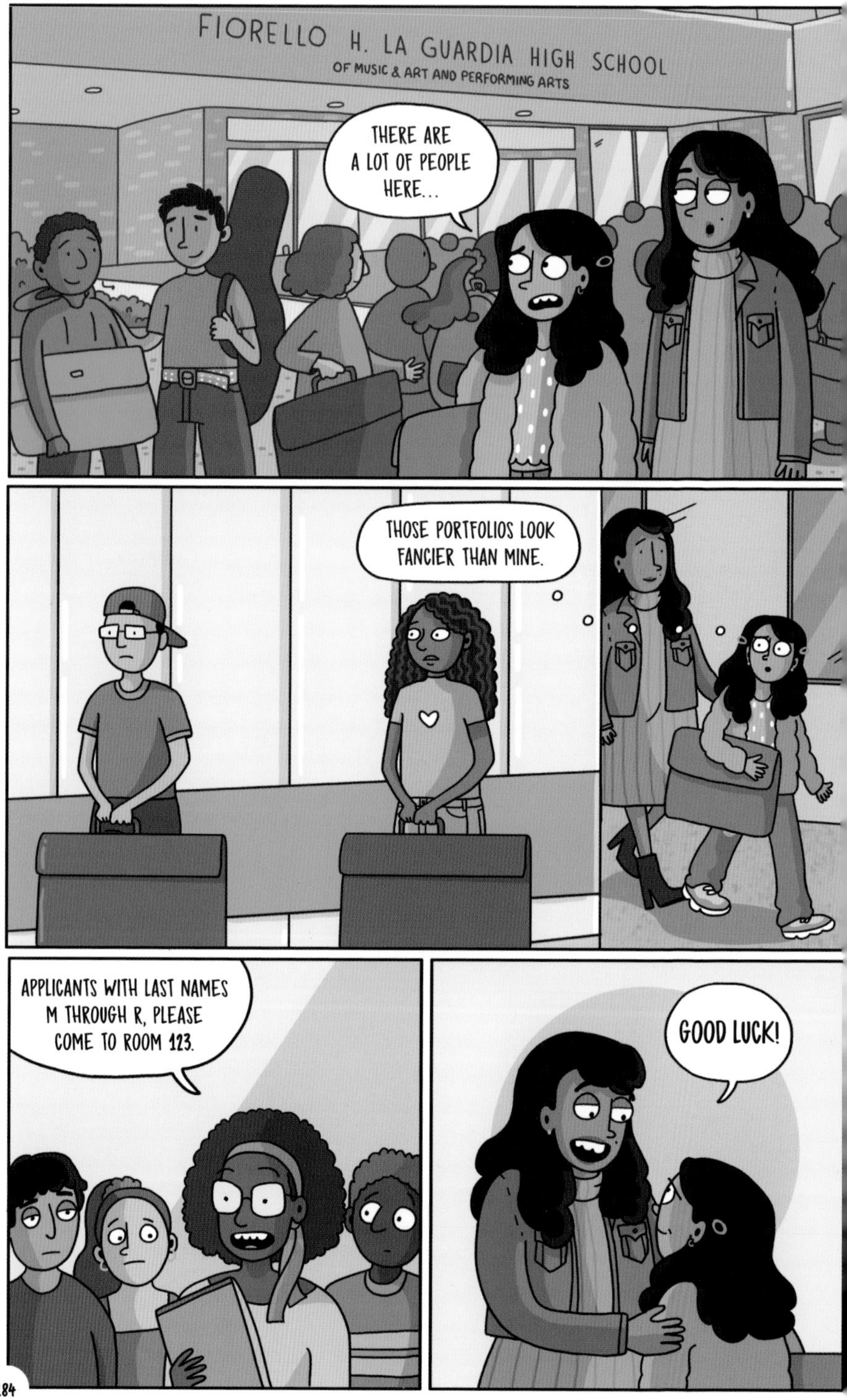
FIORELLO H. LA GUARDIA HIGH SCHOOL
OF MUSIC & ART AND PERFORMING ARTS
THERE ARE A LOT OF PEOPLE HERE...
THOSE PORTFOLIOS LOOK FANCIER THAN MINE.
APPLICANTS WITH LAST NAMES M THROUGH R, PLEASE COME TO ROOM 123.
GOOD LUCK!

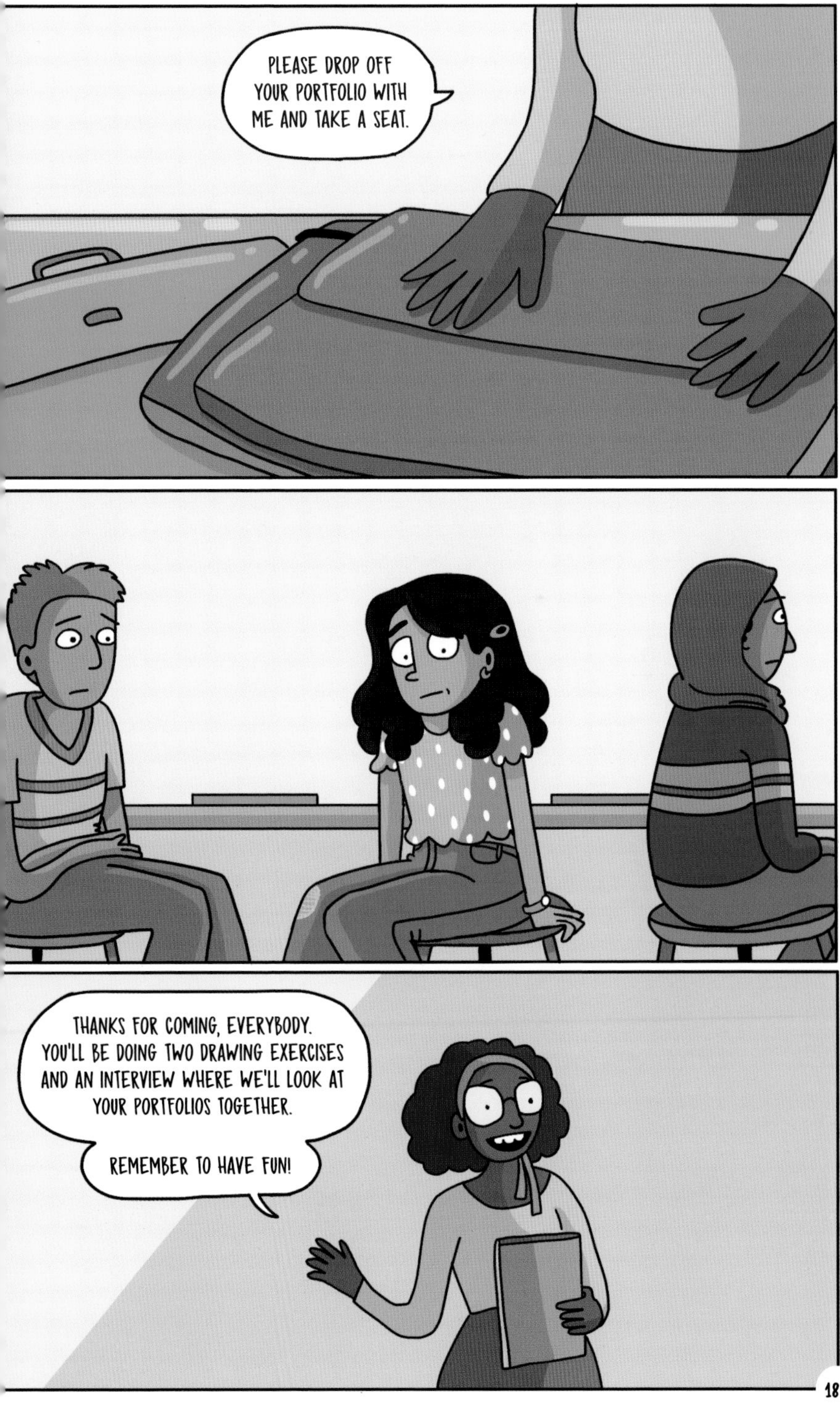
PLEASE DROP OFF YOUR PORTFOLIO WITH ME AND TAKE A SEAT.
THANKS FOR COMING, EVERYBODY. YOU'LL BE DOING TWO DRAWING EXERCISES AND AN INTERVIEW WHERE WE'LL LOOK AT YOUR PORTFOLIOS TOGETHER.
REMEMBER TO HAVE FUN!

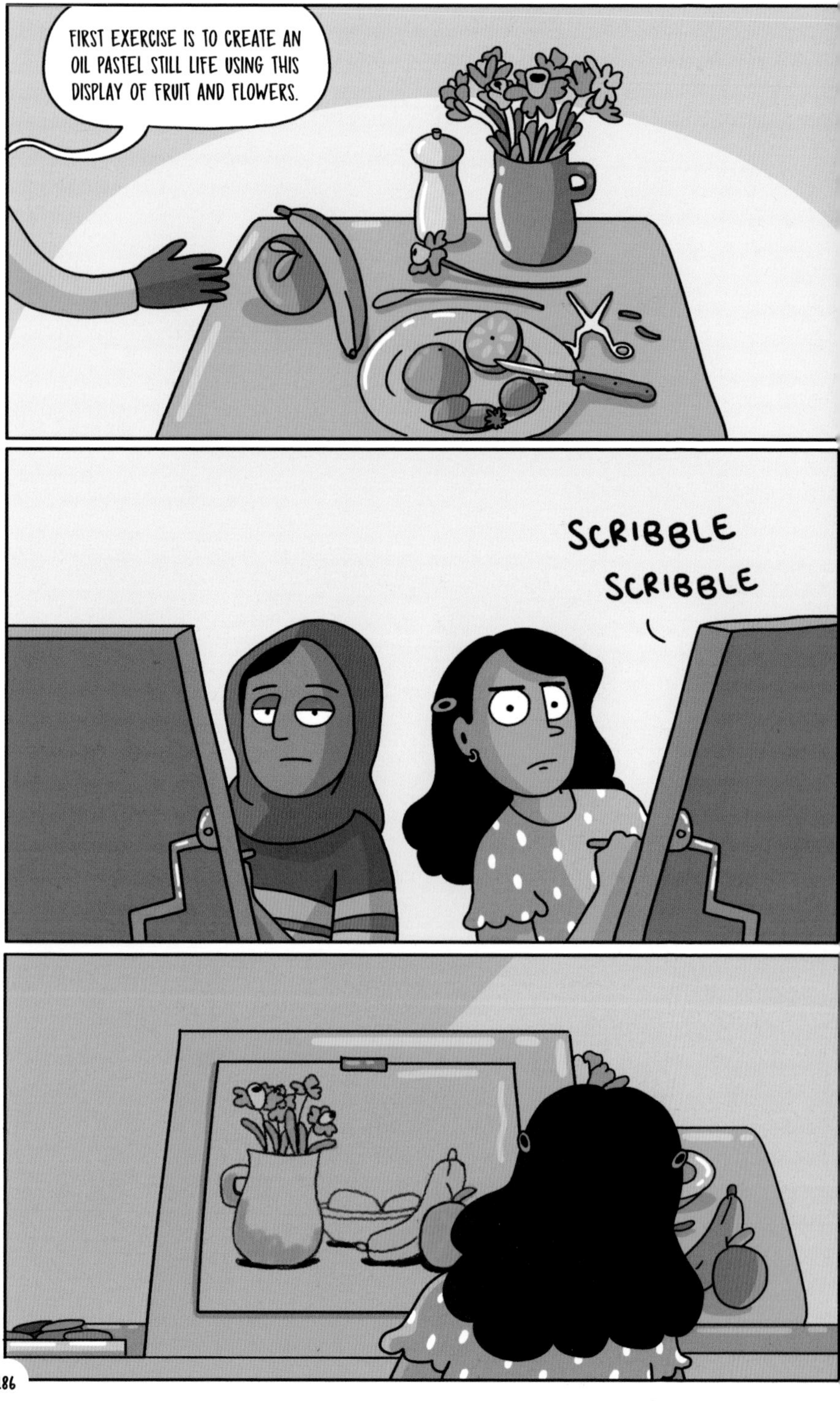
FIRST EXERCISE IS TO CREATE AN OIL PASTEL STILL LIFE USING THIS DISPLAY OF FRUIT AND FLOWERS.
SCRIBBLE
SCRIBBLE

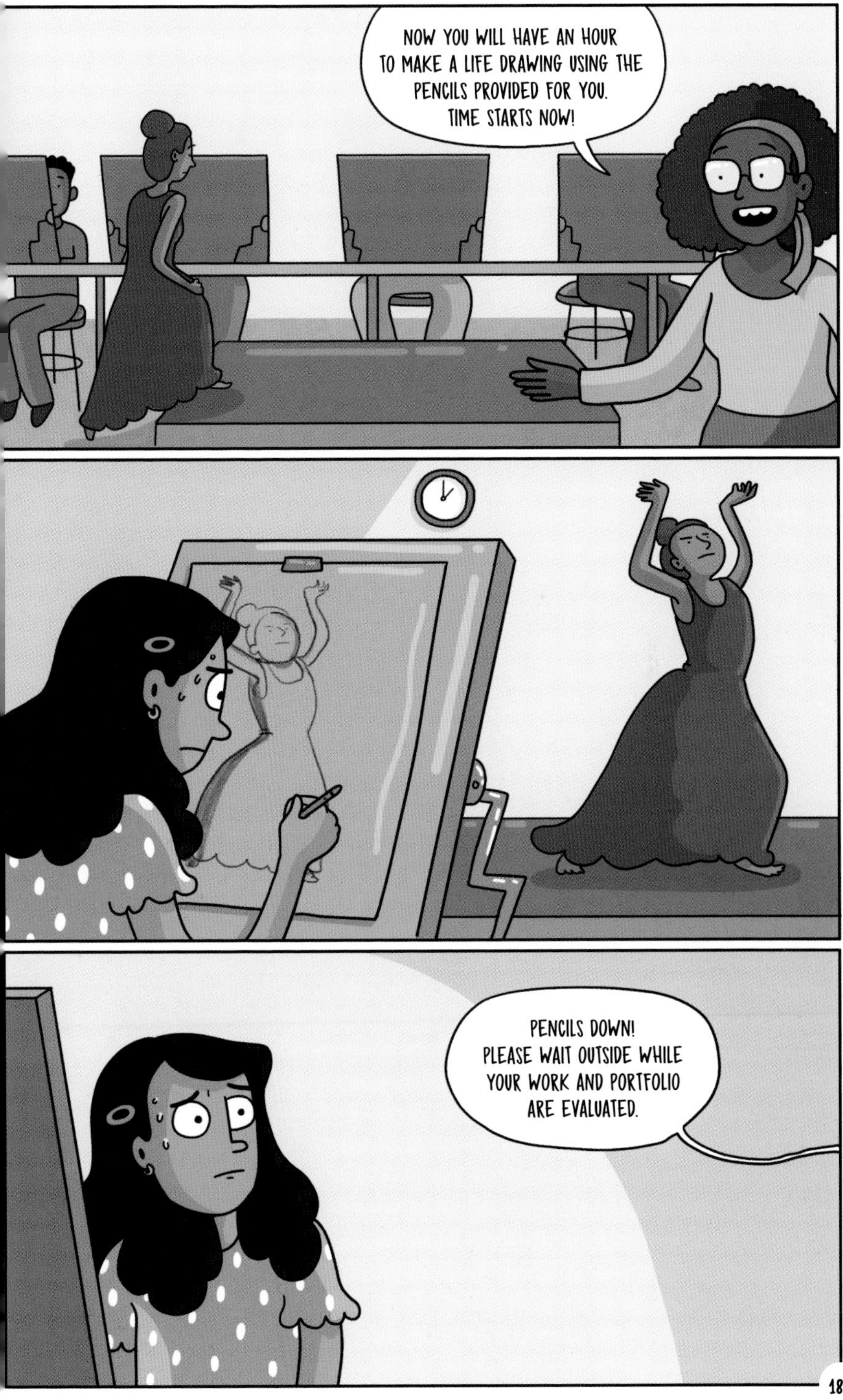
NOW YOU WILL HAVE AN HOUR TO MAKE A LIFE DRAWING USING THE PENCILS PROVIDED FOR YOU. TIME STARTS NOW!
PENCILS DOWN! PLEASE WAIT OUTSIDE WHILE YOUR WORK AND PORTFOLIO ARE EVALUATED.

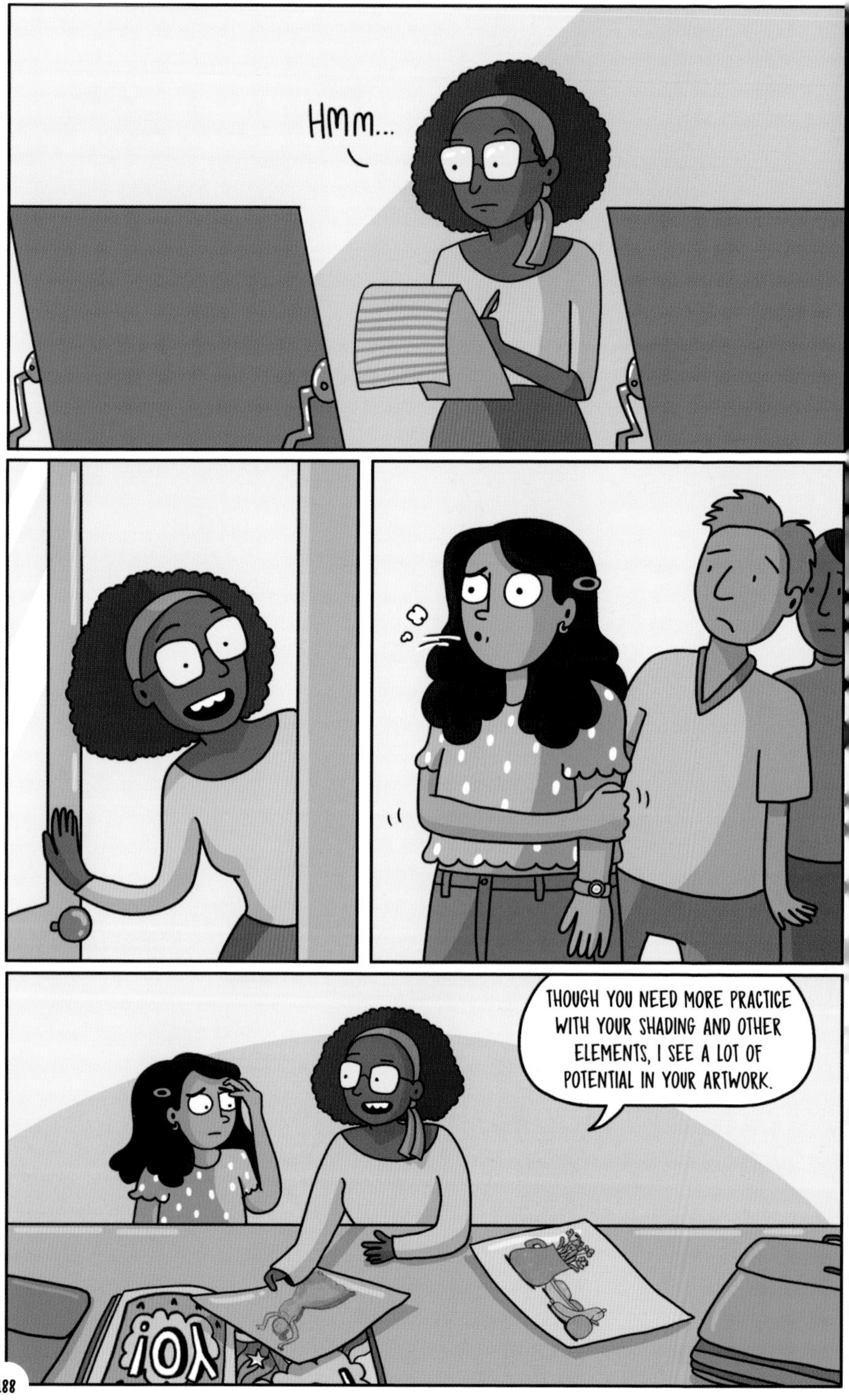
HMM...
THOUGH YOU NEED MORE PRACTICE WITH YOUR SHADING AND OTHER ELEMENTS, I SEE A LOT OF POTENTIAL IN YOUR ARTWORK.

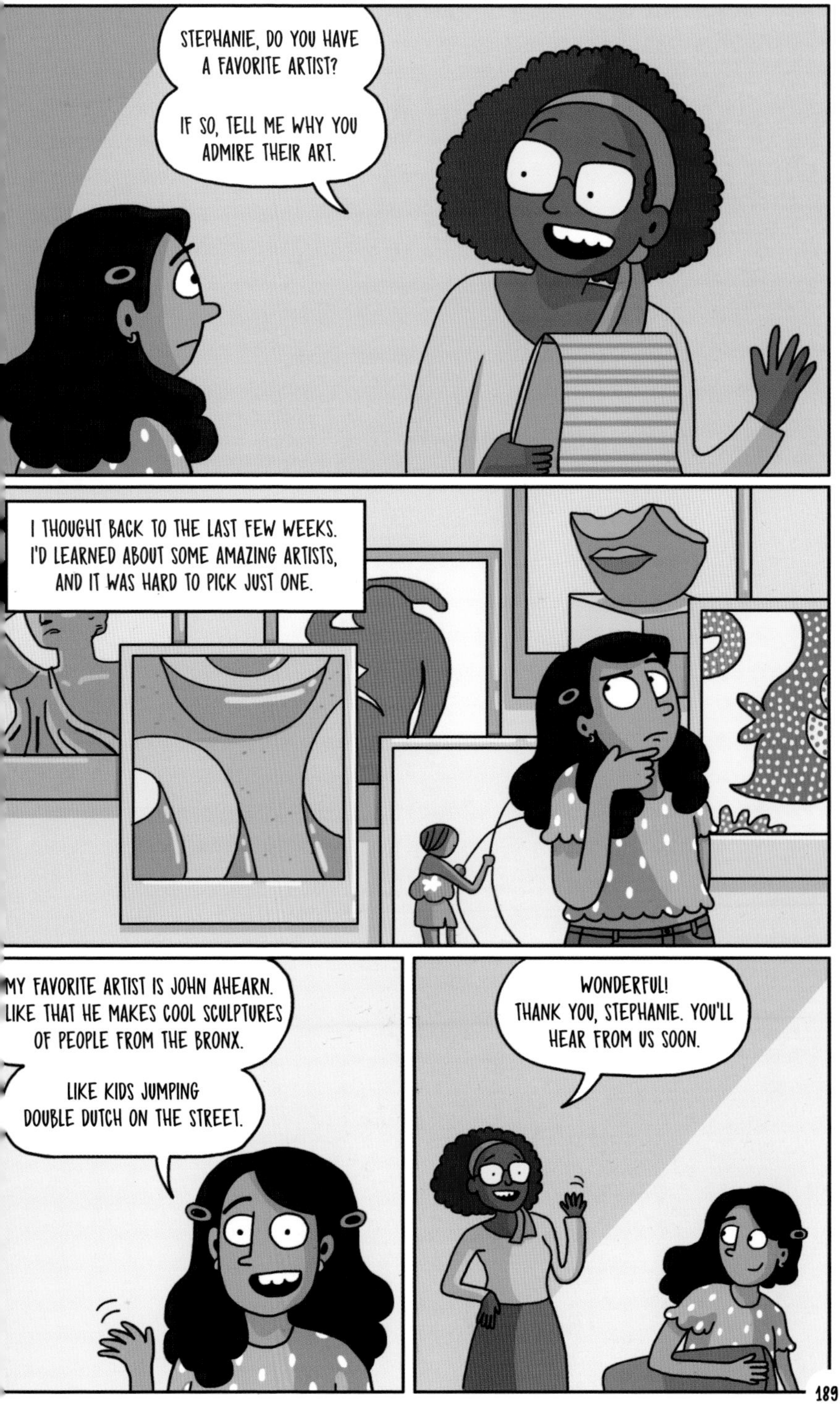
STEPHANIE, DO YOU HAVE A FAVORITE ARTIST?
IF SO, TELL ME WHY YOU ADMIRE THEIR ART.
I THOUGHT BACK TO THE LAST FEW WEEKS. I'D LEARNED ABOUT SOME AMAZING ARTISTS, AND IT WAS HARD TO PICK JUST ONE.
MY FAVORITE ARTIST IS JOHN AHEARN. LIKE THAT HE MAKES COOL SCULPTURES OF PEOPLE FROM THE BRONX.
LIKE KIDS JUMPING DOUBLE DUTCH ON THE STREET.
WONDERFUL! THANK YOU, STEPHANIE. YOU'LL HEAR FROM US SOON.

23

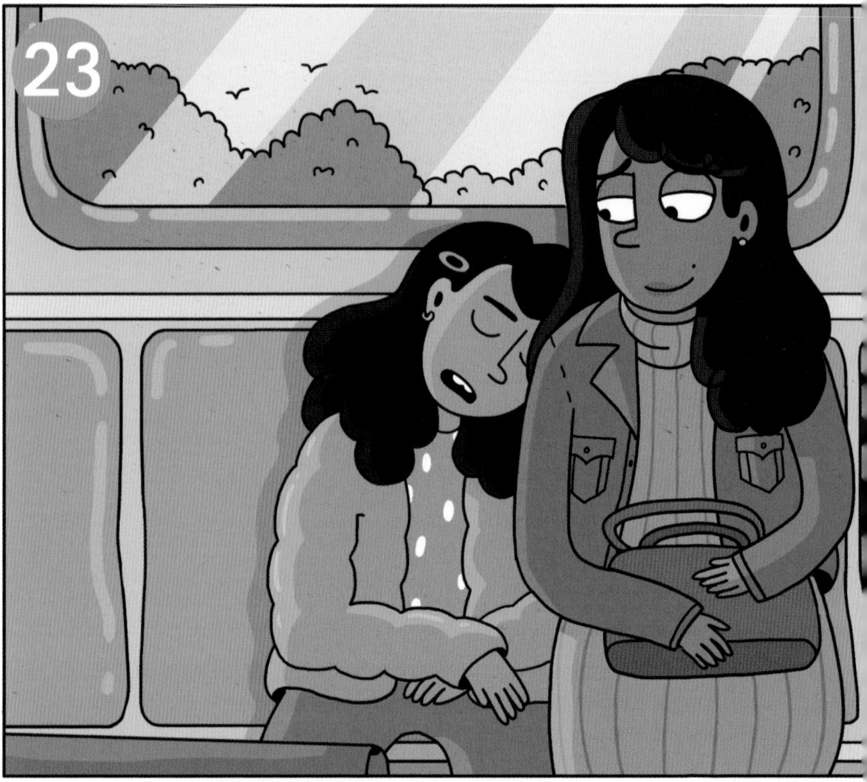

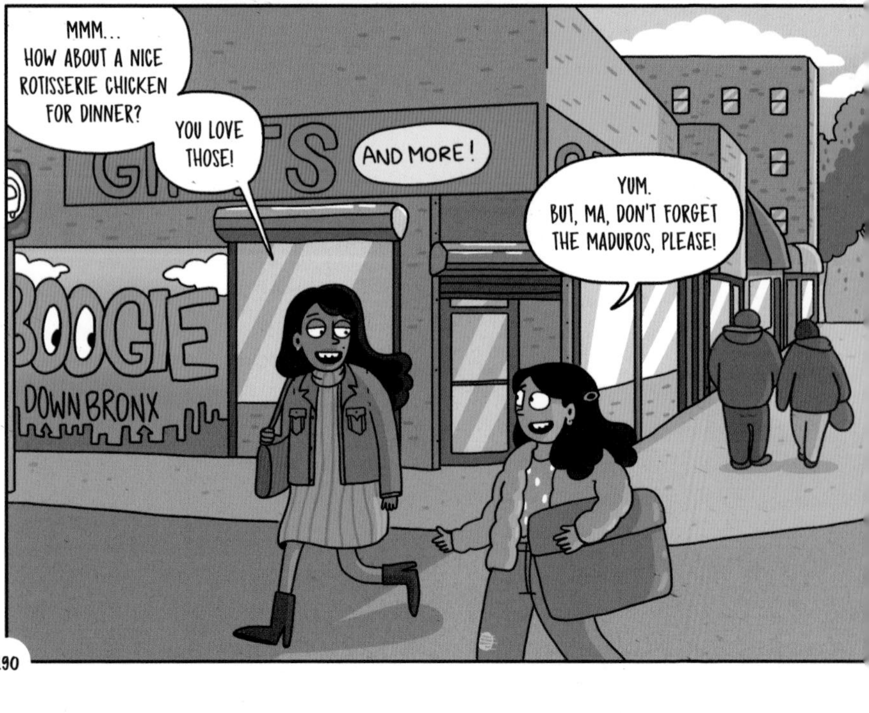
MMM...
HOW ABOUT A NICE ROTISSERIE CHICKEN FOR DINNER?
YOU LOVE THOSE!
GIFTS
AND MORE!
YUM.
BUT, MA, DON'T FORGET THE MADUROS, PLEASE!
BOOGIE
DOWN BRONX

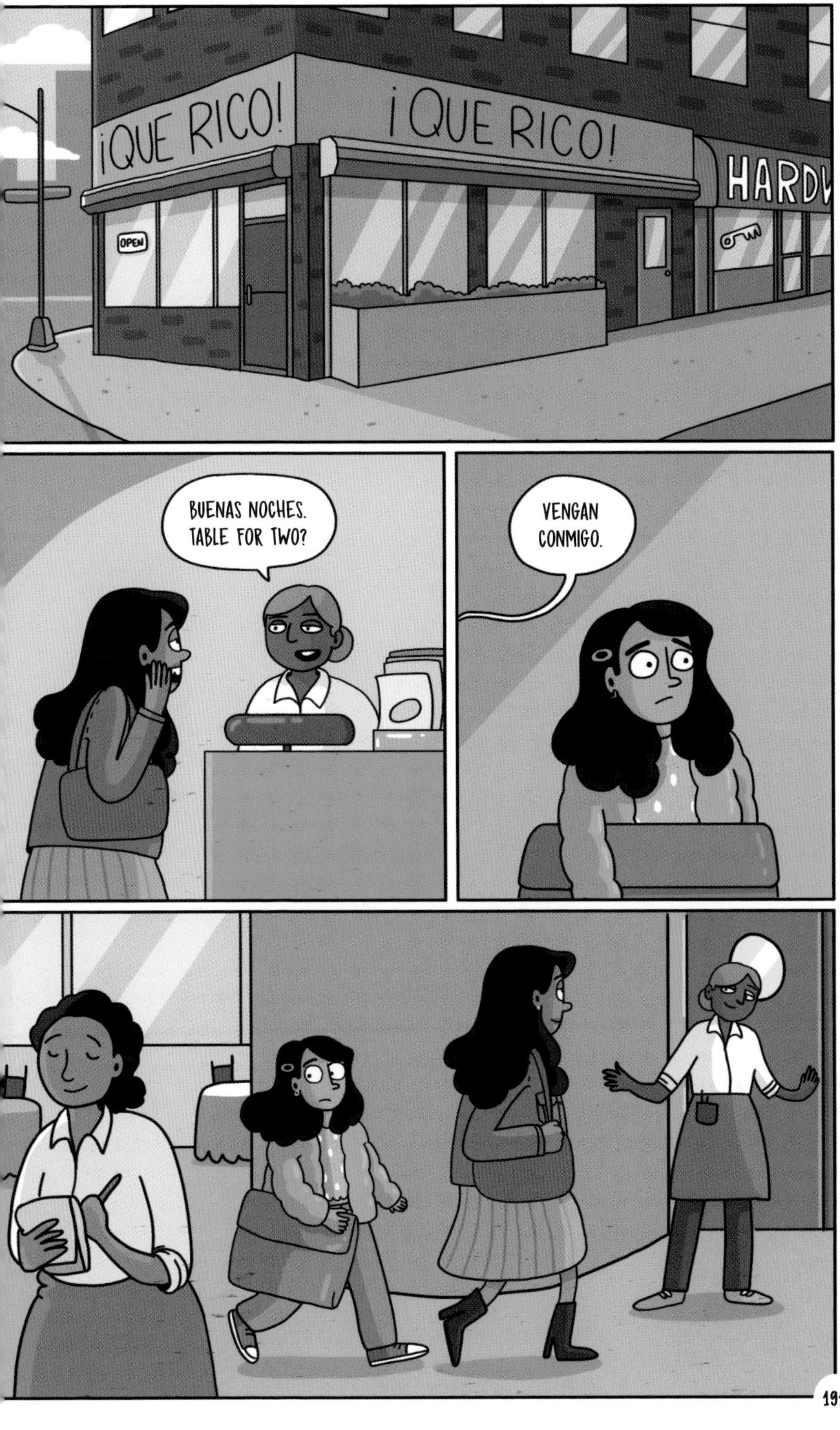
¡QUE RICO!
¡QUE RICO!
OPEN
HARDW
BUENAS NOCHES. TABLE FOR TWO?
VENGAN CONMIGO.

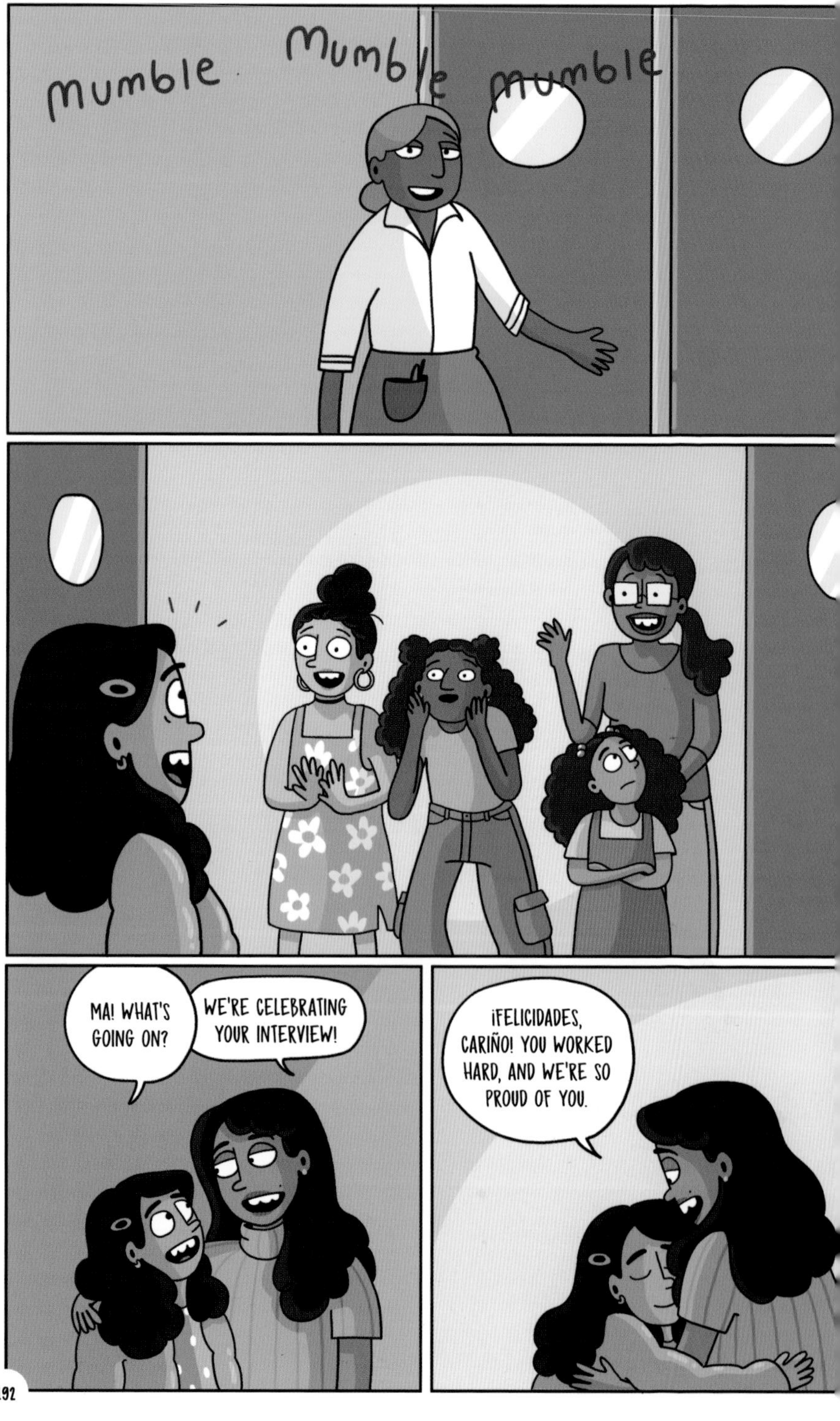
mumble mumble mumble
MA! WHAT'S GOING ON?
WE'RE CELEBRATING YOUR INTERVIEW!
¡FELICIDADES, CARIÑO! YOU WORKED HARD, AND WE'RE SO PROUD OF YOU.

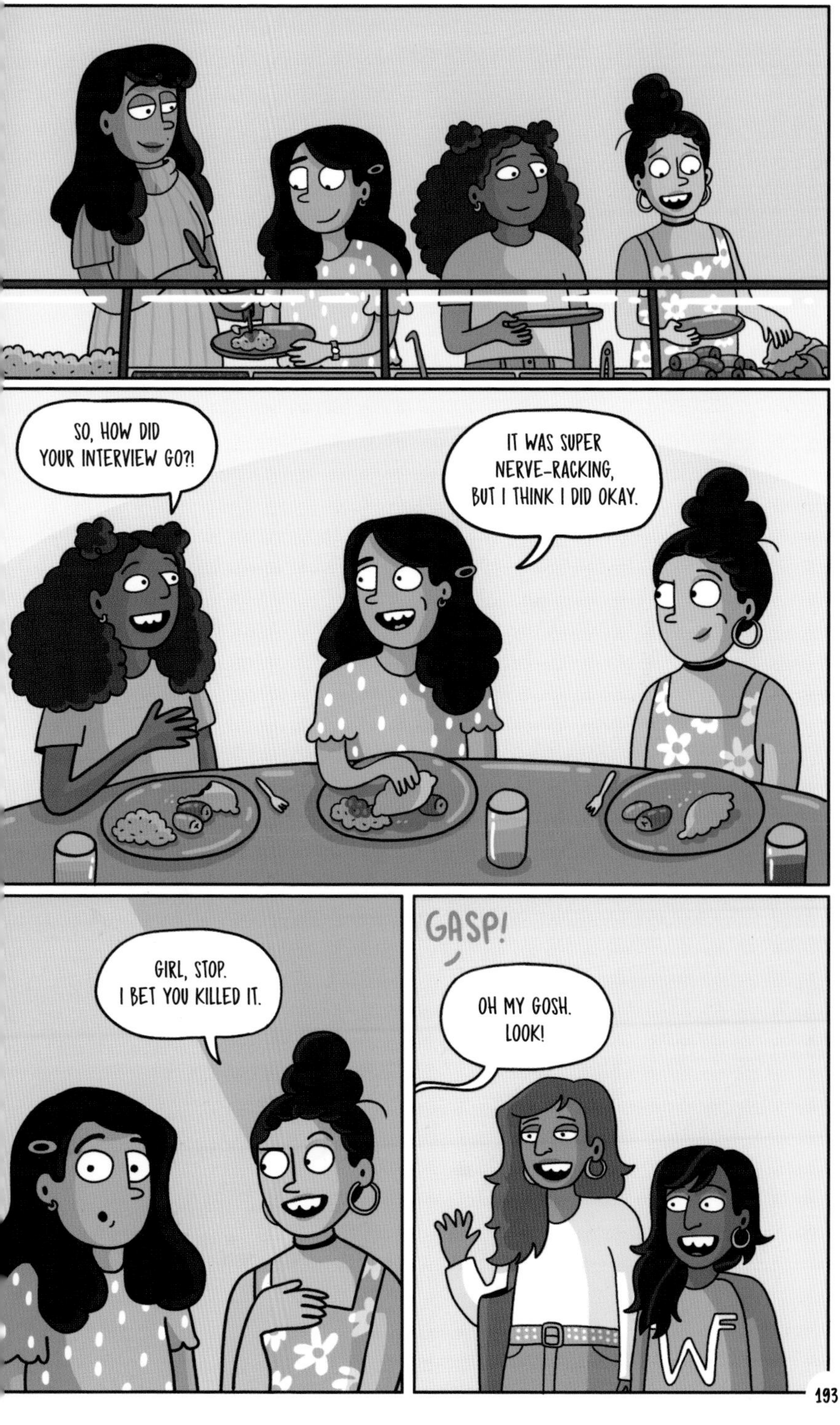
SO, HOW DID YOUR INTERVIEW GO?!
IT WAS SUPER NERVE-RACKING, BUT I THINK I DID OKAY.
GIRL, STOP. I BET YOU KILLED IT.
GASP!
OH MY GOSH. LOOK!
WF

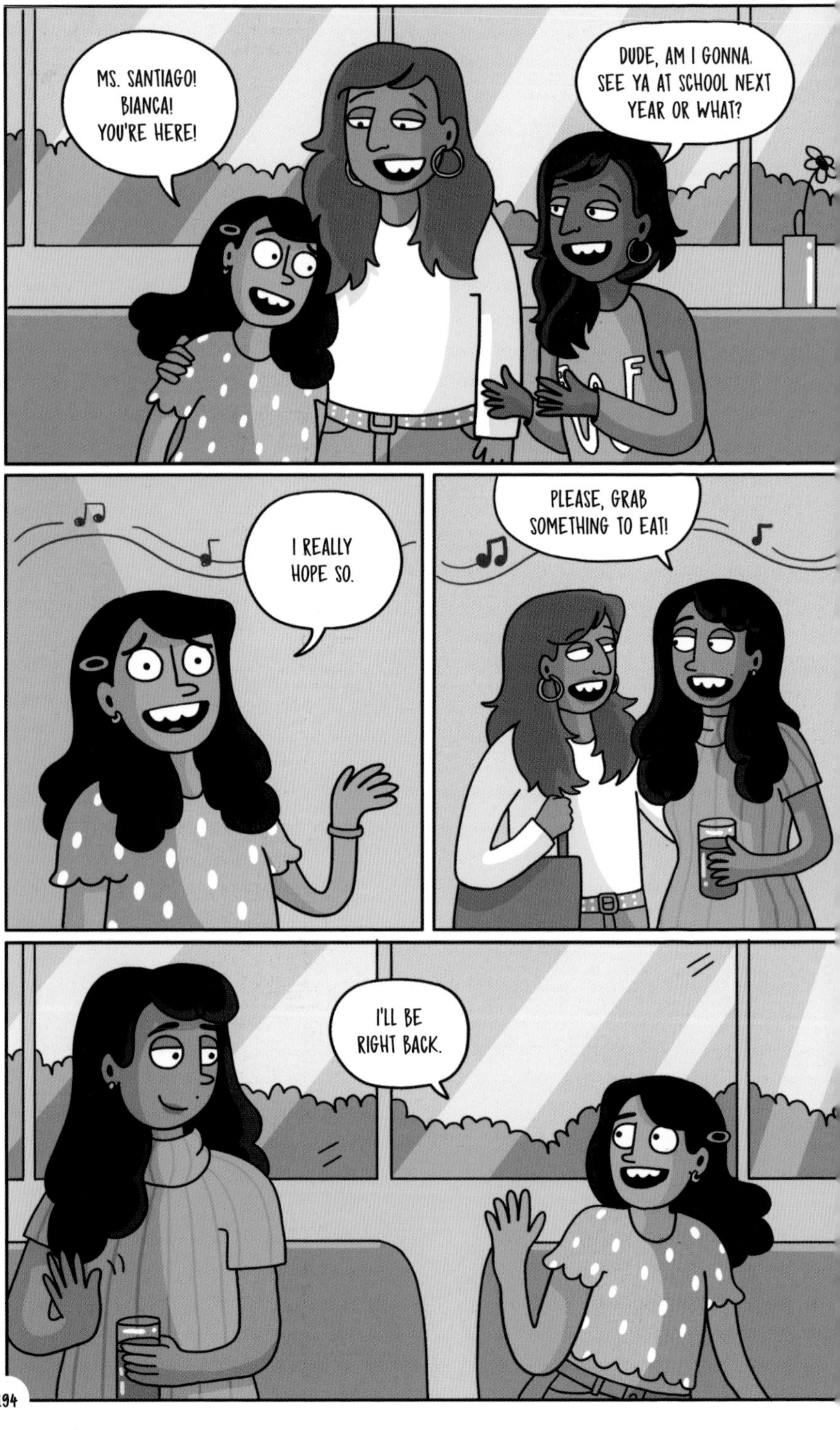
MS. SANTIAGO! BIANCA! YOU'RE HERE!
DUDE, AM I GONNA SEE YA AT SCHOOL NEXT YEAR OR WHAT?
I REALLY HOPE SO.
PLEASE, GRAB SOMETHING TO EAT!
I'LL BE RIGHT BACK.

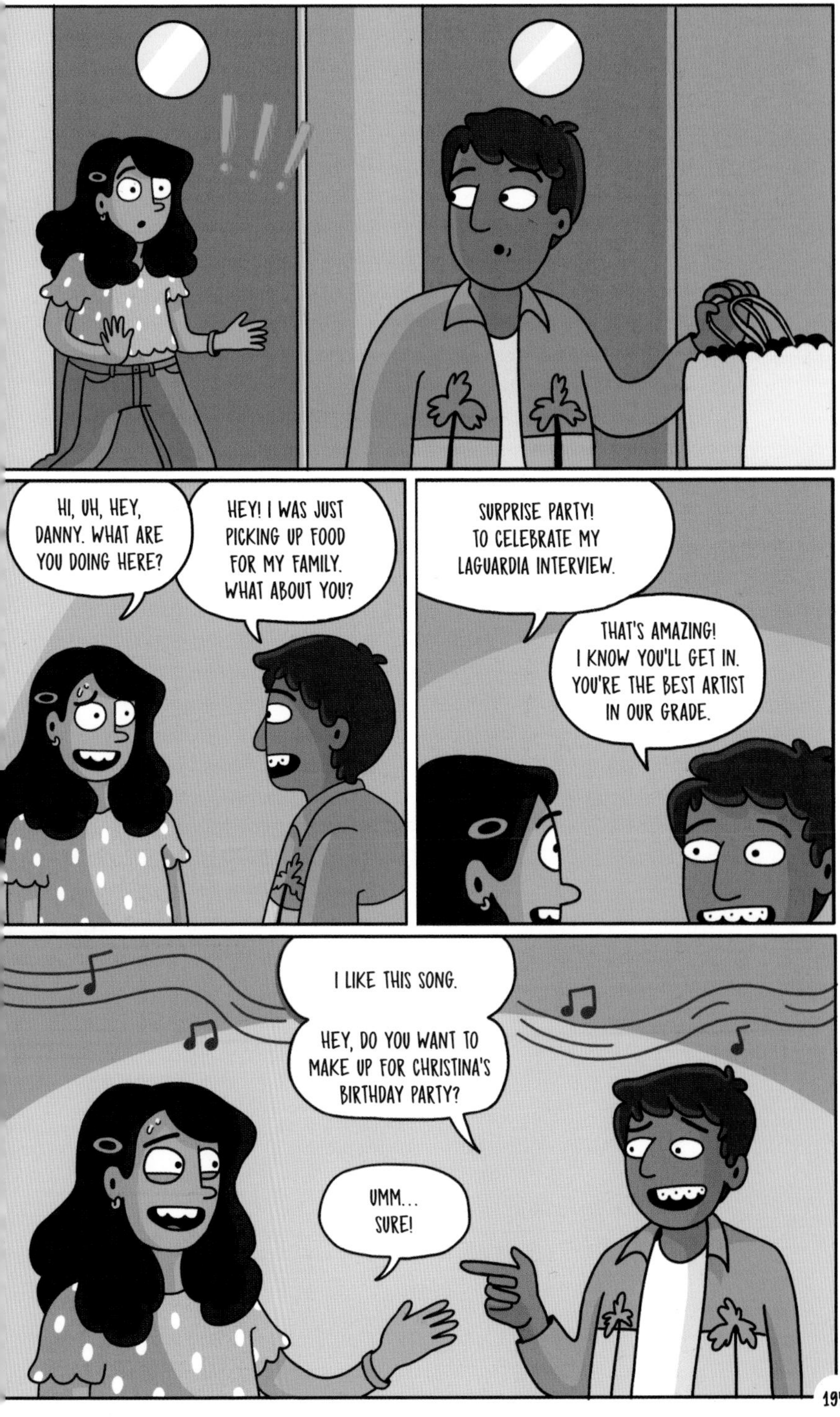
!!!
HI, UH, HEY, DANNY. WHAT ARE YOU DOING HERE?
HEY! I WAS JUST PICKING UP FOOD FOR MY FAMILY. WHAT ABOUT YOU?
SURPRISE PARTY! TO CELEBRATE MY LAGUARDIA INTERVIEW.
THAT'S AMAZING! I KNOW YOU'LL GET IN. YOU'RE THE BEST ARTIST IN OUR GRADE.
I LIKE THIS SONG.
HEY, DO YOU WANT TO MAKE UP FOR CHRISTINA'S BIRTHDAY PARTY?
UMM... SURE!

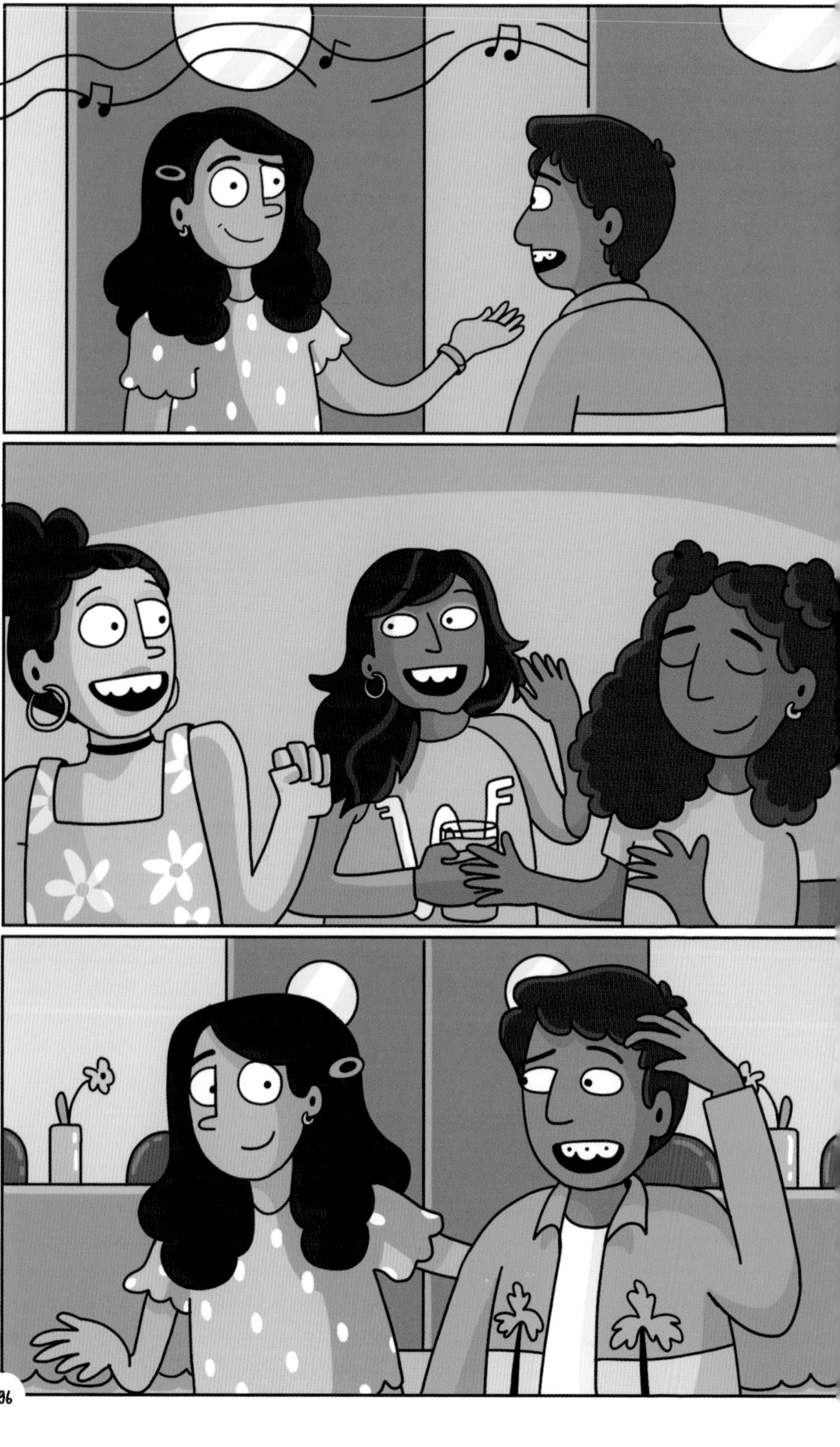

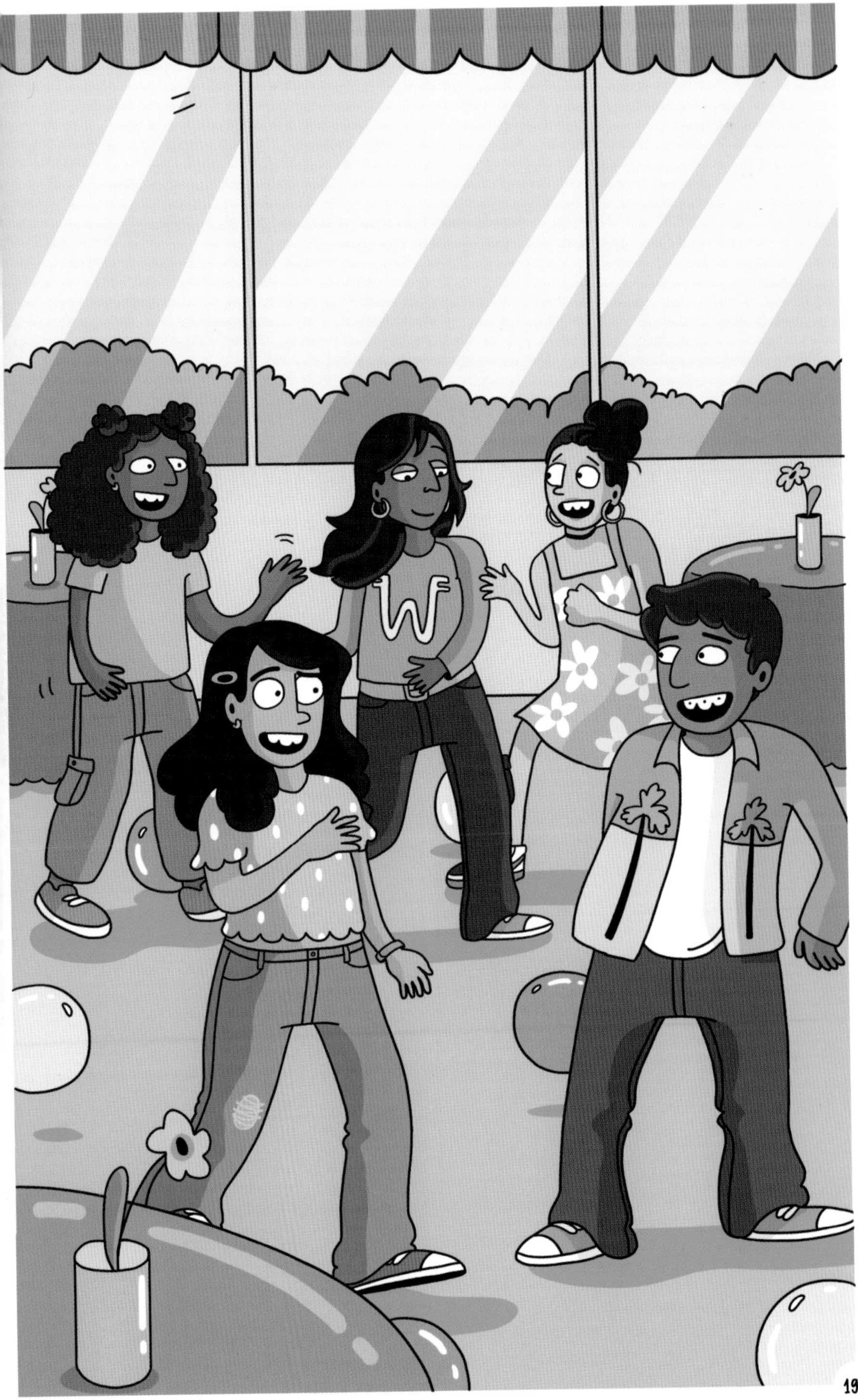
W

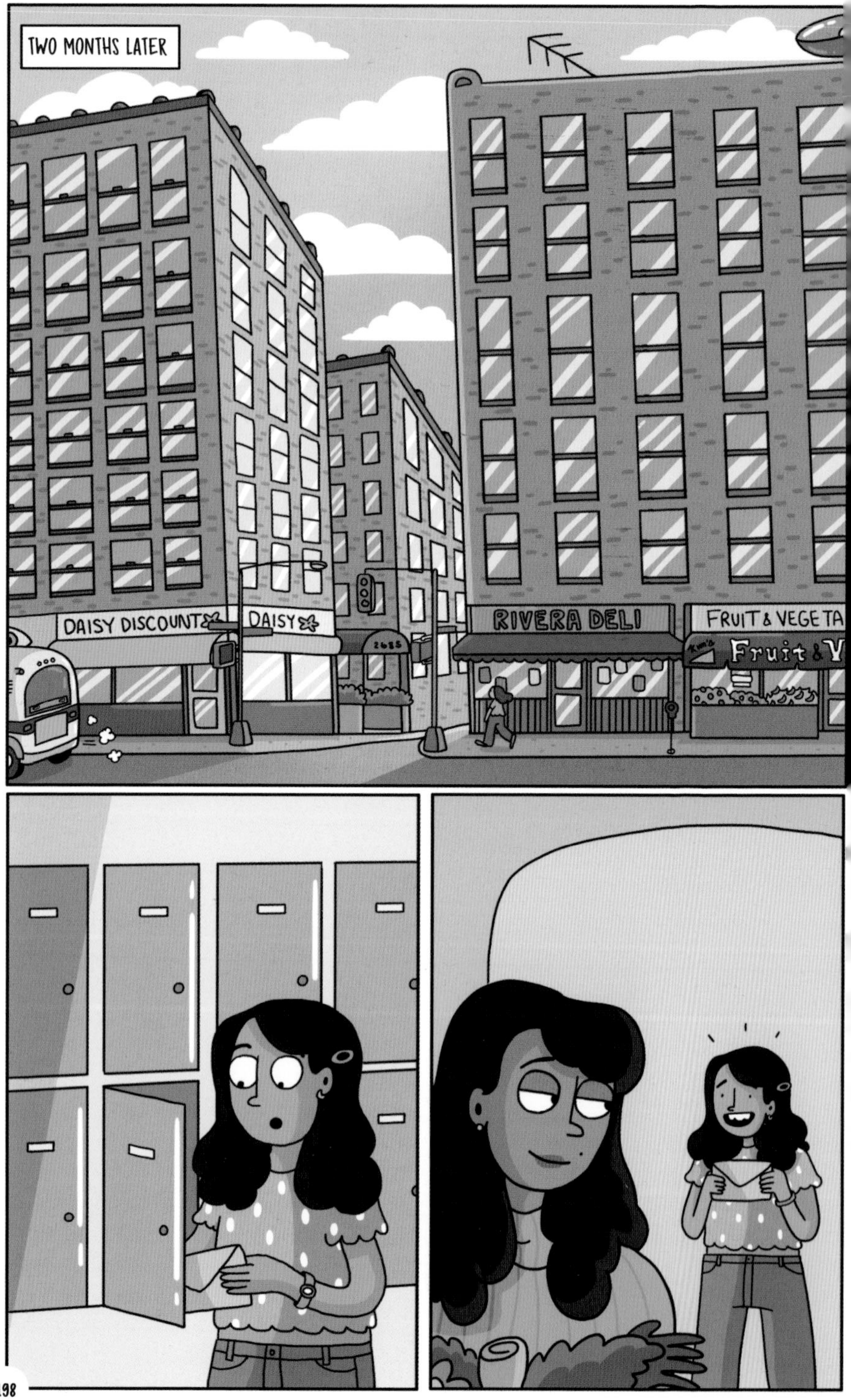
TWO MONTHS LATER
DAISY DISCOUNT
DAISY
2685
RIVERA DELI
FRUIT & VEGETA
Fruit & V

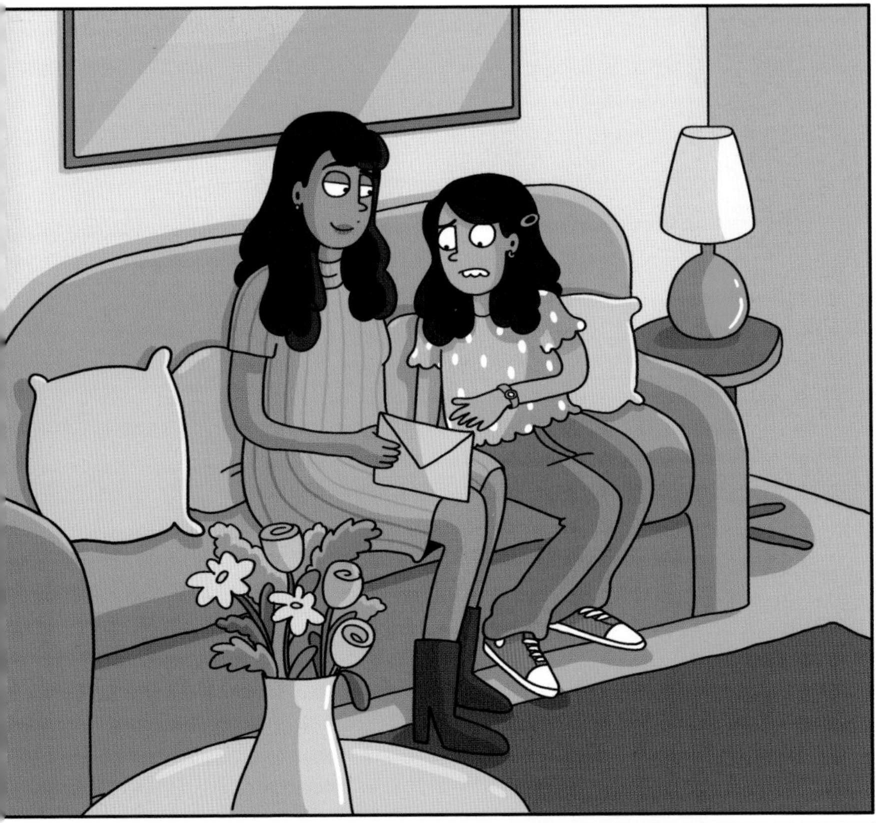

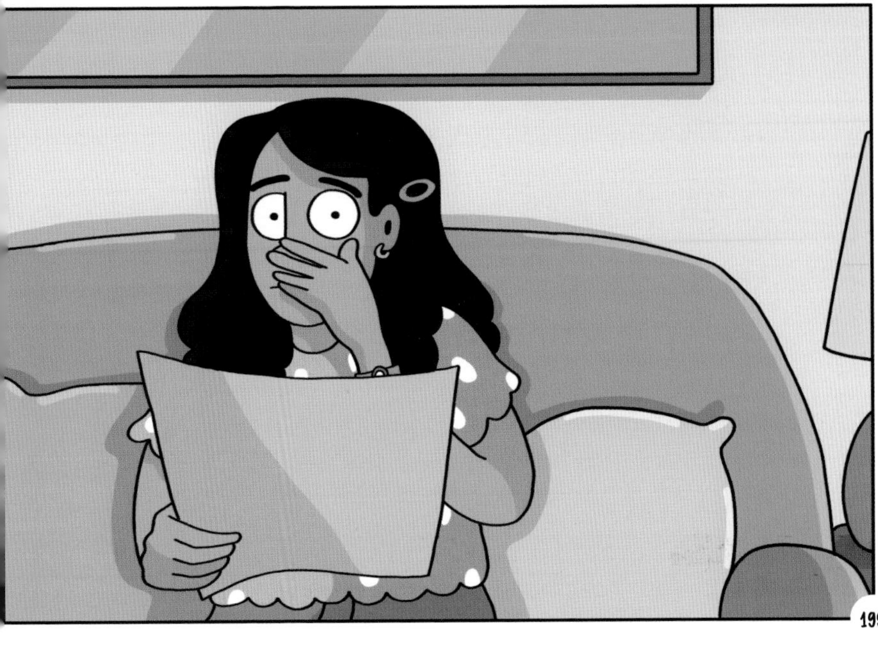

La!

Fiorello H. LaGuardia High School of Music & Art and Performing Arts

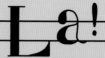

April 17, 2000

Dear Stephanie,

I am delighted to inform you that you have been admitted to the Class of 2004 at Fiorello H. LaGuardia High School of Music & Art and Performing Arts.

Should you choose to accept our offer of admission, we look forward to welcoming you at the orientation for new students on September 1, 2000.

Congratulations!

Sincerely yours,

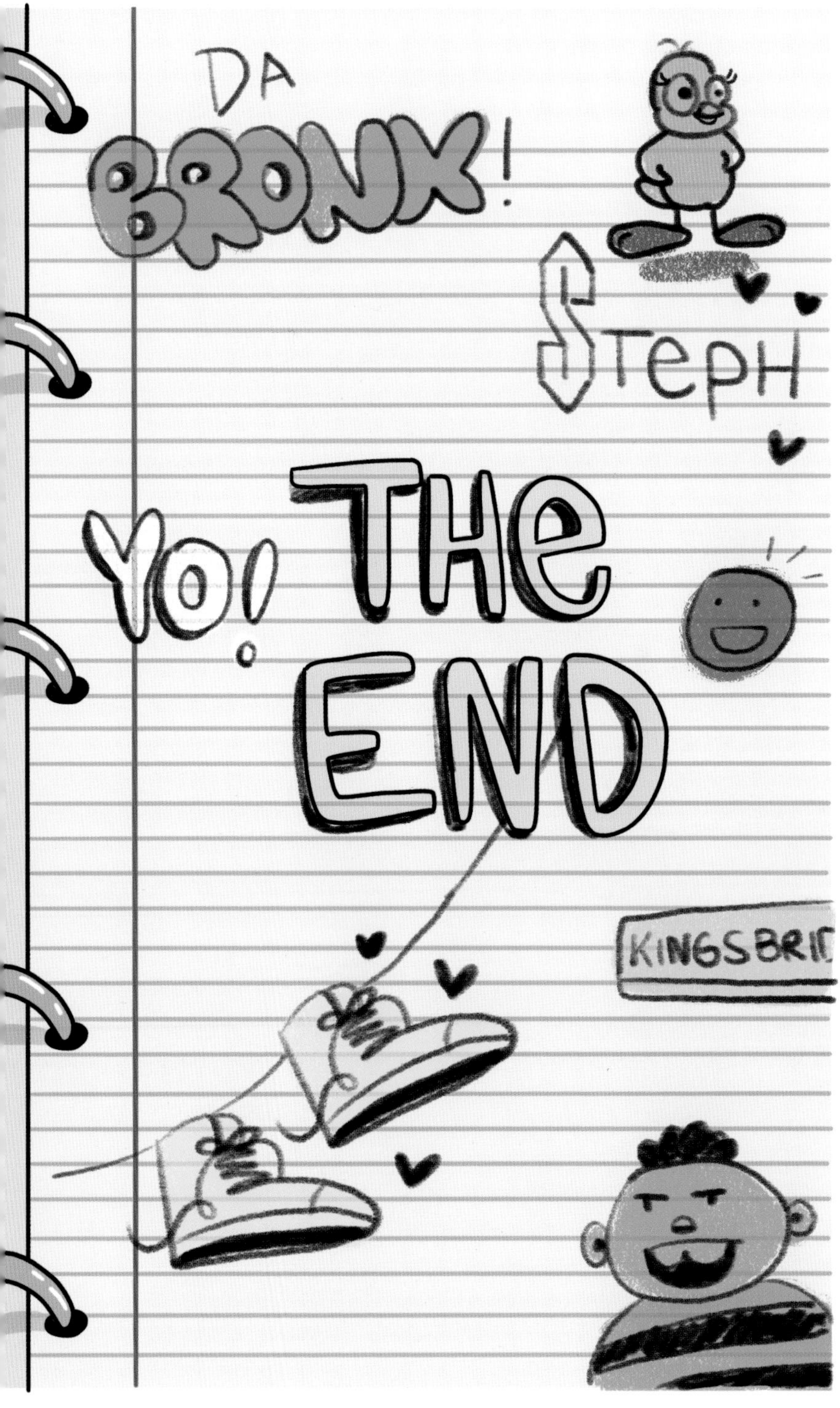
DA BRONX!
STEPH
YO!
THE END
KINGSBRID

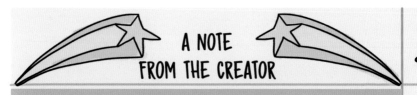

A NOTE FROM THE CREATOR

DOODLES FROM THE BOOGIE DOWN is a work of fiction based on my life growing up in the Bronx. That's me in the photos! I always dreamed of becoming a professional artist, and in the eighth grade, I learned about arts high schools in New York City. I decided that I had to go to one.

Like Steph, I faced many obstacles, including my mother's disapproval and a lack of knowledge of the application process. Also like Steph, I had a mentor in the eighth grade, though she was my English teacher.

In real life, I didn't get to go to LaGuardia. Instead, I started self-publishing short comics about my life, and that led me to creating this graphic novel. I wrote and illustrated this book to honor a childhood memory and the big, complicated questions young people are asked to grapple with. How do we balance being an American tween with the expectations and traditions passed down by our immigrant families? What's it like to do something that no one in our family has done yet? How do we open ourselves to the art that's all around us?

To the young artists reading this book: Don't get discouraged by people who don't understand your dreams. Look for the people who do. You have your talents for a reason—trust yourself and good things will come.

FAVE BOY BAND = ☆NSYNC

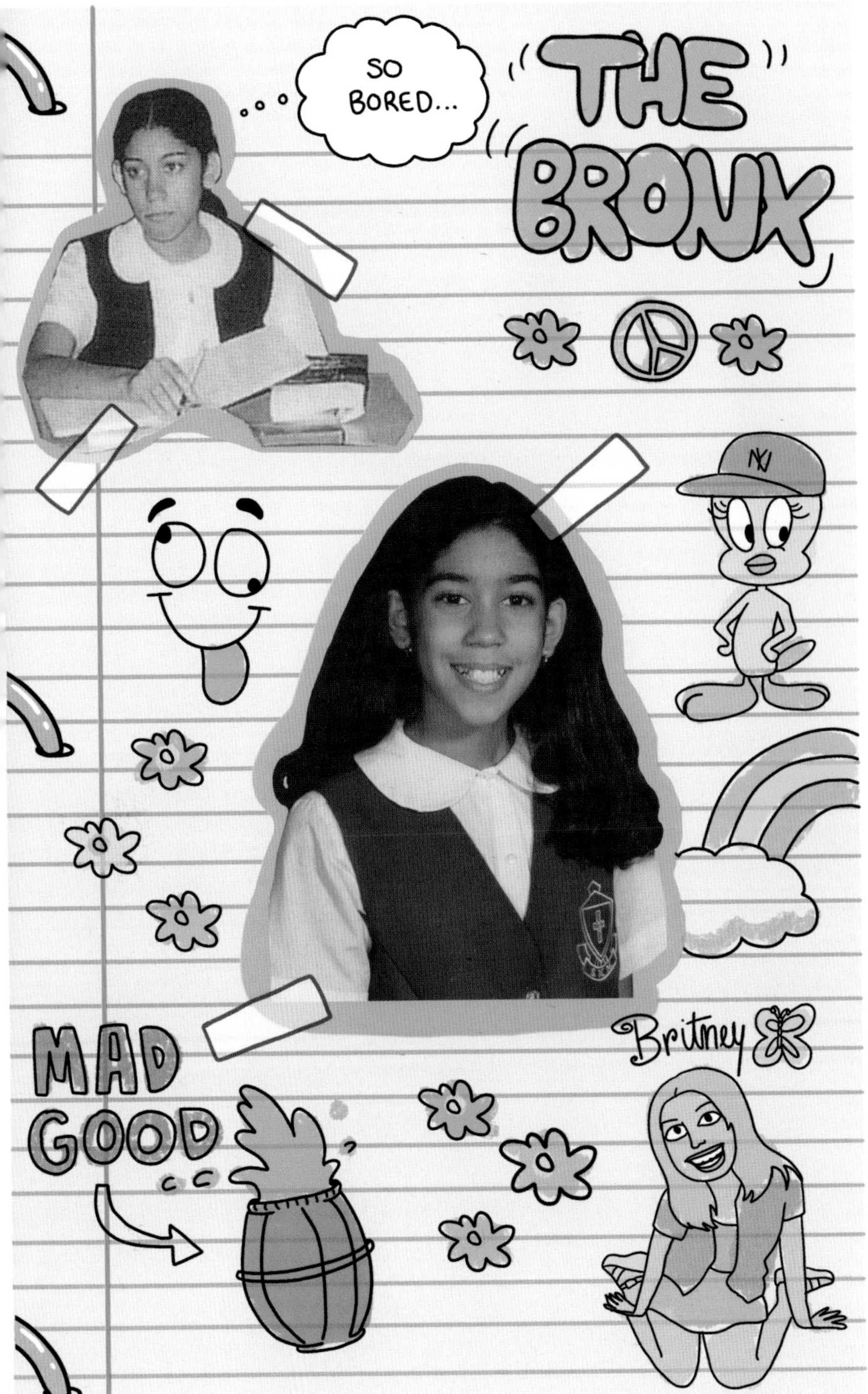
SO BORED...
THE BRONX
NY
MAD GOOD
Britney

ACKNOWLEDGMENTS

Thank you to my family, who understood how special this story is to me and supported me throughout the whole process. To my editor, Joanna, I couldn't have a better person on my side. Thank you for believing in my story and guiding me through the writing process. To Jasmin, my art director, who has been the best cheerleader and supporter of everything Boogie Down Bronx. To my color assistant, Andrea Bell, thank you for bringing *Doodles* to life with your color expertise and moral support. Thanks to my agent, Linda, for all the guidance and for sharing publishing industry knowledge.

To my friends Liz, Kat, Kelly, Breena, and so many others: Thank you for being the biggest supporters of my work. You held me up when I wasn't doing so great, and I will forever be grateful for all your advice and love.

My partner, Morris, who has gone above and beyond to support me in the making of this graphic novel. Thank you for always lending a listening ear and encouraging me to take walks when I needed it most. You're the real MVP!

Lastly, thank you to everyone who followed my work and purchased a comic or zine over the years. Your kind words and enthusiasm have given me the strength and confidence to keep pushing.